S0-ERK-037

FIC MAV
Mavro, George
War and destiny.
30206000315538

01/2014

PROPERTY OF:
SHERRARD PUBLIC
LIBRARY DISTRICT

DATE DUE

FEB 2 5 2014	
MAY 2 4 2014	
MAR 3 1 2015	

WAR AND DESTINY

Special Limited Edition

FIRST EDITION

WAR AND DESTINY

George Mavro

TotalRecallPress.com
www.totalrecallpress.com

TotalRecall Publications, Inc..
1103 Middlecreek
Friendswood, Texas 77546
281-992-3131   281-482-5390 Fax
www.totalrecallpress.com

All rights reserved. Except as permitted under the United States Copyright Act of 1976, No part of this publication may be reproduced, stored in a retrieval system, or transmitted in any form or by any means electronic or mechanical or by photocopying, recording, or otherwise without prior permission of the publisher. Exclusive worldwide content publication / distribution by TotalRecall Publications, Inc..

Copyright © 2013 by: George Mavro
Edited by: Tammy Mavro
All rights reserved
ISBN   978-1-59095-571-0
UPC: 6-43977-25724-7

Graphics used by permission from
http://www.asisbiz.com/Battles/Balkans-Campaign.html

Printed in the United States of America with simultaneous printings in Australia, Canada, and United Kingdom.

FIRST EDITION
1   2   3   4   5   6   7   8   9   10

This is a work of fiction. The characters, names, events, views, and subject matter of this book are either the author's imagination or are used fictiously. Any similarity or resemblance to any real people, real situations or actual events is purely coincidental and not intended to portray any person, place, or event in a false, disparaging or negative light.

The scanning, uploading and distribution of this book via the Interner or via any other means without the permission of the publisher is illegal and punishable by law. Please purchase only authorized electronic editions, and do not participate in or encourage electronic piracy of copyrighted materials. Your support of the author's rights is appreciated.

I want to thank my wife Tammy who spent endless hours editing this book

About the Author

George Mavro is a 24 year Air Force, Security Force veteran. He was stationed over 22 years in Europe, eight of those in Greece. He holds advanced degrees in Government and International Relations. He presently lives in Florida with his wife and two sons.

About the Book

When the young New Yorker, Markos Androlakis, visits the island of Crete in the summer of 1940 for a sabbatical, he unwittingly puts himself on a trajectory to test the fates of destiny. War soon engulfs the tiny peaceful nation of Greece and the Greek army does its best to hold off the Fascist hordes. Markos soon finds himself on the Greek and allied side of the war while fighting for survival and for the liberation of his ancestral homeland.

On 20 May 1941, Germany launched Operation Merkur (Mercury), the largest airborne invasion in history to capture the strategic island of Crete from the allies. Markos is tasked by the allied commander to help evacuate the Hellenic King to the island's south coast where he will be transported by the Royal Navy to Egypt. Unbeknownst to Markos the German Reichsfuhrer Heinrich Himmler has dispatched a ruthless SS officer Georg Mueller to capture the King and return him to Germany. Markos manages to evacuate the King and journeys to Cairo where he is recruited into the US army and the COI, which would soon become the OSS, Office of Strategic Services, under the leadership of "Wild Bill Donovan." Markos returns to America to help organize a cadre of Greek American agents to help the Greek resistance fight the ruthless and bloody Nazi occupation.

List of Characters:

Markos Androlakis: Main protagonist of novel. A Greek American student visiting Crete, Greece on an archeological sabbatical in summer 1940.

Antonis Mavroyiannis: A Greek American OSS agent and officer. Childhood Friend of Markos and his executive officer in Cairo, Egypt.

Sergeant George Papadakis: A Greek American OSS agent and explosive expert. Works for Major Markos Androlakis

Georg Mueller: The main antagonist. A brutal and ruthless high ranking Nazi SS officer. He is tasked to kidnap the King of Greece during the airborne invasion of Crete and bring him back to Germany as a prize for Hitler. He will remain in Greece as Himmler's security commander and in charge of the extermination of all Greek Jews.

Willi Bruner: A Nazi SS NCO, thug and body guard for Georg Mueller.

Hans Lantz: Mueller's assistant and executive officer

Sophia Maniakos: Georg Mueller's Greek mistress.

Wild Bill Donavan: Head of the United States Office of Strategic Services (OSS)

Benito Mussolini: Italian Fascist dictator

King George II of the house of Glucksburg and King of the Hellenes

General Bernard Freyberg: The allied commander on Crete.

Acknowledgment

To my mom and dad who told me about the their experiences in occupied Greece as teenagers

Preface

Over70 years have passed since the invasion an brutal Nazi occupation of Greece. I am writing this book to keep the memory of all those that gave their lives to free the world of Nazi tyranny and keep us free.

Introduction:

General Karl Student, the commanding general of the *XI. Fliegerkorps* looked at the map of Crete hanging on the wall in his room at the Grand Bretagne Hotel, German military headquarters in occupied Athens, Greece. The latest news from Operation Merkur (Mercury), the largest airborne assault in history to capture Crete was not good. Over ten thousand men had dropped on to the island. Losses in men and material were enormous. Contact had been lost with the forces that had dropped to seize Rethminon and Iraklion and were presumed to be dead or captured. The only success had been at the allied airfield in Maleme. The Fallschirmjager (paratroopers) and Gebirgsjagers (mountain troops) glider troops had managed to gain a toe hold on one end of the air strip. If the allies counter attacked in force, before the Luftwaffe managed to bring in reinforcements all would be lost. It would be the greatest military defeat that Germany would suffer and Student was in command. He would rather put a pistol to his head than face Hitler, if they suffered defeat His honor would not let him do otherwise. However, there was still hope, another wave of troops were enroute to Maleme.

Chapter 1

Melame Airfield Crete, Greece
19 May 1941, 1500hrs

Markos Androlakis, a Greek American from New York City, a handsome young man with a thick brown mustache, a tanned face and a pair of dark intelligent eyes, watched in dismay as the last RAF Hurricane fighter took off and headed south, bound for Egypt. The island was now totally devoid of any RAF air cover to face the impending German onslaught that was sure to come; not that the dozen or so RAF planes would make any difference against the hundreds of fighters and bombers that the Luftwaffe had available to unleash against them. It had been the allied commander, General Freyberg's decision, to send the few remaining planes back to the Middle East where they would be needed to defend the vital Suez Canal and Egypt from Rommel and his Afrika Korp.

Markos thought back on his decision to remain on Crete after hostilities had broken out between Greece and Italy. He Wondered if it had been a mistake. A Greek American from New York City and a student of history and archeology, he had decided in the summer of 1940 to take a sabbatical from NYU to study the ancient Minoan civilization that had once flourished on the island his parents had emigrated from. Even though war had broken out in Europe, both Greece and America had remained neutral. He figured that there was no way that a small nation like Greece would become embroiled in the war since Greece had very good relations with Germany and furthermore, its leader, General Metaxas, was a dictator himself.

Markos took passage from New York to Chania, Crete, on the Flora, an old Greek tramp freighter that had seen better days during the Great War. The weather was nice and the seas calm during the long voyage. They crossed the Atlantic without incident; the Captain making sure the Greek flag was prominently displayed during the day and lit up brightly at night to avoid any German U-boat attacks. One night during the crossing, they had heard explosions and seen a ship burning in the distance, a victim of one of the numerous German subs that were prowling the Atlantic. The captain went looking for survivors the next morning, but except for some wreckage, and a couple of bodies, none were to be found.

Markos finally arrived on the island in early July of 1940 and moved in with his grandparents, who lived on the western end of the island, in a small town halfway between the City of Chania and Maleme. It had taken him some time to get used to the inconvenience of having no electricity or running water and the daily summer temperature of 95 degrees or more. But he eventually adapted and quickly settled into his studies, even participating in an archeological dig. Unfortunately, this all came to an abrupt end when Greece was suddenly pushed into the abyss of war.

Benito Mussolini, the Italian Fascist dictator, not wanting to be a side show in the stream of German successes in the summer of 1940, needed a resounding victory for Italian arms. Characteristically, he turned his attention to the Balkans, toward Greece, where the prospects of adding to the new Roman Empire seemed more promising. Throughout the 20th century, Italy had been coveting Greek territory, especially the Island of Corfu and the Epirus region bordering the Adriatic which he considered an Italian lake. Thus, at 3 am, 28th October 1940, Greece's dictator, General Ioannis Metaxas, was awakened and presented with an ultimatum by the Italian ambassador. The ultimatum, which was to expire in three hours, demanded that Italian troops occupy unspecified strategic points in Greece. His reply was OHI, NO! Greece suddenly found itself at war with the 2nd strongest axis power, Italy.

What was supposed to have been an easy victory for Italian arms, quickly turned into a humiliating disaster of epic proportions! The tiny nation of only 6 million people astonished the world. Not only did the Greeks manage to hold the Italians in the Pindus Mountains, but they rapidly launched an offensive that had the Italian army reeling back into Albania. The Greeks captured thousands of prisoners and tons of badly needed military supplies and heavy equipment that was quickly turned against the invader. To a world that had witnessed a string of axis victories on the European continent, the Greek achievements carried with them the hope that victory may still be possible to a war weary British public that was experiencing the height of the German Blitz. In a speech to the House of Commons that fall, the British Prime Minister, Winston Churchill, honored the Greeks by stating that "heroes fight like Greeks."

Unfortunately, this euphoria was not going to last. It was unthinkable to Adolf Hitler to allow his Axis partner to be humiliated and defeated and as such Germany would come to Mussolini's aid. In December 1940, Hitler issued the orders for Operation Marita, the invasion of Greece via Bulgaria. With all indications that Germany was going to intervene in the Balkans, the Greeks had no illusion they could stop the German Wehrmacht alone. They reluctantly accepted British aid in men and material.

As a citizen of a neutral country, Markos could have still returned to the US, but he quickly got caught up in the euphoria and decided to stay on Crete to assist in the Greek war effort. He took a job as an interpreter with the British military liaison office that was set up in Chania in late November. Several weeks later, Markos was approached by the Hellenic army garrison commander and offered a Brevet commission to 2nd lieutenant in the Hellenic army. As a civilian, he was not privy to secret defense plans, as a Greek officer, he was. Besides his services were desperately needed by the Hellenic army, since there was no one else that had the mastery of Greek and English as he did. Markos accepted the offer and after two weeks of rudimentary firearms and other military training he was assigned as the Hellenic Army liaison to the allied headquarters staff.

The weeks managed to pass by quickly as Markos settled into his new role. Not that there was really much for him to do except translate the daily orders and attend boring staff meetings. The promised military aid and troop reinforcements for the island had not materialized. They were all diverted to the mainland in hopes of stopping the Nazi Blitzkrieg, which from all indications, was sure to come. Unfortunately, it was too little too late.

At 0515 hrs., April 6th, 1941, Field Marshall List's 12th Army launched Operation Marita, the invasion of Greece. In their typical Blitzkrieg fashion, the Germans unleashed over 1000 aircraft and hundreds of Panzers against the allied forces. Both the British and Greeks fought like lions, but there was no way they could stop the Nazi onslaught. On the Bulgarian border, the Rupel fortresses of the Greek Metaxas defense line held the Germans up for three days, even though they were bombed by dozens of Stuka dive bombers from dawn to dusk. It was only when the defenders ran low on ammunition and the Germans brought in tear-gas dispensers that the fort's commander contemplated capitulation. Upon surrendering the fortresses, as an honor to his adversary, the German commander took no one prisoner and allowed the fort's defenders to march out with their regimental colors. On the same day, April 9th, Greece's second largest City, Thessaloniki, fell to the Germans.

From Thessaloniki, the victorious German Wehrmacht swept slowly southward, meeting heavy allied resistance, but quickly smashing through it. By the 20th of April, the Greek Army in Albania was outflanked by the Germans and was forced to surrender. General Papagos, the Greek commander, told the allies on the 21st of April, that all was lost on the mainland and advised them to evacuate. With a series of successful rear guard actions, the allies had managed to hold the Germans back long enough for the Royal Navy to evacuate 80% of the expeditionary force, but at the loss of all their heavy weapons and equipment. By the 28th, the evacuation was over, Athens having fallen to the Germans the day before. Of the more than 50,000 soldiers evacuated from the mainland, 20,000 found themselves on the island of Crete with nothing but their personal weapons. On the 30th of April, Churchill decided that Crete must be held at all costs and appointed General Bernard

Freyberg as the supreme allied commander of the island.

"Sir, you are wanted immediately at headquarters for an urgent meeting." Markos was suddenly awakened from his day dream.

"Thank you, Corporal," he replied to the military policeman who had been sent to find him.

Markos walked the short distance to the headquarters building. On the way he noticed a couple of new fighting positions being built amongst the palm trees by the small two story stone structure that served as allied headquarters. The front entrance was sand bagged and defended by a two man Bren gun crew. About a hundred meters behind the building was a Bofors 40mm anti-aircraft gun emplacement covered with camouflage netting. Not much to stop a determined assault but they were short of heavy weapons, most being abandoned on the mainland. Markos was recognized by the sentry and let through the entrance. He walked into the commanding General's office and was met by Colonel Smith, General Freyberg's adjutant. In the office were also three senior Hellenic army officers. One of them he knew, Colonel Pantelakis, Chief of Hellenic Military Intelligence on the island, the other two, both Generals, he did not recognize.

"Gentlemen, the commander will see you now in the briefing room," said the General's adjutant.

Markos and the three other officers entered the briefing room which had a large map of the island hung on the far wall, marked with troop dispositions. They were greeted by General Freyberg, the allied commander, and several other senior officers. The two Hellenic army officers introduced themselves as General Zannakis, the Greek Minister of War and General Skoulas, commander of Greek Forces on Crete. Both had been recently appointed to their positions by King George of Greece who had also evacuated to the island. Not that it meant anything, since all Greek troops had been placed under General Freyberg's command anyway. The General shook the hand of the three Greek officers and gave Markos a nod. Freyberg motioned for everyone to take a seat.

"Gentlemen, now that we are finished with the pleasantries let's get down to business," said General Freyberg. "Our intelligence sources on the mainland are reporting that a German airborne and seaborne invasion of the island is imminent and will probably occur within the next 24 hours. For the past week, the Luftwaffe has launched scores of raids against us to soften up our defenses. I suspect the German attack will begin early tomorrow morning. They will hit us with everything they have, gentlemen, and that is considerable. They have hundreds of fighters and bombers at their disposal. What we are lacking in heavy weapons and aircraft we will make up with our knowledge of the terrain and our will and determination to stop the enemy. At 1800hrs, I am placing the island's garrisons on full alert and that includes all Greek forces."

The General hesitated for a moment as Markos translated into Greek for the other three Hellenic Army officers what he had said. "Therefore gentlemen I am ordering that his Royal Hellenic Majesty, King George, and his party be moved to safer quarters near the village of Perivolia. I have given orders to 12th Platoon of B Company 18th Battalion to accomplish this and guard the King. The King's safety is of paramount importance."

As Markos translated what the General had said, all three Greek officers nodded their heads in agreement. "Sir, both Generals Skoulas and Zannakis agree with your decision," said Markos.

"Excellent," replied Freyberg. Not that he really cared if the two charlatans wearing General's uniforms agreed or not. As if he didn't already have enough on his plate, London had also dumped the security of the Greek King into his lap.

"Sir, General Skoulas has offered a squad of Cretan Gendarmes to be assigned as your personal body guards," Markos said.

General Freyberg hesitated for a moment before replying. "Thank the General and tell him that I'm placing them under your command, Lieutenant. You could use some command experience."

Markos was flabbergasted. "Ah, thank you, sir," was all he could say.

General Freyberg stood up indicating the meeting was over. "Lieutenant, please stay for a moment."

"Yes, sir," said Markos wondering what was up.

After everyone had left the room, General Freyberg turned to Markos. "Markos you have proven very valuable to this headquarters and god knows we can use your language skills, but you are still a Yank and America is still neutral in this war. By tomorrow this time, we will be knee deep in Germans. This is not your war yet. I am giving you an opportunity to get out of here on a Royal Navy destroyer to Alexandria leaving tonight. Go home and if you want to fight in this war, join the US army and get some real training. Sooner or later, America will be in the war."

Markos thought of what the General had said about going home and getting out of the firing line. But he knew deep down that he could not abandon Crete in her hour of need.

"Sir thanks, but I can't do that. I am also a Greek and my ancestral motherland is being invaded. I just can't run away without a fight."

"I thought you would say that. You remind me of myself in

my younger days and another war. Okay, Lieutenant. If you insist on staying, you will remain assigned to this headquarters. You will assume command of the Cretan Gendarmes squad and assist with the defense of this headquarters. You will not wander off, unless I tell you to. Is that understood?"

"Yes, sir."

"I hear you have family that live close by."

"Yes, sir, my grandparents. They live in a small town about 10 miles from here."

"Well, take my car and driver and go visit them. It may be a long time before you see them again. Report back here by 0500hrs."

Berlin Reich's Chancellery
19 May 1941, 1600 hrs.

Obersturmbanfuhrer (Lt. Colonel) Georg Mueller could have been the poster boy for an SS recruitment campaign. The tall, stocky blond and blue eyed 33 year old, dressed in a black SS uniform, had just finished his third cigarette as he waited in the stuffy foyer of the Reichsfuhrer's office. He had received orders summoning him to Berlin for a meeting with the Reichsfuhrer, the second most powerful man in Nazi Germany. He wondered what was desired of him. He had been sent to Paris by "special request", from the Reichsfuhrer himself, to head the Gestapo's anti-partisan detail. Mueller, a former Berlin detective, had developed quite a reputation in the SS for his ruthless methods and success in tracking down and arresting terrorists. He had joined the SS just after Germany marched into the Rhineland in 1936, but showed much promise especially, after the outbreak of war. His exploits in rooting out Jews and other enemies of the Reich in Poland got the attention of Himmler and earned him a promotion to Sturmbanfuhrer (major). After the fall of France in June 1940, he was sent to Paris to deal with the French resistance. His success there quickly earned him a promotion to Obersturmbanfuhrer.

"Herr Mueller, the Reichsfuhrer will see you now," said the Reichsfuhrer's secretary.

"Thank you, Maria."

Mueller marched into the ornate wood paneled office decorated with numerous works of art whose former Jewish owners were either dead or in concentration camps.

"Heil Hitler."

Heinrich Himmler returned the Nazi salute from behind his large wooden desk and motioned for Mueller to have a seat. "Welcome to Berlin, Mueller."

"Thank you, sir," he said, as he handed Himmler a package containing a bottle of expensive French cognac, knowing that Himmler had a fondness for the drink.

"Oh, thanks for the gift, Mueller," he said, as he opened his bottom desk drawer and pulled out two glasses and a bottle opener. Opening the bottle he sniffed the contents, "Mm mm."

"It's nothing special, Herr Reichsfuhrer."

"Oh, you are too modest, Mueller. This smells wonderful," he said, as he poured both of them a drink.

"And how is Paris these days?"

"Paris is a decadent and morally corrupt city, sir. It's no wonder the French collapsed so easily when they were faced with German superiority. Although, there still are some elements that do not want to accept the "New Order" and the enemies of the Reich are being dealt with swiftly and harshly!"

"I have read the report of your exploits in dealing with the French terrorist scum, Mueller."

"I was just doing my job, Herr Reichsfuhrer."

"I would expect no less from an officer of the SS. Now I

have another important task for you."

"How can I be of further service to our glorious Deutsches Reich, Herr Reichsfuhrer?"

"I am sure you have been monitoring our successful Greek campaign?"

"Yes, sir. It was another glorious success of German arms and a humiliation and loss to the corrupt and decadent British Empire and their allies.

"That is correct, Mueller. Only the island of Crete remains under British control and that will very soon change. We cannot let them establish heavy bomber bases on the island that could threaten our oil supplies in Romania. In less than 24 hours, "Operation Merkur" (Mercury) will commence. It will be the largest airborne operation in history. Thousands of Luftwaffe paratroopers and glider troops will assault and seize the strategic island."

"That is a very bold plan, her Reichsfuhrer. Lightly armed airborne troops assaulting an enemy fortified stronghold and holding long enough for reinforcements to arrive."

"I, too, have my doubts, Mueller. General Student has convinced the Fuhrer it can be done. The British lack heavy weapons having lost them all on the mainland and we will have total air control. We also have a few surprises for the British. Our troops will be taking to the island a new type of 75mm gun so they will have some heavy weapons with them. But, yes, it is a gamble which we will win. The German soldier is superior to the British!"

"We will beat the British just by the sheer audacity of the plan," said Mueller.

"Well, Mueller, this is where your services come in. Our intelligence sources are telling us that King George, the Hellenic monarch, is on the island and staying in a villa near Maleme air field, one of our main objectives. Your mission will be to capture the King and bring him back to Germany. It will be a great propaganda coup for us and a major blow to the allied cause."

"I am sure, Herr Reichsfuhrer; the King is under heavy guard."

"Our sources tell us that there is a platoon of British infantry assigned to guard him. You will be transported to the island by glider, along with a specially chosen squad of SS troops and with a platoon of Luftwaffe paratroopers to assist you. They will attack the British guards while you seize the King. He is to be taken alive. You will have the element of surprise on your side. The British will never suspect that we will attempt to kidnap the Greek King. You will be further briefed by Obersturmfuhrer (First Lieutenant) Johann Lantz, your second in command, while in route to Greece. There is a Luftwaffe Heinkel 111 standing by at Templehoff to transport you and your men to Greece. It is a very daring plan, but it just may succeed. Well, Mueller, what do you think?"

"It is an ambitious plan, as is the whole operation. I will do my best Herr Reichsfuhrer."

"This is why I like you, Mueller, you are honest. I know there are too many variables that can cause the mission and the entire operation to fail. I know you will do your best. Our main objective is to capture the island. If we manage to capture the King, it will be a feather in our cap. Once the island is secured, your other mission will be to round up all subversives and establish an occupation security force. Cretans have a reputation of resisting authority; you will teach them to respect German power."

"Yes, sir."

Himmler stood up and raised his glass." A toast to our

success and to our illustrious Fuhrer, Adolf Hitler." Mueller nodded in acknowledgement and raised his glass. Both men quickly downed the cognac.

"At least the French do something well," said the Reichsfuhrer as both men laughed.

"Now, Mueller, your transport and men await you on the Tarmac at Templehoff. Your gear and supplies will be waiting for you in Greece. Good luck and good hunting."

Knowing he was being dismissed, Mueller rose to his feet gave the Nazi salute, marched out of Himmler's office and preceded to the waiting vehicle that would take him to the airfield.

Chapter 2

15,000 Feet over the Adriatic Sea
19 May 1941, 2340 hrs

Mueller, who had been sleeping soundly, was awakened by a sudden bout of turbulence. He glanced at his watch; they had been airborne for less than two hours after leaving Ancona, Italy, where they had stopped to take on fuel for the final leg to Elefsis Greece.

The Heinkel-111 was a sturdy plane; Mueller had flown on many during the plane's "commercial" debut in the Reich's re-armament program. He wondered whether his next ride on the DFS 230 Fallschirmjager glider transport would be as carefree; he had never been onboard an aircraft in a combat zone, let alone an unarmed transport glider. Mueller looked around the crowded aircraft cabin; most of his men were fast asleep trying to get some rest before tomorrow's attack. He had met his squad as they all boarded the aircraft back at Templehoff, eight enlisted men, under the command of an Obersturmfuhrer (First Lieutenant). Every one of them had seen combat and had been a volunteer for the SS Einsatz Commando (special operation groups). Oberscharführer Willi Bruner, an older grizzled man and the senior NCO squad leader, had impressed Mueller the most. Bruner had fought both in Poland and France and had been in charge of an Einsatz (special) Commando group which rounded up Jews and other undesirables in Warsaw. With men of this caliber and with the element of surprise on their side, they might just pull it off, he reasoned to himself. Mueller noticed his second in command, Obersturmfuhrer Johann Lantz, leaving the cockpit with two mugs in his hand.

"Sir, would you like some coffee?"

"Yes, thank you, Hans."

"The pilot says we will be landing in Elefsis, Greece in about 90 minutes. Our gear will be there waiting for us," said Lantz.

Mueller took a sip of the hot coffee. "Man, this is good. This is the real thing not ersatz coffee (roasted acorn)."

"It's Italian, sir. We got it during our refueling stop in Ancona, as well as some delicious Salami sandwiches. I saved you one."

Mueller had fallen asleep from exhaustion once they had become airborne and had slept right through their short refueling stop in Italy. "I must say the Italians still excel at some things, save for their fighting capabilities," said Mueller.

Both men laughed at the anecdote directed at their Italian ally. It was because of Italy's failure to overcome Greek resistance that Germany was now involved in the Balkans.

"Sir, I have radioed ahead to ensure our gear will be ready when we arrive in Greece. There will be hot food and showers available, courtesy of the Luftwaffe."

"Excellent, Lantz, I could sure use a shower and a fresh change of clothes before we depart for Crete. Any new updates on our target?"

"Last report sir, has the target staying at the same location with no change on the status of the guard garrison. There is one Platoon with light weapons guarding the house. Our agent will mark the landing spot with smoke. If we manage a complete surprise and catch the British totally off guard, we may just pull this off, sir."

"Let's hope so, Lantz, or this could turn out to be a fiasco if surprise is not achieved. Our orders are to take the target alive at all costs. If the King is injured or god forbid killed, this could totally turn much of the Greek populace and world opinion against us."

"We will do our best, sir."

One of the flight crew had left the cockpit and approached the two men. "We will be landing in less than an hour, Herr Obersturmbanfuhrer."

"Thank you, lieutenant."

"Lantz, wake the men up. I want everyone wide awake when we land. We will have something to eat, grab our gear and load up the glider."

"Jawohl, Herr Obersturmbanfuhrer." (Yes sir).

Melame airfield, Crete, Allied Headquarters
20 May 1941, 0500 hrs.

Markos rubbed his sleep deprived eyes as he entered the blacked out headquarters building which was bustling with activity. He made his way to the conference room and spotted the allied commander, General Freyberg, with a couple of his staff standing over a map of Greece dotted with pins, showing the location of various Luftwaffe airfields. He noticed that the general was dressed in a wrinkled battle dress uniform which meant that he probably had slept in it and had spent the night there. Freyberg turned and noticed Markos.

"Ah, Lieutenant, I hope your brief stay with your grandparents went well?"

"Yes, it did. And thank you very much for the opportunity to see them, sir," said Markos as he pulled out a small bottle containing a clear liquid and handed it to the general. Markos thought back at the tearful goodbye at his grandparent's home. His grandmother in tears and his grandfather beaming with pride as his grandson went out to fight their homeland's invader.

"This is from my grandfather, to show his gratitude for allowing him to see his grandson one more time before the battle and to thank our brave allies who are willing to risk their lives to defend the island. Those were his exact words, sir."

"This must be some of that Raki that Cretans are known for," General Freyberg said, as he stuffed the small bottle into one of his battle dress pockets.

"Thank you, lieutenant, and please thank your grandfather for me when you see him again. Tell him it is an honor and a privilege to fight side by side with our brave Greek allies."

"I will, sir."

"Anyway, I am sure I will need a stiff drink before the day is over," he said, garnering a laugh from the other officers present.

"I am glad you're here, Markos. I have a special mission for you."

"Sir?"

"The security of His Majesty, King George of Greece. Since the fall of the mainland, the King has been on the island and has established a government in exile. The Germans know this and we suspect that they may try to capture him. If they manage to do that, it would be a great propaganda coup for Hitler and a humiliation to the British government." He now had Markos' full attention.

"This is where you come in, lieutenant. The King and his entourage were moved yesterday to a secure location at the village of Perivolia, a few miles south of Chania. You are to proceed there and report to Lieutenant Ryan commanding the 12th Platoon of B Company. You will be his second in command. You will also be in charge of the Gendarmes squad that was sent to be my bodyguards. I relieved them of their duties here and sent them there last night as an additional security measure. You will guard the King with your lives and if need arises, he will be evacuated to Egypt, when and if that becomes necessary. He is not to fall into German hands. Is that understood?"

"Yes, sir."

"Do you have any questions, lieutenant?"

"What about communications there, sir?"

"There is a wireless at the house; you will be able to communicate with headquarters. Ensure that you give hourly status checks. When the invasion begins, you may only have minutes to get the King away safely, therefore, you must be alert. I am sure the Germans have agents watching the house as we speak. There are a lot of internal Greek politics at play here. I know the King was not very well liked on the island. This is one of the reasons I am sending you there. Lieutenant Ryan is a capable officer, but he does not understand Greek," said Freyberg.

"I will do my best, sir."

"I know you will, son. You also speak the language and understand the culture better than all of us here. I expect you to try and solve any problems that do arise with his Majesty and the local population. It will not be an easy task. His safety is of paramount importance to the allied cause."

"I understand, sir."

"Anything else, lieutenant?"

"Any news on the Germans, sir?

"From all our intelligence sources on the mainland the Germans are massing troops and aircraft at assembly points and air fields. We believe that an invasion is imminent and may even begin sometime this morning. Therefore, speed is of the essence. There is a vehicle waiting outside to take you to your charge. In it you will find your battle kit, your orders, and a bag containing 100 Gold Sovereigns in case you need to purchase any supplies or assistance to accomplish your mission. Good luck, lieutenant."

"Thank you, sir.

Markos saluted and turned to leave, "Markos stay safe, let Lieutenant Ryan deal with matters of defense. He and his men are well trained and have combat experience. You don't. If the King needs to be evacuated, you will go with him to Egypt. Once there, you should go to the US embassy and ask to be repatriated to the United States. Go see your family, Markos. America will be in this war soon enough. Your skills and knowledge of Greece will be needed there. Now go. Lieutenant Ryan is expecting you."

Elefsis Airfield, Greece
20 May 1941, 0530 hrs.

After landing at Elefsis airfield, 20 miles southwest of Athens, Mueller and his men were all escorted to one of the few aircraft hangers that the Luftwaffe had constructed on the airfield after capturing it in April. There, they all had hot showers, breakfast and changed into their battledress uniform.

Each one armed themselves with a MP 38 submachine gun, 150 rounds of 9mm ammo and three Model 24, "Potato Masher" grenades. Afterwards, he briefed his men on the newest intelligence that had been received on the target's location, movements and anticipated resistance.

An hour before departure, the Luftwaffe Fallschirmjager platoon arrived. They were vital to the success of the mission. They would attack the enemy security force guarding the compound as Mueller and his men went for the target. Mueller was immediately impressed by their commander who introduced himself as Captain Gerhard Schmidt. The tall blond and well-built officer radiated an aura of both cockiness and confidence as did the rest of his command. Mueller spent twenty minutes briefing Captain Schmidt on last minute mission details and then, after posting guards at the hanger entrance, he addressed all the men present.

"Comrades, today the Fatherland embarks on one of the boldest combat operations in the history of modern warfare. We will be launching the greatest air assault in history to capture a very large piece of real estate surrounded by water and occupied by the enemy. The world and the Fatherland will be watching. We have been assigned a mission of vital importance to the Reich, the capture of the King of Greece. We know where he is being kept and the element of surprise is on our side. He is being guarded by a platoon size detachment at the villa where he is staying which is located 20 kilometers south of Chania. If we pull this off it will be a tremendous blow to allied morale and a humiliation to that pig, Churchill, and to the Jews that run and finance the British government. I know each man will do what the Fuhrer and the Reich expects of him. Heil Hitler."

The large cavernous hanger erupted with shouts of "Heil

Hitler" as everyone present joined in the Nazi salute "Everyone outside! The trucks that will take us to the aircraft are here," shouted Captain Schmidt.

The airfield was beginning to hum with activity as Mueller and his men boarded the waiting trucks to take them to their aircraft for the flight to Crete. Dozens of Junker 52 transports, some with their engines running, where standing by to transport hundreds of Luftwaffe paratroopers and their equipment to their targets on Crete

"Sir, we are here," said the Luftwaffe driver as he stopped next to a DS230 glider.

"We are going to Crete in that?" Mueller asked. The glider was even smaller and flimsier than he had imagined.

"Yes, sir, first class transportation, it fits nine fully armed troops and the pilot."

"We will be sitting ducks," Mueller replied.

"The Luftwaffe is providing fighter escort and hopefully, sir, the enemy will be surprised and you will reach the ground quickly and safely."

"I hope so, Sergeant. If not, we are screwed."

Mueller hopped out of the passenger side of the truck and walked over to where Lantz and his men were forming up. There were numerous other trucks stopped by several adjacent Junker 52s unloading the Luftwaffe Fallschirmjager troops that would be assisting them on the mission.

"Oberscharführer! Prepare the men for boarding," shouted Mueller.

"Jawohl, Herr Obersturmbanfuhrer!"

Bruner quickly had the men stow most of their gear in the glider except for their small arms. Many of the transports were beginning to taxi to the runway to begin their flight to Crete. Mueller was last to board as the hatch was closed behind him.

Within a few minutes, the tri motor Junkers 52 transport began its takeoff roll towing the glider behind it.

Ten minutes later, they were cruising at 5000 feet over the crystal blue waters of the Saronic Gulf which was dotted with dozens of small rocky islets. Mueller glanced out the window and spotted several ME 109 fighter escorts taking position alongside their aircraft. Above them, a flight of JU 87 Stuka dive bombers were also heading towards the island to soften up the targets that the paratroopers were supposed to seize. All around them, at various altitudes, were hundreds of Junker 52 aircraft, some towing gliders, others containing paratroopers to be dropped over strategic targets once they were over the island. The huge air armada was winging its way southward and toward harm's way.

The flight would take a little more than 2.5 hours if everything went according to plan and there were no RAF fighter interceptors in the neighborhood. So in the interval Mueller decided to take a short nap. He asked the pilot to wake him 30 minutes before their arrival over the island so he could be fully awake and alert upon landing. The pilot agreed and Mueller pulled down his cap and closed his eyes, quickly falling asleep to the drone of the hundreds of aircraft engines of the massive airborne fist that was soon to strike and attempt to seize the last free piece of Greece.

CHAPTER 3

Perivolia, Crete
20 May 1941, 0630hrs

Arriving at the heavily guarded villa where the King of Greece and his court were housed, Markos observed that the security force had already assumed combat positions and had established both an outer and inner security perimeter. Driving up to the gated entrance, he was greeted by the sentries, a New Zealander Sergeant and a Cretan Gendarmes Warrant Officer. Markos, dressed in battle fatigues and armed with a Thompson submachine gun, identified himself and was allowed to enter the compound.

"We've been waiting for you, sir. I am Warrant Officer Kostas Manolakos of the Cretan Gendarmes. Headquarters radioed ahead and told us you were on your way. Lieutenant Ryan is having breakfast and wishes you to join him. I will escort you to him. My men and I have only been here a few hours."

"Thank you, Kostas. Call me Markos," he replied to the short, stocky middle aged man who was armed with a long barreled Austrian Mannlicher rifle of World War One vintage.

"Markos, we will find Lieutenant Ryan on the other side of the grounds," Kostas said.

"Let's go then, I would not mind some breakfast."

The villa, surrounded on all sides by several lush palm trees, was an elegant two story stone building, built around the turn of the century. It presently belonged to Mr. Tsouderos, the Greek Prime Minister, who had been appointed to the position by the King of Greece after the fall of the mainland. Markos, despite his lack of military experience, observed that there were sentries posted every fifty feet around the villa's perimeter stone wall which had a height of five feet. A Bren gunner had also been posted on the 2nd floor front balcony that covered the frontal approaches to the house. He was impressed with the thoroughness of Lieutenant Ryan. As they approached the back of the villa he saw several men around a campfire in a clearing between some of the tall palm trees. A slim, dark haired young man with a pencil thin mustache rose from a stool he had been sitting on and approached Markos holding out his hand. Warrant Officer Manolakos left the two men and went back to his post.

"Hello, I am Lieutenant W.H. Ryan, commander of this motley crew. We've been expecting you," he said with a friendly smile.

Markos immediately liked the man. "I am Markos Androlakis, commander of, well, I have not seen my crew yet."

Both men broke out into a laugh. "A Yank? The General only said that my second in command spoke excellent English.

You're a long way from home."

"It's a long story. I came to the island last summer to study Minoan archeology. I also have family on the island. Suffice to say, just like you, I am stranded here for the duration!"

"Very interesting, oh I am sorry. I am being rude to my guest. Would you like some coffee and a bite to eat?"

"Sure, that would be great."

"Corporal Davies, would you bring a cup of coffee to the lieutenant here and something to go along with it."

"Sure thing, sir."

Within a couple of minutes, Markos was handed a steaming cup of black coffee and a tin containing some fried bully beef mixed with powdered eggs. Markos took a swig of the coffee.

"Ah, that hit the spot," he said, as the strong hot liquid gave him a quick jolt.

"Try the bully beef with scrambled eggs. Its Davies's own recipe," said Ryan. "I will take you around to meet your men, and to meet his Majesty and his entourage as soon as you finish eating."

"Yes, I would like that very much, and the Corporal's scrambled eggs are indeed quite good," replied Markos between mouthfuls of the hot food.

"I told you," said Ryan with a grin. "Enjoy it. It may be the last hot meal we have for a while. All our intelligence sources indicate that an invasion is imminent, probably in the next few hours."

"I heard. That's what General Freyberg told me right before I left his headquarters. The entire island's garrison is on alert."

"We need to be ready to move with our charges at a moment's notice," Ryan added.

"Your men and your expertise in Greek and the local customs will come in handy if we need to get out of here quickly.

A few minutes later both Markos and Ryan were walking the villa grounds. Lieutenant Ryan introduced Markos to the rest of his men from the Cretan Gendarmes who were posted around the house in various locations. He was impressed with what he saw of the Cretans. Most of them were armed with WWI rifles or 19th Century French single shot GRAS rifles. What they might have lacked in modern weaponry they made up in their zeal to fight the enemy that would soon be coming. Markos thought that he would be resented by his men when they found out he was a Greek American, but on the contrary they were proud to serve under a fellow Cretan who came all the way from America and stayed to fight for their island.

Lieutenant Ryan looked at his watch it, was 7:10am. "About time I introduce you to our charges; they should all be dressed and finished with breakfast.

Berlin, Reich Chancellery, Fuhrer Bunker
20 May 1941, 0715hrs, (0605hrs Berlin)

Reichsfuhrer Heinrich Himmler put his hand up to his mouth trying to suppress a yawn. He usually hated these early morning meetings with the Fuhrer and the General staff, but this morning was different. If everything went to plan he would present the Fuhrer with a wonderful gift which would exemplify the power of the German Reich to all those that still opposed it. Of course, he would not tell Hitler anything of the special mission until he had confirmation from Mueller that the target had been captured and was on the way to Germany. There were just too many possibilities of the mission failing, or the target being killed during the attempt. At this moment, the head of the General Staff, General Oberst Franz Hadler, was briefing Hitler on the commencement of "Operation Merkur."

"My Fuhrer, at approximately 0700hrs Berlin time the

Luftwaffe, under the command of General Wolfram Von Richtofen, will begin neutralizing targets in the Melame airfield/Chania area and be there to provide any needed air support. The General has over 180 fighters and 150 dive bombers at his disposal. We expect little or no British RAF opposition. At 07:15hrs, 5000 men, the first wave of General Student's vaunted Fallschirmjagers under command of Major General Eugen Meindle, will be jumping to seize the critical Maleme airfield located at the west end of the island. This airfield must be secured for our attack to succeed. It is vital for bringing in the reinforcements and heavy weapons that will be needed to continue the attack and capture of the island. Later in the day, Fallschirmjagers will also drop in the Heraklion and Rethminon sectors to secure the middle and eastern ends of the island."

"What about the Royal Navy?" asked Hitler.

"I have been assured by General Richtofen that any sortie of the Royal Navy near the island or the Greek mainland will be met by the full might of the Luftwaffe. We enjoy complete air superiority and the island is not far from our southern-most mainland bases. It will be very costly to the Royal Navy if they decide to venture out. Actually, my Fuhrer, it would prove beneficial for us if some of their major units do sortie so we can destroy them!"

"Excellent, General! This will be one of the greatest feats of German arms! The greatest airborne operation in history! We will teach that Jew lover Churchill a lesson. We will drive them out of Crete and the Mediterranean. If our Italian allies had a bit more stomach for fighting, this would have already been accomplished. I did not want to get involved in this Balkan mess. That fool Mussolini would have been defeated by the Greeks, especially after the British began sending them aid. I could not have a major Axis ally being humiliated by a poor, backwards country. I wish we had the Greeks as allies instead. Even after a thousand years of being invaded and occupied by so many races, they still are a warrior race!"

"My Fuhrer, the Cretans are a special breed of Greeks. Along with the British, they will openly oppose us," said Admiral Canaris, chief of German intelligence.

"I will not tolerate our troops being attacked by civilian bandits! Hadler, issue an order stating that any German soldier that is murdered by a Cretan bandit will result in ten Cretans being shot!"

"Yes, my Fuhrer!"

"Heinrich, you have been quiet this morning."

"There is not much to say, my Fuhrer. I have though sent a squad of Special SS troops under the command of Obersturmbanfuhrer Mueller to the island. They will assist in setting up a civil administration and rounding up undesirables and trouble makers," replied Himmler.

"Ah yes, I know Mueller. Good man. He did brilliantly in Paris rooting out French resistance scum and other trouble makers. He could also assist the Luftwaffe in dealing with any actions committed by any bandits against our troops"

"Of course, my Fuhrer, he is one of my best."

"General Hadler, I am going to take my breakfast now. Contact me immediately once you have any news."

"Yes, my Fuhrer."

"Heinrich, join me for breakfast.

"Everyone in the room stood in attention and rendered the Nazi salute as Hitler and his arch henchmen Heinrich Himmler left the operations center.

Perivolia, Crete
20 May 1941, 0740 hrs.

After finishing their post checks, Markos and Ryan went inside the villa and found the King and his entourage consisting of his cousin, Prince Peter, Colonel M. Levidis, Master of Ceremonies, Prime Minister Tsouderos and Kyriako's Varvaressos, Governor-in-Exile of the Bank of Greece, were still sitting around the table having breakfast. Lieutenant Ryan introduced Markos to the King and his associates. His Royal Majesty, a tall, balding middle aged man dressed in a General's uniform, invited both men to join him in a cup of a coffee. The King was a bit surprised to see a Greek American wearing a Hellenic Army uniform, but was deeply satisfied after Markos explained to him the circumstances leading to him joining the Greek Army.

"Markos, I am deeply honored that you chose to serve your motherland in her hour of need."

"Thank you, your Majesty, but any Cretan would have done the same."

"Your Majesty, we must be ready to move quickly if we have to. Our Intelligence sources have told us that the German invasion of the island is imminent," said Lieutenant Ryan. "I need you to change out of your uniform, it is too conspicuous. We can't have anything happening to you. Your capture or injury by the Germans would be greatly detrimental to the allied cause."

"I understand your concern, Lieutenant Ryan, but I am the King of the Hellenes and I will not show cowardice in the face of my country's enemies. Thousands of my countrymen have already given their lives and thousands more may die in the next few days."

"Please, Your Majesty. No one would ever accuse you of being a coward. Lieutenant Ryan is right. Just imagine the German propaganda coup your capture would be."

"Okay, Lieutenant Androlakis, since both of you insist, I will change into something more inconspicuous."

"Thank you, Your Majesty," Markos replied.

"Lieutenant Ryan!"

"What is it, Sergeant Smith?"

"Sir, it's a message from headquarters. The airfield is under very heavy air attack."

"Thank you, Sergeant."

"It's begun. The Jerries are softening up the airfield before their troops arrive. Your Majesty, I need you and your entourage to be ready to move at a moment's notice."

"Don't worry about us, Lieutenant Ryan. We will be ready to move when you give us the say so." The King and his entourage quickly got up and headed upstairs to prepare themselves, in case they quickly needed to evacuate.

"Markos, let's go alert the troops," said Ryan, as they quickly exited the house. But that would prove to be unnecessary since everyone could hear the explosions coming from the vicinity of Chania. Far in the distance, coming from the direction of the sea, they could hear a droning noise.

"Markos, round up your men and position them inside the house. They'll be our last defense if the perimeter is breached."

Markos quickly took off running to find his Gendarmes troops as the droning sound became louder.

1000 Meters above the Mediterranean Sea
20 May 1941, 0825hrs,

"Sir, we are 15 minutes from the target zone." Mueller was awakened from his semi sleep by the glider's pilot. He looked out the glider's window and could see the island's brown coastline outlined by the bright blue Mediterranean Sea quickly approaching.

Mueller, who was sitting behind the pilot, looked back and hollered to his second in command, who was sitting in the rear of the cramped glider, loud enough to be heard above the din of the towing plane's engines.

"Lantz, make sure all the men are up and ready to go, we arrive in 15 minutes."

"Yes, sir"

As the coastline got closer, Mueller watched in awe as the nimble ME109 fighters zoomed in and out of the huge formation. The larger, less agile, JU 87 Stuka dive bombers swarmed past to attack targets on the ground. He could see smoke rising from several locations inland that the Stukas had already hit. The five plane formation carrying Mueller's strike force turned a few degrees east to avoid flying over Souda Bay and the city of Chania hoping to avoid any potential antiaircraft defenses. Several minutes later, they crossed the rocky coastline at 500 meters (1500 feet). Mueller could see small whitewashed houses and many people running and pointing skywards.

"Sir, another five minutes to the target," said the glider pilot.

Tracers from several well camouflaged antiaircraft positions filled the sky as they crossed over several olive groves. Mueller saw one of the lumbering Ju 52s that was towing one of the gliders containing his Luftwaffe Fallschirmjagers begin to pour out flames and smoke from one of its three engines. As the fire quickly began to spread to the wing, the JU 52 began to rapidly lose altitude. The glider pilot, not wanting to crash with the transport, released the towline and began the glide toward the ground. Mueller watched in horror as the Junkers 52 crashed into a rocky hillside and burst into flames.

"What a way to start the mission, 25% casualties before we even landed," he said to the glider pilot.

A few minutes later, the pilot pointed to a clear field a few miles ahead. The field was situated between several olive groves and vineyards. A large house was located about 500 meters east of the field.

"That must be the target, but I don't see any smoke. Oh, I see it, there it is. Tell the other planes we are going in," said Mueller.

The formation went into a wide 360 degree climbing turn. At 1000 meters, they released their tow lines and the gliders began their descent.

Perivolia, Crete
21 May 1941, 0840hrs

Ryan's platoon had assumed their battle positions and waited to see what would transpire. It was evident from the airstrikes that the German invasion had most likely begun. Markos had his men placed both inside and outside of the house as a last ditch measure to buy the needed time to evacuate the King and his associates if that became necessary. Both Markos and Ryan scanned the horizon with a pair of binoculars from the second floor balcony that served as a machine gun nest and observation post. From what both men could observe, much of the aerial traffic was headed towards Maleme. It was Markos that noticed several small aircraft a few miles to the north headed their way.

"Ryan, look!" said Markos pointing skywards. Those aircraft have no engines and are headed our way. There are no military targets in this area."

"Those are gliders and we're the target! Corporal Jones, alert everyone, we are going to have company real soon,"Ryan said.

"Should we evacuate the King?" Markos asked.

"No, there is no time. Jerry will be here in a few minutes. Let's ensure they get a good welcome. There can't be more than ten men in each of those gliders. That's about equal odds. Let's better them a bit." Ryan took another glance skyward.

"They're going to pass almost overhead in about a minute. I want you to give them all you got," he said to the Bren gunner.

Ryan stood out on the balcony and yelled down to his men.

"Lads, when the gliders pass overhead, give them all you got. Don't forget to aim slightly ahead. Once they are down we will take them out. I want Alpha and Bravo Squad ready to move once Jerry has landed. Remember the honor of New Zealand is at stake. We were sent here to protect the King of Greece and that's what we will do to our last breath! Now get ready."

"Here they come!" Markos yelled.

"Open fire."

All they heard was a whoosh as the 4 gliders passed about 100 meters to the left of the house. Simultaneously, the villa grounds erupted with small arms fire. The Bren gunner took aim slightly leading the first glider and opened fire. The .303 caliber rounds ripped through the cockpit killing the pilot instantly. With a dead man at the controls, the glider immediately nosedived into a clump of trees, killing everyone on board. Several bullets from the concentrated small arms fire also scored hits on the other gliders wounding or killing several more of the raiding force, including Captain Schmidt, the Luftwaffe liaison officer. Seeing the first glider go down, two of the glider pilots attempted to maneuver away from the incoming small arms fire causing them to miss the open field that was their intended landing spot and crash land into an adjacent olive grove. The last glider carrying Mueller and his men passed through the small arms fire relatively unscathed and made the landing field.

"I think we have just bettered our odds, my friend," said Ryan with a big grin to Markos whose ears were still ringing from the din of the small arms fire.

"I will take two squads and go and clear out the remaining Jerries that landed in the groves. You stay here with the remainder of the platoon and hold this house and safeguard the King till I return. Get a message out to the force commander at Maleme and brief him of our situation here and ask them for instructions. Tell them the Jerries probably know the King's location. Why else would they be landing here?"

"You're probably right," Markos said.

"It's all yours, mate. I'll be back as soon as I deal with the threat."

"Good luck, Ryan."

"Thanks, I may need it."

Perivolia, Crete, glider landing site
21 May 1941, 0847hrs

When the glider carrying Mueller and his men stopped rolling down the field, Mueller cracked the hatch open and quickly got out followed by the rest of his troops. So far the mission had been a total fiasco; over 50% of his raiding force had been lost before they even had set down. In the distance he could see one of the gliders carrying the Luftwaffe troops smashed against the trees. Several troops had gotten out and were helping the injured. The rest were beginning to form up.

"Lantz, form the men up quickly," screamed Mueller.

Before Lieutenant Lantz could give the command the olive grove where the Luftwaffe troops had crash landed was inundated with small arms fire. Most of the Fallschirmjagers had been quickly cut down while offering little or no resistance.

"Sir, we must assist them," said Lantz.

"No, they have not spotted us yet. Their sacrifice may be the diversion we need to get to our target. Let's move quickly into the trees."

Grabbing their weapons and gear, Mueller and his men with the Luftwaffe glider pilot in tow, ran towards an adjacent olive grove. They were able to reach the tree line without being spotted and quickly dropped to the ground for cover. Intense small arms fire could still be heard coming from the olive grove. Ryan and his men had found the other glider.

"This is our chance. There must be at least two squads out there, maybe another two guarding the villa. We can rush the house," Mueller said to Lantz and Bruner.

Both men agreed it was a good idea. "We will need a small diversion. Lantz, take two men and our Luftwaffe guest who now is an honorary SS man." That drew a laugh from the men. At least morale was still good, thought Mueller.

"I need you to get as close as possible to the front gate and start shooting. Move around. I want them to think that there are at least two squads assaulting them. I will take the rest of the squad and hit them from the back after you hopefully draw away some of the guards. I also need you to provide us covering fire once we have our target."

"You can count on me sir," Lantz replied.

"Hopefully, some of the Fallschirmjagers have survived and will assist us, but don't count on it. Let's get moving before the enemy returns to the villa."

Perivolia, Crete, at the Villa
21 May 1941, 0900hrs,

Markos had gone upstairs where the radio operator had setup the wireless and made contact with Melame. The news from there was not very good. The airfield was under heavy attack by German fighter bombers and Fallschirmjager troops. After briefing headquarters on the situation at the Villa, Markos was given the order to begin evacuating the King to the South coast of the island for eventual pick up by the Royal Navy. Markos found the royal party in the villa's large ornate living room. They had all heard the ongoing fire fight. He gave them the news that General Freyberg was ordering their evacuation from the island. The conversation was suddenly interrupted by a burst of automatic fire, accompanied by several rifle shots coming from the vicinity of the front gate.

"Everyone, take cover."

Several more bursts of sub machine gun followed by a loud explosion came from the front of the house. "Sir, the front gate is under attack, we need to reinforce it. I will take my squad to assist, said Corporal Jenkins, Charlie squad leader."

"No, Corporal that will leave us with only five Gendarmes as our last ditch defense in the house. What if it's a diversion? Send three men. They will have to fend for themselves. Lieutenant Ryan should be on his way back. I want the rest of your men to take positions at the back windows."

"Yes, sir."

Mueller had reached the rear boundary wall of the Villa undetected. They had picked up on the way another six Fallschirmjagers that had survived the initial landing. A couple had been lightly wounded, but still combat capable. This greatly improved their odds for success. The attack on the front gate had pulled some of the guards to the front of the building, but not all. A Greek Gendarmes guard was still guarding the rear of the building. He would have to be quickly taken out.

"Bruner, on my signal, you will take out the guard. We have 10 meters of open ground to cover till we reach the wall. Once over the wall, we run like hell, it is another 10 meters to the house. There are three windows. We will head towards the center window. There are probably guards posted on all of them. I will fire several bursts to smash the glass in the center window. Hans and Carl will fire a couple of bursts on the left window. You two," said Mueller pointing at two of the Fallschirmjagers, "will fire on the right window to keep the guards head down, the rest of you will take out any opposition we meet. The King is not to be harmed. You all saw his picture before we left the mainland. He is to be taken alive at all costs. Now let's move it. We only have a few minutes before the rest return."

Mueller gave Bruner the signal to shoot. Bruner, in a single motion, brought up the KAR 98 sniper rifle he was carrying, aimed and fired. As the guard fell, Mueller and his force ran the 10 meters to the wall, jumped over and entered the villa's grounds. Mueller fired on the run shattering out the glass in the center window and killing the two guards that had been posted there. The rest of the team fired on the other windows, wounding two of the guards and forcing the remaining guards to keep their heads down, giving Mueller the opportunity to reach the window unscathed. Mueller quickly leaped inside, falling on the ground.

Markos had heard the guards he had posted at the villa's rear windows yell out a warning before all the window panes were smashed by a steady stream of bullets.

"Hurry, everybody run upstairs," he screamed, as he grabbed the King and pulled him toward the large staircase.

Mueller quickly got up and saw another guard rushing into the room, pistol drawn. Mueller thought he would be dead in seconds. A burst of automatic fire from one of his team members took the guard out. Mueller nodded in thanks.

"Hurry, let's find the King before the rest of the guards return. Be careful, I am sure there are more guards here." But as two of the Fallschirmjagers rushed into the hallway, they were instantly cut down by rifle fire by two of the Gendarmes posted at the foot of the stairs. Mueller and his team were now effectively pinned down and time was running out.

"Damn it, they are upstairs." He could still hear firing going on outside which meant that Lantz was still occupying a good part of the guard force.

"Bruner, take them out! We need to get upstairs in the next couple of minutes or it's over."

"Jawohl, Herr Obersturmbanfuhrer!"

Perivolia, Crete, 500 Meters west of the Villa
20 May 1941, 0910hrs,

Except for a few survivors that were still returning fire, Ryan and his men had killed most of the glider troops that had survived the crash landings in the olive groves. In the distance they could hear shooting coming from the direction of the Villa. Ryan suspected that it had to be the troops of the third glider.

"Okay, lads, let's head back. From the noise I think Lieutenant Androlakis has his hands full and may need our assistance." Little did Ryan know, how right he was.

Back at the Villa, Mueller and his men had forced the guards up the stairs and were beginning to fight their way up. Markos had locked the King in one of the bedrooms and stood outside armed with a Thompson sub machine gun. The Germans had entered the house and had fought their way to the staircase; most of his men were either pinned down, injured or dead. All that stood between the Germans and the King were two of his Gendarmes and himself.

"Sir I am almost out of ammo. Georgos is almost out too,"

yelled Sergeant Mitsakis, which was followed by a burst of automatic fire coming from the bottom of the stairs, taking out one of the Gendarmes.

Markos peeking around the corner could see that one of the Germans was almost halfway up the staircase. He had to act quickly or they would soon all be dead. He had only fired the Thompson once and remembered that the gun was hard to control. He checked the safety and brought the gun up to his chest, peeked around the corner and fired a two second burst. Several of the 45 caliber slugs hit the German, knocking him down the stairs. Markos had no time to contemplate that he had just killed a man. The Germans downstairs began firing at his location. Plaster and bullets flew all around him and he figured he had only seconds to live when he remembered that he had a Mills bomb attached to his web gear. Taking the grenade, he pulled the pin and tossed it over the landing and down the stairs. He heard someone scream something a few seconds before the grenade exploded. Markos' ears rang from the explosion, but the firing coming from below had suddenly stopped. Shooting could still be heard coming from outside Markos heard someone shouting his name.

"Markos, are you alright?" It was Ryan. They had arrived and pulled his nuts out of the fire.

"Ryan, I am up here. Where are the Germans?"

"They pulled out and took off running when we arrived."

Ryan ran up the splintered and scarred staircase and saw Markos.

"Are you injured? Where is the King?

Markos, whose ears were still ringing from the gunfire and grenade explosion, had stood up and was brushing the dust and plaster off his clothes. "I am okay, Ryan. At least, I think so. You arrived in the nick of time. For a minute, I thought I was a goner. The King and his party are locked up in a back room."

Ryan looked around at all the damage and bodies that littered the stairs and bottom floor and shook his head in disbelief. He had been joined by Warrant Officer Manolakos.

"Well, looking at this place, it seems you did okay in your first baptism of fire."

Markos stared at the dead Germans and body of the dead Gendarme. "Well, I had a lot of help. Those guys, Ryan, saved my ass," he said, gesturing to the Cretan Gendarmes.

"Kostas, what are our casualties?" Markos asked.

"Two of my men are dead, one of them Georgos," he said pointing to the dead man.

"Another two, lightly wounded. Two of Ryan's men were killed and another wounded."

"Thank you, Costas. Make sure the wounded get the medical attention they need."

"Let's check on the King," Ryan said.

The two men walked to the room where the King was holed up and knocked on the door. "It's Markos, Your Majesty, open up the Germans have left for the time being."

The door opened and both men saw the King holding a British Army Webley Service revolver in his right hand and the two Greek officers in his party were armed with rifles. "Your Majesty, you're safe. The Germans are gone," said Markos.

"I was not going to be taken alive and be paraded in Berlin like an animal," said the King, as he and the others put their weapons down.

"It was Markos and the Cretans who stopped the Germans from grabbing you, sir."

The King gave Markos his outstretched hand. "Thank you, lieutenant. I will not forget what you and your men did here."

"Thank you, Your Majesty. Just doing my duty"

"Gentlemen, we need to hurry and get out of here. The area will soon be crawling with Germans," Ryan said.

"Where will we go, Lieutenant Ryan? Certainly not to Melame. The airfield would be one of their main targets."

"Just before the German attack on the Villa, Melame ordered us out of here. We are to go to the South coast where you will be evacuated by the Royal Navy to Egypt," Markos replied.

"But there are Germans everywhere!"

"We do not have a choice, Your Majesty. The Germans know you are here. Back at the olive groves where the Germans landed we spotted a small signal fire still burning. This was no chance encounter. You were their target. Get packing, sir. Just take what you will need for the journey. We are leaving in 20 minutes. And gentlemen, please dress inconspicuously."

"We definitely will, Lieutenant Ryan," said the King."

Chapter 4

Perivolia, Crete, One Kilometer North of the Villa
20 May 1941, 0945hrs,

After quickly exiting the villa the same way they had entered, the survivors of the German assault team headed north through the surrounding fields trying to distance themselves from Ryan and his New Zealanders. Mueller was beside himself. The raid had gone bad from the very minute they had crossed the coast. Losing the first glider had just been bad luck, but the loss of another and the enemy attack on their landing site had been a disaster. But still, he had come so close, only to be stopped by a few Greeks, armed with museum pieces. His men had been almost to the top of the stairs when someone had tossed a grenade. That had taken out three of his men, but he still could have pulled it off, had the New Zealander Lieutenant and his men not returned, thus forcing them to retreat toward Chania. He looked at what remained of his once platoon size force which was now resting in a grape vineyard. Only a quarter now was left. One of his SS men had been killed and another lightly wounded by grenade shrapnel. Most of the Luftwaffe Fallschirmjagers had been killed on landing, or on the attack on the house. If the rest of the attacking German forces met the same resistance as they had, the attempt to capture the island would be in jeopardy.

"Sir, The enemy is not following us," said Lantz who had just returned with Bruner from the direction of the Villa.

"At least something is starting to go right. We are in no shape to fight off a large sized assault. We'll head to Chania and link up with our forces there and commandeer some men and go after our quarry again."

"But sir, we will lose track of them. I am sure they will be leaving the house after our attack. They are aware that we know who they are protecting."

"This is why I want you, Lantz, to pick two men give them the spare radio and you will instruct them to stay out of sight of the enemy. They are to follow them wherever they go. They will give us a report every couple of hours."

"Yes, sir."

"Once we have some more troops we will go after them and finish the mission."

"If I were the enemy commander, sir, I would head south. There is no way they can go towards Chania or Maleme and not run into our patrols."

"You are probably correct on that assumption, Lantz. They would never take the chance with the King. They would also be moving a lot slower in the rough terrain with the King and his party in tow, so we should be able to catch up with them fairly easily. Now, go pick your two men to track our target."

"Yes, sir!

Mueller looked towards his senior NCO who was covered in dust and blood from several shrapnel cuts received from the grenade that had ruined their plans. They could all hear the heavy fighting that was going on just north from their present position, which meant that German troops were close by.

"Bruner, get everyone ready, we are moving towards Chania. According to my map, the main coastal road is a couple of kilometers from here. We should run into our forces there."

"Send a couple of men to scout ahead. We don't need any more surprises."

"Jawohl, Herr Obersturmbanfuhrer!"

Perivolia, Crete, the Villa
20 May 1941, 1030hrs,

Once Ryan and Markos had ensured that the surrounding area had been cleared of Germans, they gave orders to begin preparations to evacuate the villa. Before dismantling the radio, they had received another message from headquarters confirming their orders to evacuate to the South coast to be picked up by the Royal Navy. Their journey would be long and dangerous. The Germans had already made one attempt against the King. They would have to travel over 50 kilometers and across the Lefka Mountain range to get their charges away from the clutches of the Nazis.

They quickly loaded the few pack mules they had with food, ammunition and the remaining Greek gold reserves that had been evacuated to Crete to be used to run the exiled Greek government.

"Markos, I want a couple of your men to travel ahead and act as scouts. They will be our eyes and ears. We will need the assistance of the local population if we are going to pull this off. We have almost 50 clicks to travel and must go over a mountain range before we make it to the south coast," said Ryan. "I am sure we have not seen the last of our German friends. Those guys were professionals. One of the dead was wearing SS insignia. Those guys don't give up easy. They are elite fighting troops."

Markos remembered how close he had come to meeting his maker. "Yeah, I heard of them in old news reels when I went to the movies back home. Those guys knew exactly what they were doing. I think our friends may be going for reinforcements and coming after us."

"You may be correct on that assumption, Markos. The King is too valuable a prize for the Germans to let him get away. That's why we need to put some distance between us and this house."

Ryan glanced at his map. "I think we'll spend the night here at Therisso," he said pointing at a spot on the map approximately 15 kilometers south of the villa. It should take us the rest of the morning and most of the afternoon to get there. I don't want to be out traveling at night unless we have to. We need to try to stay off the main roads to avoid any German aircraft spotting us."

Markos turned to the surviving Cretan Gendarmes who now numbered only eight men from the original ten men that had deployed to the villa earlier that morning. A few of them had taken the MP38 machine pistols, KAR 98 Mauser rifles and stick grenades off the dead Germans and had dumped their antique rifles. One of them had his left arm bandaged, but still carried his weapon. Markos told them what the intended plan was and they too agreed that it was probably the best course of action. Markos then dispatched two of them ahead of the group to act as scouts as Ryan had requested.

At that moment, the King and his party exited the house. They were all dressed in plain clothes and were wearing hiking boots. "Your Majesty, I see you are ready to leave?"

"We are all ready, Lieutenant Ryan. May I ask where we are headed?"

"Why of course, sir. We will spend the night at a village called Therisso. It's about 15 kilometers from here."

"That should take us the rest of the day to get there barring any unforeseen circumstances such as the Germans", said the King. "Then let's get moving. We don't have any time to waste."

"We will, your Majesty, but before we go I need to ensure we are not being followed by our German friends. Corporal Smith!"

Smith, who had just finished loading the mules, turned around, "Sir."

"Take two men and watch our rear. I do not want anybody sneaking up on us. Make sure you remain about 500 meters behind us. I will send you a replacement every couple of hours"

"Yes, sir!"

"Now let's get moving, we have a long way to go."

Four Kilometers South of Chania
20 May 1941, 1210hrs

After walking for about an hour, Mueller and what was left of his team had reached the east-west coastal road a few kilometers south of Chania. The din of battle could be heard coming from the direction of Crete's second largest city.

Remnants of the heavy fighting that had taken place littered the area. Many Fallschirmjagers, still in their chutes, were lying motionless in the nearby fields, killed before they had even reached the ground. The road was littered with several destroyed trucks and Bren gun carriers, apparent victims of Luftwaffe bombing and strafing attacks. The smell of burning rubber and flesh still lingered in the air.

The tired SS men and Fallschirmjagers hunkered down in an orange grove adjacent to the road to have lunch. Mueller ate his fieldportionen (field rations) hurriedly, bland tinned sausage and cheese with hard Zweiback biscuits. Washing down the last bite of his rations with a gulp of tepid water from his canteen, he spotted Bruner returning from the direction of Chania. He tossed the senior NCO a pack of rations.

"Here have something to eat, Willi."

"Thank you, Sir. We made contact with some of our units about fifteen hundred meters to the east of us. They are General Sussman's men under the command of a Major Heidrich," said Bruner.

"The General and his staff are dead. Their glider came apart and crashed into a hillside soon after takeoff."

A shiver ran through Mueller's spine as he thought of what could have happened to him on the way to this god forsaken island. This whole operation had not gone very well from the start. "Let's go meet the major and see if we can salvage our part."

"Sir!"

"What is it, Lantz?"

"We just received a radio report that the target is moving south."

"Just as I thought, they are not sticking around and taking the risk of being captured. If they are moving south, I suspect they are going to the coast to be evacuated. The King is now too much of a liability to the British."

"You're probably correct, sir. Our men are following at a safe distance."

"Good work, Lantz. Now let's get moving. Everyone, be alert! There are enemy troops in the area. Avoid contact with them, if possible. We can't afford any more casualties."

A half hour later, they made contact with a large detachment of General Sussman's troops. Mueller observed that many of the Fallschirmjagers had been wounded, but their morale was still good. He asked them where their commanding officer was and they directed him and his men to a temporary command post which had been set up in an olive grove. The sporadic sounds of gunfire could be heard coming from several hundred meters north of the command post. The area was hot, intermittent enemy mortar rounds were landing near the grove. Reaching the command post, he spotted an MG-34, manned by two Fallschirmjagers covering the approach. A group of officers were hunched over a map and an NCO was talking into a radio. Several seriously wounded Fallschirmjagers lay nearby and were being treated by the unit medics.

"Who is in command here?"

"I am, "replied a tall, stocky man wearing Major's insignia.

"Major Heidrich, at your service."

"I am Obersturmbanfuhrer Georg Mueller on a special mission for the Reichsfuhrer and I require your assistance."

"And what may that be, Herr Obersturmbanfuhrer?"

"I require the service of 20 of your men to finish my mission. Most of my troops were killed when we landed."

"That is presently out of the question. As you can see, the situation here is still very fluid. The enemy is on the other side of this olive grove." As if to press the point, a couple of mortar shells landed in the grove, killing and wounding several of the Fallschirmjagers that were positioned there.

"We are barely holding. Half the battalion is dead or wounded. General Sussman and most of our staff is dead. This entire operation may fail. We were given bad intelligence and we landed on top of them. The enemy was waiting for us and slaughtered my men!"

"Are you finished, Major? I don't want to hear any more of your traitorous defeatist talk! You will do as ordered. This mission is of vital importance to the Reich!"

"I am not under your orders, Herr Mueller. I don't have 20 men to spare! We may be overrun at any minute."

"I don't give a damn, Major!" Mueller's voice had gone up several octaves.

"This mission is vital to the fatherland!"

For a fleeting moment, Mueller thought about pulling his service pistol and shooting the stupid fool, but reconsidered due to the MG-34 only 50 feet away. He did not want to test the loyalty of Heidrich's men for their commander. Mueller thought of another option. Heidrich would be dealt with in another way.

"Major, would you at least give us the use of your radio for a few minutes?"

"Of course you may use it."

Mueller had the radio operator contact Wehrmacht Headquarters in Athens and had his request passed on to the senior SS liaison officer. Thirty minutes later, a message arrived for Heidrich. After reading it, he appeared pale and nervous.

"Sir, I must apologize for the misunderstanding. I will give you Sergeant Smelling and two squads. Will that be sufficient, sir?"

Mueller was amazed at the sudden change of heart, but the

SS did have certain methods of expediency it could call on when in a pinch.

"That will be enough for now, Major."

In less than 30 minutes, Sergeant Smelling and twenty men with an MG 34 had joined Mueller's ranks. Ten of the men were Alpine troops which could prove useful once they entered rough terrain.

"Lantz, let's get moving. I will brief the new men on our mission once we are well on the road.

Berlin, Reich Chancellery, Fuhrer Bunker
20 May 1941, 1330rs, (1230hrs Berlin Time)

Himmler watched in silence as the Fuhrer vented his rage at the fat fool and commander of the Luftwaffe, Herman Goering and the Chief of Staff, General Oberst Franz Hadler. The latest reports from Crete were bad and getting worse by the moment. Casualties amongst the Fallschirmjagers had been extremely severe and losses of transport aircraft had also been heavy and were still mounting. The Fallschirmjager and glider landings at the center and eastern end of the island had almost been wiped out. They had landed right on top of prepared enemy defenses. Even the islanders had taken up weapons and were using gangster methods to murder German troops. They would pay later; he would make sure of that. The only bright spot, if it could be called that due to the heavy casualties suffered by the airborne forces, was at Maleme airfield at the west end of the island. There, the Fallschirmjagers were barely holding and that was with the nonstop assistance of the Luftwaffe. If they could keep their tenuous hold on the airstrip and get some more reinforcements flown in, the operation could still succeed. But at the moment, that seemed very iffy.

"Heinrich!"

"Yes, my Fuhrer."

"Have Obersturmbanfuhrer Mueller and his men arrived safely on that damned island?"

"Yes, my Fuhrer. He and his men made it."

Himmler was relieved when he got the radio message from Mueller, but disappointed at the news that the mission had initially failed. From what he had read and heard all morning, he was not surprised that Mueller had lost half his command before he had even landed. So far, "Operation Merkur" had been a bloody disaster. The intelligence information had been all wrong. The British were on the island in force and had made defensive preparations and did have antiaircraft defenses and artillery, albeit not in great quantity. Not that he thought Mueller had much of a chance of succeeding; the odds were heavily stacked against him. But Mueller had asked for his assistance in obtaining more men so he could give it another try. The man was persistent. He would have to give him that. Well that was the reason he had chosen him. He had quickly typed up a message ordering that idiot Luftwaffe major to give Mueller anything he wanted, even his first born, if Mueller made the request.

"One bit of good news in this fiasco," said Hitler. "I want Mueller to go after these bandits that are killing our soldiers and teach them a lesson!"

"Yes, my Fuhrer. I will relay to him your orders."

"Hopefully, Mueller will stay alive long enough to implement them," thought Himmler.

One Kilometer, North of Therisso
20 May 1941, 1700hrs,

Except for an occasional German Fiessler Storch reconnaissance plane flying overhead, the journey to the village of Therriso, which rested at the foothills of the White Mountains, had been uneventful. They had mostly avoided the main roads to prevent the royal party from being spotted by the hundreds of refugees that were leaving the coastal areas where the fighting was going on. Ryan could not take the risk of anyone sympathetic to the Germans observing them and turning them in. They had stopped approximately one kilometer outside the village of Therriso and waited for the return of their scouts. Markos had sent them to check out the village and make contact with the two Cretan Gendarmes that had travelled ahead of the party and were supposed to have made arrangements for their overnight stay. Thirty minutes later, the two scouts and one of the Gendarmes had returned and made contact with them.

"Sir, the village is quiet. No one has spotted any enemy activity. The villagers said many planes have flown overhead, but so far they have been ignored by the Germans."

"What about quarters for the night?"

"Lieutenant Androlakis, I spoke with the village mayor. He will let us use his home and barn for the night and give us some provisions for our journey. Even though his political sympathies are not with the royalists, he is a patriotic Greek and will do his duty."

"Thank you, Takis."

"Let's get moving then and try to keep the King and the rest of his party out of sight, Markos. I don't think he is the most popular guy around here," Ryan said.

Fifteen minutes later, they had reached the outskirts. Therisso was your typical Cretan village that survived by sheep herding and agriculture. Most of the houses looked pretty old and alike, built of stone and topped with a red tile roof. Many of the town's men were gone, having taken their flocks to higher altitudes for the summer grazing season. They were met at the entrance of the village by the mayor and a group of townsfolk who cheered them on.

"Welcome to our village. I am Manolis Kiriakakis, Mayor of Therisso. We are honored that our allies, who are bravely fighting the German invaders, chose to stay here for the night and also share our food," the mayor said..

"We are all very grateful for your hospitality. We'll not stay too long and put you in danger. We will leave early in the morning," replied Markos in Greek.

"We, Cretans, are not worried about danger. Everyone here is a patriot. We have been fighting invaders for hundreds of years," said a large burly man sporting a long Mustache who was standing by the mayor.

"You speak English," said Ryan rather surprised.

"Yes, a little bit. I am Stavros Maniakos. Before the war, I was a tourist guide. I have escorted many British tourists through Samaria gorge that is how I learned my English. We are all happy that you are here. My grandfather fought the Turks and I will fight the Germans too, if necessary,"

"Thank you, Stavros, but I hope that it does not have to come to that. But if it does, we will welcome your assistance," said Ryan.

They were escorted to the mayor's home which was a large two story structure located in the center of the village. Ryan and Markos quickly whisked the King and his party inside to keep them out of the villagers view. The King and his entourage were going to bed down for the night in the house while the rest of "12 Platoon" took over the empty adjacent barn for their use. Ryan and his men were pleasantly surprised with the Cretans hospitality. They were brought fresh bread, cheese, eggs, olives and wine to wash it down. For security, Ryan took the necessary precautions and posted sentries around the house and at the approaches to the village. Unfortunately, Mueller's men were observing their moves and relaying their position to their commander. The two Germans would not live through the night. They would be detected and taken out by Ryan's men who had set up an observation post 500 meters south of the village, but the damage had already been done.

CHAPTER 5

6 Kilometers south of Therisso
20 May 1941, 2050hrs

All day they had headed south. The sounds of battle had gone on for most of the day; they could hear the sirens of the Stukas that were working over the enemy coastal positions. By nightfall, the noise of battle began to taper off. Mueller had kept his team off the main roads to avoid enemy traffic and being spotted by the locals. Finally, he had decided to call a halt for the night. It had gotten too dark for them to continue trekking through unfamiliar territory and risking injury or worse bumping into an enemy patrol. Mueller had them set up camp in a grove of citrus trees that ensured they remained camouflaged from prying eyes. He did not allow them to light any fires and risk being spotted. They would have to eat their rations cold and use the red lenses on their flash lights to see through the darkness. The last radio message they had received from the scout team had informed them that the target had stopped for the night at a village called Therisso, approximately six kilometers north from their present position.

"Sir, the men are bedded down and sentries have been posted."

"Thank you, Lantz. We will leave at daybreak. I don't want the enemy to get deep into the highlands. Then it becomes more difficult to stop them and they can easily set up ambushes in the confined mountain paths."

"Our men are keeping an eye on them, sir."

"I know, Lantz, but that can change. The English are not stupid. You should never underestimate your enemy. Their commander is a very competent officer, as is the Greek Lieutenant that Bruner noticed during the firefight in the house. They bloodied our noses pretty bad back there. I am almost certain they suspect we are looking for them."

"Yes, sir. Any officer worth his salt who is responsible for the security of such a high value asset would take the proper precautions. They will have sentries and patrols out scouring the adjacent country side. I hope our men are well hidden and do not take unnecessary risks."

"I hope so, too. We can't afford to lose track of the target. Now we need to get some rest. Everyone had a hard day. Tomorrow, I suspect, may be more trying."

"True, especially if we have to trudge up in the mountains after the Tommies, sir."

"We may have to, Lantz, that's why I need everyone rested. I will take the first three hour shift. You will take the next and Bruner the last. I need people I can trust on watch. I have ordered the sentries to avoid any type of contact unless absolutely necessary. We can't jeopardize the mission fighting an unnecessary engagement with an enemy patrol.

"Jawohl, Herr Obersturmbanfuhrer."

Therisso, Crete
21 May 1940, 0530hrs

The smell of frying sausages and freshly baked bread permeated the morning air around the village. The royal party and the men of the 12th Platoon had just completed their breakfast of freshly baked bread eggs and sausage and were getting ready to head out. Ryan and Markos were in a hurry to leave and wanted to put as much distance as possible between them and the village. The night had not been uneventful. One of their listening posts had detected two Germans that were apparently tracking them. Ryan's men had quickly dispatched the Germans, but had found a radio amongst their positions which signified that the Germans were still after them and probably knew their location.

"Ryan, everyone is packed and is ready to move. We now have a local guide to lead us through the mountains. Stavros has volunteered his services," said Markos.

"That's good news, Stavros will come in very handy. I am sure our friends are not far behind."

"I am honored to assist our gallant allies, Lieutenant Ryan. I do know a couple of shortcuts through the Lefka Mountain range and to the coast, but the trail is very rough and your pack mules will not make it. It will also be cold at the higher altitudes," said the guide.

"We really don't have much of a choice, Stavros. We can't take the regular road; the Nazis will catch us for sure. So any route you know that can save us some time and maybe lose our German tail would be appreciated right now. We will take our pack animals with us as far as we can."

"I really hate to abandon these people. The Germans know

we were here and two of their men are dead. They may not take that very well."

"I agree with you, Markos, but as I said, we don't have much of a choice. Our main mission right now is to get the King to the coast and safely evacuated."

"You're right, Ryan."

"Sir, the men are ready to go."

"Okay, Sergeant Thomas. Let's move. Stavros, lead the way."

Therisso, Crete
21 May 41, 0800hrs

It was a warm sunny morning when Mueller and his men entered the village of Therisso, weapons at the ready. The smoke of cooking fires was evident in the air. Two squads had checked out the village earlier and reported back that the town was empty of enemy soldiers. Most of the inhabitants upon seeing the Germans had locked themselves in their homes, too frightened to come out. Mueller was in a seething rage. Sometime during the night, they had lost radio contact with his surveillance team which most likely meant they had been discovered by the enemy and killed. Not only did their quarry have a head start on them, they now knew that he was after them. He had no patience to play games with these people; he needed answers and wanted them now.

When they reached the village square, they were met there by the mayor and the village priest. "Welcome to our humble village, sir," the Mayor said in broken German.

"I am Manolis Kiriakakis, Mayor of Therisso."

"I am Obersturmbanfuhrer Georg Mueller. We have been following a band of English soldiers in company with several Greeks. Do you know where they have gone?"

"A group of soldiers did pass through here yesterday, but I

don't know where they went."

Mueller got up into the Mayor's face. "Passed through you say?"

"Yes, as I said before, about 50 soldiers passed through here yesterday, late afternoon, Herr Mueller."

"Ja, passed through!" Mueller backhanded the Mayor knocking him to the ground.

"You are a lying sack of shit! Two of my men are missing and are probably dead. Before they went missing, they reported that the English bedded down for the night in your town," screamed Mueller in a bout of rage.

The Mayor now visibly frightened, got up and defiantly spat on the ground. "We are at war and you are the enemy!"

Mueller began to reach for his pistol, but hesitated for a moment, calmed down, looked at Mayor and smiled.

"Lantz, Bruner. I want you to round up twenty villagers and bring them here to the square. I will demonstrate to these fools what happens to enemies of the German Reich."

"Jawohl, Herr Obersturmbanfuhrer," replied Lantz.

Fifteen minutes later, Lantz and Bruner returned with 20 of the villagers, a mixed bag of men, women and children of all ages. Mueller, who had not said another word to the Mayor, unbuckled his holster, pulled out his pistol and walked toward the group of villagers that had been lined up against the church wall.

"So Mayor, I want to show you and the rest of your countrymen what happens when you decide to defy us."

"Lantz, bring me that old man," said Mueller pointing to one of the villagers that Mueller's men had lined up against the church.

Bruner grabbed the man who was wearing a woolen shepherd's jacket and a traditional Cretan head scarf and shoved him towards Mueller. The old man, losing his balance, fell to the ground in front of Mueller. Getting up slowly, he stared at Mueller defiantly.

Without a second's hesitation, Mueller raised his pistol and shot the man between the eyes. The sound of the gunshot reverberated throughout the square. The old man fell dead at Mueller's feet.

"Ilias, Ilias!" screamed one of the women being held hostage by the church. She tried to go to the body, but was held back by one of Mueller's men.

"What did you do?" yelled the Mayor in anguish. The priest had left the Mayor's side and went to help the man. Seeing he was dead, the priest administered last rites.

"It is your fault this man is dead. Had you told me what I wanted to know from the beginning, he would still be alive. Let this be a lesson to all of you. This is what happens to enemies of the German Reich. Now please translate to your people what I just said."

The Mayor quickly translated into Greek what Mueller had said. Someone in the group yelled "German murderers!" The mood of the hostages had changed from one of fear to anger. The woman who had been crying for her murdered husband now stood in silence and stared at Mueller with hatred in her eyes.

"Now, I will try this again. I have some questions and I will not tolerate any more insolence! Where did the British that stayed the night in your village go?"

"I do not know. They did not tell me anything."

"You are lying! Mueller nodded at Bruner who in turn pistol whipped the Mayor across the head, knocking him down and giving him two kicks to the rib cage. Two of Mueller's men, both SS, picked up the Mayor who was bleeding from a cut on his forehead.

"Since you do not know anything, let's ask your town's people. Now translate!"

The Mayor translated Mueller's question, but not one of the hostages came forward.

"I see that I must make myself clearer. Lantz, pick five hostages and shoot them."

"Herr Mueller, you can't do that," pleaded the Mayor. "That is murder."

"Murder? Greek civilians were killing German soldiers as they came down hanging from their parachutes yesterday. Two of my men are missing. Maybe they were murdered by Greek bandits from this very village?"

"We have harmed no one, Herr Mueller. But it is war and we Cretans do have the right to defend our lands from invaders. We have done this for centuries."

"You are right, this is war. So I can do as I please and I will shoot them all if I have to. It's now up to you, Mayor."

Lantz had lined up three men and two women against the church wall and was in the process of preparing the firing squad, when one of the selected male hostages to be shot began singing the Greek national anthem. He was soon joined by the rest of the Greeks in the square.

"See, Herr Mueller, Cretans are not afraid to die for their country."

"As you wish, Mayor." Mueller nodded to Lantz who had selected the firing squad which was now facing the five hostages that were to be shot.

"Firing squad, attenhut! Ready, aim," commanded Lantz. The ten man firing squad brought their rifles up and took aim. Lantz looked at Mueller, waiting for his nod to give the order to fire.

"Wait, please!" screamed a women in English who was running toward the square followed by one of Mueller's men.

Mueller motioned for Lantz to have his men to lower their rifles. "Please don't kill these people."

"And who are you, Miss?" he said to the young and quite attractive dark haired women who stood across from him panting heavily as she tried to catch her breath.

"My name is Sophia Maniakos. My father, Stavros Maniakos, is guiding the English and Greek soldiers through the Lefka Mountains. He was a tour guide before the war. He knows the mountains very well."

"I am Obersturmbanfuhrer Georg Mueller."

"Shut up, Sophia!" yelled the Mayor. Bruner quickly silenced him with a rifle butt.

"No, I will not idly sit by and watch these people murdered to protect the King. What has he ever done for Crete, except terrorize us and throw us in jail?" she yelled to be heard by everyone in the square.

"When did they leave?" asked Mueller.

"They left about 5:30 this morning and headed into the mountains."

"Do you know anything about two German soldiers that were following the English?"

"I heard the English soldiers talking about one of their patrols finding and killing your soldiers last night."

"Thank you for the information, fraulein Maniakos. At least their families will know now that they gave their lives for the fatherland."

"Please, sir. Let these people go. They have not done anything."

"That depends, fraulein. My men and I do not know these mountains. Your father is helping enemies of the Reich. Two of my men are already dead."

"Please don't harm him. I will help you if you promise not to hurt my father or anyone else."

"And how will you do that?"

"I will guide you and your men through the mountains. I know them very well. I used to accompany my father when he guided British and German tourists through them. That's how I know English and I do speak a little of German."

Mueller thought it over for a moment and decided to accept her offer. He would take a different approach with her since she was volunteering her services. What did he have to lose anyway? She was very attractive and if she betrayed him he would make her regret the day she was born.

"I will accept your services, fraulein, but we must leave immediately. The enemy has over a two hour head start."

"Yes, but I must go home and change first to something more appropriate for the terrain.

"Of course, two of my men will escort you to your house."

"Thank you, but I don't need any assistance."

"I insist, fraulein."

"Lantz, let the rest of these fools go and detail two men to escort the girl to her house to change. She will be guiding us through the mountains"

"Mayor, I want your people to provide us with some rations. Make it quick, we are leaving in twenty minutes."

Lefka Mountain Foothills, Crete
21 May 1941, 1145hrs

By midmorning, the royal party had reached the lower slopes of the Lefka Mountains. Above them loomed high ridges that were still covered with snow. With Stavros as their guide, they had made good time in the rugged terrain. As they climbed higher into the mountains, the temperature had cooled and the topography switched from the dry Mediterranean brush to lush evergreen trees. The thin mountainous air carried the faint sounds of heavy fighting that was coming from the North coast. According to the last radio report, they had received from allied headquarters, the battle for control of the island had so far gone very badly for the Germans; except for a small foothold at Maleme airfield, they had suffered thousands of casualties and had nothing much to show for it. The next 24 hours would be crucial for both the invaders and the defenders. If the Germans managed to expand their foothold at Maleme and bring in reinforcements and artillery, the battle could be lost to the allied cause.

Markos had taken position in the middle of the party providing security for the King and his party. He had sent Warrant Officer Manolakos with two of his men to hang back a few hundred meters to ensure they were not being followed. Markos was not too worried, they had at least a three hour head start and the Germans would not know which route they would be taking through the mountains. He was beginning to worry about the King and his companions. A few of the older men were beginning to show signs of fatigue. He decided to go ask Lieutenant Ryan to stop and take a rest break.

"Ryan, we've been on road since 0530hrs this morning, we need to take a break and give the animals and the men a rest. The King and his party are starting to tire. Most of them are middle aged men and are not used to this pace."

"You're right, Markos, but only for 20 minutes. I want everyone to grab a quick bite to eat. No fires, I don't want any smoke to give us away. We don't know how far behind the Jerries are."

"Thanks, Ryan. I need a break too. Not used to this either.

In New York, I took the subway wherever I wanted to go in the city."

"Stavros, give it a rest for 20 minutes. Grab something to eat," yelled Ryan to the guide who was about 30 feet ahead of them.

"Okay, Ryan. There is a small stream about 200 meters ahead that is a good place to rest and also get fresh water."

"Sure, Stavros, take us there."

Both men turned and saw King George of Greece approaching them. He was alone. Markos and Ryan gave him a salute.

"Please, gentlemen, let's dispense with the courtesies until we are finally safe and sound. You have all put your lives in danger for my behalf and I want to thank you and your men for that.

"Your Majesty, we are all just doing our duty and we will keep doing it till you are safely evacuated," said Markos

"I know you all will and I and my companions appreciate that."

"Sir, how are you and your party managing? We have been really moving at a grueling pace," Ryan asked.

"We are not young men anymore, but we are managing fairly well. Knowing that the Germans may be following us, gives everyone that added bit of energy," the King replied.

"We will probably have to abandon our pack mules pretty soon, the terrain, according to Stavros, will be pretty rough and it will be getting much colder as we reach the snow line in a few hours," added Markos.

"We will help you carry the cargo and supplies."

"Thank You, Sir. Hopefully that will not prove necessary, my men should be able to carry the, the gold, extra ammo and food," said Ryan.

"Gentlemen, we have arrived at our rest stop." The party had reached a small clearing surrounded by tall pine trees. From the side of the mountain, a spring was gushing ice cold water.

"Thank You, Stavros, this place is beautiful. Let's stop for a rest, grab a bite to eat and quickly move on. Markos, have the men grab some fresh water and food and then post some sentries."

"Will do, Ryan."

Lefka Mountains, Crete
21 May 1941, 1310hrs

With Sophia as their guide, Mueller and his men had set a grueling pace. Mueller was surprised that the young women could keep up with the best of his men who were trained Gebirgsjagers (mountain rangers). In actuality, he was the one having a hard time. He had become soft with all the time he had spent in Paris, drinking Cognac and chasing the French girls. He had to stop a few times to rest and catch his breath as his breathing had become labored in the thinner air. One of the Gebirgsjagers had advised him that he would acclimatize to the thinner air in a couple of days. Unfortunately, that was a luxury he did not have.

As they climbed deeper into the mountains, Mueller was impressed with the beautiful natural scenery that was all around him. Lush pine forests and snowcapped mountains. It reminded him of his early days, training in Bavaria. On the way up the mountain trail, they had passed a couple of sheep herders, but none of them had seen any English or Greek soldiers. Even if they had, he did not expect them to tell him so. Earlier in the morning, they had been able to follow the tracks that the enemy soldiers and pack animals had left. Now as the terrain became rockier, it was getting harder to find their tracks. They could not be more than an hour ahead of them, he thought. There was no way that the allied troops, straddled with the royal party, could make the same time that he and his men had made up the mountain. Mueller glanced at Sophia who was several paces in front of the group; she looked completely stunning in the tight pair of pants she was wearing. The girl had been completely true to her word. She had taken them this far without a single complaint. Maybe he would spare her father as a goodwill gesture. From the last radio reports they had received, the fighting was still going badly for Germany's forces, but the Fallschirmjagers had established a foothold at Maleme airfield and reinforcements were starting to come in. Maybe the Luftwaffe might just pull off this mad endeavor of theirs, capturing an enemy held and fortified island by air.

After another ten minutes of walking, they reached a clearing with a spring gushing fresh cold water out the side of the mountain. Sophia turned around and smiled at Mueller. "They were here not too long ago," said Sophia, pointing to boot and hoof marks that were left in the mud, in addition to several empty tin cans that had contained British army rations.

"This was one of my father's favorite resting places when he took tourists through the mountains. The spring has some of the best water on the island." She took a metal cup out, filled it with water and handed to Mueller who took a sip.

"This water is ice cold!" He quickly drank the rest down.

"Thank you, fraulein. It's very good," he said to her while handing her the cup back. She smiled at him as she took the cup filled it and drank.

"Once they reach the top of the mountain, my father will take them through the Samaria gorge."

"Are you positive, fraulein?"

"Yes, that is the route my father will use at this time of the year."

"I want to thank you, fraulein, for helping us."

"I hate the royalists, Herr Mueller. They arrested my brother and put him in prison as a subversive. He was a Venezalist and a nationalist. He was allegedly killed while trying to escape. At least that's what they told us. My mother died a year later from her grief."

"Venezalist? I am not familiar with Greek history."

"Eleftherios Venizelos was a Cretan nationalist who fought the Ottomans and later became prime minister earlier this century after Crete was joined with Greece. He is the father of modern Greece. He built up the Greek army and with couple of successful wars, he doubled Greece's size."

"Yes, he was just like our Fuhrer, Adolf Hitler. He united Austria and the Sudetenland with Germany."

"Yes, something like that. But in the end, he was stabbed in the back by the royalist traitors who later caused the destruction of the Greeks of Asia Minor in 1922. They had been living there for over 2500 years."

"I remember that in history class," said Mueller.

"Our Fuhrer would never let that happen."

"Germany is lucky to have such a powerful leader and military," said Sophia.

"Yes, we Germans are fortunate that we have our great Fuhrer, Adolf Hitler. Now please excuse me, fraulein. I must take care of some military business. I really enjoyed our chat."

"I did to," she replied.

"Lantz, post some guards and have the rest of the men get something to eat and fill their canteens with fresh water. I want everyone with a full stomach for what lies ahead," said Mueller.

"We will be leaving in 20 minutes and need to make good time to catch up with our quarry. They can't be more than a couple of miles ahead. I want a squad of Gebirgsjagers to forge ahead. They should be able to follow their trail now. Advise their Sergeant that once the enemy party is found to report back immediately with the news. They must not be detected by the enemy or our plan will not work. I do not want to take the enemy head on. If we can get ahead of them and set a trap, possibly at the Samaria gorge, we may be able to capture them and avoid casualties on both sides. I do not want the King harmed."

"Jawol Herr, Obersturmbanfuhrer!"

Lefka Mountains, 1600 meters
21 May 1941, 1630hrs

After trudging for several more hours, the party had left the tree line and was now traveling through a rocky landscape, devoid of trees and fauna. Markos wondered if this is how the surface of the moon looked like. He had once looked at the moon through a telescope while in college and this terrain looked very similar. It had gotten noticeably cooler and by nightfall, they would be at the snowline where it would be at least 25 degrees cooler than the valley. They would spend the night there, a prospect he was not looking forward to, since they all lacked cold weather gear.

The bolder strewn track had become more difficult for them to negotiate as they progressed higher up the mountain. Ryan had gotten rid of their pack animals a couple miles back and had distributed what extra gear they absolutely needed amongst the men. Even the royal party had volunteered to carry the spare ammo. The view at this altitude was stunning; they could see for miles down into the valley and all the way to the coast. Columns of smoke could be seen rising from the direction of Chania and the faint sound of occasional explosions carried through the thin mountain air. With no more trees to conceal them from prying eyes, the party was now visible from the air. Several times, they were over flown by Fiessler Storch observation planes, but were ignored. Markos hoped their luck would last. But unbeknown to them, Mueller's Gebirgsjagers scouts had found them and were on their way back to brief him.

The trail had narrowed to the point that they could only walk two a breast up the steep path. Markos and several of his Gendarmes had taken point with Stavros, their guide. As the party approached an area that was heavily strewn with very large boulders, a shot rang out followed by another. Everyone quickly dropped to the ground, looking for cover. Markos looked around, but could not see where the shots had come from. Within a minute, Lieutenant Ryan had joined Markos.

"Do you see anything, Markos? Where did those shots come from?"

"I don't see anyone. The shots came from up ahead."

"We can't stay here forever, Markos."

Ryan was about to dispatch a squad to try and flank the shooters when one of the ambushers yelled down to them in Greek. "Who are you? Germans? Do not come any closer or we will shoot."

"They are Greek," said Markos.

A couple of Ryan's troops tried to move in an effort to outflank their ambushers, but another shot rang out. The bullet struck the ground near one of the soldiers causing rock chips to fly. The soldiers immediately went to ground.

"I said, do not come any closer."

"We are Greek and allied soldiers. Stop shooting at us before someone gets hurt," shouted Markos in Greek.

"How do we know you are not Germans? Germans can speak Greek too," replied someone else in Greek that was hiding up the rocky path with the shooters.

"We are wearing Greek and British uniforms. We can show ourselves to you if you promise not to shoot. My name is Markos Androlakis. I am an officer in the Greek army."

"Okay, Markos, stand up slowly and show yourself, no weapons, please."

Markos got up very slowly with his hands raised in the air. "I will be walking towards you if that is okay with you. I am wearing a Greek officer's uniform."

"Okay, don't try anything funny."

Markos walked up the path for several meters before he was told to stop.

"That's far enough, turn around a full circle."

"Markos turned a full 360 degrees. He spotted one of the men pointing a rifle at him. Seeing that he was not carrying a weapon, they ordered him to walk toward the man holding the rifle.

"Okay, stop." Markos froze in his tracks. The man holding the rifle put the weapon down and another man frisked Markos and found his Hellenic Army ID card.

"You can put your hands down. Indeed, you are a Greek officer. Thank God, you are not Germans. We are not very heavily armed. I apologize, but one can't take any chances. I am Stathis Mavrakis," said the man, offering his hand to Markos.

Markos shook the man's hand and called out to Ryan that everything was okay. "Well for a moment, you had us worried, Stathis. We know there is a group of Germans following us."

Several more men, who had been hiding behind some of the larger rock formations, came out and greeted them.

"Zito English ally," yelled one of the men and offered Ryan a swig of Raki, the local Cretan drink.

"What did he say?" Ryan asked.

"He said long live our English allies."

Ryan smiled. "We are not exactly British, but I'll drink to that," he said taking a good swig of the alcohol. "Wow that's powerful stuff. How do you guys drink that, Markos?"

"It's a man's drink, Ryan. And I thought you Kiwis were hard core drinkers?"

"Guess it takes some getting used to," said Ryan, as he took another swig.

They were soon joined by the royal party, but the Cretan guerillas were so overwhelmed with patriotism and fighting a common enemy, the Germans, they did not seem to mind the King and even offered him a drink which he accepted.

"Markos, tell our new friends that this is a great party but we need to get moving," Ryan said.

Markos explained to Stathis and his men that they loved his company, but had to leave. The Germans were not too far behind.

"Markos, can you spare any weapons for us? We are woefully short and we need them to fight the Germans," asked Stathis.

Markos translated to Ryan what Stathis had said. Ryan thought it over for a few seconds. "Well we could give them one of the Bren guns and some ammo and a few grenades. They are getting pretty heavy to lug over these mountains."

Markos told Stathis what Ryan had offered and the guerilla leader jumped with joy. "OH, thank you, sir. We will kill many Germans with them."

"I am counting on it," replied Ryan with a smile.

"Sergeant Jones, give these men one of the Bren guns, some

ammo and any grenades we can spare. I am sure they will be put to good use soon by our friends here."

"Yes, sir."

After a quick instruction on the use of the Bren machine gun, Ryan turned it over to the guerillas, along with some spare ammo and a dozen grenades. Markos had also given them the old rifles that Cretan Gendarmes had swapped for K98 Mausers and MP 38 sub machine guns they taken from the dead Germans back at the villa. Saying goodbye to their new friends, they all parted ways. According to Stavros, their guide, they would need another two hours to reach the summit and camp for the night.

Berlin, the Reich Chancellery, Fuhrer Bunker
21 May 1941, 1800rs, (1700hrs Berlin Time)

Reichsfuhrer Heinrich Himmler had just finished reading a message that had been sent from Mueller. According to the message, he was in pursuit of the royal party and their New Zealander escorts somewhere deep in the mountains of southern Crete. The man was amazing, he thought. After almost being killed upon landing and losing most of his men, Mueller had not only quickly recovered from his situation, he now was in pursuit of his quarry. He needed more men like this in his personal service. They get things done. Well that was why he had picked Mueller for this mission. He still had not said anything to Hitler about Mueller's special mission. The possibility for failure was still very great and he did not want to be embarrassed in front of the Fuhrer.

The door to the Fuhrer's conference room opened and both he and Goering came out smiling. The Fuhrer's mood had changed drastically for the better. The situation on the island was stabilizing, but still critical. The Luftwaffe Fallschirmjagers had succeeded in partially securing Maleme airfield, one of their main objectives, and had managed to fly in some reinforcements. One good British counter attack on the airfield could still cause the entire situation to quickly go south, but except for a few minor attacks for some reason that had not yet happened. Losses of men and material had so far been extremely heavy, but the situation now was not entirely hopeless.

"Ah, Heinrich there you are. You missed Herman's briefing."

"Sorry, my Fuhrer, I have a splitting headache," said Himmler. He was in no mood to be in the same room with that pompous idiot Goering and hear all his bragging and stupidities if he didn't have to.

"The situation has slightly improved. The fighting ability of the German soldier is superior to the drunken English and new Zeeland louts that we are facing. If we can hold the airstrip for another 48 hours, the island will be ours and the British will have to swim to Egypt," said Hitler.

"The Luftwaffe will sink any Royal navy ships that approach the island!" added Goering.

"Of course, my Fuhrer," replied Himmler, not wanting to remind him that the Royal Navy still ruled the Mediterranean and that the Italian Navy was useless and could not stop the British from evacuating their men from Crete if they decided to. Granted the Luftwaffe had caused the British the loss of some ships, and could still make it very painful for them, but it could not single handedly stop the Royal Navy from reaching the island.

"I am going to my office to take a couple of aspirin and get a bite to eat," said Himmler.

"I hope you feel better, Heinrich."

"Thank you, my Fuhrer."

Lefka Mountains, Crete
21 May 1941, 1830hrs,

Mueller and his men had halted at the end of the tree line for a ten minute rest. The terrain that awaited them was strewn with large rock formations, huge boulders and mostly devoid of any trees and brush. It would slow their progress, but it would also slow down their enemy even more. During their short rest break, two of the Gebirgsjagers that had scouted ahead returned and told him they had located the enemy party just a couple of kilometers ahead. They would wait until the enemy camped for the night and then they would bypass them and move ahead to set a trap. He was exhausted and so were most of his men, but they were so close now. Earlier, they had all heard shots and thought that his scouts had been detected, but when the Gebirgsjagers had returned, he was relieved that they had not been found, otherwise his plan would have go down the proverbial toilet.

"Lantz, we need to move fast and get in front of them and trap them in the gorge. I will talk to the girl."

"She is our only chance for success, sir. She knows these mountains very well and we don't."

Mueller called to the girl. "Fraulein, may I have a word with you."

"Of course."

"My men have found the enemy. They are about two kilometers ahead of us. I am sure they will soon be stopping to rest for the night. Can you guide us past them? If we can trap them in the gorge, we can solve this with little or no bloodshed. This would be better for all and especially for your father. If we have to fight, I can't guarantee his safety"

"It will be dark soon, Herr Mueller."

"Please call me Georg."

"As I was saying, Georg," She smiled as she said his name.

"It will be getting dark soon. I have an idea where my father will stop for the night on the mountain summit. We will have very little light with no moon. It will be very dangerous, but it can be done."

"We don't have a choice, fraulein."

"Please call me Sophia."

Now Mueller smiled. "It has to be done, Sophia."

Mueller turned to Lantz. "She will help us. Let's get moving, we don't have time to waste."

"The men are exhausted, sir."

"So is the enemy, Lantz. We are soldiers of the greater Deutsches Reich! The German soldier is superior to a bunch of New Zealand drunks and old men. Now let's get going."

"Jawohl, Herr Obersturmbanfuhrer."

It was now all up to the Greek girl, Sophia, to guide them past the English without being detected. Unbeknownst to Mueller, as they moved into the open landscape, they were spotted by Stathis guerrilla band. The Cretans realized that these were the Germans that were after the British and the King of Greece. Unfortunately, they did not have the fire power to take on the Germans single-handed. The Greeks would follow them at a safe distance and intervene if the Germans attacked their friends.

Chapter 6

Lefka Mountains
21 May 1941, 2100hrs,

The allied party, exhausted from the grueling 14 hour trek through the mountains, had stopped and set up camp for the night on one of the numerous summits of the Lefka Mountain range. At an altitude of almost 2000 meters (6600 feet), the snow was still on the ground even at this time of year which made for a very cold night, especially since they were also lacking cold weather gear. The night sky was crystal clear and Markos could see the millions of stars that made up the Milky Way. He shivered from the cold air that penetrated through his uniform jacket. They could not light any fires to stay warm fearing they would be seen by the Germans. It would be a very uncomfortable night for all.

Markos had the first watch and was making a post check to ensure their sentries were alive and awake. It had been a long hard day and the men were all exhausted. Fortunately, he did not have to worry; Ryan's soldiers were all professionals as were the Cretan Gendarmes. His steps made crunching sounds as he walked on the semi frozen snow. As he came around the bend of the foot path to check on the last sentry post, he was challenged by one of the guards in broken English and Greek.

"Sergeant Mitsakis, It's Lieutenant Androlakis."

The man visibly relaxed and lowered his weapon and saluted. Markos returned the salute. "How is it going Sergeant? I know you are tired, so I won't ask that silly question." Both men laughed.

"Fine, sir. I am managing. The cold and the thought of the Germans following us is helping keep me awake."

Markos looked at the glowing dials on his watch. "You will be relieved in about an hour and you can go to sleep."

"I can't wait till morning so we can get out of here. By tomorrow this time, you should be on your way to Alexandria and away from here."

"You can come too, Sergeant. Greece will need soldiers with your experience."

"I have family here, lieutenant. A wife and two kids. I can't leave them to face the Germans alone. I'll still fight the Germans here on Crete. If they take the island there will be armed resistance. Cretans will never sit by and let enemy occupiers rule us. Anyway, sir, some of the younger single men might join you in Egypt."

"Well, Sergeant, hopefully we will throw the Germans into the sea and not have to face that possibility. So far, except for a foothold on Melame airfield we have defeated most of their landings."

Markos knew that if the Germans didn't get pushed off the airfield very soon by an allied counter attack and they managed to fly in a large amount of troops and artillery which the allies lacked, the battle for control of Crete would be lost.

"I pray to God, we do, sir."

"I'll see you later," said Markos, as he took off up the icy trail back to the camp.

Once back at the encampment, Markos checked on the King and the rest of his party. A small tent had been put up for his Royal Majesty to use. It would keep out some of the elements but not provide much warmth. He found the King arguing with one of Ryan's Sergeants.

"Is there a problem, Your Majesty?" Markos asked.

"No, lieutenant. I am just telling the sergeant that I don't need the tent. Sleeping outside is fine."

"That will be all, sergeant. I'll take it from here."

"Thanks, sir," said the NCO, obviously relieved that someone else now could argue with the King.

"Please Your Majesty, use the tent. The men can guard you easier."

The King sighed, "Okay, Markos, if you insist."

"Thank you, sir."

"No. I thank all of you for what you are doing for us."

"As I said before, Your Majesty, we are all doing our duty."

"I know you are. That's why I would like you to join my staff once we get to Egypt. The Greek Army needs to be rebuilt. Greece needs men like you."

"I am a Greek, but I am also an American. My family is in New York and I have not seen them in almost a year. The US will soon be involved in this war. I may be more useful over there."

"Just think about it."

"I will, sir. Have a good night."

"You too, Markos."

Markos saluted the King and walked towards Ryan's tent where he found the young New Zealander with Warrant Officer Manolakos sharing a bottle of Raki. The three men discussed the next day's strategy. Hopefully they would pass through the Samaria gorge without incident and reach Aghia Roumeli on the coast where they would be picked up by the Royal Navy and hitch a ride to Alexandria.

Lefka Mountains
21 May 1941, 2330hrs

The night grew colder and Mueller's lungs burned from the chilled mountain air. Higher and higher they climbed along the narrow trail. Everyone walked in complete silence not wanting to give their position away to any nearby enemy scouts. Finally they had reached a point a hundred meters below the main ridge. Sophia pointed to the faded trail that continued to the summit. Mueller signaled for everyone to wait there, while he and Sophia forged ahead. Reaching the summit, Mueller lay down next to Sophia and looked across the top of the ridge. It was clear of any English troops. Sophia assured him that the enemy party was camped about a kilometer from their present location. Mueller motioned for the Gebirgsjagers to scout ahead.

An hour later, they were climbing down the south side of the mountain. The night air was laced with the thick scent of pine. They had left the snowline a few minutes back and the going had become much easier. A half hour later, Sophia had taken them to a gulley that was surrounded with thin strands of conifer and not visible from the main path. She indicated that they should camp here for the night. Everyone was exhausted, having been on their feet for almost 20 hours. Mueller had Lantz and Bruner set up the sentry watches and then quickly set up his small tent as did most of the rest of the men. Needing to relieve himself, he got out of his tent and walked to a clump of tress where he emptied his bladder. The temperature at this altitude had to be just above freezing; early morning dew was beginning to settle on the ground.

On the way back to his tent, he spotted Sophia. The girl had laid out a thin blanket on the damp pine needle covered ground and had another thin blanket to use as a cover which was now damp. Sophia was beginning to shiver. Mueller felt a tinge of pity for the girl, she did not have the thick sleeping back he had back in the tent to stay warm in these harsh elements. He invited her to share his small tent for warmth. At first she politely refused, but as the mountain breeze began to pick up she began to shiver harder. Mueller took her hand and pulled her towards him. She came willingly and they both walked the short distance to his tent. They both removed their jackets and boots and went inside the small tent and he zipped it closed to keep out the elements. The girl was now shivering uncontrollably.

"I am so cold," she whispered through her chattering teeth.

"Here, get under the covers. Your shirt is wet my dear. Take it off and put it over us to dry."

He unzipped his sleeping bag and covered both of them. The shivering girl had taken off the damp shirt and snuggled up to him. He put his arms around her for added warmth. She was wearing nothing underneath. He could feel her cold skin and smell her feminine scent. He cupped her ample breasts and the girl shivered this time, but it was not from the cold. She turned around and their lips brushed. Mueller pulled her harder toward him and their mouths met.

"I am virgin. Please go easy."

He was not surprised. Most of the girls on the island kept their virginity until they were married. To do otherwise would dishonor her family and could result in an honor killing. Sophia was no Parisian whore. She was a beautiful woman and he would go gently and savor the moment. The girl let out a muffled cry as he entered her but, soon she was enjoying the act. They made love a couple of more times before they fell asleep in each other's arms from sheer exhaustion.

Lefka Mountains, south Slope, Samaria Gorge
22 May 1941, 10:30hrs

Markos admired the natural beauty of the Samaria gorge scenery that surrounded them. The narrow ravine was surrounded by steep cliffs that reached heights of 1000 meters or more. It was also home to the famous Kri- Kri mountain goat that had inhabited the island since antiquity. The group had just entered the gorge to begin their long descent to the sea shore. Europe's largest canyon began at an altitude of 1250 meters and stretched 16 kilometers to the shores of the Libyan sea in Aghia Roumeli. Throughout Crete's violent history the Samaria gorge was used by the Cretans to hide from enemy invaders. The steep sides made it almost impregnable to anyone trying to enter it from the outside.

The news they had received on the radio from the front was not good. Attempts to dislodge the Germans from their foot hold at Maleme airfield had failed. The invaders had been able to bring in more reinforcements with artillery. It was not boding well for the allies. Both Markos and Ryan were relieved that everyone's morale had improved immensely since they left their encampment. Lacking cold weather gear had made an extremely miserable night for all of them. The thin morning mist that had soaked everyone had not helped. With a clear sky and the warm sun shining down on them and with their journey almost over, their morale began to rapidly improve.

Markos walked to the front of their procession where both Ryan and their guide, Stavros, were having a friendly chat. "Hey Stavros, how much farther to Aghia Roumeli?"

"If we continue at this pace, maybe five hours, Markos."

"Why are you in a hurry to leave this beautiful quiet scenery and get back to a war?" Ryan asked.

"This place makes me nervous. Two guys with a gun can keep us pinned down in here for days."

"Oh don't worry, Markos, we'll be out of here in a few hours. By nightfall, we should be on our way to Alexandria."

"I hope you are right, Ryan."

Samaria Gorge, Crete
22 May 1941, 1200hrs

Stathis and his guerrilla band had spent most of the night forging ahead of the Germans. He was amazed at the enemy's determination and stamina. His men were from the area and knew the mountains well, but their respect for the Germans had gone up several notches. Once the enemy troops had entered the gorge, it had become difficult to trail them and remain undetected. He sent one of his best men to observe the German movements. Stathis had finally realized that the Germans were up to no good when they left behind ten men to help set the trap for their friends. The rest of the Germans finally halted in a very narrow area of the gorge and set up an ambush for the approaching allied party. Markos and the rest of their friends would be trapped and slaughtered in the gorge.

Stathis and his men did not have the fire power to attack the Germans head on. They would wait till the Nazis made their move. Once the enemy was preoccupied, they would intervene and hit them from the rear. Hopefully, together with the allied soldiers they would defeat them.

Samaria Gorge
22 May 1941, 1240hrs

Mueller had set the trap which would soon be sprung. The enemy would not have a choice but to surrender or be slaughtered. He had positioned snipers that could keep them pinned down in the gorge for days. Mueller had promised Sophia that he would not harm her father and gave orders to spare the man. His rear guard had radioed that the enemy party had just gone past them.

"Lantz, is everyone is ready?"

"Yes, sir."

"I do not want a fire fight unless we are given no choice."

"The men have been briefed, sir."

"Here they come. Everybody get ready," said Mueller.

As the allied group approached the German position, Mueller gave the signal for his men to go into action. One of his snipers fired, the bullet striking inches from Ryan. Immediately everyone took cover.. One of Ryan's men tried to get up to move, but was hit by sniper fire.

"I think we are in deep shit. We need to go back," said Ryan.

"Everybody back into the gorge," Markos yelled.

But that was stopped short with a burst of machine gun fire coming from the rear.

"You are right Ryan, we are in deep shit and we are also trapped in here. We can't go forward and we can't go backwards," Markos said.

"This is Obersturmbanfuhrer Georg Mueller. You are surrounded. You have no chance to resist. You can't get out of here alive."

"Okay, Ryan, what do we do now?"

Before Ryan could answer, one of the Cretan Gendarmes got

up, ran a few meters forward, firing his machine pistol. A single shot rang out, the bullet hitting him in the leg and dropping him in his tracks.

"The next one that tries anything will be shot dead" To show them that he meant business, Mueller motioned to his machine gunner who let off a burst, the bullets striking the ground just in front of them.

"Okay, we get your message. What do you want?" yelled Ryan.

"Send out all the Greeks, put down your arms and we will let you go."

"Sorry, I can't do that," Ryan replied.

"Your position is untenable. If you don't comply, you will all be killed. To demonstrate, a 50mm mortar round was fired and landed 30 meters from their position.

"You have five minutes to comply. You can discuss this with the King. We will let three of you stand to talk with each other as long as you are not holding a weapon. If you try anything, you will be shot by one of my snipers. Do we have an agreement?"

Ryan and Markos still wanted to make a fight of it but before they could reply, the King stood up with his hands over his head. "We agree to your proposal," he said walking over to Ryan and Markos.

"You have five minutes," Mueller replied.

Southern Samaria Gorge, Crete
22 May 1941, 1350hrs

Stathis, the partisan leader, had heard the firing which meant that the Germans had sprung their trap on the King's party. There was no choice now but to intervene and hope that between them and the allied force they could stop the Germans and get their friends through the pass.

"Antonis, we will attack the Germans in ten minutes. I guess we will see how good this Bren gun works. Get everyone ready. We will creep up to them and hit them first with grenades and then rush them," said Stathis to his second in command.

"Let's hope the English are able to join the fray or we are all dead," Antonis replied.

"We'll soon find out, my friend."

Samaria Gorge, Crete, allied position
22 May 1941, 1354hrs

"Please, Your Majesty, do not do it."

"Lieutenant Ryan, we are all trapped here and we have no choice. They will kill us all otherwise. That would be a needless waste of life."

"I will be with you, sir, whatever happens."

"Thank you Markos," the King said.

"Mueller! This is King George. I want you promise, that you will not harm any of these men if we surrender to you."

"You have my word as a German officer, Your Majesty."

"Okay, we are coming out," the King replied.

A minute later, the Hellene King followed by his entourage, Markos and the Cretan Gendarmes reached the German positions. Several of the German soldiers were standing and covering them with their weapons. Mueller had a pistol pointed at Markos.

Mueller came to attention, clicking his heels. "Greetings, Your Majesty. I am Obersturmbanfuhrer Georg Mueller. You are now a guest of the German military."

"You gave your word you will not harm anyone. I expect you, as a German officer, to honor it," replied the King.

"I will let the Commonwealth soldiers pass once they turn in their arms."

Mueller noticed Markos. "What a surprise. This is the Greek lieutenant that ruined my plans back at the villa," said Mueller, as he stared Markos down.

"Just doing my duty," replied Markos in English before the King could answer Mueller.

"What do we have here? An American? Your country is neutral. This is not your war."

"My name is Lieutenant Markos Androlakis and yes, I am a Greek American. I volunteered to fight the enemies who have invaded Greece. Greece is the country of my forefathers, therefore, it's my war too."

"Very noble of you, but your war is now over."

Markos stared at the young woman that joined Mueller at his side. She was very pretty and most likely Greek. "Sophia! What are you doing here?" asked Stavros in Greek.

"Just helping the Germans catch our real enemy, the Royalists. It's time they pay for what they did to my brother and your son!" replied Sophia in English.

"Sophia has been very helpful guiding us through these mountains and this is one of the reasons I will spare your life," said Mueller.

"You don't know what you done, Sophia."

"I know very well what I have done, father. This royalist scum should pay for what they did to my brother and to this nation. Greece does not need them or the British. The British have imposed these non-Greek Kings on us for the last hundred years and have betrayed us when our armies were fighting in Asia Minor. We now have a powerful friend, Germany. Georg has promised that Germany will protect Greece from any external enemies if she joins a greater Europe that Germany is trying to create."

Before anyone could stop him, Stavros slapped Sophia. "You traitorous whore!"

Two of Mueller's men grabbed Stavros and held him. "You are a fool, father, and a traitor to Crete for assisting the royals!"

Stavros spat at his daughter. "You are no longer my daughter. You are a whore of the Germans."

"I have no more time for this. Lantz, get this fool out of my face and take the King and the Prince along with you. Bruner, shoot the rest of them."

"Jawol, Herr Obersturmbanfuhrer."

"Mueller! You gave your word as a German officer no one would be harmed if we surrendered," yelled the King."

Before Bruner could carry out his orders, several explosions intermingled with a fusillade of gunfire hit Mueller's men, taking out several of the snipers and the mortar team that had been covering the allied soldiers. Caught by surprise Bruner hesitated for a moment. Markos seized the opportunity and jumped on the German NCO, knocking him to the ground. Both men struggled, but the brawny SS man had years of experience of street fighting, battling communists and anarchists during his early brown shirt Storm Trooper days. Bruner head butted Markos and then began to choke him. Markos began to weaken and his vision started to blur. From the corner of his eye, he spotted a large stone. He quickly reached for it, grabbed it in his left hand and struck Bruner in the head. The German released his grip on Marko's throat and collapsed.

Markos took a deep breath as his head cleared and looked around. He could not see the King anywhere. He figured that the royal party must have taken cover. Ryan had seized the opportunity given to them by the Cretan guerrillas and ordered his men forward. Caught between the crossfire, the Germans began to fall back towards their rear guard. Markos picked up Bruner's MP38 machine pistol and began crawling forward hoping to find the King.

As soon as the firing had started Mueller had grabbed the King and he with Sophia began moving toward the German rear guard positions. "It's over Mueller. You don't stand a chance. Surrender and you will be treated honorably. Something that you would not have done," said the King, as Mueller pushed him forward.

"Shut up! You Bourgeoisie, pampered ass, tin soldier. What do you know of war and honor? I will shoot you myself before I give you back to the English," replied Mueller.

"Your family almost destroyed this country and lost us the war with Turkey. The royalists also murdered my brother and are responsible for my mother's death," added Sophia.

"I am sorry to hear that, young lady. But why are you betraying your country?" asked the King.

"Shut up!" Sophia yelled, as she pointed a gun that Mueller had given her at the King. "I am helping my country get rid of vermin like your kind. I should kill you myself! But I will take more pleasure seeing you paraded as a trophy in Berlin."

Before the King could reply, a man jumped from behind a tree and pointed a rifle at them. Sophia recognized the man as her father. "Drop your weapon, Mueller." Mueller did as he was instructed.

"Your Majesty, come over here. Take this pistol and get out of here quickly."

The King took the offered weapon, thanked Stavros, and headed toward the direction of the gunfire. "You fool you don't know what you just did," Mueller said.

"Father, Georg is right. The royalists are our enemy and

responsible for my brother and mother's death."

"Shut up, you whore. You disgraced your family. You are not my daughter. I will kill you and your Nazi lover."

Stavros raised the rifle and shot Mueller. Sophia rushed to Mueller's side. Before Stavros could work the Mauser's bolt to chamber another round and turn the rifle on Sophia, she fired her pistol, hitting him in the chest. Stavros stood there for a moment, looking at his daughter in total shock, before his legs gave out and he dropped dead to the ground. Mueller groaned, he was still alive. He was bleeding from a wound on his right side. She reached into one of Mueller's utility uniform pockets and found a first aid pack. She quickly opened it, took out a bandage, placed it on the wound and staunched the bleeding. If she could get him to a doctor, he might live.

After being rescued by Stavros, King George, with weapon in hand, cautiously headed toward the direction of the fighting. On several instances, he had to hide from surviving Germans that were retreating back into the gorge. Another couple of hundred meters and he would be back to safety.

"Halt! Drop your weapon."

The King dived to the ground, his weapon spitting out lead, hitting one of the three German soldiers in the process. He had decided that he would not be taken alive. Rifle bullets started landing all around him. At least he thought history would record that he fell fighting his nation's enemies. A burst of automatic weapons fire suddenly brought the rifle fire to a halt.

"Your Majesty, are you injured?"

King George II, of the house of Glucksburg and King of the Hellenes, let out a long sigh. "You pulled my nuts out of the fire again, Markos."

"I'm just doing my duty, Your Majesty."

CHAPTER 7

Aghia Roumeli, Crete
22 May 1941, 1620hrs

After the brief but bloody firefight, the surviving Germans retreated northward back into the gorge. Ryan and his men owed their salvation to the Cretan guerrillas. Stathis' intervention had saved all their asses. Over two dozen Germans had been killed and five taken prisoner at the cost of six wounded commonwealth soldiers, and the loss of two Cretan guerrillas. While looking for wounded, they had also found the body of their guide, Stavros which they buried in his beloved gorge. Unfortunately, Mueller had gotten away.

A couple of hours later, the party had finally reached the south coast and the picturesque village of Aghia Roumeli. The village was located about a kilometer from the shore overlooking the Libyan Sea. During the Venetian and Turkish periods, the abundant timber and the river flowing through the gorge that was used to power saw mills had made Aghia Roumeli an important ship building center. Now it was a quiet little fishing village with a few dozen white washed houses with small gardens where the locals grew their own vegetables. This was soon to change.

As they reached the village outskirts, they were met by Colonel. J.S. Blunt and his staff, the British military attaché to Greece who had arranged the evacuation of the King and his party. He advised them that they would be picked up within the next couple of hours by the HMS Decoy, a Royal Navy destroyer that would be transporting them to Alexandria. Markos had a little while to say good bye to his command. Ten minutes later, Markos and his surviving Cretan Gendarmes were sitting outside the village Kaffeneion (coffee shop) having a well-deserved drink of Raki, the local Cretan drink.

"Well men, last chance. Mr. Manolakos has volunteered to come along. Anyone else want to come to Egypt? asked Markos. "We will be rebuilding the Greek army there and will need experienced men like you." During the trip through the gorge, Markos had thought about what the King had said to him and decided to take up the offer and join his staff.

"We would all like to, sir, but we have families here. We will fight the invader here on Crete. The Germans will never feel safe on this island," Corporal Galanakis said.

"I understand," Markos said.

Markos raised his glass. "In the short time I had the honor to command you, I have never seen a bunch of braver men willing to risk everything for honor and country. To our fallen comrades that did not make it."

They all downed their drinks and ordered another round.

They were soon joined by Lieutenant Ryan. "Let's have a glass for the lieutenant," said Markos to the Cafe owner.

"Thanks, Markos. I could sure use it. We should be boarding within the hour."

Ryan pointed at two ships that were barely visible in the horizon. "There is our rides. Those ships must be doing 30 knots. They're hell bent on picking us up and getting out of here before the Luftwaffe pays us a visit."

"It was a close thing, my friend."

"Yes, it was Markos." Ryan raised his glass.

"To you and your men, Markos. These Cretans are some of the best fighters I have seen."

"And to you and your men, who made this possible."

Markos translated and they all downed the strong liquor. "You will make a good officer, Markos. You have both the leadership and the audacity needed to succeed in time of war."

"Thanks, Ryan, but I don't want to make this a career. I will fight till this war is over. Where's the King?"

"The King and his party are at the shore. I have a squad covering them and also one covering the pass just in case our friends decide to try something."

Markos stood up and saluted his former command. "Well men, good luck and have a safe trip back to your families, 'till we meet again."

Markos turned to warrant officer Manolakos. "I think it's time we headed to the shore, Kostas."

"I'll see you on the beach," Ryan said.

Samaria, Gorge
22 May 1941, 1710hrs

The small weary band of German survivors, with Sophia and Lantz in the lead, was slowly making their way back up the steep gorge. The once elite Fallschirmjagers and Gebirgsjagers had become completely demoralized after their defeat at the hands of the Cretan partisans and commonwealth troops. A few of the soldiers were wearing bandages from having been wounded during the engagement. One of them was Bruner, who had a large bloody bandage wrapped around his head. His injury though did not stop him from taking turns carrying the stretcher they had constructed to transport the seriously wounded Mueller. Fortunately, Sophia had been able to stop the bleeding but Mueller needed a doctor soon, if he was going to make it back to Chania. Hopefully, within the next two hours they would reach the Village of Omalos at the top of the gorge. She knew there was an old retired doctor living there and he would have to operate on Mueller.

"How much longer Fraulein?" Obersturmfuhrer Lantz asked, in heavily accented English.

"About an hour and a half to two 'till we reach Omalos. I am worried too, Hans. He has lost a lot of blood. He needs a doctor real bad."

"Thank you, fraulein, for everything you have done for us and for the Obersturmbanfuhrer. If it wasn't for you he would be dead now."

"I would do the same for you."

She thought back to the moment when her father shot Mueller and tried to kill her. It was funny, but she did not feel any remorse for having killed her father. He was a fool for having helped the royalists that were responsible for her brother's death. Now the only man she had ever felt anything for was slowly bleeding to death from her father's hand. She had done her best to stem the bleeding after he had been shot. But she and Mueller had walked almost a kilometer till they had run into Lantz and the rest of the surviving Germans and that had not helped to stem the blood loss. She prayed that Mueller would last till they reached Omalos.

Aghia Roumeli, Crete
22 May 1941, 1750hrs

Anchored 500 meters (1700ft) off the beach were the two Royal Navy destroyers, HMS Decoy and the HMS Kelly, which would transport them to Alexandria. After saying his goodbyes to the Cretan Gendarmes that remained behind, Markos and Warrant Officer Kostas Manolakos went down to the beach where they boarded the small tender that was ferrying everyone to the HMS Decoy. After they had all climbed aboard the destroyer, the tender was raised and secured. Both warships immediately weighed anchor and set course at flank speed for Alexandria, Egypt. Markos noticed that the crew was at combat stations. The captain was not taking any chances. They were all well within the range of the Luftwaffe.

Twenty minutes later, as the island slowly faded from view Markos noticed several black specks coming in from that direction. It wasn't too long afterwards that the action station bells were sounded and Air Action imminent was heard over the Tannoy. The four specks in the sky were now much closer; they were identified as Ju 87 Stuka dive bombers. There was not much Markos could do except hug the deck and try to shoot at the oncoming planes with his Thompson sub machine gun. Ryan had his three Bren guns deployed to also add to the ship's fire power. The four planes split into two groups and each group targeted one of the destroyers. By now both ships were putting up a hail of antiaircraft fire and zig zagging to throw off the aim of the pilots. Markos watched in dread as the first plane began its dive. He was transfixed at his spot, unable to move as he watched the dive bomber grow larger. The noise was deafening as the Stukas' siren, which was meant to terrorize and instill fear to those on the ground, also added to the din of the antiaircraft guns. The pilot let go of his bomb as the ship began a hard turn to port. The bomb landed 75 feet off the starboard side and exploded, sending a large plum of water on top of them.

As the plane came out of its screaming dive the rear gunner raked the ship with 7.92mm machinegun fire killing two crew men. Markos glanced across the short distance at the HMS Kelly. The first Stuka had scored a near miss and was trailing smoke, as it headed back towards the mainland. The near miss had sprung several of her hull plates, forcing the ship to slow down making her an easier target. The second Stuka had now begun its dive on the HMS Decoy, but fortunately for the destroyer, the attack ended quickly when an antiaircraft shell struck the bomb the Ju 87 was carrying, blowing it out of the sky. Now it was going to be the Kelley's turn.

Major Stefan Krantz, a Luftwaffe veteran pilot of both the Spanish civil war and the Norwegian campaign, was determined to pay the British back for the loss of his squadron mate. He located the target through the bomb site window on the cockpit floor and at 4600 meters (15000ft) he moved the dive lever to the rear, limiting the "throw" of the control column. The dive brakes were activated automatically, and then he set the trim tabs, retarded his throttle and closed the engine cooling flaps. The aircraft then nosed into a steep dive. Red tabs protruded from the upper surfaces of the wing as a visual indicator to the pilot that, in case of a g-induced black out, the automatic dive recovery system would be activated.

Though hurt, the destroyer's fighting ability was not hampered. The sky above the HMS Kelly filled with black puffs of smoke as she tried to knock the aircraft from the sky. The

Stuka dived at a 90° angle, holding a constant speed of 500–600 km/h (300-370 mph) due to dive-brake deployment, which increased the accuracy of the Ju 87's aim. When the aircraft was reasonably close to the target, a light on the contact altimeter came on to indicate the bomb-release point. The pilot pressed the bomb release at 450 meters (1500ft) and initiated the automatic pull-out mechanism by depressing a knob on the control column. An elongated U-shaped crutch located under the fuselage swung the bomb out of the way of the propeller, and the aircraft automatically began a 6g pullout.

Markos watched in horror as the Ju 87, miraculously unscathed from all the flak the HMS Kelly had put up, released its bomb and headed for home. The 250 Kilo (550 lb.) bomb continued on its deadly path and plowed right through the thin deck adjacent the smoke stack. The bomb tore through the bowels of the ship and went off inside the engine room. The crippled warship immediately lost power and took on a 15 degree list. Without power and fires out of control in the engine room, there was no way the HMS Kelly could be saved. Her captain immediately gave the order to abandon ship. Within minutes, the HMS Decoy was alongside the stricken ship to take on survivors. Fifteen minutes later, the HMS Decoy was back on her way at full speed, but not before putting a torpedo into the HMS Kelly to ensure she did not fall into enemy hands. Markos and the rest of the evacuees finally were able to relax and stretched out on the deck, quickly falling asleep from exhaustion.

Omalos, Crete
22 May 1941, 2230hrs

The small band of German survivors had reached the tiny village of Omalos just around sunset. Sophia quickly located the doctor's home and knocked on the heavy wooden door. A skinny, older man answered and was shocked to see the heavily armed enemy soldiers at his door step. He identified himself as doctor Petros Soufakis. Sophia quickly explained to the man their predicament. He had Mueller brought inside and quickly examined him and the wound. The doctor advised Sophia that Mueller needed a hospital and surgery to remove the bullet and that he did not have the facilities to treat him there. After some "convincing" from Bruner, the doctor agreed to perform the surgery with Sophia's help.

The surgery proved to be successful; the bullet had missed Mueller's internal organs and he would fully recover. After removing the slug from Mueller's side, the doctor advised Sophia that he was not to be moved for at least 48 hours to keep the wound from opening up and bleeding. Anymore loss of blood could be fatal to him.

Sophia wiped the sweat from Mueller's forehead as he lay in bed in the doctor's home. Mueller stirred and opened his eyes.

"Oh my head, where are we?"

"We are in the village of Omalos at the top of the gorge. You are in the village doctor's house and just had surgery to have the bullet removed.

"We need to get out of here and back to Chania." Mueller tried to rise and he fell back into the bed.

"Georg, don't be foolish. You've lost a lot of blood and are lucky to be alive. The doctor said you must not be moved for at least 48 hours so the wound can close. If you start bleeding again you may die."

Mueller grasped Sophia's hand and squeezed it. "Okay, whatever you say, my dear. At least I have a pretty nurse taking care of me. I thank you for saving my life and for the aid you have given us."

Sophia began to cry. "What is it my dear?"

"I have no one left and nowhere to go. My father is dead and the Greeks see me as a traitor."

Mueller gently pulled the girl toward him. "You will come with me back to Germany and I will show you the wonders of Berlin, soon to be the capital of all of Europe!"

"Really? You will take me with you?"

"Of course, my dear. How can I not, after all you have done for me. You saved my life back there."

"Oh thank you, Georg." Sophia gave him a quick kiss on the lips. "Now please get some rest so you can get well."

Reich Chancellery Berlin, Germany
26 June 1941, 1400hrs

After recuperating for a couple days at Omalos, Mueller's strength had improved and his wound had stabilized enough for him to travel. The trip down the mountain had been hard, but Sophia had procured a horse from one of the villagers to make the journey easier for him. Once they reached the valley, the journey had become more dangerous. With Sophia's help, they avoided allied forces that were retreating to the south and eventually made contact with the advancing Germans several kilometers east of Maleme.

By the 26th, Maleme airfield had been secured by the Germans and was being used to fly in massive reinforcements. Mueller was transported to the local field hospital at the airfield where he was seen by a German military doctor who noticed that one of his sutures had ripped and ordered him to be evacuated to the mainland for further treatment. He was loaded aboard a JU 52 Medical transport, marked with red crosses to avoid being attacked by enemy aircraft, and evacuated to the mainland along with Sophia, Bruner and

Lantz. Before their departure Mueller sent a detailed report to the Reichsfuhrer of their failed mission.

When the Junkers 52 transport arrived at Elefsis airfield, just south of Athens, it was met by the airfield commander, a Luftwaffe colonel. He notified Mueller that he was being ordered back to Berlin by the Reichsfuhrer himself, on the next transport for recuperation and treatment of his wounds. The colonel had Mueller transported to the base hospital, to have his wound cleaned and re-sutured. Accommodations were also made for Sophia, Lantz and Bruner to spend the night. The next morning, they all boarded a JU 52 transport for the long flight to Germany. When they landed at Templehoff airfield, Mueller boarded a waiting ambulance to transport him to a military hospital for further treatment. Before going in, he asked Lantz to put Sophia up in the Hotel Bristol at the ritzy den Unter den Linden district. Lantz also took a room there while Bruner stayed at the nearby SS Liebenstandarte barracks. (Hitler's Body Guards)

A couple of days later, Mueller joined Sophia and took her shopping for new clothes. Berlin was a lively city, even though there was a war going on. Sophia had never experienced the theaters and nightclubs that city life offered. Time passed quickly while Mueller recuperated. Then, a summons to see the Reichsfuhrer was delivered by SS courier. He was to report to Himmler's office with Sophia the next day.

They had been both waiting in the outside foyer area of the Reichsfuhrer's office for over 20 minutes. Mueller was wondering if Himmler was angry at him for the mission failure. It was not a good career move to fail the Reichsfuhrer. He was dressed in his SS uniform, which hung loose on his frame having lost over five kilos (12 lbs.) during his recuperation from his wounds. Sophia admired Georg in his Black SS uniform with its ornate dagger hanging from his side and the silver deaths head insignia on the collars. In fact, he looked very intimidating.

The door to Himmler's office opened and the Reichsfuhrer walked out into the waiting area in the company of Obergruppenführer *(Lieutenant General of the SS)* Reinhard Heydrich *Reichssicherheitshauptamt, (Reich Main Security office,).* Mueller immediately snapped to attention and rendered the Nazi salute to both senior officers.

"Ah, Mueller, I hope you are well. Sorry to have kept you and you're very lovely friend waiting. I am sure you know the Obergruppenführer?"

"I am much better, Herr Reichsfuhrer. Yes, I met Herr Heydrich at an SS function last year."

"I have heard of your recent exploits, Mueller. It was a pity your target escaped with help of bandits," said Heydrich.

"Please step into my office, Mueller, your friend may join you. Herr Heydrich will be joining us."

"Thank you, sir."

They entered Himmler's ornate office where Mueller observed an SS photographer standing in the room and to his total surprise, so was the Fuehrer, Adolf Hitler. He immediately snapped to attention and saluted. Sophia was in total shock as she had only seen Hitler in newspaper clippings. Now she was in the same room with one of the most powerful men in the world.

"At ease, I have something for you, Mueller."

"Heinrich, please, the award."

The Reichsfuhrer pulled out a small case from his desk and handed it to Hitler. He motioned for the photographer to come over. The Fuehrer opened the case and pulled out an Iron Cross 2nd Class and approached Mueller, who was now in complete shock, as he was expecting a reprimand for his failure.

"This little token is for your gallant effort to serve the Reich during the invasion of Crete. Despite suffering heavy casualties upon your arrival on the island, you never stopped pursuing the quarry. You managed to reconstitute your team and persisted to carry on the operation. Had it not been for the intervention of local bandits, you would have succeeded in your mission. The Fatherland bestows the Iron Cross 2nd Class to Standartenführer Georg Mueller."

Hitler went behind Mueller and put the medal around his neck while the photographer took pictures. Upon securing the medal, the Fuehrer held out his hand. "Congratulations Standartenführer. Your promotion is effective immediately."

Mueller shook Hitler's hand followed by Himmler and Heydrich.

"I …I… don't know what to say, my fuehrer."

"Well, you could start by saying thank you," said Hitler as he started to laugh.

"That will be all," said Himmler to the photographer.

"Yes, yes, thank you, sir."

"Relax, Mueller. Just, joking," Hitler said.

"The mission may have failed because of bad luck and bandit activity, which is another issue the Reich's Fuehrer will discuss with you. But you, Mueller, succeeded in other ways. You showed the leadership that all SS officers should aspire to."

"I was not alone, my Fuehrer. I could not have done anything without the assistance of both Obersturmfuhrer Lantz and Oberscharführer Bruner."

"They too were recognized for their actions this morning. They both received The Iron Cross 3rd Class and a promotion. Bruner was promoted to Hauptscharführer (Master Sergeant) and Lantz to Hauptsturmführer (Captain)"

"Thank you, sir. They deserve it." Hitler turned his glance to Sophia.

"So this is the pretty Sophia that assisted our gallant forces. I am glad to meet you young lady. We need more like you in greater Europe to help defeat the rot and corruption caused by greedy Jewish bankers and the corrupt British Empire."

Hitler took Sophia's hand and kissed it, causing Sophia to blush, she was almost at a total loss for words.

"Thank you, Herr Hitler."

"No, the pleasure is mine, young lady."

"Without her, we did not stand a chance to even attempt the mission, my Fuehrer. She also saved my life after the bandit attack and she cared for my wounds."

Mueller purposely left out the part that she had shot her own father in the process to spare her any pain.

"Thank God for that. As a reward to show our appreciation, I am bestowing honorary German citizenship to you, Sophia, for your actions in assisting German forces and for saving such a valuable officer of the SS."

"Thank you, sir. I would do it again for Georg."

"I am sure you would, young lady. We need many more like you for the "New European Order." Now please excuse me. I must attend to state business and receive a briefing on our Russian endeavor. Our forces are crushing the Bolshevik scum on all fronts. Good luck, Mueller."

As the Fuehrer departed the room with two of his SS Liebenstandarte body guards, everyone came to attention and rendered the Nazi salute.

"Now that the formalities are over, everyone please have a seat," said Himmler. "Let's get back to business. I have a proposal for you, Mueller. Obergruppenführer Heydrich and I have been discussing the rise of bandit activity in our occupied territories. He has experience crushing bandits in Czechoslovakia. You also did well in Paris. I would like to send you back to Greece to build an apparatus to track and destroy all anti German activity. Are you interested?"

Mueller quickly glanced at Sophia. He still didn't know what had come over him, but he had fallen in love with this girl. "Of course, Herr Reichsfuhrer, I will go anywhere to fight the enemies of the Reich."

"That's the spirit, Mueller. Of course, Sophia can join you and she can act as a liaison interpreter for you."

"Thank you, sir. When do we leave?"

"Leave as soon as you wish. Take two weeks leave and show Sophia our beautiful Fatherland."

"I will, sir."

"Mueller, please stop by my office tomorrow morning. I would like to talk to you about my experiences and maybe you could share some of the tactics you used in Paris to crush the bandits," said Heydrich.

"I will, sir."

"Standartenführer Mueller, your orders will be ready, after your leave is over," Himmler added."

CHAPTER 8

Cairo, Egypt,
Allied Headquarters for the Middle East
10Aug 1941, 1000hrs

Allied Headquarters Middle East was located in a large block of commandeered flats surrounded by barbed wire, located in Garden City, a suburb of Cairo situated between downtown and the Nile. Both Markos and Ryan stood at attention in the large, hot and dusty parade ground that was full of Greek and New Zealand flags, waiting to be decorated by the King of Greece. Markos was dressed in a Hellenic army uniform sporting captain's insignia. The national anthems of both Greece and New Zealand were played by a military band followed by the citations being read by a British army brigadier general. Afterwards, King George II of the Hellenes approached the two men and pinned Greece's highest decorations, the Gold Cross on Markos and the War Cross on Ryan.

After the ceremony was over, everyone went over to the officers club to celebrate with a drink. Markos was amazed at the opulent decor of the club. The walls and ceiling were covered in teak and the walls were also adorned with paintings of famous battles and portraits of past British military commanders. The British Empire was still alive and well here in Egypt. Ever since his arrival to Egypt, he had been on a whirlwind tour throughout the prosperous Greek community of Egypt that had been there since the days of Alexander the Great. Greece needed a hero and he was it, for the time being. The King to show his gratitude for all Markos had done promoted him to the rank of captain and attached him to his staff. Markos could not complain, he had a great time, attended lots of parties and met many women. This was not what he really wanted. He had thought that his real job would be to help rebuild the Hellenic army. Many new people had arrived, but it seemed the only thing they were interested in was gaining rank and positions and taking part in political intrigue. The friction was growing daily between the Royalists and Republican officers. The King had passed an amnesty allowing officers that were cashiered under the Metaxas regime to rejoin the army for the unity of the nation. Markos was not seeing too much of this unity at the moment.

"Hey, Markos, how about a drink?" It was Ryan and it seemed that he had already had a few.

"Sure, Ryan, I'll have a beer."

Ryan motioned to the Egyptian bartender. "A pint for my friend here."

"On the way, sir."

"This was a big day for us Markos, might as well enjoy it. I am getting shipped out shortly to join the army in the desert. Seems this new Jerry Commander, Ernest Rommel, whom everyone is calling the Desert Fox, is beginning to give us a run for the money with his Afrika Korps."

"I have heard of him; hope you guys are able to stop him."

"We will."

Markos got his beer and raised it to a toast. "Good luck to you, my friend and may God watch over you as he did on Crete."

"Thank you, Markos, same to you." Ryan emptied his glass and was pulled over to another table where other New Zealanders were sitting.

"May I have a seat?"

Markos looked up and saw a thin older man wearing a US army uniform with colonel rank.

"Sure, sir, have a seat."

"I am Colonel William Eddy, US Military attaché observer."

Markos took the man's hand and shook it. "I am Captain Markos Androlakis."

"I know who you are and I know you are also an American from New York City, serving in the Hellenic army and on the King's staff."

Markos was surprised. Not that any of this was secret information, but this officer was quick to let it be known that he was not your average military attaché. He was most likely an intelligence officer.

"Am I in any trouble?'

"No, on the contrary, we are very impressed with you."

"We?"

"I also represent the COI, Office of the Coordinator of Information, which is run by a civilian and prominent New

York lawyer, Colonel William Donovan, a former Medal of Honor winner and friend of the president and of mine. We served in the Great War together in France, he was a major and I was a captain."

"COI? Never heard of it."

"It's a brand new organization that was started last month to coordinate US intelligence gathering and to better prepare us for the upcoming war. Sooner or later we will be involved. German subs are sinking American merchant ships and we can't let the Nazis win."

"What can I do?"

"You have experience, you fought the Nazis and you managed to pull off evacuating the King of Greece."

"I had a lot of help, Lieutenant Ryan and his men and my detachment of Cretan Gendarmes."

"Well, captain, I really would like to discuss a few more things with you in a more secure environment. Could you come by my office at the US embassy, say around 1500hrs tomorrow?"

Markos thought it over for a moment. What did he have to lose? "Sure, sir, I'll come by."

"It's at 8 Kamal El Din Salah Street, here in Garden city at embassy row."

"Thank you, sir. I am sure I'll find it."

"I will let the marine guards know you are coming and they will escort you to my office. See you tomorrow, Markos."

As the Colonel turned to leave, Markos spotted Costas who was now wearing a Greek Army infantry lieutenant's uniform.

"Hi Costas, sit down, I'll buy you a beer." Costas took a seat at the table.

"Markos motioned to the waiter for another beer.

"Congratulations for your award, captain."

"Thank you. You deserved your medal too and promotion."

"A lot of good it does. No one here is interested in fighting the Germans; they are more interested in receiving promotions, titles and fighting each other."

"I have the same sentiments, Costas. I see it too, every day. We have been getting recruits and many ex-military are making their way here from Greece."

The beer arrived and Costas raised the glass, "to the liberation of our nation."

Both men drank their beers and Markos rose from the table. "See you later, Costas, got to go do my daily paperwork drills and see who is getting promoted today," he said sarcastically.

"I know exactly what you mean, Markos."

US Embassy, Cairo, Egypt
11 Aug 1941, 1505hrs

The taxi from the military compound had only taken about 10 minutes to reach the American embassy. The embassy building was surrounded by a stone wall, topped with several strands of barbed wire. Markos noticed that there were marine guards patrolling the grounds. He handed his ID card to the marine guard at the gate and told him he had an appointment with Colonel Eddy. The sentry let Markos in and gave him directions to the colonel's office which was on the second floor. The sign at the door said Military Attaché. He knocked on the door, entered and was greeted by the colonel's aid, a US army major, who escorted him to the colonel's inner office. Colonel Eddy rose from his cluttered desk and shook Markos' hand.

"A pleasure to see you again, Markos. I am glad that you came by."

"Thank you, sir. I am still an American and if I can assist the United States in any way, I am at your service. Oh and by the way, I did have you pegged as an intelligence officer from the get go."

The colonel grinned. "I was right about you, Markos, you are very sharp and have potential to go far."

Markos glanced up at the painting of Picket's Charge hanging above the colonel's chair. The Confederacy's hopes had depended on Picket's desperate charge, breaking through the Union lines at Gettysburg, giving them a victory and hopefully the ability to negotiate an end to the civil war. Markos wondered if his future depended on his reply.

"How so, sir?"

"Let's not kid ourselves. As I told you yesterday, the United States will soon be in this war whether we like it or not. We need people like you that have knowledge of the enemy, that have been to different places in the world and speak other languages. We need a special unit that can harness these abilities and turn them against our enemies. This is what Colonel Donovan is hoping to accomplish."

"And how will he cut through all the red tape and accomplish that?"

"He has the full support of the president."

"Sounds very interesting, colonel, but I'm already committed to the Greeks."

"You know as well as I do that is going nowhere for the time being. There is too much political infighting amongst them. The Royalists against the Republicans, right against left. The British are going to have a fun time getting that mess straightened out before they have any Greek forces in the field. Your talent is being wasted here. Need I also remind you that your loyalties should also lie with the United States? Great Britain can't win this war alone. Even with the Soviet Union involved now, the war's outcome still looks bad for the allies.

The Germans are destroying one Soviet army after the other and have killed, wounded and captured over a million Russians, if the casualty figures are to be believed. If you wish to see Greece liberated, the US will have to get involved. Our industrial might will tip the balance against Germany."

Markos thought for a moment about what the colonel had said. He was an American first and it was true that his efforts in Egypt were going nowhere. Maybe he could help Greece more this way. He also had not seen his family in New York for over a year. "What you are saying about the Greek military problems here in Egypt is true. The Brits are not very happy with them at the moment. So what do you propose I do, colonel?"

"I believe you should think about returning home and joining us."

"I would also be deserting the Greek cause and the King who has his faith and trust in me."

"I think I could take care of that, I have spent many years in this city and know many people in the Greek community in Egypt. You can make tours of the Greek community wearing your Hellenic army uniform to stir up their patriotism. Besides the money donations you can help collect for Greece's cause would go a long way to getting Red Cross aid into the country. I will also guarantee you the rank of captain once your initial training has been completed."

Markos paused and thought it over for a moment. It was an excellent offer. "Well sir, in that case, if you can arrange it, I may just take you up on your offer to go back home and become part of the COI."

"Well, give me a couple of weeks to get the wheels turning and I will contact you."

Markos got up from his seat and shook the colonel's hand.

"I'll be waiting to hear from you sir."

German Headquarters
Grande Bretagne, Athens, Occupied Greece
18 Aug 1941, 1300hrs

Standartenführer Mueller had just finished his lunch and began shuffling through the daily reports he received from the local Gestapo. Terrorist activity was still very low, but he knew sooner or later that would change as allied agents infiltrated the country. He had been in Greece for only 10 days since his return from Germany. His leave had been a fairy tale. He and Sophia had gone to southern Germany and hiked the Alps. Sophia, was a natural mountaineer and he often had a hard time keeping up with her. The weather had been beautiful in the mountains and their love had blossomed even more. He had taken her to the Bavarian capital, Munich, and shown her the sights and the beer hall where National Socialism had been born. Well, it was now back to business.

Upon their return to Greece, Mueller had taken up residence in the Hotel Grand Bretagne which also served as the German Headquarters in Greece. Ironically, this elegant hotel had also served as the allied headquarters prior to their defeat and evacuation from Greece. Now it was teeming with German military and civilian staff that were needed to govern the occupied nation. Germany had allowed Greece to form a government which had pledged loyalty to the Reich, but in reality, it was subservient to the German Commander. Mueller had been appointed head of the SD (Sicher Dienst), the SS security service in Greece. He had been given a small office that once had been an elegant bedroom. He had a window overlooking the palace and the Tomb of the Unknown Soldier. The furniture had been removed, but not the elegant décor and wallpaper. He now reported directly to Obergruppenführer Heydrich. Mueller had also brought along both Obersturmfuhrer Lantz and Oberscharführer Bruner. Lantz was now serving as his aid and Bruner would serve as both his and Sophia's security detail. Sophia had also joined him and taken up residence in the hotel for her safety. The Greeks did not look upon it too kindly when their women were cohabitating with the enemy. There was a knock on the door.

"Come in." It was Lantz and he was holding a manila envelope.

"This just came by courier for you, sir. It's addressed to you."

"Thank you, Lantz. That will be all."

Mueller waited for Lantz to leave, he then took the letter opener from his desk drawer and opened the envelope. There were several photos and a note indicating that they were recently taken by an Axis agent outside the American Embassy in Cairo. The photos were of an individual wearing a Greek Army uniform. Mueller looked at the man's face in one of the photos which had been enlarged. He recognized it. It was the Greek American, Markos Androlakis that had ruined his mission on Crete. Mueller wondered what he was doing at the US embassy. Was possible he just wanted to go back home? But why wear the uniform to the embassy? Maybe he was working with the Americans. He was positive that sooner or later, the US would join the war. The Jew loving war monger Roosevelt had done his best, short of declaring war against Germany, by giving war material and assistance to the British Empire. American warships had been escorting British convoys halfway across the Atlantic and there had been numerous incidents between the US Navy and Kriegsmarine U-boats that had resulted in casualties. It would be catastrophic for Germany if

America came into the war on the side of the allies. America's entrance into WWI had cost Germany the last war. No nation could compete with America's industrial might. Fortunately, that was not his decision to make, it was the Fuehrer's. He would make a note to the Abwehr (German Intelligence) to have this Greek American in Cairo eliminated. The Americans would need assets like him to form a cadre to prepare their soldiers for the war that was sure to come. He would ensure that would not happen.

Cairo, Egypt
27 August 1941, 2100hrs

Hassan had been following Markos for the last couple of days. He had been hired by an Italian businessman to have the Greek American eliminated. Hassan figured that the Italian was probably a spy, but he did not care, as long as he was being compensated well enough for his services. He had received 100 gold sovereigns, a hefty sum for a simple job. He figured that the Greek must have pissed someone important off for him to get paid this well. No matter, the job would get done.

The Greek was sitting and having dinner in one of the numerous dining establishments in the Garden City section of the city. He would follow his target after he left and quickly make short work of him with his knife in one of the darker side streets he would have to take on his way back to the base. It would look like a robbery, a common enough event in Cairo.

Markos had finished his lamb kebab and pilaf (rice) dinner and motioned to the waiter to bring his bill. He had spoken to Colonel Eddy's aid, Major Thomas, who had come by his office, just this morning. The major had advised him that Colonel Eddy had used his connections and spoken to King George about his returning to America to "better help" the Greek cause and war effort. The King had agreed with the Colonel that he could better serve Greece in the US. In fact, he had a meeting with the King tomorrow morning. The colonel was also arranging transport for Markos's trip back to the States, not the easiest thing to do in wartime. Hopefully, within a week, a US Naval destroyer would be docking in Alexandria bringing a new crew of marines and supplies to the embassy. It would be his ticket back to the US. The waiter soon arrived with the tab. Markos paid the bill and left a tip, got up and walked out and headed back toward the Greek compound which was a brisk twenty minute walk.

Ten minutes later, Markos was walking through a dark residential area with very few streetlights on. He turned his head and thought he caught a glimpse of someone. He picked up his pace, but had a feeling he was being followed. Turning a corner, he waited for the assailants. He looked around and saw a medium size rock which he picked up and balled it in his fist. Markos held his breath and waited for a moment. Hassan had ducked in a doorway when his quarry had turned his head and looked back. He was sure he had not been seen. He was dressed in black and using the shadows to hide. The Greek suddenly began walking faster and turned a corner. Hassan pulled out his knife and sprinted toward the street corner. As he turned the corner he was struck in the jaw. He dropped his knife and staggered for a moment, but years as a killer and many a street fight put him into instant survival mode.

Markos saw the gleaming knife fall from the assailants hand as he struck him in the face. He attempted to punch him again, but the man blocked it and went for his knife. Markos sensing that he was in trouble, jumped on the assailant and the two began to struggle on the ground each, attempting to stop the other going for the knife. The assassin butted Markos on the head, temporarily stunning him, which gave him the opportunity to break free and pick up his knife. Hassan lunged at Marko, but before he could plunge the knife in, a gunshot rang out in the usually quiet Egyptian neighborhood. The heavy caliber bullet struck Hassan in the chest, knocking him to the ground. Markos shook his head a couple of times to clear it and looked up to see who his savior was. It was Colonel Eddy's aid, Major Thomas, and he was holding a US army issue 45 ACP.

"You?"

"You're welcome, captain. Oh, and that was a pretty good attempt to take this guy out. With a little bit of training, you would have taken him out with your first hit. You don't get a second chance in this line of work."

"Ah... thanks for saving my ass, major. But how did you know?"

Thomas bent over Hassan and felt for pulse. "He is dead, let's get the hell out of here before the cops show up."

Fifteen minutes later, they were sitting in a coffee shop situated near the Greek compound, sipping on a cup of hot Turkish coffee. "Well, major, I am all ears."

"We've had you followed. Word on the street was that someone paid a lot of money to hire a hit man to kill a Greek officer. My men observed that this guy, a known criminal, had been trailing you for the last couple of days. We know the embassy is being watched by German and Italian agents. Obviously your photo was taken and sent to Berlin. Somebody does not like you there and wanted you eliminated. I am sure you must have pissed off some pretty high ranking people during your escapades on Crete."

Markos thought back at the German officer that had tried twice to capture the King and was thwarted the first time by his actions. "Yeah, sort of and I think I might know who. There was an SS officer, an Obersturmbanfuhrer Mueller that was in command of the team trying to capture the King. I ruined his first try. He was pretty pissed off at me."

"It may be him," said Major Thomas. "The SS is a pretty nasty group of thugs. I've read several reports on their actions against partisans in Poland and France. They are ruthless. I'll run the name and see what we come back with. For now, I think you need to stay at the embassy for your safety. We'll let the Greeks know about the attempt on your life."

"That's not necessary, sir. I'll be fine."

"I insist, Markos. Your life is in real danger now."

"Well okay. I'll stay."

"Then let's get out of here."

"I'll hail a cab."

"No, I have a car."

Thomas raised his hand; a car that had been parked down the street started its engine and drove up to them. A marine corporal was at the wheel and a marine sergeant was in the front seat. Both men were armed with Colt 45 caliber automatic pistols and a Thompson was under the front passenger's seat. The marine sergeant opened the door and let both officers in.

"Can't take any chances in this town, Markos."

"Yeah, you do have a point."

Fifteen minutes later, they arrived at the embassy. Markos was met by Colonel Eddy and given a room on the third floor where he settled down for the night. They would get his personal belongings in the morning.

USS DAVIS, DD395
7 Sept 1941, 1300hrs

Markos leaned on the starboard side rail of the ship and looked across the deep blue Mediterranean towards the North.

He could make out the hazy outline that represented Franco's Spain, a potential ally of Nazi Germany. His transport, the USS Davies, a US navy destroyer had departed Alexandria, Egypt, for the US three days ago, after dropping off supplies and a new contingent of marine guards for the US embassy. After the attempt on his life, Markos had spent a week as a guest of Colonel Eddy. True to his word, the colonel had spoken about him to the King of Greece. The King had wholeheartedly accepted the colonel's proposal and sent Markos a letter, releasing from his obligations.

The day before his departure for America, Markos had been invited to dine with the King. His Majesty had thanked Markos again for all that he done for him and wished him luck in his new role. As a reward for his services, Markos was allowed to keep his commission, a captain in the Hellenic Army. Markos had promised the King of Greece that he would speak out for the Greek cause in America and let the Greek community there know of Greece's sacrifices against the Axis forces. The next morning, Colonel Eddy had personally transported Markos to the dockside in Alexandria, where he handed him over to Lieutenant Commander Jordan, the Destroyer's captain.

The seas had been calm and the voyage been uneventful, except for a couple of over flights by both Italian and German reconnaissance aircraft. The planes quickly departed the area after spotting the large red, white and blue American flag the USS Davies was flying. Not taking any chances, the captain had initiated general quarters and had all the ship's antiaircraft manned and fortunately for all, it proved unnecessary. By early morning, they would be docking at the British naval base in Gibraltar to take on fuel and supplies for the long voyage across the Atlantic. Markos had been given a bed in the executive officer's small cabin. The executive officer, Commander

Fleming, was a middle aged man from Boston and had done his best to make Markos feel at home. The commander had told Markos many sea stories over coffee to make the time pass, but was fascinated with Markos' experiences fighting the Germans on Crete. He thought that America would soon be in this war too. Germany could not be allowed to win. Markos hoped that this would happen very soon.

Gibraltar, British Military Naval anchorage
8 Sept 1941, 1200hrs

The USS Davies had arrived at the great strategic naval base of Gibraltar, and dropped anchor under the famous rock earlier that morning. Captured by the British in 1704 during the war of the Spanish Succession and ceded to England under the treaty of Utrecht in 1713, the Rock, as it was called, controlled the approaches into the Mediterranean. Since then, Gibraltar had survived sieges and several wars, but had remained in British hands.

Markos had gone ashore earlier and walked around the famous fortress which was brisling with anti-aircraft guns. He was amazed at the huge tunnels that had been built into the rock to withstand a modern siege, in case they were attacked by the Germans or the Spanish. The only supplies the garrison received were from Britain, since Spain claimed the Rock and blockaded the base by land. Most of the town's inhabitants had been evacuated to England or other places for their safety in case the fortress came under attack.

Upon returning to the Destroyer, Markos was invited for lunch in the Davies' wardroom where the ship's officers were enjoying a lunch of grilled steaks they had picked up at the base NAAFI store. Though frozen, they still were pretty good. Surprisingly, for a place being surrounded by hostile forces, the

Brits were pretty well stocked with food and other supplies.

"So Markos how was your jaunt this morning around the Rock?"

"Pretty interesting place, captain. The Brits really have put a lot of effort in making this place impregnable with lots of antiaircraft guns, many tunnels and guns. This is a very valuable asset. It controls the access into the Mediterranean. If Gibraltar ever falls, the Germans would control the Mediterranean and Egypt would be in deep trouble. All supplies would have to go around Africa."

"If Franco decides to side with Hitler, there is not much the Brits can do to hold this place," said the Davies' commanding officer. "If the Germans bring lots of airpower to bear, the British can only last so long. The Royal Navy can't come close to shore to support the fortress with their big guns because they will be vulnerable to German airpower. So the garrison would mostly be on their own."

"That is true sir. I saw what airpower can do to ships back on Crete. One of the destroyers that had come to pick us up was blown out of the water by a Ju 87 Stuka dive bomber. But the British will put up a good fight, just as they did in Greece and are doing so now in the desert. The Germans and Spanish will pay dearly to take this place."

"I hope they last long enough until we join this war," said Commander Fleming, the ship's executive officer."

"They will, sir. The Germans now have their hands full fighting the Russians," Markos said.

"I hope you are right, Markos. The Russians are losing millions of men and giving up lots of territory to the Germans."

"Napoleon had taken Moscow and still lost the war, captain. I think the Germans will…" Before Markos could finish his sentence a huge explosion, followed by another two from across the bay, rocked the USS Davies.

Everyone jumped out of their seats and rushed outside to see where the explosions came from. They looked across the anchorage and two tankers and a cargo ship were burning furiously and settling quickly in the water.

"What the hell is going on?"

"Looks like they were torpedoed, captain."

"You are probably right, Fleming. Sound general quarters. I want to finish loading supplies and get the hell out of here."

"Aye, Aye, sir."

Several hours later, the USS Davies slipped her moorings and headed out into the Atlantic Ocean. Prior to their departure they had learned from the British that the three merchant ships had been sunk by Italian navy frogmen using manned torpedoes.

Athens, Occupied Greece
9 Sept 1941, 1500hrs

Napoleon Zervas, a heavy set man of medium height and a former Hellenic army officer, in the company of two of his friends, Leonidas Spais and Ilias Stamatopoulos, had just announced to the Greek nation and the world, the formation of EDES (The National Republican League) resistance organization. Leaflets had been printed proclaiming the establishment of EDES and sent out to various areas of the country to be distributed. Like many other resistance movements founded during that time, the political orientation of the National Republican Greek League was Republican, with a strong dislike towards the exiled King George II. The founding charter of EDES that Zervas had helped author, explicitly demanded the "establishment of a Republican regime, of Socialist form in Greece." The charter had acknowledged the prominent exiled Venezalist and anti-royalist General Nikolaos Plastiras as its nominal political head, but the general was in exile in Nice France, thus power would in reality default to him.

Zervas, a lifelong republican, anti-monarchist and staunch anti-communist, had spent most of his career supporting the republican Venezalist cause and had been ousted from the army in 1935 during a pro Venezalist coup attempt. He now saw himself as a potential political savior of Greece and thus found his niche. The organization's vague program nowhere mentioned armed resistance. He was in no particular hurry to take to the hills and begin fighting the invaders especially with the onset of winter. First he needed to make contact with the British in order to receive money and weapons to begin building the organization. That in itself would require his presence in Athens. He knew he had a lot of hard work before him. He prayed that God would give him the wisdom to save Greece from the communists and royalists.

German Headquarters,
Grand Bretagne Hotel, Athens, Occupied Greece
10 Sept 1941, 1100hrs

Mueller was reviewing the latest reports from the various Gestapo precincts throughout the city. Except for some black marketing activities and some thefts of Wehrmacht supplies, where the culprits had been caught and executed, there was not much to report. Mueller was very surprised that the Greeks were behaving. He wondered how long that would last. The reports he received from Sophia, who regularly mingled with the local population, were dire and spoke of possible starvation of thousands of Athenians this coming winter. Because of German military confiscations of vehicle transport and food supplies to take care of German military needs, farmers were not able to bring their products into the capital. Reports coming from the countryside also related that farmers refused to accept occupational currency for their produce which added to the food shortage in the capitol. Mueller was fuming at the incompetency of the occupational and local government. Not that he cared if the Greeks starved, but if that did happen this winter, there would surely be more acts of rebellion and sabotage against the German occupation forces.

On another note, he had received an Abwehr report that the assassination attempt in Cairo, against the Greek American officer that had ruined his mission on Crete, had failed. He was not at all surprised. The kid was competent and smart. The assassin's body had been found by the Egyptian police. The autopsy had revealed that he had been shot and killed by a 45 caliber bullet, most likely from a US. army issued pistol. He had been correct to surmise that the kid was probably now working for the Americans and would prove to be a very valuable asset to them. He had a feeling that sooner or later he would be running into Markos Androlakis again. This time, he would kill him personally.

CHAPTER 9

New York City
18 Sept 1941, 1700hrs

The USS Davies had arrived and docked earlier that morning at the Philadelphia naval yard. As soon as the gang plank was lowered, a representative of the COI came on board and made contact with Markos. The COI agent handed Markos a train ticket to New York and a hundred dollars spending money. The agent advised him that he was to report in two weeks to COI headquarters in Washington DC where he had a meeting with William Donovan, director of the COI.

Not having many possessions, Markos grabbed his duffle bag, said his goodbyes and was given a ride to the 30th Street station by the COI agent. There he caught the 12:13 pm

Southerner to New York. Several people on the train gave him odd stares, not recognizing his Hellenic Army uniform. After answering several questions from a couple of the passengers about his uniform, he was treated as a war hero for the rest of the trip and was bought round after round of drinks till the train pulled into Penn Station at 1:50 pm. Feeling a bit tipsy from all the drinks, he caught a cab to his home in Brooklyn. Forty five minutes later, he was dropped off in the Flatbush section of Brooklyn where his family lived in a three bedroom apartment in a tenement house, near Ebbets field, home of the Brooklyn Dodgers. His parents did know he had left Egypt. The entire time there, he had only received one letter from them.

Markos climbed up the flight of stairs and rang the doorbell. His mother opened the door and for a moment was in shock, when she saw her son standing in front of her dressed in a Greek army uniform.

"Markos!" She immediately hugged him and showered him with kisses.

"Hello, Mamma." Now both his sister Maria and his father had joined his mother in hugging and kissing him.

One of the neighbors down the hallway, Mrs. Papadakis, opened her door and peeked outside to see what all the noise was about.

"Markos, you are back!" She yelled, rushing over to also give him a hug.

"Let's go inside," his father said.

"You're just in time for dinner. We are having baked chicken and potatoes."

"That's great, mama. I really missed your home cooking."

For the first time in more than a year, Markos was at his home and having dinner with his family. He could tell his father, a slim man in his fifties, and a baker in trade, gleamed with pride, as he asked him questions about his wartime experiences on Crete. His dad had served with the Greek army during WW I and during the disastrous war with Turkey in 1919. "Markos, did you kill anyone?" asked his sister Maria.

"Maria, don't ask your brother those questions."

"That's okay, Mom."

"Yes, Maria, I did. It was kill or be killed. The Germans were in the house and coming to capture the King and kill us. I shot a man and tossed a grenade which stopped the attack. I also had to kill two German soldiers when we were attacked on our way to the coast to save the King after they had him surrounded and were shooting at him."

Both his mother and sister were silent and just stared at him. His father broke the silence. "Markos, you are a true warrior and Cretan. You killed the enemies of our people, just like your grandfather and his father who fought the Turk. You are also a hero for saving the King twice and receiving the Greek nation's highest award for valor."

"I am not proud of it, Father but that is war. Kill or be killed. I just did my duty. I lost some brave men, too, and we lost the island to the enemy."

"I know, my son. I fought in WWI and in Asia Minor. I saw some horrible things there, too. Now you are safe at home."

His mother now openly crying, hugged him. "Markos you are now safe. No more war for you."

"Mother, the US will soon be in this war. We can't let the Germans win. Grandfather and Grandmother are still on Crete. The night before the German invasion, I promised them I would be back to see them. I intend to keep that promise. Crete and all of Greece will be liberated."

"Spoken like a true warrior," said his father.

"I have a meeting with a Mr. William Donovan on Monday. He is in charge of a new intelligence agency called COI. They want people with my experience to help build an intelligence organization to prepare this country for the impending war that we will soon be involved in. That is one of the reasons I am back here."

"He's right Mom," Maria said.

"America will soon be at war too. Markos would be drafted anyway. He can serve the country better this way and as an officer doing what he knows best."

His mother stopped crying and looked at Markos. "Then may God always watch over you, my son."

Holy Trinity, Greek Orthodox Cathedral
W24th St., NY City
21 Sept 1941, 1100hrs

Markos was in his full dress Hellenic army uniform, adorned with the medals that were awarded to him by the King of Greece. He had been given the podium by Archbishop Athenagoras to address the congregation during Sunday morning services at Holy Trinity Cathedral, the head of the Greek Orthodox Church in America.

"Good morning, my fellow Greeks. I am extremely honored to be here today and I want to thank the Archbishop for giving me the opportunity to speak to you. My name is Markos Androlakis; some of you may know me. I grew up here in New York City. I just returned from the Middle East where I was serving the Greek government in exile and was attached to King George's staff. Prior to that, I was on Crete, fighting the Nazi invaders. I personally witnessed the destruction, death and brutality inflicted on the peace loving Greek people. I was sent here to speak to you by the Hellenic King, George II, whom I personally escorted to safety off the island to Egypt. Enroute, we had to fight off two German attempts to capture him. Thanks to the help of brave Greeks and our allies, the mission succeeded. Greece today is occupied by a most brutal enemy. The country has been divided amongst the Axis powers and its resources looted. The Greek people are facing starvation, disease and other untold hardships. What the King asks of you is to open your wallets and donate generously to the Greek cause. All proceeds will be given to the International Red Cross so food, medicines and other aid will hopefully reach the country. Also, write your congressmen. Ask them to help the allied cause. America needs to join the war against the Nazis. With the arsenal of democracy on the side of the allied cause, Germany will surely be defeated and Europe will be quickly liberated from Nazi oppression. Long live Greece! Thank you."

The church erupted in wild applause which turned into a standing ovation. Markos turned to leave the podium. Archbishop Athenagoras stood up and motioned for silence.

"Markos, would you mind taking questions from the congregation?"

"Of course not, your Eminence."

Markos went back up to the podium and began to take questions. The first question came from an older man that Markos knew since he was a little boy. "Markos, tell us about the German soldiers are they as good as everyone says?"

"Yes, Mr. Kostas, the Germans are excellent soldiers, well trained, ideologically motivated, determined and totally ruthless. They will do anything to achieve victory. But they can be defeated. We defeated them in battle. Crete should not have been lost. If we had we better equipment and communications, the Germans would have lost. We were defeating them. History will be the judge."

"Markos, how did the Greek soldier fight? Were all the stories we heard true?"

"Mr. Theofanis, I am glad you are well." Markos noticed the pretty young girl by his side. That must be his daughter Anna, he thought.

"Yes, the stories are all true. The Greeks fought like lions. Short of modern equipment, lacking modern aircraft and armor, they managed to defeat Mussolini's hordes in Albania and slow- down the Germans. I personally saw them fight on Crete and sacrifice their lives against the invader. I am sure it won't be long before there is a home grown resistance fighting the Axis occupiers. The Germans will be very brutal. They will shoot many hostages and burn many villages before this war is over. We were already receiving reports of German atrocities on Crete, but we could not verify them. What I did see of the Germans, makes me believe those reports."

The last question had been for Markos to tell his account of the King's rescue. After relating his experience of the trek and fight across the island, Markos received another standing ovation. After services, he was invited for coffee and cake at the church reception hall. There, he bumped into Anna Theofanis. He could not stop staring at her. She had grown more into a woman since he last saw her, and she was prettier than ever. Long dark brown hair, green eyes and a knockout figure.

"Hello, Markos. You look so handsome in your uniform and medals. I am glad you are back home safe. We all missed you."

"So am I, Anna, it's good to see you. What have you been doing with yourself?"

"I have been helping at my dad's restaurant and taking night classes at NYU."

"Would you like to go out and catch a movie? I still have over a week before I have to report to Washington."

"Why don't you come by my dad's place tomorrow night and we will go catch a movie. My dad would love to talk to you about your experiences." Markos smiled. "Sure, Anna, I'll come by around 7pm."

"Okay, see you then."

"Hi, Markos." Markos recognized the voice. He turned and saw his childhood friend, Antonis Mavroyiannis.

"Antonis!" Markos hugged his friend.

"How are you, my old friend?"

"I saw you talking to Anna. She is a knockout."

"Yes she is. Anyway what have you been up to?"

"Oh, helping my dad and learning the shoemaker business. So, was it really bad?"

"Had some good times, but towards the end, we were fighting for our lives."

"So what are you going to do?"

"Stay in the army for now. War will be here soon, my friend. There is no way of avoiding it. Germany is hell bent on conquering the world. They must be stopped."

"So you are staying in the Greek army?"

"No. I will be transferring to the US army."

"Well, stop by for a beer."

"I will, Antonis. See you later."

Markos went looking for his parents, ready to go home. He spotted them by the cathedral's entrance. They were speaking to Archbishop Athenagoras.

"Ah, there you are my son. Your speech was very moving. We collected $100 for the Red Cross. That is pretty good for a normal Sunday service."

"Thank you, your Eminence. I just spoke from my heart. Greece will soon need all the help it can get. The coming winter will be very hard for the Greek people."

"I know my son. We will do anything we can to aid in their suffering and help save some lives."

"I will also do my best your Eminence to collect donations and supplies for them."

"I know, my son. May God always watch over you."

"Thank you your Eminence," said Markos' mother. "So far, God has been watching over him."

Markos hoped that his luck would last. He was sure that in the future he would need the Lord's assistance to stay alive.

Kaisariani, Athens, Occupied Greece
27 Sept 1941, 1900hrs,

In a run-down tenement slum in the poverty stricken Athenian district of Kaisariani, the Greek communist party, represented by Lefteris Apoustolou, along with the representatives of three other leftist parties, announced the creation of (EAM), the National Liberation front. EAM's charter called for the "liberation of the Nation from foreign yoke" and the "guaranteeing of the Greek people's sovereign right to determine its form of government". At the same time, while the door was left open to cooperation with other parties, the Communist Party of Greece (KKE), due to its large size in relation to its partners, assumed a clearly dominant position within the new movement. KKE's well-organized structure and its experience with the conditions and necessities of underground struggle would be crucial to EAM's success. George Siantos was appointed as the acting leader, since Nikolaos Zachriades, the KKE's proper leader, was interned in Dachau concentration camp by the Germans.

EAM would soon announce its political manifesto and aims to the Greek people. It would use the autumn of 1941, to expand its influence throughout Greece, either through preexisting Communist cells or through the spontaneous actions of local 'people's committees'. EAM would also establish a youth movement, the "United Pan-Hellenic Organization of Youth" (EPON). The next and final step would be the formation of its military arm.

Washington D.C, COI Headquarters
6 Oct 41, 1500hrs,

Markos had taken the 09:54 am Royal Blue Express from the Liberty Street station and had arrived at Washington's Union Station at 1400hrs. From there, he took a taxi to the 2430 E Street, N.W which was the address for the COI office which was headquartered in a complex of buildings west of the Lincoln Memorial on what is known as "Navy Hill", originally the site of the Old Navy Observatory, built in 1843. He called the day before and scheduled an appointment with Colonel Donovan at 1500hrs.

The taxi dropped him off in front of the building. He grabbed his duffle bag, paid the driver and walked inside where he was met by an armed military policeman. The guard noticed Markos' rank on his uniform and saluted him. Markos showed him his Greek Military ID card which was printed in both English and Greek and his US passport. The guard looked at his clip board.

"Sir, I see you have an appointment with Colonel Donovan. I will take your ID and issue you a badge. The Colonel's office is on the second floor. Oh and sir, you can leave your duffle bag here. You can't take it upstairs. Don't worry it's secure here with me."

"Thanks, Sergeant."

Markos clipped the badge on and walked up the stairs to the director's office. He walked inside and was met by the receptionist, a middle-aged woman that checked his badge and told him to have a seat. His uniform felt a little tight. He had gained a few pounds the last two weeks eating his mother's good food. His leave had ended too soon. One thing he was able to accomplish though, was to turn in his sabbatical paper and finish his bachelor's degree with NYU. He had also spent a lot of time with Anna and his feelings for her had grown. Markos hoped she felt the same way for him. Last night's kiss at the movie theater, while watching the Wizard of Oz, made him think that she also had feelings for him. He had scored some points with her father when he visited their restaurant telling him his war stories. Besides, if the old man did not like him he would never let his daughter go out with him. He would take it slow with Anna, she was a good girl and he was serious about her. The rest of his leave was spent with his family and friends. He also did get a chance to visit another Greek church where he raised $200 for aid to Greece.

"Captain Androlakis, Mr. Donovan will see you now." Markos was suddenly jolted back into the present.

The secretary opened the door to Donovan's office and Markos walked in. He was met inside by a stocky, grey haired, energetic man of 58, who immediately offered his hand to Markos.

"Captain Androlakis. Welcome to Washington. Colonel Eddy has told me many good things about you."

"Thank you, sir. I am glad to be here to offer my services if they can be of any use?"

Donovan grinned. "Have a seat, young man. Would you like a drink?"

Markos thought about it for a second, but figured it would be rude to say no to his future boss.

"Sure, sir."

Donovan pulled out a bottle of Old Grouse scotch and two crystal glasses from his drawer and poured an inch of scotch in each glass and handed one to Markos. Donovan raised his glass. "Here's to a fruitful relationship."

Both men downed the liquor. "Well, Markos, you asked if your services can be of use. I am here to tell you that you are a valuable asset to this nation. We will soon be at war. You happen to have fought the Nazis and have high connections in the Greek exiled government. This nation lacks an effective intelligence service. The President has given me a mandate to quickly build a cadre to prepare for the coming war. We need men like you, Markos, who can think on their feet and take quick action when needed. Are you with us, son?"

"Yes, sir. That's why I am here. Tell me what you need me to do?"

"I like your spirit, Markos. Well, the first thing I want you to officially do is sign your commission papers into the US army at the rank of captain. Then we will be able to talk more since your security clearance will be in effect."

Markos was caught by surprise. "Security clearance?"

"We ran a security clearance on you after you left Egypt. You passed with flying colors. You are cleared up to Top Secret. Anything you hear or read in this office will never be repeated to anyone, unless they have a need to know. Do you understand?"

"Of course, sir."

Donovan picked up the phone and one of his aides, a major, walked in with a stack of paperwork. Fifteen minutes later, Markos had signed all the necessary documents and taken the oath of service.

"Congratulations, Markos, you are now a captain in the US army. After we are finished here, please go see the admin NCO.

He will take your picture and make your ID card. The office is down on the first floor."

"Thank you, sir."

"Now that you are official and under US military jurisdiction we can talk. I am assigning you to the Greek section. You will be working for Colonel Eddy whom you have already met. He has spent many years in that area of the world. You also speak Greek and know the area and the culture. Additionally, you have combat experience that no one else has. I want you to help build the section and recruit other Greek Americans. I intend to take the war to the Germans, once war is declared."

"The Greeks will resist the occupiers, sir. It is only a matter of time before they take up arms and form resistance groups."

"You are right, Markos. What intelligence we are getting from our embassy in Rome and from various Italian sources is that starvation is setting into the capital. The Axis forces, especially the Germans, have looted food warehouses, confiscated transportation resources and caused rampant inflation, making the Greek currency worthless. All this has caused food and goods to stop flowing into Athens. The embassy is predicting that tens of thousands will starve this winter unless they somehow find a way to get food into Athens and to some of the islands. This of course, though unfortunate will instill additional hatred against the Axis occupiers and cause more acts of resistance."

"I heard the same thing when I was in Cairo, sir."

"You will be allowed to keep your Hellenic army commission. It may prove useful in the long run. I do want you to build relationships in the Greek community. Did you do any training with the British while in Egypt?"

"I did take a three week infantry officer leadership combat

course, which included hand to hand combat and light and heavy weapons training."

"Good. When you go get your ID, card pick up the army officers manual and read it."

"I will, sir."

"Do you have a place to stay here in Washington, Markos?"

"I was going to get a room at the Hay-Adams until I find a place to stay."

"Nice place, but not worth the money. There are some rooms available upstairs if you don't mind staying here for now until we get more suitable quarters for the staff."

"Sure, sir. I don't have a problem with staying here."

"Well it's 1600hrs; I want you to meet someone. Wear your Hellenic Army dress uniform with all your medals and meet me downstairs at 1800hrs."

"Yes, sir."

Donovan picked up the phone and dialed the admin NCO. "Sergeant Jacobson, I am sending Captain Androlakis down. Fix him up with a new ID and get him a room upstairs."

"See you at 1800hrs, Markos."

White House, Washington, D.C
6 Oct 1941, 1800hrs

Markos left his room which was located on the third floor in the building's east wing and walked down the two flights of stairs. He had been pleasantly surprised with his lodging; the room was of decent size and had its own bathroom and small kitchenette. He met Donovan in the lobby at 1800hrs and they both walked outside and entered a waiting 1941 Buick Series 60 army staff car.

"Where are we going, sir?"

"We are going to meet the boss."

Marcos wondered who that was when the sedan entered Pennsylvania Avenue. A couple of minutes later, it pulled up to the White House gate. They showed their IDs and were allowed to enter. That was when Markos realized that the boss was the President of the United States. The sedan pulled up to the rear entrance where they were met by a couple of secret service agents and escorted to the Oval Office. Franklin Delano Roosevelt the 32nd president of the United States, was sitting behind the famous HMS Resolute presidential desk with an electric heater keeping his crippled legs warm. Both Markos and Donovan entered the room and Markos saluted. Roosevelt returned the salute with a smile.

"Ah, so this is Captain Androlakis of the Hellenic army whose escapades you have told me about Bill?"

"Yes, Mr. President. As of this morning, Markos is also a captain in the US Army.

"Well Markos I heard of your exploits saving the Greek King on Crete and the attempt on your life in Cairo."

Markos was almost at a loss for words. The President of the United States had heard of him and he was having a conversation with him.

"I was just doing my duty, sir and trying to stay alive in the process."

"Good answer, son. That's what any good soldier would do. Tell me about the Germans. Are they as tough as everyone says they are?"

"They are very good soldiers, well trained and well equipped. They are very highly motivated and determined to win at any cost. They are ruthless and do not abide by the rules of war. Many Cretan civilians were shot because they were caught helping allied soldiers."

"I heard those reports too. Will the Greek people resist,

Markos? We are getting reports that starvation is hitting the capital," said FDR, as he put a new cigarette in his holder and lit up.

"Yes, Mr. President. The Greek people will never willingly accept an occupier. No matter what the cost. The Axis occupiers have looted food stores and vehicles. The Greek government in exile had heard these reports too. Tens of thousands may starve. This will only make them resist even more."

"If it's any help, I did ask the American Red cross to send aid. But I fear war will soon break out between the United States and Germany and we may not be able to get too much aid in."

"Anything will be of help at this point, sir."

"Bill Donovan thinks your services will prove vital to our future war effort, Markos. The United States must be prepared to act quickly once war breaks out. This is why I authorized the creation of the COI. Intelligence gathering and sabotage behind enemy lines will be a critical component in the defeat of Nazi Germany. Building a Greek network is one of our priorities. There is still a lot of antiwar sentiment in this country. It is slowly shifting with each atrocity the Nazis commit. We can't let the Nazis win this war. They are evil. If they win in Europe, the US will be all alone. It would only then be a matter of time till we were next on Hitler's agenda.

"I will do whatever is necessary, Mr. President. The Germans can be beat. We almost defeated them on Crete."

"I know you will, son. You have got what it takes. You proved that on Crete and by God we will beat the Nazis when the time comes. Good catch, Bill."

"You have to thank Colonel Bill Eddy, Mr. President."

Roosevelt took a puff from his cigarette and smiled at

Donovan. "Well Bill, Eddy works for you, so you get the credit. Shit rolls downhill. When something goes bad in the country the president always get blamed. So enjoy the credit. We will talk again Bill. I expect a lot from you and your agency. We don't have long to prepare, war can break out any day."

Donovan knew he was being dismissed. Good night Mr. President. You can count on us."

"I am, Bill."

Athens, occupied Greece
17 Oct 1941, 1900hrs

Mueller and Sophia were sitting down in the Grand Bretagne dining room enjoying a Wiener schnitzel while hundreds of people were suffering and dying of starvation throughout the capital. Sophia was filling Mueller in on the scuttlebutt she had picked up on the street.

"Georg, people are getting very angry and blaming Germany for the lack of food in the capital and systematic looting of Greek properties. They are calling for protests and demonstration against the puppet government and occupation authorities."

"My dear, they are right, but the British naval blockade is also preventing food supplies from getting in. I have spoken to Günther Altenburg, the Reich Plenipotentiary for Greece, to see if he can do anything to help the situation, but it seems no one really cares The Reich states Greece must pay the costs of the occupation."

"Can't you do anything, Georg? Thousands of women and children will starve. The Greek people will blame the Germans and turn against them."

"I know, my dear. The fools are not listening. I will talk to some of the senior Wehrmacht commanders to see if they can hand out some supplies to the neediest women and children, but that will barley scratch the surface."

"Anything will help and may save some lives. It will also portray the German army in a better light to the Greeks. I have heard Georg, that the communist party has formed a political resistance group called EAM (The National Liberation Front). Cells are beginning to spring up everywhere. They have just published their manifesto; I managed to get a copy. I will translate it for you"

"Good work, Sophia, that's very interesting information, my dear. The communists will want to eventually control the labor movement and call strikes to resist us. I will advise the SD headquarters in Berlin to this effect. We will need to watch them closely."

"Thank you, Georg. If we can prevent a mass famine in Athens, we may steal the noise from the communists, at least in the capital."

"I will send an army food kitchen to various schools every day throughout the capital along with photographers to show the Greek people that Germany cares. That's the best I can do, Sophia."

"I will be there and judge the people's reaction."

Mueller leaned over and gave Sophia a peck on the check. "You are brilliant my, dear. This is another reason I love you so much."

She reached over and gave him a long kiss. "Let's go back to our room."

Mueller smiled. "I always like dessert."

CHAPTER 10

New York City, COI Office
10 Nov 1941, 1300hrs

Markos sat behind his desk, located in the new COI New York office, awaiting his next interview. He had been sent by Donovan to New York City to help set up the new COI headquarters there. The office, which had only been open for a couple of weeks, was located in Room 3603 of Rockefeller Center, which had been the former operations location of the British MI6 New York office. Donovan had asked Allen Dulles, a former diplomat, to head the new headquarters. Markos immediately liked Dulles. The man was very intelligent, a great organizer and a fervent anti-Nazi. Dulles had given Markos a desk in the cramped office to help with his recruiting effort.

The phone rang. "Captain Androlakis, your appointment is here."

"Thank you, Jane, please send him in."

The door opened and his friend, Antonis Mavroyiannis, stepped inside. The slim, dark haired young man was wearing a thick jacket to ward off the damp New York November cold.

Markos got up from behind his desk and shook his friend's hand. "Hi Antonis, glad you could come by."

"My dad's store wasn't very busy."

"Would you like a coffee and donut?"

"No thanks, Markos. I stopped by Katz's kosher deli and grabbed a Pastrami sandwich for lunch."

"Wish I had one, their food is great. Anyway, Antonis, I asked you to come by so I can show you our organization. I was hoping I could interest you to join us."

"Join the army? My father would have a heart attack."

"Our ancestral homeland is occupied and being ravaged by the Nazis. Thousands are dying of starvation as we speak. The United States will need Greek speakers, like us, to aid in building intelligence gathering networks and resistance movements in Greece.

"Sooner or later, this country will be at war with Germany and you will probably be drafted into the army anyway. Now you have the opportunity to pick where to go instead of ending up in the infantry."

"You do make a good point there, my friend. So what will I be doing if I decide to join the COI?"

"I am offering you the Signal Corps Officer Candidate School at Fort Monmouth, New Jersey. You will learn all about radios and communications which will come in handy when we are sent to Greece. After you graduate, you will report back to me and be my aid and communications officer. We will need to recruit more Greek speakers to build a cadre. Once we are at war with Germany, some of us will be sent to occupied Greece to aid the resistance."

"What resistance, Markos?"

"We heard from the government in exile in Cairo that, so far, they have heard of a Republican group called EDES headed by a Napoleon Zervas and a political movement called EAM that has been started by the communists. They are both in their infant stages but plan to have men in the field by summer fighting the Axis occupiers. This is your chance, Antonis, to help make a difference."

"Sounds pretty interesting, Markos. Count me in!"

Markos held out his hand. "Welcome to the COI. There is a person I would like you to meet. First though, I need you to sign your recruitment paperwork. Are you sure about this, Antonis? Last chance to back out."

"Yes, sir. I am sure I want to do this. I am looking for some action. I am a bit tired of the shoe repair business anyway."

"I will be back in a few," said Markos.

A few minutes later, Markos appeared with a stack of papers and an older, thin graying man in tow.

"Antonis, this is Mr. Allen Dulles, the New York COI director."

Dulles shook Antonis' hand. "Pleased to meet you, young man."

"If you are ready, Antonis, raise your right hand and repeat after me," said Markos.

A couple of minutes later, after taking the oath of enlistment, both Markos and Dulles were congratulating Antonis. "Welcome to the COI Antonis, I am looking forward to working with you," said Dulles.

"Thank you, sir."

"And to the US army," Markos added.

"I am sure Markos told you how important it will be for the

United States to have an intelligence gathering organization in place once war breaks out. Your knowledge of Greek will be vital in building a network in Greece."

"Yes, he did, sir. I am looking forward to working with everyone."

"Well, for starters, you will report to Fort Dix on Monday, to attend a six week basic training and weapons course, " said Markos. "Afterwards you will come back here."

"Yes, sir."

Fort Monmouth, New Jersey
8 Dec 1941, 0600hrs

Antonis was beginning to doze off as he paced his section of the Fort Monmouth perimeter. He was cold and miserable as the freezing rain mixed with snow flurries hit his face. Even though he was wearing a poncho, the rain had seeped through, causing him to shiver. His shouldered Springfield rifle began feeling heavier as he made his rounds. He still had another hour before being relieved.

Antonis had quickly adapted to the routine of Officers Training School and had actually started to enjoy the army life, when everything had suddenly gone to hell with the dastardly Japanese sneak attack, on the US Naval base at Pearl Harbor Hawaii. Rumor had it that thousands had been killed or wounded and that the Pacific fleet had been seriously damaged to include several battleships being sunk at their moorings. If that wasn't enough, the Japs had also attacked the US army and naval bases in the Philippines, causing serious damage to military assets and large loss of life.

The country had suddenly found itself at war. Even though Fort Monmouth was thousands of miles from the Pacific and Hawaii, the base had been placed on alert immediately following the Japanese attack and the officer cadets were called to pull guard duty against any potential Japanese saboteurs, which he thought to be ridiculous. Not that he minded the guard duty, it was just very cold. He figured that he had better get used to it, because several months from now, he could find himself on some Greek mountain top. That is, if the United States ever went to war against Germany. He was really worried that instead of Greece, he might find himself on some Pacific island fighting the Japs. Little did Antonis know that the Germans would very shortly solve his problem for him.

US State Department, Washington DC
11 Dec 1941, 0930hrs

The German Chargé d'Affaires, Dr. Hans Thomsen, and the First Secretary of the German Embassy, Mr. von Strempel, called the State Department at 8:00 A.M. and requested a meeting with the US Secretary of State, Cordell Hull. The Secretary, having previous engagements, directed that they be received by the Chief of the European Division of the State Department, Mr. Ray Atherton. Mr. Atherton promptly received the German representatives at 9:30 A.M.

"Good morning, sir, "said Dr. Thomsen. "I am here to deliver a note from my government. A copy of this note is also being delivered to your Chargé d'Affaires in Berlin this morning by my foreign ministry." Mr. Atherton opened the note and proceeded to read it.

MR. CHARGÉ D'AFFAIRES:

The Government of the United States having violated in the most flagrant manner and in ever increasing measure all rules of neutrality in favor of the adversaries of Germany and having continually been guilty of the most severe provocations toward Germany ever since the outbreak of the European war, provoked by the British declaration of war against Germany on September 3, 1939, has finally resorted to open military acts of aggression.

On September 11, 1941, the President of the United States publicly declared that he had ordered the American Navy and Air Force to shoot on sight at any German war vessel. In his speech of October 27, 1941, he once more expressly affirmed that this order was in force.

Acting under this order, vessels of the American Navy, since early September 1941, have systematically attacked German naval forces. Thus, American destroyers, as for instance the Greer, the Kearney and the Reuben James, have opened fire on German submarines according to plan. The Secretary of the American Navy, Mr. Knox, himself confirmed that-American destroyers attacked German submarines. Furthermore, the naval forces of the United States, under order of their Government and contrary to international law have treated and seized German merchant vessels on the high seas as enemy ships.

The German Government therefore establishes the following facts: Although Germany on her part has strictly adhered to the rules of international law in her relations with the United States during every period of the present war, the Government of the United States from initial violations of neutrality has finally proceeded to open acts of war against Germany. The Government of the United States has thereby virtually created a state of war.

> The German Government, consequently, discontinues diplomatic relations with the United States of America and declares that under these circumstances brought about by President Roosevelt Germany too, as from today, considers herself as being in a state of war with the United States of America.
>
> Accept, Mr. Chargé d'Affaires, the expression of my high consideration.
>
> December 11, 1941.
> RIBBENTROP.

Atherton's expression quickly turned from one of surprise to anger. "Dr. Thomsen, in accepting this note from your government, I am merely formalizing the realization that the Government and people of this country have faced since the outbreak of the war in 1939. The threat and purposes of the German Government and the Nazi regime toward this hemisphere and our free American civilization have just been realized."

"Sir, Germany considers herself in a state of war with the United States. I am asking that the appropriate measures be taken for my departure and the members of the German Embassy, and my staff from this country. The Swiss Government will take over German interests in this country. Dr. Bruggmann has already received appropriate instructions from his Government."

"My Government will arrange for the delivery of your passports. I assume we will be in communication with the Swiss Minister very shortly. You must realize, sir, that the physical difficulties of the situation will demand a certain amount of time in working out this reciprocal arrangement for the departure of the missions of the two countries."

"Of course, Mr. Atherton. Thank you for the meeting and have a good day." With that, both men left the State Department and returned to the German Embassy where the staff had been burning their classified documents. Both men were sorry that it had come to this. They knew that Germany had made a fatal mistake by declaring war on the United States. As Churchill had stated after the attack on Pearl Harbor and America's entry into WWII, a sleeping giant had just been awakened.

COI Headquarters, Washington DC
17 Jan 1942, 1333hrs

With the US now at war, the tempo at COI headquarters had changed drastically. Never expecting to be in a two theater war, COI now had to find agents that had experience in the Orient. In the last couple of weeks, there had been an influx of many new recruits. Markos helped as much as he could, assisting many of the new recruits in getting situated in the organization. As a result of the German declaration of war, the Balkans department, which Markos was part of, had been ordered to quickly catch up on the state of Greek affairs and recruit more Greek speaking agents. His supervisor, Col Bill Eddy, had invited him back to Egypt to meet with the Greek government in exile and with the Greek intelligence community. Markos had spent much of the early morning getting his affairs in order and finishing packing when the phone in his room rang. "Sir, it's Sergeant Jacobson in admin, the "Colonel would like to see you."

"I'll be right down, Sergeant."

Ten minutes later, Markos was sitting down in Donovan's office enjoying a glass of Old Grouse scotch. "Well, Markos, are you packed and ready to go?"

"I am, sir. All my bags are packed and I'm ready to go."

"There will be a C-47 transport leaving for England from Washington National at 1700hrs. Orders have been cut for you to have a seat. When you get to England, you will catch a ride with the RAF to Cairo. Colonel Eddy will meet you there."

"I am looking forward to seeing him and all my old friends there."

"We want you to mingle with the Greeks there and find out what's happening in Greece in terms of resistance groups. Word has it that the Communists are the best organized. That does not surprise me since they always had to operate underground to survive. If you can get a meeting with the King that would be the icing on the cake."

"I will do my best, sir."

"I know you will. Give my regards to Bill Eddy. Now grab your stuff and get one of the drivers to take you to the airport. Have a good trip."

"Thanks, sir."

Libyan Sea, 50 miles South of Crete
20 Jan 1942, 1600hrs,

The flight to England had been long and tiring. The C-47 transport had departed Washington and after a seven hour flight landed in Gander Newfoundland, for refueling and crew rest before taking off on the long 16 hour fight to RAF Mildenhall England. The flight across the Atlantic had been uneventful and after spending a day resting, Markos boarded an RAF Wellington bomber that was going to take him to Cairo, Egypt. After a 6 hour flight the bomber landed at Gibraltar where it picked up fuel and took off for the long stretch to Cairo Egypt. As their only passenger, the flight crew had invited

Markos to sit in the cockpit.

Markos gazed at the empty blue Mediterranean Sea passing below them. From 15000 feet, the view was pretty spectacular. In more peaceful times, the sea would have been dotted with fishing boats and ships plying their trade as they did for thousands of years. "Hey, Markos, that dark smudge off to the right is Crete. Hopefully, we don't run into any Luftwaffe fighter patrols, the nearest German airfield is only sixty miles away," said Lieutenant Morgan, the bomber's navigator.

"Wish I could drop in and visit my grandparent's. How much longer 'till we arrive?"

"Three more hours," replied the navigator.

"Well Yank, you may just get your chance. The tail gunner just spotted two twin engine Messerschmitt BF 110 fighters coming in from the North to intercept us."

"What can I do to help?" Markos asked.

"Go inside and assist the waist gunner and pray," replied the pilot.

Markos ran to the inside of the plane as the starboard side 7.7 mm machine gun opened fire on the first BF 110 making its pass on the Wellington. It was basically a futile gesture against the heavily armed fighter bomber. The German fighter opened fire as it passed over the bomber. The inside of the plane erupted with chunks of the fuselage flying everywhere, as numerous machine gun bullets and two 20mm canon shells ripped through the bomber, taking the head off the waist gunner. Markos, covered in the gunner's blood, grabbed the waist gun as the second fighter made its pass straight at the bomber. He let loose with a long burst of fire just as the BF 110 opened fire. The German fighter ran into his stream of bullets, several ripping into the cockpit, instantly killing the pilot and wounding the gunner. But the bomber had been hit too. One of the German fighter's canon shells had hit the port engine, causing smoke to pour out of it. The stricken fighter, with a dead man at the controls, plunged toward the sea 15000 thousand feet below.

The bomber was now in a shallow dive towards the ocean three miles below. With flames pouring out of the port engine, Markos ran up to the cockpit which was in shambles. Both the pilot and navigator/ radio operator were dead. Pieces of flesh and blood littered the cockpit floor and instrument panel. The copilot though seriously injured was trying to keep the plane in the air.

"The waist gunner's dead."

"So are we, Yank, unless I get this plane flying straight and level again. Hurry, give me a hand, grab the yoke and pull."

Markos quickly removed the dead pilot's body and jumped in the seat.

"Pull!" the copilot yelled.

Slowly the large bomber pulled out of its dive and leveled off at 5000 feet. The copilot had feathered the damaged engine and managed to extinguish the fire.

"I am making for that cloud bank to the north if we get there, we may lose the fighter."

"Here he comes!" screamed the rear gunner. The pilot of the BF 110, bent for revenge, made another pass at the lumbering bomber. The Wellington shuddered as it was hammered by machine guns bullets and cannon shells.

"I got the bastard," yelled the nose gunner, as the fighter passed underneath the stricken bomber.

Markos could see smoke coming from one of the fighter's engines before it disappeared from site as the bomber entered the cloud bank. The remaining BF 110, itself damaged and losing sight of the bomber, turned for home, minus its wingman.

"We made it!" Markos said.

"We are not out of the woods yet, mate. We are leaking fuel and that last pass must have damaged our control lines. I've lost communication with the tail gunner. Go back there and see what's going on."

Markos exited the cockpit and made his way to the rear of the plane. He observed that the fuselage was riddled with dozens of holes and he wondered what still kept it flying. When he reached the tail gunner, he saw that the man was dead; the Plexiglas was riddled with holes and splattered with blood. What he did notice was that a large piece of the tail rudder and part of the elevators had been shot away. He immediately turned around and went back up to the cockpit and gave his report to the copilot.

"It seems, Yank, you're going to get your wish after all. We will never make it to Egypt in this plane. We are starting to lose altitude and I will not be able to keep her airborne much longer. We are heading for Crete. Hopefully we can find a boat that can take us to Egypt."

Markos was shocked. He could not believe that he was going back to the Nazi occupied island. But looking at the wounded copilot and the state of the plane, he knew they had no other choice. The nose gunner, Flight Sergeant Harrison, who probably was no older than twenty, had also entered the cockpit with a first aid kit.

"Sir, I need to try and patch you up and stop the bleeding."

"Do what you can, Sergeant. I have to keep us in the air a few more minutes," said the copilot as he picked up the radio mike and began issuing a mayday call.

Ten Miles South of Loutro, Crete
20 Jan 1942, 1740hrs

The Lefka Mountains of Crete could now be seen clearly in the waning light from the cockpit. The wounded copilot was struggling to keep the doomed plane airborne long enough to ditch near the coastline. Feeling faint by the loss of blood, he knew that he had to get the plane down fast before he passed out.

"Okay, everybody this is it. When we hit the water this plane is not going to stay afloat long. I was able to get a mayday and our location to Cairo so they know our status. They are sending an RAF Sutherland. I want both of you in the back and secure your selves to your seats and brace for the crash. Harrison, once we are down, grab the dingy and throw her out. Now get back there."

"Yes, sir."

"Where are we?" Markos asked.

"Just off the coast of Loutro and Chora Sfakion," replied the copilot.

"Captain, follow me quickly. We don't have much time."

Markos followed Harrison inside where they both secured themselves to their seats and waited for the impact. They did not have to wait long. The damaged bomber hit the water hard and quickly came to a stop. Water began filling the interior. The numerous holes from the air battle only speeded up the process. Harrison quickly undid his seat belts and ran to get the life raft.

"Sir, go help the pilot."

Markos unstrapped himself, the sea, pouring in, was now up to his waste as he ran up to the cockpit. He found the copilot slumped over the controls and quickly released him from his seat and carried him to the exit of the rapidly sinking plane. "Captain, hurry up and jump, the plane's going under," screamed Harrison."

Markos inflated the copilot's Mae West vest and pushed him into the water. He quickly jumped into the cold water, inflated his vest, grabbed the wounded copilot and swam towards the rubber life raft. Reaching the raft just as the plane sank under the waves, Markos pulled himself inside the raft and both he and Harrison hauled the injured copilot in. Harrison opened the survival kit and pulled out a couple of blankets giving one to Markos and covering the injured copilot with the other

"Sir, here is one of the pistols in the survival kit." Markos took the Webley 38 caliber revolver.

"I am sure someone saw the ditching, hopefully it was not an enemy patrol. We're about two kilometers from the shore. We'll wait until it's dark to land if we're to stand any chance on avoiding the German patrols."

"Sir, I managed to staunch the bleeding, but Flight Officer Jeffries needs medical attention pretty soon if he is to survive."

"I know, sergeant. Let's get ashore safely and we will get him some help."

"Sir, Jeffries said that a Sutherland was on its way."

Markos hesitated for a second. See that light, Sergeant? Said Markos, as he pointed to the direction of the shore.

"Looks like a boat headed our way, sir.

"They're probably Germans. No Greek would have the fuel to run their boat. They're about ten to fifteen minutes away. It's dark and they can't see us. I suggest we head out to sea and then double back. They will think we are headed towards the shore and search for us in that direction. So row, sergeant like your life depended on it."

"Yes, sir. I don't want to be a guest of the Germans."

Fifteen minutes had gone by and, they had paddled about a kilometer from where they had ditched the plane. The German patrol boat had just reached the area and was shining its searchlight in the water. Not finding anything, the boat turned and began searching the waters closer to the shore.

"You were right, sir."

"Lucky guess, Sergeant. Let's paddle for another few minutes and then just drift. Hopefully the Krauts will think we reached the shore and stop searching for us on the water."

Twenty minutes later, another patrol boat had joined the search, both men could see light flashes coming from the beach, where the German patrols were searching the coastline.

"I think we need to put some more distance between ourselves and the Germans."

"I could not agree more with you, sir."

Loutro, Southern occupied Crete
20 Jan 1942, 2205hrs

Markos and Harrison had rowed several kilometers down the coastline of southern Crete and drifted for a couple of more hours until they could not see the lights of the German patrols anymore. The wounded copilot had been in and out of consciousness and was in need of immediate medical attention if he was to stand a chance to live. Not having seen any sign of the Germans for several hours, Markos decided it was safe to go ashore. They landed on a sandy beach just west of the small fishing village of Loutro. Markos and Harrison hid the rubber dinghy and moved the wounded copilot several hundred meters inland away from the beach. They found an olive grove where they decided to hunker down for the night. Markos was shivering in his damp army utility uniform and wet jump boots. He was glad that he wore that instead of his dress uniform and low quarter dress shoes which were now at the bottom of the sea with the plane.

"Sir, Jeffries started bleeding again. He is not going to make it till morning."

"I'm going for help, sergeant."

"There might be Germans in the village, captain."

That's a risk I will have to take. Jeffries is not going to make it unless we get him to a doctor, we don't have much of a...." Before he could finish his sentence they heard the throb of aircraft engines coming from the southeast.

"That's probably the Sutherland, sir."

The plane turned on its landing lights as it flew low over the water searching for survivors from the crashed Wellington bomber. Several seconds later, a stream of tracers arched out to sea from one of the patrol boats that had been searching for them. The plane doused its lights, went to full power and climbed for altitude.

"So much for rescue," Markos said.

"He is heading this way. I am going to signal him."

Before Markos could reply, Harrison took out one of the survival flashlights and began signaling in Morse. The Flying boat zoomed overhead and turned its lights on and off in acknowledgement.

"They saw the signal, sir. They are coming around for another pass."

Harrison continued flashing the light as the plane made a slow circle over their position until Harrison had completed the message. The Sutherland then turned toward the south and headed back to Egypt.

"I gave them a full report on our status, sir."

"Let's hope the Germans didn't see the light. I am going to the town, I know someone there. Stay put. I'll be back with help as soon as I can."

"Yes, sir. I'll be here watching over Jeffries."

Markos took off towards the lights of the small fishing village less than a kilometer away. He prayed that there were no Germans stationed there and that he could get help for the injured copilot. Markos reached the first few buildings and saw an old woman carrying a pail of water. She looked up at him in surprise.

"Grandmother, are there any Germans in the village? "he asked in Greek.

"No, my child. They are in Sfakion, the next village from here. Are you Greek?"

"Yes, I am Greek-American and I need your help. I have a wounded man. Our airplane was forced down by the Germans and we crashed into the sea."

"Come with me to the Kaffeneion (Coffee house), most of the men are there, they will help you."

"Thank you, Grandmother."

Markos followed the old woman to the village's sole Kaffeneion where several men were playing cards and drinking Tsikoudia, the local version of Raki. When Markos entered the Kaffeneion, everyone looked up at the stranger in uniform. "English?" asked one of the men who had been playing cards.

"No, I am not British, I am an American officer," said Markos in fluent Greek.

"An Americanos here on Crete!" said another older gray haired man who stood up from his chair and approached Markos.

"I am also a Cretan and a Greek officer. I need your help. Our plane was shot down by the Germans and there are two other British airmen just east of the village. One of them is seriously wounded."

"What is your name young man? The man asked.

"My name is Markos Androlakis."

"Markos!" One of the men that had been sitting down and playing cards jumped out of his seat and hugged him.

"Sergeant Mitsakis, my friend!" said Markos returning the hug.

"It's good to see you again, Markos."

"We have all heard of you from Pavlos. You are the Greek American officer that commanded the Cretan Gendarmes detachment that helped the King escape from the Germans."

"Yes, I'm the one," Markos replied to the man.

"The older man held out his hand. "I am Thanasis Petrakis, mayor of this small village. You are a brave patriot and a Cretan warrior. As much as we hated the King, we are all now united fighting a common enemy, the Germans. We will help you."

"Thank you. We hope to be gone as soon as possible as to not put you in any danger."

"Nonsense! You will stay as long as need be. Ilias, Pavlos, go with Markos and bring the injured English flier here. Thanasis, go find the doctor."

COI Headquarters, Washington DC
24 Jan 1942, 0910hrs

William Donovan, head of the COI, was reading the latest message that had come in from Col Eddy in, charge of COI operations in the Mediterranean theater at the Cairo embassy. It gave a report on the shooting down and ditching of the plane that had been transporting Markos to Egypt and a report from a RAF rescue plane that had been sent to pick up survivors. The plane had picked up a Morse code message sent by flashlight from one of the surviving crew members. Two crew members, including Markos, had survived the crash and had safely reached the island. Now Donovan had to find a way to get him off Nazi occupied Crete. Markos was too valuable an asset to lose. He would have to turn to the British for assistance. They had SOE (Special Operations Executive) agents on the island. He would talk to his counterpart at the British Embassy and get the wheels moving. He was confident that Markos could take care of himself and stay out of the hands of the Germans. Hopefully, he could make some connections that could bear fruit for future operations against the Germans on the island. Unfortunately, the recruiting and training of Greek American agents would fall behind because of Marko's absence. Maybe he could get Antonis Mavroyiannis out of training from Fort Monmouth a week or two early. Donovan picked up the phone.

"Sergeant Jacobson, get me the military attaché office at the British embassy and bring me another coffee, please."

"Yes, sir."

He wondered what the British would ask for in return. Nothing was free in the intelligence business.

CHAPTER 11

Chania- Hora Sfakion road, Crete
24 Jan 1942, 1717hrs

Standartenführer Georg Mueller glanced at his military issued Longines DH wristwatch. It was indicating 1720hrs. The sun was quickly setting and it would be dark soon. The ride in the army Kubel Wagen (Wermacht Jeep equivalent) was beginning to take a toll on him. They had been on the road from Chania to Hora Sfakion, for more than four hours since leaving the airfield with a strong SS security escort. The bumpy potholed dirt road was fit for goats rather than vehicles. He and Hauptsturmführer Lantz had arrived at Maleme airfield via a Luftwaffe Junkers 52 transport from the mainland. Bandit activity had begun to pick up and he was on an inspection to check the SS forces and security procedures on the island.

They would soon be arriving at the small town of Hora Sfakion where he would inspect the small garrison stationed there. A report had crossed his desk that an RAF Wellington bomber had been forced to crash land just off the south coast near Hora Sfakion, but Wehrmacht forces were unable to find any of the survivors. He was sure the survivors were being hidden by the locals whom he would deal with shortly.

Mueller was glad to be out of Athens for a while, though he would miss Sophia, the Greek girl he had fallen in love with. He had left Bruner there to keep a watchful eye over her. Sooner or later violence would pick up and a Greek girl seen with a German in Athens could be a death sentence. The city itself had become a place of death, as thousands had already died from lack of food and hundreds more were dying daily of starvation. Not that Germany had done any of this deliberately. Lack of transport, made it almost impossible for farmers to transport goods into the city. The collapse of the currency and the British naval blockade had all made for an explosive situation where in the end starvation had prevailed. He had tried to better the situation by sending reports to Germany, but all his cries had fallen on deaf ears. This would, for sure, stoke the fires of hatred against Germany and resistance was sure to increase with the coming of spring.

Stavros Mavrakis and his men had been waiting most of the day to ambush German vehicles that traveled on the Chania-Hora Sfakion road. His hit and run tactics had begun taking a toll on the German occupiers, but not without repercussions. His last attack had resulted in the execution of several Cretan partisans that were being held by the Germans. They had been strung up in the middle of the town square of Chania. But Cretans were used to hardship and cruelties that had been committed on them by the various invaders that had occupied their island through the centuries. All the Germans had accomplished was to increase the hatred and create more Cretan partisans who flocked to his or other bands that roamed the mountains to exact their revenge on the occupier. He would not have to wait long. He could see several German vehicles that were making their way up the narrow mountain road. His men had cut down a couple of trees and placed them across the road which would force the Germans to stop and clear the road.

The lead SS motorcyclists had reached the road block and came to a stop as did the rest of the convoy. That was when the Cretan partisans opened fire. The two motorcyclists were quickly cut down by a grenade before their sidecar machine gunners could bring their weapons to bear. Mueller heard the grenade explosions and ducked as the windshield was shattered by bullets.

"Get out of the vehicle," Mueller screamed.

Both he and Lantz opened the door and fell to the ground, taking cover. The truck that had been carrying the SS security contingent had been stitched with bullets, killing or wounding several of the men that had been inside. The rest had jumped out and began returning fire. Mueller looked around for the Obersturmfuhrer that had been in command of the detachment. He spotted the man slumped over in the front seat of the Kubel wagen they had been riding in. "Lantz, I am going for the machine gun," said Mueller, pointing at one of the rider less sidecars.

"Sir, you will be killed."

"We will all be killed if we don't do something fast. Take charge of the survivors and when I give the order, open fire at that high point where they have the machinegun and I will make a run for it."

Mueller used what little cover was available and inched

toward the sidecar. When he was about twenty meters from it, he motioned to Lantz to open fire. The partisan machine gunners, inundated by rifle fire took cover, giving Mueller the break he needed. By the time the other partisans switched their fire toward the running figure, he had reached the side car, pulled back on the charging handle of the MG 34 and opened up a withering fire on the partisan positions. Lantz took the opportunity and had a squad outflank the partisan machine gun, taking it out with a grenade. With the gun no longer operational, the partisans could not hold their own against the highly trained German troops and quickly retreated up the mountain leaving their dead and seriously wounded behind.

With the fighting done, Mueller quickly took stock of the situation, four men had been killed and five wounded. Two of their three vehicles were still running so they would not have to walk the rest of the way.

"Sir, come here, one of the bandits is still alive."

Mueller walked to where Lantz and his men had dragged one of the wounded partisans and had laid him against a tree. He could see in the waning daylight that the man had been hit in the gut with grenade shrapnel. "What is your name?" He asked the man in accented Greek which he had learned from Sophia.

The man refused to answer him. Mueller put his foot on the man's stomach and pressed until the man screamed and spit up blood.

"Sir, it's getting dark and we need to leave. He does not have long to live he is bleeding out."

Mueller unholstered his 9mm Walter P38 service pistol leaned down and placed the barrel against the man's temple. "I will ask you one more time. What's your name?"

The man looked at Mueller than spat at him. "Go screw

yourself, Nazi pig, we will kill you all on this island."

"Okay, as you wish." Mueller pulled the trigger, splattering the man's brains all over the tree he was leaning against.

"You are right, Lantz, it's getting dark. Let's get the wounded loaded in the vehicles and get the hell out of here. We will deal with these scums later."

Loutro, Crete
24 Jan 1942, 2310hrs

Markos and Flight Sergeant Harrison were sitting in the village mayor's smoke filled kitchen where a burning cooking fire also served to provide some warmth against the night chill. They were enjoying their late evening dinner of village sausage and fried eggs, washed down with generous glasses of the local red wine. The copilot was upstairs, hidden in the loft, recovering from the shrapnel wounds he received during the Luftwaffe fighter attack. Pavlos had left the day before for the Lefka Mountains to make contact with the resistance forces there and their British SOE advisors. Markos was hoping that they would soon be contacted by the British Liaison officers and smuggled off the island. The town's people were risking their lives by aiding the allied soldiers and he did not want to put these people at more at risk.

"Do you want some more wine gentlemen?" asked the mayor.

Both men nodded yes and the Mayor refilled their glasses. The mayor raised his glass, "to victory against the Germans."

Before they could finish the toast they were interrupted by a knock on the door. The mayor opened the door. It was one of the townspeople, "the Germans are here."

Markos and Harrison immediately ran out of the house and down a narrow alleyway where they were spotted by several

German soldiers coming from the other direction.

"Halt!"

"Shit! Captain, they've seen us."

Both men turned and ran the other direction followed by several shots. They ducked inside a barn. "Harrison, get out of here, I will hold them back."

"No, sir. I am staying."

"It's an order. Get out of here. Head for the mountains and find the guerrillas. Now go!"

"Ok, good luck, sir. And oh for a Yank, you are a pretty good guy."

Markos peered outside and saw the advancing German soldiers and fired several shots in their direction making them duck for cover. Taking the opportunity, Harrison exited the barn and ran into the darkness. Markos waited several seconds and stuck his head outside, but this time he was met by a hail of gunfire that struck the building, barely missing him. He knew he was in trouble and hoped that Harrison had gotten away.

"You are surrounded. Surrender and you will be treated as a prisoner of war."

Markos checked his Webley revolver. It only had three more bullets in the chamber. His options were not looking very good at the moment.

"This is Hauptsturmführer Lantz, you have no chance. Surrender now. You will not be harmed."

"Oh shit, SS troops," he said to himself.

The Germans had also brought up a vehicle and had focused its lights on the barn. He did not have much of a choice. His only option was to surrender or be killed. At least if he was alive, there was always a chance of escape.

"Okay, I am coming out. I am throwing out my weapon."

Markos tossed out his pistol, put his hands in the air and

walked out taking a few paces toward the vehicle.

"Halt!"

Markos stopped dead in his tracks. He was immediately surrounded by armed German soldiers. He was approached by an officer.

"I am Hauptsturmführer Lantz." He stared at Markos' uniform and was confused for a moment.

"What do we have here, an Americaner?"

"I am Captain Markos Androlakis, US army. I expect to be treated as a prisoner of war."

Lantz stared at Markos and smiled. He recognized the name. He turned to one of his men. "Heinrich, find the Standartenführer and tell him I have a surprise for him."

"Jawol, Herr Hauptsturmführer."

The soldier did not have far to go. He ran into his commander less than one hundred meters from where Markos was being held. Mueller had been on the other side of the village. He had heard the shots and was on his way there to see what had happened. Lantz saw Mueller approaching and snapped into attention. "Sir, I have a surprise for you," and gestured toward Markos.

Mueller immediately recognized Markos.

"You? The Greek American who ruined my operation to capture the King of Greece. I see now you are wearing an American uniform with captain's rank. My, you get around."

"Just doing my duty, colonel."

"Well, your career is now over."

"Sir, my men tell me there was another man with him," said Lantz.

"So captain, where is the other man?"

"I don't know. Hopefully far away from here," said Markos with a smug grin.

Mueller's day had started out pretty bad; being ambushed and almost killed by the local partisans had put him in a terrible mood. Once he reached Hora Sfakion, one of the local collaborators had paid him a visit and told Mueller that rumors were floating around that several allied airman had washed ashore near Loutro. So he had mobilized the local garrison and mounted a night operation by land and sea so he could catch some of the bandits, or allied soldiers and airmen that were being hidden by the locals, by surprise. His hunch had paid off, but he was in no mood to be mocked, especially by this particular American POW.

"Who helped you here?"

"No, one."

"You are lying. You could not survive without food and assistance."

"I will ask you again. Where is the other soldier and who helped you?"

"Go to hell."

"Mueller lost it and slapped Markos."

Markos broke free of his guard and lunged at Mueller. Before he could strike the SS Officer, he was hit in the head with a rifle butt knocking him out.

"Lantz, put him in the barn and post a guard. I want no one coming in or out of this village. We will tear it apart in the morning. Anyone we catch aiding enemy soldiers will be executed!"

"Jawohl, Herr Standartenführer!"

Five Kilometers Northwest of Loutro, Crete
25 January 1942, 0615 hrs.

Flight Sergeant Harrison was utterly exhausted by his trek through the rough Cretan terrain. Daybreak had found him about five kilometers from Loutro in a pine forest about a thousand meters above the village. After managing to sneak through the German cordon around Loutro, he headed towards the Lefka mountains as fast as he could. During their stay at Loutro, he had memorized a map of the island and thought he was now heading in the right direction. The smell of burning wood permeated the cold morning air. He hoped that the smoke came from some Shepherd's cooking fire. Pulling his pistol from his pocket, he headed towards the source of the smoke. The sound of a bolt going forward froze him in his tracks. Harrison dropped his weapon and slowly raised his hands.

"Do not move," someone shouted in heavily accented English.

"Don't worry, mate, I am not moving an inch."

Two men came toward him from out of the bushes. They were armed with MP38s and dressed in heavy winter clothing, wearing knee high leather boots. One of them picked up the pistol Harrison had dropped and then searched him.

"You are English? RAF?"

"Yes, my plane was shot down a few days ago."

"Okay, you can put your hands down. Thanos, give him his weapon back and take him to the commander"

"Follow me, sergeant."

A few minutes later, they came to a small clearing where more than a dozen men were having coffee and breakfast around a fire. One of the men who was wearing a leather fleece lined jacket, probably in his mid-twenties, noticed them and walked toward their direction.

"Hello, sergeant, I am Major Monty Woodhouse," he said holding out his hand.

"I am Flight Sergeant Harrison, sir."

Harrison noticed another man who looked vaguely familiar walking over with a tin of hot coffee in his hand. It was Pavlos Mitsakis, the former Gendarmes Sergeant and now turned Partisan.

"Harrison, how are you?" He said, handing the cup of hot coffee to him.

"Where is Markos?" he said in broken English.

"Well, sergeant, where is the American captain? The Americans are very keen on getting him back, according to the latest messages from Cairo. We were on the way to pick you men up."

"Sir, I have bad news. The Germans came in by water and land last night. The captain held them off and ordered me to escape and find the resistance."

Another man had joined them and asked Woodhouse something in Greek. Woodhouse answered him and he could see the concern in the other man's face.

"Oh, excuse me, this is Stathis Mavrakis, the leader of this motley band of fighters."

Harrison acknowledged Stathis and held out his hand. The partisan leader took his hand and shook it with a firm grip.

"Gentlemen, we are running out of time. Let's move it and save our American ally and your copilot.

Loutro Crete
25 January 1942, 0735hrs

Markos opened his eyes and saw the sunlight streaming in through a window. He was lying in a pile of hay and he surmised that the Germans had locked him in the barn that he had been hiding in. He had an excruciating headache and a large bump on his forehead where the rifle butt had struck him. He rose slowly to his feet and walked to one of the corners of the stone building which was filled with hay and bags of wheat and relieved himself. He could hear shouting outside and wondered what the Germans were up to. Obviously, it could not be good knowing the reputation of the SS and Mueller. He did not have long to wait. The door burst open and two SS men brandishing MP 38 submachine guns, rushed in, grabbed him, hauled him out the door and escorted him to the small Warf where Mueller and a couple dozen of his men had set up a mobile command post. Markos figured that the German force had to be at least platoon size (40 men) The Warf was devoid of any of the town's people.

"Good morning, captain. I hope you slept well?"

"Oh, just like a baby, colonel," replied Markos sarcastically.

"Would you like some Ersatz coffee (Ground corn and Chicory coffee substitute)? Of course, it's not as good as your American coffee. Germany has been at war for over two years so we are a little short on coffee beans."

Markos nodded his head. "Sergeant, please give our American guest a cup of coffee and some breakfast."

"Jawohl, Herr Standartenführer."

The German NCO grabbed a cup and filled it with the hot liquid that had been brewing on the cooking fire and gave it to Markos. Markos took a swig of the bitter brew. It was barely drinkable, but at this point beggars could not be choosey. The NCO returned with a slice of black bread and a piece of Dauer Wurst (hard sausage) and handed it to Markos. Though not hungry, Markos forced himself to eat the food not knowing when he would see more from his captors.

"How did you like your breakfast, captain?" Mueller asked.

"This is standard German army fare."

"It hit the spot. Thank you," Markos replied.

"Now it's time to get back to work. While you were

"sleeping" captain, my men were busy searching the village for bandits and allied soldiers. We found your copilot and the people that were hiding him."

Mueller saw the look of surprise on Markos' face.

"Don't worry, captain. He will be treated as a prisoner of war. He is on his way to our hospital in Chania for further treatment. But now I must make an example for the rest of these villagers. They must learn what the cost of resistance against the German armed forces is."

"What do you mean?" asked Markos.

"You will see soon enough."

"Sergeant Schmitz, have Hauptsturmführer Lantz bring the prisoners. The rest of you bring the town's residents here. I want them to see what happens to enemies of the Reich."

"Yes, sir."

Several minutes later, Lantz and a squad of SS troops in the company of a man wearing a hood arrived with the village Mayor and his family. By now, Mueller's troops had rounded up most of the town's people and brought them to the Warf. Mueller said something to one of his NCOs and the man went to one of the boats tied to the Warf and brought back several pieces of rope and began tying a hangman's knot. When he finished it he slung it over one of the branches of a large Cretan Plane tree.

"What are you doing, Mueller?"

"I am going to hang them. You brought this upon them, captain."

"You bastard" Markos tried to lung at the SS Officer, but several of Mueller's men quickly subdued him.

Mueller gestured to the man wearing the hood. The man approached Mueller and the SS officer spoke to him in English for Markos' benefit.

"Please translate to these people that the penalty of aiding the enemies of the German Reich is death. The wounded British airman was found hidden in the Mayor's house. Therefore the Mayor will be executed. Yesterday, I was attacked on the road by Greek bandits and several of my men were killed. I should burn this entire village and hang every man. I will show mercy. Germany is not the enemy of Greece. I will not execute his entire family. I will let him choose which one of his two sons will be hung with him."

The masked collaborator translated into Greek what Mueller had said to the villagers. The Mayor was in shock upon hearing his fate. Not that he wanted to be hung, but he would die for his country if he had to. But to choose which one of his sons would live or die was incomprehensible. He dropped to his knees and begged Mueller for his sons lives.

"So, who will it be, Mayor?"

"I can't choose!"

"I will then choose for you. I will hang you all."

"No, please."

"Mueller, you can't just murder these people," yelled Markos as he was restrained by two of Mueller's men.

"They are enemies of the Reich and they will be executed as an example. Sergeant, hang the Mayor first."

The mayor was grabbed by the two burley SS men and taken to the tree where one of the ropes was hanging. The Mayor had stopped fighting and calmly waited his fate as the Germans placed the noose around his neck.

"Do you have any last word?" asked Mueller.

"Long live Hellas! Death to the Germans!"

Mueller nodded and two soldiers pulled on the rope, hauling the Mayor off the ground. His wife screamed and fainted as the hanging man gasped for air and kicked his feet.

Two minutes later, he had stopped moving.

"Sergeant, prepare the other two."

"Jawohl, Herr Standartenführer!"

Outskirts of Loutro, Crete
25 January 1942, 0826hrs

Perched on a rocky ledge overlooking the village, Major Woodhouse watched through his binoculars in horror at what was taking place on the wharf less than 300 meters away.. His men had not been in position to intervene and save the man that had been hanged. He would though try to save the rest. They had force marched the five kilometers to Loutro to rescue the American officer that London and Washington wanted back. Stavros and his men were now in place and were awaiting his signal to attack.

"Sir, here is the rifle."

"Thank you, Giorgos."

Woodhouse put the binoculars down and picked up the scoped Enfield Sniper rifle. He looked through the scope and saw a teenage boy being dragged by two German soldiers toward the same tree where the other man had just been hung. His body was still dangling from the tree. Woodhouse took aim at one of the two Germans and slowly squeezed the trigger. The rifle barked once and the .303 slug tore through the German's chest spinning him around. Hearing the signal to attack, several other weapons opened fire, taking out several more Germans.

Markos heard the first shot and dropped to the ground as all hell broke loose. Several of the Germans had been hit and the others were quickly seeking cover. He saw his opportunity and dove for a MP-38 that had belonged to one of Mueller's men who had been hit. He grabbed the weapon and let off a burst, hitting one of the Germans who was blocking his escape route. Markos took off running toward the direction the shooting was coming from. He ran between two houses and ducked behind a stone wall. Mueller saw what happened, drew his service pistol and ran towards the direction of where Markos had gone, leaving Lantz in charge to organize the defense. Markos lifted his head up over the wall and saw Mueller less than 50 feet away. Both men looked at each other for what seemed eternity before Mueller raised his gun and fired, prompting Markos to take cover. Markos, raised his weapon, fired a burst and took off running towards the direction of the partisans. Mueller watched as Markos jumped over a stone wall and tossed a potato masher grenade towards the fleeing American. The grenade exploded several meters from Markos, showering him with dirt. Markos felt a sharp pain on his right thigh, but kept running. Mueller reached the wall and carefully peered over it. He cursed his luck, the American was gone. He was sure they would meet again. The sound of firing was intensifying so Mueller turned around and headed back towards his men.

   Markos kept running uphill through thick underbrush which hid him from the Germans view. He headed toward the high ground where lots of gunfire was coming from, he prayed that he would not get hit by a stray bullet or be shot by one of the attackers. The pain in his thigh was becoming sharper. He reached down, touched the area and felt wetness. That is all he needed, a wound at this time. Hopefully, it was not too bad, he could still walk. Markos dived to the ground as a burst of fire hit the area around him. Looking behind him, he saw that no one was following him. Mueller must have given up his pursuit after he had thrown the grenade. For some odd reason, his and Mueller's fates were somehow intertwined in this perverse world of war. Hopefully, next time he ran into

Standartenführer Mueller, it would be in his gun sight. Markos was now less than 100 meters from the partisan lines, but was pinned down from heavy fire coming from both sides. He started yelling in both Greek and English to get the partisans attention.

Woodhouse had seen and heard the grenade explosion and was worried that the American had been killed. He had seen him bolt once the firing had started, but had lost sight of him in the melee.

"Americanos! Americanos!"

Woodhouse had heard Markos' shout above the din of the weapons fire.

"Hang on Yank. We're coming."

"Okay men, let's rescue the American and kick some German ass."

Woodhouse gave the signal and he and the partisan force started heading down the hill toward the village. Woodhouse spotted Markos and ran toward the American with Pavlos the former Gendarme NCO in tow. Markos looked up and saw Pavlos; a thin fair skinned younger man crouched over him with another man beside him.

"Thank God for the cavalry," said Markos

"You okay, Yank?" the other man asked.

"I am Captain Markos Androlakis. I' m okay, just have a bit of shrapnel from the grenade in my thigh, but I can walk."

"I am Major Monte Woodhouse and I know who you are. There is a lot of interest in both London and Washington in getting you off this island."

"I didn't know I was that important," said Markos.

"You must have friends in very high places. Let's get moving." Woodhouse helped Markos up and they headed down the hill.

The Partisans had continued their assault. The Germans, having suffered serious casualties, jumped in the boats they had used in their initial assault and pulled out of Loutro. When the partisans reached the wharf they were met by several of the town's people, who were rejoicing at the apparent defeat of the Germans. The Mayor's two sons had cut down his body. Markos went up to them and paid his respects to the family. "Your father was a very brave man. But you can't stay here, the Germans will be back with a vengeance. If they find you here they will kill you," he said to the two boys.

"We are not afraid to die," said the older of the two boys.

"I know you aren't, but you need to come with us. You can fight the German as partisans."

"Please, my sons, go with Markos. Don't let your father's sacrifice be in vain. I will bury your father."

The two boys looked at their mother and nodded. "Okay, Mother," said the youngest with tears in his eyes. She hugged both her sons.

"Go fight the invaders and avenge your father's murder like any Cretan would do."

"We need to get out of here, Markos before the Germans come back in force, but first let me take a look at that wound," said Woodhouse.

Chapter 12

COI Headquarters, Washington, DC
27 January 1942, 0915hrs

James Donovan, the COI director and coordinator of all US Intelligence services, had just gotten off the phone with his British counterpart in the United States. He felt relieved for the first time in over a week. Markos had been found and secured by British SOE agents on Crete. He had been slightly wounded in the thigh by grenade shrapnel, but he was now okay and fit to travel. The British were planning to get him off the island by submarine in the next couple of days and have him transported to Egypt. He would have Colonel Bill Eddy put Markos on the first transport back to England. Hopefully, within a week, he would be back in Washington. Knowing Markos, he had put his time on Crete to good use and developed some contacts.

They would be needed shortly. God knows, the war was going badly. Rommel was pushing the British back in the desert, the Philippines were under siege by the Japanese and could possibly fall, and the allies were losing hundreds of thousands of tons of shipping in the Atlantic to German submarines. Given enough time, things would change. The United States was just beginning to mobilize. It would soon start producing tens of thousands of planes and tanks, much more than all the Axis powers put together could produce. What was needed was time and he planned to use his organization to buy that. By the summer, his agents would be spread throughout Europe and reeking-havoc on the Axis occupation forces.

Lefka Mountain Range, Crete
27 January 1942, 1312hrs

After leaving Loutro, the hike up to the partisan camp had been very painful and exhausting. Woodhouse had managed to dig out the piece of grenade shrapnel, but after trudging uphill for several hours, his strength had given out and he had to be carried the last few miles. The partisan camp was located just below the snow line of Mount Pachcnes, an 8000 foot peak in a thicket of trees, which made it hard to detect from the air. The Partisans had built some lean-tos and had set up several tents to provide shelter from the cold and inclement weather. It was bitterly cold and Woodhouse had given Markos a sheep fleece coat to stay warm. At the camp, Markos had met up with the RAF gunner, Flt Sergeant Harrison, and thanked the man for finding the partisans and getting him rescued.

A couple of days later, Markos was sitting in the small tent that he and Harrison were sharing, killing time until they could return to Egypt. He had just received word from Major Woodhouse that he would soon be leaving the island. A Royal

Hellenic navy submarine, the Triton, was coming tomorrow night to pick him and Harrison up and transport them to Egypt. Markos had hoped that he would have some more time on the island to visit his grandparents, but he was told Colonel Donovan wanted him back in the US. He would send them a letter through Woodhouse's partisan network. His wound was much better; he could now walk on it with very little annoyance. Markos looked up and saw Pavlos approaching.

"Come on over and get some hot food, Markos. One of the men shot a wild boar, it should be delicious."

"Sure, I am hungry and wild pig does sound good."

They both walked over to the cooking fire and grabbed some meat and a piece of semi stale bread. They sat down on some rough stools that one of the partisans, who had been a carpenter had built and ate their food. "This is pretty good," said Markos as he bit into the hot meat and washed it down with some watered down wine.

"I told you that it would be good."

Markos looked at his friend for a moment. "Pavlos, I know you have family here, but why don't you come with me?" You have been fighting the Germans for months. We need men like you."

"I don't know, I have family here."

"You know you're probably wanted by the Germans. Don't put your family at risk by going there. Someone may turn you in for a reward and the Germans will execute your entire family."

Pavlos thought about it. "What would I do?"

"Train other Greek and allied agents and help build a larger network. I work for Colonel William Donovan. He is head of the American intelligence services. We are training hundreds of agents to take the war directly to the Nazis in the occupied countries. Greece is one of those countries."

"So you are a spy, Markos?" said Pavlos with a smile.

"You can kind of say that more a special forces saboteur."

"Okay, my friend. I will do it."

"I will try to get you a commission as an officer in the Greek army."

"I would really appreciate that, Markos."

"You earned it, Pavlos. They were giving away commissions to any idiot with some political connections in Cairo. We leave for Egypt tomorrow night."

"I always did want to see the pyramids."

"You will soon get your chance, my friend. I will let Woodhouse know that you are coming along."

Gestapo Headquarters, Athens occupied Greece 28 Jan 1942, 1400hrs

Mueller had just finished interrogating the prisoner, a skinny, dark haired youth of twenty years. He was now positive that the prisoner had acted alone. He was beaten bloody and would be shot the next morning. He had been caught sabotaging Wehrmacht military vehicles. The stupid fool entered the military depot, but did not know that Alsatian guard dogs patrolled it. By the time the guards got to him, he was ripped to shreds. Mueller was finished here; he would go back to his hotel and see Sophia. Maybe they would go out to a theater. He spotted his driver, an SS Scharführer (Staff Sergeant), approaching.

"Herr Standartenführer, your vehicle is ready."

"Thank you, Schultz, I will be right out."

Leaving Gestapo headquarters, Mueller was thankful that anti occupation activities on the mainland were still very low, not like on that godforsaken island of Crete where he almost lost his life. Sophia was correct; the Cretans are not like your average Greeks. They fight like madmen. To make matters worse, on his last trip there, he ran into that damn Greek American, Markos Androlakis. His trip had turned into a fiasco. The attack on Loutro by the Partisans had cost him seven men and resulted in a humiliating retreat by sea. Later of course, he made the Cretans pay by executing over 50 of them, but he knew that only stoked the hatred and revenge. The occupation forces could not show any weakness. They had to be ruthless and sow fear into the local inhabitants. Crete would be a problem in the future, he was sure of that, and special measures would have to be taken to deal with the threat.

Libyan Sea, Crete
28 January 1942, 2304hrs

The Royal Hellenic navy submarine Triton had surfaced under a dark cloudy sky a few kilometers from the coast of Aghia Gallini, a small fishing village on the south coast of Crete. The sub had been built in France fourteen years earlier and it could not be compared with the more modern axis boats, but it could still do the job it was designed for, hunt and kill enemy shipping. The Triton had been on patrol in the Aegean sea when her captain, Lt. Commander E. Kontoyiannis, received a message from allied naval headquarters in Alexandria to proceed to Crete and pick up several allied personnel.

Lieutenant Yiannis Vassiliou, the boat's executive and weapons officer, was standing watch on the sub's conning tower, scanning both the sea and sky around him for any enemy activity and for the signal light that would indicate that their passengers had arrived at the coast. A submarine was most vulnerable when caught on the surface and he was not going to let that happen. He would also be leading the landing party. It had been a while since he had last set foot on Greek soil. The thought of it made his mind race to his parents and sister on the mainland. Yiannis hoped they had left Athens for the village where food would be more plentiful. He had heard about the starvation in the capital. He wondered how the Germans could be so inhuman to let tens of thousands of people starve, many of them women and children. Yiannis was glad that his commander and crew had decided to fight after Greece's surrender. They had taken the boat to Alexandria where several other units of the Hellenic navy had fled. Yiannis thought he had noticed a flash of light coming from the coast line. There it was again. "Captain, I see the signal," hollered Yiannis down the conning tower hatch.

A few seconds later, the sub's captain emerged from below. "Sir, there's the signal again."

Lt. Commander Kontoyiannis looked towards the shore and saw the signal. "Okay, give them the response."

One of the signalmen gave a quick response back to shore and it was answered correctly. "Sir, they responded correctly."

"Thank you petty officer," replied the sub's captain. "Yiannis, get the raft launched and go pick up those men so we can get out of here and in deeper water."

"Shore party on deck," yelled Yiannis down the sub's conning tower. "I want the shore party armed with Thompsons."

Markos had seen the signal light which meant the sub had arrived to pick them up. He and his party had been escorted to the beach by six of Stathis' men. They had stayed off the beaten path and had managed to avoid the German patrols. Fifteen minutes later, they could hear oars slapping in the water. Markos flashed his light once.

"We are here," he called out in Greek.

The dark shape of a rubber raft carrying men dressed in black, armed with sub machine guns, became visible. As soon as the boat touched the sandy shore, one of the men jumped off and walked up to meet them.

"I'm Lieutenant Vassiliou, executive officer of the Hellenic navy sub Triton," he said, holding out his hand.

"Pleased to meet you. I am Captain Markos Androlakis, United States army and former captain in the Hellenic army. This is Sergeant Pavlos Mitsakis of the Cretan Gendarmes and Flt Sergeant Harrison of the RAF."

Yiannis was taken by surprise, an American and a former Greek officer? The US just entered the war. Markos was an interesting individual, he thought. Hopefully, they would talk on the trip back to Alexandria. "Climb aboard, let's get out of here," said Yiannis.

The three men climbed aboard the raft and quickly began to row into deeper water. When they were about 100 meters from the shore, a shot was heard followed by several more.

"Damn it! We've been discovered, row like your lives depended on it!" Yiannis shouted.

A flare lit the sky. "We are too close to shore, we are sitting ducks, "said Markos

Bullets began to land in the water. Markos could see the muzzle flashes from the Germans firing at them. He grabbed one of the Thompsons and fired a burst. He knew that he was out of effective range for the Thompson, but it made him feel a bit better being able to shoot back.

"Ah!" Markos looked back, one of the sailors rowing had been hit in the shoulder.

Harrison pulled the wounded man to the bottom of the raft and began to row. The flare finally went out. "Row men, row faster," screamed Yiannis.

Another flare lit the night sky over them, silhouetting them and making them a perfect target. Even though they were 300 meters from the shore, the Mauser K98 rifle could still reach out to over 500 meters. Bullets began hitting the water all around them. It wasn't long before one hit the rubber raft, causing an air leak. Markos put his hands on the leak, but it was like the little Dutch boy putting his finger in to plug the dike.

Suddenly, a flash of light lit up the night sky. The sub had fired a star shell from its 3.9 inch deck gun. Several seconds later, another loud boom echoed across the water. Markos heard the shell pass overhead and explode on the beach scattering the Germans. The sub fired another four shells and ceased fire. The Germans had gone to ground. In the interval, they had rowed out of range. The rubber raft was slowly sinking, but Lt. Commander Kontoyiannis had fired up the Triton's engines and maneuvered the sub closer to pick them up. He had arrived in the nick of time as water began to fill the raft.

Yiannis grabbed the rope that had been thrown to the raft and pulled them next to the hull. Everyone quickly abandoned the sinking rubber raft and climbed aboard the sub. The wounded sailor was helped below and the damaged raft pulled aboard to be repaired. Markos and the rest of the group were met on deck by the boat's captain.

Yiannis introduced Markos to the sub's captain. "Sir, this is Captain Markos Androlakis, US Army."

"Thanks, you saved our asses back there."

"Well, I was not about to lose a good executive officer and four men," he said smiling.

"Let's get out of here before the Germans send out a night fighter or patrol boat. Giorgos, flank speed due south get us into deeper water."

"Yes, sir, "replied the deck officer who called down the orders to the engine room. Within a few seconds, the sub's 1420 hp diesels roared to full power and pushed the boat southwards into the Libyan Sea at 13 knots.

"Please follow me below, gentlemen," said the Triton's captain. "I am sure, after all this excitement you would like something warm to drink. We will arrive in Alexandria in about 30 hrs. if we have no problems on the way"

Libyan Sea
29 January 42, 0809hrs

Markos and the rest of the passengers were given bunks by some of the on duty crewmen and were able to catch a few hours of sleep. The sub made its way towards Alexandria at a leisurely 12 knots, not to strain the old diesel engines. Markos had heard that subs were cramped and confined, but this was the first time in his life he had ever been in one. He had to hand it to the officers and crew; it took a special person to be a submariner. There was no way he could do this for long and keep his sanity. The crew had been kind enough to lend him a pair of overalls and a shirt while his uniform was washed and dried. He made his way to the galley through the sub's cramped confines and found Lieutenant Yiannis Vassiliou having breakfast. Markos sat down at the same tiny table and was served a chunk of bread, butter, marmalade, a boiled egg and a steaming hot cup of coffee by one of the mess assistants.

"Good morning, Yiannis. I did not get a chance to thank you and your men for risking your lives to rescue us. That was pretty close last night. I hope the Partisans got away."

"I am sure they did. They know the land better than the Germans. As for the rescue, it was our job. You would have done the same."

"So you said that you are Greek American and were also a Greek officer. How is that?"

"I was born in the USA. I am from New York City. My family is originally from Crete. I was visiting Crete on an archeological sabbatical when the war broke out. Since I speak both English and Greek fluently, my skills were needed for the Greek war effort. I volunteered to be an interpreter liaison for the British and Greek staff in Chania and later Maleme. Because I would be dealing with secret documents, which no civilian would be allowed to see, I was offered a Brevet commission to second lieutenant. I was placed on General Freyberg's staff after he arrived on the island. A day before the invasion, I was given command of a squad of Cretan Gendarmes and sent to guard King George of Greece. The Germans landed next to the house with gliders. They had been tipped off by their agents who had been watching the King's movements of his location. The paratroopers attacked the house, but we managed to barely hold them off, losing two Gendarmes in that attack. We were also ambushed by the same group on the way to the island's south shore to evacuate the King, but with the help of the partisans, we managed to save him from capture and scatter the Germans.

"Wow, what a story," said Yiannis, now further impressed by the young Greek American officer.

"Well, there is more," said Markos. "When we arrived in Cairo, the King awarded me the Gold Cross, promoted me to captain and attached me to his staff.

"Congratulations, Markos. I salute you for receiving Greece's highest decoration for valor, you are a real hero."

"I don't know about that, I was just trying to save my ass."

Yiannis laughed and was soon joined by Markos. "When you think about it, anybody would do the same, but you managed to save His Highness' ass in the process too."

"Believe me, Yiannis, when the Germans were coming up the stairs, I was not thinking of any other ass than my own. Thankfully, I came out of it unscathed, but I lost two men."

"The responsibility of command, Markos."

"I couldn't even tell their families they died as heroes. We gave them a quick burial and had to flee before the Germans came back in force."

"I'm sure their comrades let their families know."

"I really hope so. Once the war ends, I intend to go back and tell them that their sons or husbands died saving their comrades."

"I think we will see a lot more death and destruction before this war is over. Anyway, how did you become an American officer?"

"I was approached by a senior American officer who told me I could help both the Greek and American cause if I went back to America and joined a "special" organization that organizes resistance groups to fight the Nazis in the occupied countries. I was also disgusted at the Greek political infighting and lack of action in Cairo. Everyone cared more about receiving rank and position rather than fighting the Nazis. So I took his offer, and here I am."

"Were you on a mission? All we were told was to pick up some important passengers."

"No, I was on my way to Cairo to speak to the Hellenic army intelligence boys to see what was going on in the mainland and help organize the Greek resistance movement. The RAF plane taking me there was jumped by two German fighters just south of Crete. We managed to shoot one down, but his wingman got us."

"You are lucky to be alive."

"Hopefully, my luck does not run out. What about you Yiannis?"

"My family lives in Athens. My father was a naval officer and fought in the Balkan wars of 1912-13 on the battleship Averoff under admiral Koundouriotis. He took part in the naval battles of Limnos and Elli where the Averoff almost single handedly defeated the Turkish fleet. He retired from the navy ten years ago. I decided to follow in his footsteps. After graduating the academy, I was gunnery officer on the Destroyer Velos. Then I volunteered for the submarine service. I am both the Triton's executive and weapons officer. We were out on patrol when the Germans invaded. After the surrender of Greece, our captain decided to continue the fight so we fled to Alexandria. I know though what you mean about those seeking rank and status. I saw it in Alexandria too."

"Any news from your family?"

"I have not seen my family or heard from them since last March. I hope they left Athens and went to the village. My mom is from Korinthos. My grandfather is a farmer. There will be plenty of food there. We all heard about the famine in the capital."

"I am sure they're fine, Yiannis. Your dad will know what to do."

"I sure hope so."

Suddenly, the boat's klaxon went off. "General quarters man your battle stations," came over the tannoy.

Let's go to the control room," Yiannis said.

On the way to the control room, they passed Pavlos and Harrison. "Markos, what do we do?"

"Just sit by your bunks and if the crew needs anything, give them a hand," said Yiannis.

As they entered the control room, the sub's captain, Lt.

Commander Kontoyiannis, was assuming his battle station next to the periscope.

"Take us down to periscope depth."

"Yes, sir," replied the helmsman.

The diving klaxon sounded. Markos felt a slight tilt as the sub began submerging.

"Nine meters, sir."

"Thank you, chief petty officer."

"What's up, sir?" asked Yiannis.

"There's smoke on the horizon. We are still a warship and we are going to check it out."

The commander raised the periscope and looked through the eye piece. "Chief takes us down to 30 meters and set an intercept course of 155 degrees, half speed."

"Sir, course set at 155 degrees, setting depth to 30 meters, half speed."

Markos watched the depth gauge slowly wind downward to 30 meters. The sub was traveling at four knots to conserve batteries. It could do nine knots in an emergency, but that would quickly drain its batteries.

"Thirty meters, captain."

Twenty minutes later, the sub was back up to periscope depth. Lt. Commander Kontoyiannis was scanning the horizon.

"It's an Italian convoy of three steamers and a Spica class destroyer escort. Probably taking supplies to the Afrika Korps. Let's see if we can prevent some of them from getting there. Prepare a full spread all bow tubes."

"Yes sir, all tubes are loaded and ready, sir" said Yiannis.

"Range 3500 meters. Adjust heading to 140 degrees.

"Adjusting heading to 140 degrees, sir," said the helmsman.

The captain lowered the periscope. Even though the periscope barely broke the sea's surface, an alert observer could see its wake and give them away.

After ten minutes, the captain raised the scope. The convoy was not even zigzagging. The Italians were getting very cocky. "Range 1600 meters" He set his sights on a fat merchantman probably in the 3000 ton range. Mark 1500 meters, the firing computer quickly calculated the torpedoes course and speed.

"Fire one."

Markos heard the hiss of the compressed air pushing the torpedo out of the tube and so did the Italian ASDIC (sonar) operator of the Regia Marina (Royal Italian Navy) destroyer escort, Circe.

"Fire two."

The sequence was repeated one more time. As the 3rd torpedo left its tube, the captain lowered the periscope.

"Take us down quickly, 70 meters, the escort is turning. Turn to a heading of 045 degrees. Rig for silent running"

"Yes, sir," replied the boat's navigator and chief engineer, Ensign Petropoulos.

Libyan Sea, 200 miles North of Tobruk, Libya
29 January 1942, 0845hrs

The Italian convoy of three steamers and a Spica class destroyer escort, under the command of *Capitano di Corvette* (Lt.Cdr.) Palmas, had left Taranto harbor with a load of Ammunition and 20 Panzer Mark IV tanks bound for Derna Libya. The port city of Tobruk had fallen to the British on the 22nd. The supplies were critical for the success of the Axis forces trying to hold back the British 8th Army advance into Libya. They had been sailing the last two days at a leisurely speed of 13 knots. By late morning tomorrow they would be arriving at their destination.

Lt. Commander Palmas was quite blissful, he had another

convoy under his belt without an incident, and his promotion to commander was practically assured. That was until his ASDIC operator announced that he had detected a sub just to their west at a distance of approximately 1800 meters and that he had just heard the sound of torpedoes being fired. So much for his promotion, he thought. The Circe's captain picked up his binoculars, looked to the west and saw the wake of three torpedoes heading toward his charges.

"Sir, the torpedoes came from a heading of approximately 320 degree.

"Helmsmen, blast our horn quickly. Officer of the bridge, sound battle stations." The Circe gave three quick blasts of her horn, a signal for the convoy to scatter as the general quarter's klaxon reverberated throughout the small warship.

"Helmsman, turn to a heading of 320 degrees, give me 25 knots. We will get those bastards."

The Circe quickly picked up speed and headed in the direction from where the torpedoes had been fired. The hunters would very soon become the hunted.

Two Hundred miles North of Tobruk, 250 feet beneath the Libyan Sea 29 January 1942, 0847hrs

"Sir, high speed screws heading in our direction," said the ASDIC operator.

" Captain Androlakis, I think you will experience your first depth bomb attack. Pray this Italian commander is incompetent and received his command with Fascist party connections."

"Ten seconds to first torpedo impact," said Yiannis.

Ten seconds passed. "Miss, on number one, five, four three, two one."

They all felt the loud boom in the water as the second

torpedo struck, followed soon by the third.

"Great shooting, two hits, captain," said Yiannis.

They all felt another loud explosion. "Must be munitions going off. Poor bastards", replied Lt. Commander Kontoyiannis.

"Ship breaking up and sinking, sir," said the boats' ASDIC operator.

"Sir, depth bombs in the water."

Markos held his breath, too terrified to move. He prayed that the Triton would not become his iron coffin. The sub was suddenly jolted by several nearby explosions.

"That wasn't too bad," captain."

"This is only the beginning, my American friend. They will run patterns trying to guess where we are so they can launch their depth bombs."

"How long does this last?" asked Markos.

"Until they sink us, or run out of bombs."

That was not what Markos wanted to hear.

"High speed screws, sir, bombs in the water."

Markos could clearly hear the propellers of the Italian warship as it raced overhead and dropped its depth bombs. Several second later, two large explosions punched the sub, causing the lights to momentarily go out and pipes to spring leaks.

"That was too close, take down to 100 meters. Turn to a heading of 90 degrees."

"Sir, that is past our operating depth, "Yiannis said.

"Either we get crushed by the sea, or blown to pieces by the depth bombs."

"One hundred meters, sir."

Everyone could hear the sub's hull plates groaning at the pressure the sea was exerting on the hull. One slight crack in the pressure hull and they would be crushed like an eggshell. "All stop. Let's drift with the current."

"All stop, sir."

"High speed screws sir, they are dropping depth bombs."

Several nearby explosions rocked the sub, but they were not as severe as the last bunch. For the next 45 minutes, the enemy warship dropped its depth bombs, but they were getting more distant. The entire crew either sat in their bunks or stood their watch, not making any movements or sounds that could give them away to the enemy ASDIC operator.

"Thomas, what is their distance?"

"Three thousand meters, sir," replied the boat's ASDIC operator.

"All ahead slow."

The Triton's electric motors came to life and started turning the propellers and giving her a speed of two knots. At that slow speed the propellers' cavitations were minimal and with the sea stirred up from all the depth bombing, it was hard for the Italian ASDIC operator to hear the sub. Slowly, the Triton was able to make her escape to the east.

After an hour of fruitless searching, *Capitano di Corvette* (Lt.Cdr.) Palmas gave up. Maybe the sub had been destroyed, but he doubted that because there was no sign of its demise such as an oil slick or debris. More than likely, it had made its escape, and in the process, ruined any chance of a quick promotion. He quickly rounded up his surviving charges and continued his voyage to Tobruk, minus one ship which had been carrying 12 tanks, munitions and fuel.

Two hours later, the Triton blew her ballast tanks and surfaced. The hatch was opened with a loud hiss as the stale air below, under pressure, rushed to escape. Her diesels were started and she set course once again for Alexandria. As soon as the watch reported all clear, Markos climbed up to the conning tower to get some air and was soon joined by Yiannis. It had been a harrowing experience for him and he was still shaken from it.

"How do you do it, Yiannis? Sail in these sardine cans under the water and get bombed from above and not crack?"

"I was terrified too. Any man who says otherwise is a liar. I guess you get used to it. There is a thrill to sneaking up on the enemy and putting a fish in them. But there are those moments that make you want to regret that you ever volunteered for sub duty."

"I prefer the dry land. You can keep your sub."

"Another 20 hours and we'll be in Alexandria."

"Amen for that," replied Yiannis.

CHAPTER 13

US Embassy, Cairo, Egypt
30 January 1942, 1500hrs

True to Yianni's estimate, the Triton docked at the large British naval base in Alexandria, Egypt at 0530hrs. Markos thanked Lt. Commander Kontoyiannis and his crew for risking their lives to save him. He also said his farewell to Yiannis Vassiliou and hoped to meet up again with him on his next trip to Egypt. Markos had been met at the pier by a marine embassy driver. He said his good bye to Flt Sergeant Harrison who was also met at the pier by an RAF staff car. Markos would make sure that Harrison received an award for his actions in the air and on the island. He had also invited Pavlos to spend his first night in Egypt at the US embassy. He wanted to introduce him to his commander, Colonel Eddy. Pavlos, with his connections and knowledge of Crete, could turn out to be a valuable asset for both the COI and Greek Special Forces. He would also personally take Pavlos to the Greek delegation in Cairo and ensure he was given a commission and put in the Hellenic Army Special Operations Section.

The short drive to Cairo had been uneventful, not much had changed except for the presence of more troops and armor. Rommel and his Afrika Korps were being pushed back into Libya after the Axis siege of Tobruk had been lifted, one of the only successes of the war so far. At the embassy, Markos was greeted by Colonel Eddy like a long lost son. Both Markos and Pavlos were put up in the guest suites and a tailor was brought in to have Markos fitted for new uniforms since he had lost his entire belongings when the plane sank. Upon meeting Pavlos, the colonel had been impressed with the man and complimented Markos on recruiting him to the allied cause. He agreed that Pavlos would definitely be a great asset once trained and the time came to send American agents to the island. He would talk to his Greek counterparts later and insist that Pavlos be placed in the Special Operations Section.

Once settled in, Markos had been called down to the colonel's office for a debriefing. He put on a clean utility uniform he had been given by Major Thomas, the colonel's aid and fellow COI agent, and went down to the colonel's office. Markos walked inside, saluted and was asked to sit; Major Thomas was also there, sipping on a scotch. The colonel looked up at Markos and smiled.

"Let me congratulate you again on your miraculous escape from Crete. Seems it is becoming a habit with you," he said jokingly.

"Well sir, I have to thank both the British SOE services and the Greek Partisans, not to mention the Hellenic navy that got me out."

"Heard you had an interesting time as a submariner."

"Colonel, I never want to see a sub again if I can avoid it. I'll take the infantry any day over subs."

"Captain, you may not be able to avoid that. Best way to insert agents and teams into enemy territory is by sub. Anyway, there is no plan for you to ride in one soon, you are needed back in the USA to get the agent recruiting program moving. You are a valuable asset. Bill Donovan pulled a lot of strings to get you out of Crete."

"I do appreciate that, sir."

"Tell me what the situation on the island is?"

"There is plentiful food because Crete has a fishing and agricultural economy. The Nazis have consolidated their grip on the island. There is a growing resistance movement and the British SOE are helping a lot. There are some attacks on the German forces but the Germans respond ruthlessly, as I have personally witnessed."

"I read your report. Your acquaintance, Standartenführer Muller, is in action again. He is a blood thirsty bastard; we have a dossier on him from Poland. He is now based in Athens, Special Sicherdienst service (Security). What happened in Loutro was a tragedy, but the methods the Nazis are using are instilling more hatred against them from the local population."

"True, sir. The Cretans are famous for blood feuds and will pay the Nazis back, but the cost is very steep. They shoot 10 Greeks for each German killed and burn entire villages."

"That is unfortunate, Markos, but we can't let the Germans feel safe anywhere. They must be harassed. The more soldiers they use for internal security, the less there are on front lines fighting allied forces."

"I understand, sir. The Greeks feel the same way."

"What have you heard about resistance movements on the mainland?"

"Not too much, sir. EAM, the communist movement, is growing there. Very little EAM influence on Crete. The Cretans are no friends of communism. A small nationalist-royalist group, EDES, has also sprouted."

"I have heard of both, but so far nothing is being done by either one to harass the Germans."

"Sir, we need to be assisting these movements by sending in agents to help organize them. They need gold to buy food and supplies and we should be dropping weapons and explosives."

"I agree with you, captain. I need you to prepare agents to send to Greece as soon as possible. Our COI Mid East headquarters will be here. You will be the Operations Officer, and liaison to the Greeks. So get used to seeing Cairo."

"Yes, sir.

"I called my counterpart in the Greek contingent and Pavlos will be given a commission and assigned to the Hellenic army special forces. I insisted that he be assigned here as a liaison. The Greeks agreed. As soon as he finishes some special training he will take an intensive English course and come to work."

"Thanks, sir. He will be a great asset for our Crete section. He is brave, loyal and has connections on the island as well as personal experience fighting the Germans."

"That's why I want him here. I value your opinion, captain. There is small party at the British headquarters tonight. We have been invited. I have been told that King George will be there. I want you to attend. The Greeks know you are here. One of their subs did pick you up. The King personally ordered the Hellenic navy to go get you."

"I do not have a uniform, sir. I lost everything when we were shot down."

"Don't worry, the tailor promised me that he will have a jacket and trousers for you by 1900hrs. I had ordered extra fabric from the states for situations like yours. Plus, I had another set made for myself. You are about the same size as the major. I am sure he can lend you a shirt and tie. You can run to the NAFI store and buy a pair of shoes."

"Yes, sir. If my jacket is ready, I will be there."

"Good. We leave at 2000hrs," said the colonel. "Oh, and Monday morning you will meet with Colonel Kostopolous, commander of the Hellenic Army Special Forces. You are to give him a courtesy briefing on your personal experience on Crete. Your flight back to England and the US leaves Tuesday. We need you back there to get things moving. The Greeks here are more interested in politics than liberating Greece."

"They've been that way for thousands of years, sir."

"I know, captain. Now go find a pair of shoes. We have a party to go to."

British Middle East Headquarters, Cairo, Egypt
30 January 1942, 2100hrs

The American military delegation, consisting of Markos, Colonel Eddy and the US ambassador, had arrived at the British compound at 2045hrs, and proceeded inside to the ballroom. True to the tailor's word, Markos' uniform jacket and trousers had arrived at 1900hrs. He had borrowed a shirt and tie from the major and had procured a pair of shoes at the British NAFI store. Colonel Eddy had been able procure a copy of Markos' Greek military decoration which he now wore around his neck. Entering the ballroom, Markos was amazed at its lavishness and splendor indicating the wealth and power of the British Empire. Large multi-tiered crystal chandeliers hung from the ceiling and the floor was paved with expensive marble tile. He had a feeling that once the war was over, the empire's days were numbered. He saw the rise of America as the next great power. The European powers will be exhausted and broke after tearing each other's hearts out in this war. Markos was sure that the US would dominate the postwar world. He grabbed two glasses of champagne and handed one to the colonel.

"Very lavish, sir. The British spared no expenses on decorating this ballroom."

"They could have better spent their money. Now they are asking us for loans to fight this war."

"They will be broke, sir, once this war is over. Their colonies will be asking for independence. Same for all the European powers, especially those that were so easily defeated and occupied like Holland and France."

"I fear you are right on that aspect, captain. The European powers were virtually broke after the Great War. They lost their best and brightest on the battlefields charging machine guns. One of the reasons they let Hitler rise to power was the fear of another blood bath engulfing Europe."

"Well they sure have one now, sir. Hopefully, America will learn from the Europeans' mistakes and not let this happen again."

"I hope we do, Markos. First though, we must defeat the Nazis. I see the Greek delegation sitting over there. Why don't you go over there and mingle with them while I go say hello to the Brits."

"See you in a bit, sir."

Markos got another serving of champagne and walked over to where the Greek delegation was sitting. He noticed King George sitting between two senior Hellenic naval officers. He walked by the table and raised his glass in a toast.

"Long live Greece."

The two naval officers turned around, visibly upset at being interrupted by a lowly captain, but they immediately changed their attitude when they saw Greece's highest military decoration around Markos' neck. They quickly raised their glasses and repeated the toast.

"And God bless the Hellenic navy, the submarine Triton and its crew for saving my ass," said Markos, as he raised his glass again.

The King, caught by surprise, got up from his seat and gave Markos a quick hug, leaving the two officers awestruck.

"How are you my boy? I heard what had happened to you and I ordered the navy to bring you back."

"Thank you, Your Majesty. The Triton got me out just in time."

"The least I could do for the man that saved my life twice."

He looked at the two naval officers. "This is Captain Markos Androlakis, the man that saved my life twice on Crete and helped get me off the island. Now excuse me gentlemen, I need to catch up with Markos."

The King put his arm around Markos' shoulder and walked to a more secluded spot on the other side of the large ballroom.

"First I want to thank you, Markos, for all the money and supplies you collected for the Greek cause in America. I am being told by the British that they will lift their blockade to let food and humanitarian supplies in to help alleviate the tragedy that has befallen Athens and other areas."

"Just doing my duty as a fellow Greek. I have heard of the starvation, suffering and deaths of tens of thousands of fellow Greeks. The quicker the Nazis are defeated, the faster they will leave Greece."

"I know, but that will not be an easy task. Tell me what you saw on Crete. How were conditions there?"

"Your Majesty, the island has plenty food since it has an agricultural and fishing economy. Resistance is growing and there have been attacks against the occupiers. They have replied with ruthlessness and complete brutality, not taking into regard any of the rules of war. I witnessed it personally."

Markos told the King of the incident in Loutro and his capture and escape from Standartenführer Mueller.

"That man is evil. You know he heads a special team in Athens to root out resistance fighters and anyone being openly opposed to the Germans."

"Yes, I have heard that, Your Majesty."

"I don't know what has happened to the Germans. You know, when I was a young man, I attended the German military academy and left after the outbreak of the WW1. They were a totally different people then. Yes, they had the Teutonic stubbornness and superiority complex, but they were not murderers. They were honorable soldiers."

"It's called National Socialism, Your Majesty. It used all the ills and the suffering of the Germans after their loss in the Great War and has perverted their Teutonic beliefs and values. It has turned them into monsters. Not that Stalin and the communists are much better. They are our allies now. A marriage of need and convenience."

"Yes, you are right, Markos. If the Germans lose this war, and I believe they will, especially after the entrance of the United States on the allied side, they will pay dearly for their sins for generations to come. As for the communists, they are not any better. Stalin has murdered thousands. Now with the emergence of EAM in the mainland, I am being told that their influence is growing rapidly and spreading throughout the nation."

"Yes, I have heard that too, Your majesty."

"They are the best organized. General Metaxas and his Asfalia secret police had driven them under ground in the late 30s. With their infrastructure already in place, it was easy for them to come out of the shadows as patriots and future liberators of the nation and grow rapidly. With the deaths of tens of thousands of Greeks from starvation and a puppet collaborationist regime in place, unable to do anything for the people, their influence has grown tremendously in the mainland and especially in the capital. I am being told from my sources that, come this summer, they will be fielding fighters against the Germans."

"Well as long as they are fighting the Nazis that is a good thing. No one else has done anything to put men in the field."

"I hope so, but I do not trust the Stalinists of the Greek Communist Party (KKE). They are directed and manipulated by Moscow. There is also a small nationalist movement headed by a former army officer, Napoleon Zervas, called EDES, but he has been very slow in organizing. I have spoken to the British to send agents and assistance to help him organize as a counter measure against the communists. Churchill agrees. He also sees the EAM/KKE as a future threat to Greece."

"We have also heard of the EDES movement but we don't know too much about them," said Markos.

"I know you are an intelligence officer for the Americans. Please help Greece. Talk to them about assisting the nationalists or at least equally helping both sides. America is powerful and will emerge from this war as a great power. Unfortunately, they lack the knowledge and political experience of the British who have ruled a great Empire for almost 200 years."

"I will discuss it with my superiors, Your Majesty. United States official policy is not to get involved in the internal affairs of an allied country. The US will aid any group fighting the

Axis powers."

"That is all I ask. I want to ensure that after the Germans are thrown out of Greece, the political system will not be dominated by any particular group."

Your Majesty, we are preparing agents for Greece and we will need the cooperation of every Greek resistance group. I am in charge of the recruiting effort in the US. There are many Greek Americans that are willing to volunteer and help the motherland. I will be leaving for America next week but will be back. I will head operations here in Cairo."

"That's good news. I will be seeing you again then. Help the Greek cause while in America. Also, give my regards to your family and have a safe trip this time," he said with a smile.

"One thing, sir. I brought Pavlos Mitsakis back with me from the island. He was part of the Cretan Gendarmes. He has been fighting the Germans since our departure. He also helped rescue me. Please ensure he receives a commission and a position in the Greek Special Forces. We need him as a liaison. We were promised from the Hellenic staff this will happen but you know how things sometimes fall through the cracks."

"Yes, I remember the young man. I will also give him a decoration for his service on the island and I will ensure he gets what he was promised. You are right, things do have a way of being overlooked here."

"Thank you, Your Majesty. I am sure we will be meeting again soon."

Markos turned and walked over to where he had last seen Colonel Eddy. He found him sitting with a British Colonel.

"Captain, let me introduce you. This is Colonel Eddie Myers, commander of the SOE section for Greece and Crete, and this is Captain Markos Androlakis, my new Operations Officer."

Markos took the man's hand and saw that he was being sized up. The colonel, an average set man in his middle thirties, smiled as he squeezed Markos' hand in a vice grip shake.

"So this is the famous Markos Androlakis I have heard about in various Greek and British circles. I am pleased to meet you. Pull up a chair and have a seat, captain. What are you drinking?"

"I was having champagne."

"Nonsense, have a real drink."

He motioned to one of the Egyptian waiters, "Scotch, please. Make that three."

"I didn't know I had such notoriety," said Markos.

"Your exploits, saving King George's nuts on Crete, have gotten around, as well as your recent adventures."

"I was just doing my duty, sir. I do though want to thank you and Major Woodhouse for getting me off the island."

"Oh yes, Woody's a great chap. He is my second in command. Has some work to do organizing the partisans, but it's coming along. We could not leave you there, you were needed back in Washington to help get the Greek section organized. We will need your help in building a resistance movement on the mainland."

"That's what I will be doing, sir."

"We need Greek speaking agents in the field. The SOE does not have many, thus we are looking to the Americans to fill in the void. I have proposed to Colonel Eddy that we do a joint operation on Crete, maybe this summer, as a precursor of more to come."

Markos looked at his boss who nodded yes. "I don't see why we could not organize something by then."

The waiter arrived with their drinks. Colonel Myers raised his glass. "To chaos, gentlemen."

London, England
3 Feb 1942, 1900hrs

Markos had arrived in England yesterday after departing Cairo on a RAF Dakota (C-47), one of the first planes the British had received from the US lend lease program. The trip had been without incident and his flight back to the United States was not until noon tomorrow. He had been able to get a seat using his COI ID card and a Twix (Telex) that had arrived from Washington, bumping him up to priority one status. Having a day to kill, he decided to go see London and visit the sites. Having spent most of the afternoon walking around, he was amazed at the tremendous damage the city had suffered during the Blitz. Whole areas had been devastated. Entire blocks were turned to rubble. He had to hand it to the British, even with all the death and destruction, morale was high, especially now that America had joined the war on the allied side.

After having dinner at one of the numerous pubs that lined Piccadilly Circus district, he headed towards the Kings Cross Station to catch a train back to Cambridge and RAF Mildenhall. He could have taken a cab, but he needed to walk off all the alcohol he had consumed from all the numerous pints he been treated to. There were not too many American military in London, thus, he was a novelty to the British. Markos was sure that would wear off pretty quick. He glanced at his Hamilton military issue watch. It was 1910hrs and the last train would be leaving at 2000hrs. Looking at a map he had bought of London, he estimated it would take another 20 minutes to reach the station. As he walked through a blacked out, relatively unscathed residential and business district, air raid sirens began to wail. Just his rotten luck, he thought, the Luftwaffe had decided to pay London a visit the same time he had decided visit the town.

Markos began to run towards a man that was waving a flash light, most likely one of the air raid wardens. "Over here, mate. Here is the air raid shelter."

Markos walked down several steps and into an oval shaped iron corrugated shelter. It had dim lights and benches. "Is this thing safe?" he asked the warden.

"Pretty much, Yank, except for a direct hit."

Markos took a seat right next to a young blond woman. From what he could in the dim light, she was very pretty.

"Hello," he said to her as he sat down. "This is my first time in London."

She smiled. "This was a daily occurrence during the blitz."

"My name is Markos Androlakis."

"I am Susan Smith. You are an American? Never seen that uniform before."

"Yes, I am a captain in the US army."

They could all hear the humming sound of the unsynchronized engines of the approaching German bomber formations. Soon that was augmented by the sound of antiaircraft batteries that defended the city opening fire on the German bombers.

"Androlakis, a strange name."

Markos grinned. "It is Greek, actually originated from the island of Crete."

She looked into his eyes. "My husband was killed there, a corporal in the Royal Tank Regiment."

"I was there," said Markos.

"But how? You are in the US army."

"Long Story. I was visiting the island to study archeology before Greece entered the war. Once the war started, I volunteered my services to the allied cause and joined the allied staff as a liaison officer for the Greek army."

"Was the fighting bad?"

"Yes, it was terrible. Hand to hand in many instances."

"He was killed at Maleme. Do you know it?"

"Yes, I was stationed there on General Freyberg's staff."

"My husband was a gunner in one of the tanks."

"Yes, I had seen some tanks there before the attack."

"You might have seen him," she said with tears in her eyes.

They could hear the bombs starting to drop and explode. The explosions were coming closer and closer. "Perhaps, there were many soldiers there."

She put her hand on his as the explosions got closer. A large explosion rocked the shelter and the lights went out. She hugged Markos in fear. He could feel her body trembling. "Hold me, please. At least if I die, it will be in one's arms."

The bomb explosions were now getting farther and farther away. "I think it's over," he whispered in her ear.

She finally let go of him but held his hand. Finally the lights came back on and the all clear sounded. The warden opened the door and everyone climbed out into a scene of utter devastation. A stick of bombs had hit a block of houses and had demolished them. Several were burning and Markos could hear screaming and cries for help.

"I am going there to see if I can help."

"Be careful," she said.

Markos ran to one of the demolished houses where he could hear screams. It had been a three story home, now it was just rubble. Pieces of masonry and wood were coming down everywhere as flames were beginning to shoot up from a ruptured gas line.

"Please help us."

Markos ran in and went up the partially wrecked staircase. The flames from the burning building provided the light he needed to enter the demolished apartment. The fire was beginning to spread quickly throughout the rest of the building.

"Please help us before we burn alive."

"I am coming," he yelled.

Markos reached the woman, she was covered in dust and was semi naked. She had been protected from the falling masonry by a door that had fallen over her. She was clutching a small child. He pulled the door off her but one of her legs was trapped by a falling beam.

"Please take my baby to safety."

"I will get you out."

He searched for something to use as a lever and found a piece of lead piping that had come off the plumbing when the house collapsed. He had to hurry, the flames were getting closer. He rushed back to the woman and tried to move the beam. It barely budged and she screamed in pain.

"Get my baby out. Please leave me."

He knew that he had little time left to save her. The flames were closing in. He could hear the glass exploding from the heat. "Look, I will try again, but pull your leg out. It will hurt but it's the only way."

"Okay, I will try."

Markos heaved with all his strength and the beam moved several inches. "Now do it if you want to see your child grow up," he yelled.

She screamed in pain but was able to free her leg. He scooped both of them up and headed down the stairs. He reached the outside of the building with them and suddenly the world around him exploded and everything went black.

St Andrews Hospital, London
4 February 1942, 1500hrs

Markos opened his eyes and the first thing he saw was the pretty face of Susan Smith, the woman he had met in the air raid shelter. He looked around and saw that he was in a hospital room with other patients. He quickly took stock to see if all his limbs were there and rubbed his eyes, trying to clear his head.

"Doctor, he is awake."

"Let me see him, miss."

The doctor, an older white haired man, approached Markos and started taking his pulse. "Where am I?" Markos asked the doctor. Last thing he remembered was a loud explosion and that he was carrying an injured woman and child to safety.

"You are in St Andrews Hospital, young man. You received a very nasty blow to your head last night. That was a very brave thing you did, rescuing that trapped woman and her child."

"How are they?"

Apart for a fractured leg to the mother and cuts and bruises, they will make a full recovery."

"What happened? I remember carrying them outside. I heard a loud roar, then everything went blank."

"It was a delayed action bomb. It went off as you exited the building. A piece of debris hit you on the head," said Susan.

"Am I okay, doctor?"

"Except for a cut, a couple of stitches and a possible slight concussion, you will be fine."

Markos noticed another man walking into the room wearing a US army uniform sporting colonel's insignia and pilot wings. Markos tried to sit up.

"Lay down son, take it easy. I am Colonel Ralph Royce, US

army air attaché here in the embassy. How are you feeling?"

"Besides a headache and feeling that I have been kicked by a mule, okay I guess. How did you know I was here?"

"The embassy got a call from the British defense ministry that a US army officer had been hurt in last night's air raid and that he was being treated at St Andrews Hospital. They gave us your name and it was recognized by one of Bill Donovan's boys. He said that you were transiting through England back to Washington."

"Yes, sir. I came to London to kill some time until my flight, oh, damn, I missed it."

"Don't worry, captain, as soon as you are fit to travel, you will be on the next flight out. Colonel Donovan has been sent a message on your situation. Oh, and the British told us about last night. That was a pretty brave thing you did, son, risking your life to save a woman and her child."

"I could not let them be burned alive, sir."

"Guess I would have done the same thing had I been in your shoes."

The colonel turned and spoke to the doctor who was administering to another patient. "When will this gentleman be released and fit to travel?"

"I would like to observe him for another couple of days, concussions can be funny. As for being able to travel, I would say by the end of the week, barring any complications."

"Okay, captain, as soon as you have been cleared, fit to travel I want you to come by the embassy and we will get you on the next flight back to the States. Besides, I see you are in very good hands here," he said, as he looked at Susan.

"Thank you, sir."

The colonel turned and left the room. "So, Susan, how long have you been here?" Markos asked.

She took his hand and held it. "Since last night. I didn't know how bad you were hurt. You were unconscious and alone in a strange city. You risked your life for that woman and child. You did not have to. It was the least I could do."

"Thank you. I do appreciate that. Hopefully, I can make it up to you in a day or two."

"I would really like that," she said with a mischievous smile.

"Now go home and get some rest. Come back in the morning, maybe they will let me out of this place."

"Okay, I will see you in the morning."

London, England
5 February 1942, 1400hrs

Susan had arrived early the next morning to find out that Markos had been given a 24 hour pass by the doctor until the following day when he would receive his medical evaluation and hopefully be officially released. He was going to get a hotel room, but she invited him to stay over her place. Lacking any clothes, except for his uniform which had been returned to him cleaned and pressed, she offered to lend him some of her husband's clothes.

Leaving the hospital, they took a cab to her small flat which was in the Knightsbridge section, close to the center of the city. The bomb damage in the area had been moderate and her block had been pretty much spared. Her modest flat consisted of a bedroom, living room, kitchen and a small bathroom with a tub. The apartment was fairly cool due to wartime rationing of coal.

"Cozy little place, but a bit nippy."

"The heat will come on at night for a few hours and in the morning and afternoon for a few more, just enough to break the chill. That's when we have hot water. There is a war on you know?"

Markos thought of back home. Except for gasoline and tire rationing, most items could still be found. He was sure that would change as the war progressed.

"I do need a bath to get this dust off me."

"I'll heat some water up for you and put on the electric heater for you."

Twenty minutes later, Markos was basking in the heated bathroom and lying in the bathtub, soaking the soot and grime from his body when Susan came in wearing a bathrobe and holding a pot of hot water. She poured the water in and much to Markos' surprise, she took her bathrobe off exposing her ample figure and got in.

"Mustn't waste the hot water," she said with a devious smile.

"So what happens now if there is an air raid?" he asked jokingly.

"Then we shouldn't waste any time. I have not been with a man since my husband left for Greece a year ago," she said as she reached and grabbed hold of him.

Several hours later, Markos reached over the other side of the bed to touch her, but she had gotten up. He looked at his watch and it was half past five. It was starting to darken outside as the sun was beginning to set. He could smell the aroma of food coming from the kitchen. He got out of bed and put on a shirt and a pair of slacks that she had given him which had belonged to her husband and entered the small kitchen. "Mmmmm, that smells good. What is it?"

"Sausage and potatoes. Wish it could have been steak, but with rationing going on, it's hard to find good meat these days. Here, sit down."

Markos sat down by the table where she had set a plate for him. She filled his plate, then she put some food in hers.

Markos put a forkful of the food in his mouth. "It's pretty good," he said washing it down with a bottle of Fullers beer.

"Thank you. I am actually a pretty good cook when I have the ingredients available, but with rationing I guess I won't be cooking too many things until the war is over."

"My mom is an excellent cook. She usually makes traditional Greek food."

"Never have tried any foreign food. The British cuisine is not known as one of the best, but it's hearty."

"This wasn't too bad. I liked it. I will take you out tomorrow for dinner. Tell me where the best restaurants are."

"You don't have to spend your money on me."

"No, I want to thank you and have an enjoyable evening out with you."

"Then we will go to the Savoy," she said.

"Sure, anywhere you want."

"Oh, thank you," she replied, jumping on his lap kissing him.

Markos picked her up and carried her to the bedroom.

US Embassy, London
6 February 1942, 1300hrs

It had been a hectic morning for Markos. He had dropped Susan off at a nearby shop where she worked part time. Susan would meet him back at her flat where she would be ready to leave for the Savoy at six. The weather was cold and rainy and he had been given some of her husband's winter clothes to wear to keep warm. He then took a cab back to the hospital where had been officially released and cleared by the doctor to travel. A message was waiting there for him to report to the embassy immediately. Markos departed the hospital and took another cab to the US embassy at 1 Grosvenor Square and met with

Colonel Royce and advised him on his medical clearance. After a phone call, the colonel was able to obtain Markos a seat on a US army air Corps (USAAC) B-17. The bomber was flying back to the United States late Saturday afternoon, after touring several RAF air bases. The USAAC was getting ready to deploy hundreds of bombers to England to begin a sustained bombing campaign on the continent.

After securing Markos a ride back to the States, the colonel invited him to lunch at the embassy cafeteria. Markos was surprised that burgers were on the menu. He ordered a cheeseburger and a side of fries, having missed good old American junk food. The colonel ordered a bacon lettuce and tomato sandwich and a side of fries. Both men picked up their food and sat down at an empty table.

Markos got up from his seat, "What are you drinking, sir."

"Grab me a Coke, captain." Markos grabbed two Coke bottles and sat down to eat.

"I invited you to lunch to tell you that you will be receiving an award from the British tomorrow for your actions during the German bombing raid the other day."

"I didn't do anything special. Anyone would have done the same. Anyhow, that's pretty quick. Things like that take weeks, not days."

"Well, word about your heroic actions got around pretty quickly from the ministry of foreign affairs to the ministry of defense to the palace and now the morning papers"

The colonel pulled out a folded newspaper from his jacket pocket and showed Markos the front page. Under the headlines: "Yank risks life and limb to rescue trapped bomb victims," was his picture in a hospital bed with his head bandaged.

"Having an American allied officer risk his life to save

British civilians and be decorated by the King of England for his actions is a great morale booster for a war weary public and good politics for Anglo American relations."

"The King? Me?"

"Yes, captain. You will report here tomorrow at 1130hrs in dress uniform and we are due at the palace at 1300hrs. It is just as much a surprise to us. I found out about it late yesterday."

"But my baggage is still in storage in Mildenhall."

"I had it transported here this morning."

"May I bring a friend, sir?"

"That woman from the hospital?"

"Yes, sir. She is a war widow. Her husband was killed on Crete."

"I don't see why not."

"Thank you, sir. It would mean a lot to her."

"I'll have an embassy car drop you off with your bag."

"Thank you, sir."

Knightsbridge, London
6 February 1942, 1800hrs

Having been dropped off at Susan's flat, he entered the small apartment with the spare key she had given him and waited for her to return from work. In the mean-time, he took a short nap and was awakened when he heard her put the key in the door. She came into the bedroom and gave him a long kiss.

"Wake up, sleeping beauty."

"Mmmm, what time is it?"

"It's six, luv. I was thinking of getting undressed," she said, as she took her work clothes off and got under the covers.

"I don't want to go to the Savoy tonight."

He saw the look of disappointment on her face. "I have to go somewhere in the morning."

"Where?"

"To the palace to meet your King. They want to give me some medal for saving that woman and her child and you are coming with me."

"What! You are crazy! Me, a nobody? I don't have any clothes."

"You will get up early tomorrow morning and you will go buy a pretty dress and shoes. Here is 30 pounds," he said pulling out the bank notes.

"I can't take your money."

"You will do as I say, because you will spend tomorrow night at the Savoy with Britain's latest hero. We're due at the palace at 1pm."

"Oh, Markos!" She put her arms around him and began kissing him.

"We can get some fish and chips and stay in. Besides I always wanted to try them."

"Sure, luv. I will go get us some."

Twenty minutes later, she returned with a package containing fried fish pieces and fried potatoes wrapped in newspaper. The fish had a bit of vinegar poured over which gave them a tangy taste. Markos tried a piece. "Not bad at all," he said.

"My husband liked fish and chips too. We used to stop by the stand when we went out dating."

"How long were you married?"

"Only six months before he went off to war and got himself killed. Now I'm a widow at 21 and soon you will be gone and I'll be alone again."

Markos saw tears in her eyes. He took her in his arms. "I have to leave Sunday. I am needed back in Washington."

"What do you do?"

"Special Operations on the continent. I can't tell you more."

"Where? Greece?"

"Susan, I can't say, more."

"Well, it would make sense since you are Greek and speak it."

"I will be coming through London. I promise I will see you again."

"I would like that," she said.

"Now finish up and let's go to bed."

"Mmmm, yes, sir."

Buckingham Palace, London
7 February 1942, 1300hrs

The US embassy car pulled up to the front of Buckingham palace and was met by a British army honor guard. The car door was opened and the US ambassador to the court of St James, John Gilbert Winant stepped out of the 1941 Cadillac Fleetwood Limo, followed by Colonel Royce, Markos and Susan, who was wearing a stunning white evening dress with matching shoes. The commander of the palace honor guard, an army colonel saluted the ambassador and escorted everyone inside to the ceremony room. Everyone was shown where to stand for the ceremony. Markos noticed that there were several press photographers in the crowed.

Several minutes later, the King and his entourage entered and the ceremony began. First, the British national anthem was played, followed by the Star Spangled Banner. The master of ceremonies, a British brigadier general read the award citation.

> **Attention to the reading of the citation to accompany the award of the George Cross.**
> Captain Markos Androlakis, United States Army while on leave in London on the night of 3 February 1942, risked life and limb to rescue a woman and her child that had been trapped in a burning building as a result of a German aerial raid. Captain Androlakis without hesitation ran into the burning building and with flames spreading all around him was able to free the woman and her child that had been trapped under debris. As captain Androlakis exited the burning structure carrying the injured survivors, a delayed action enemy bomb detonated causing injury to him. For this act of bravery he is hereby awarded the George Cross.

With the completion of the reading of the citation, King George VI of England walked up to Markos and pinned the medal to his left breast pocket and noticed his Hellenic army medal.

"So you saved my cousin, George?"

"Just doing my duty, Your Majesty."

"Yes, young man you were," he said with a smile. "After the ceremony, please join me for a cup of tea and bring your friend."

Markos nodded yes, but at a loss for words. The King then shook his hand and took a step back and saluted. The salute was returned by Markos. The King turned and faced the US audience.

"I would like to thank our American allies for all the assistance you have so far provided and will provide to Great Britain in her hour of need. Acts like these from our brave young men is what makes democracy and freedom worth fighting for. Our alliance will prevail and the Nazi menace to freedom will most surely be defeated. Now please enjoy your refreshments."

Markos still in shock, walked over to where Colonel Royce, the US ambassador and Susan were standing. The US ambassador and Colonel Royce both shook his hand. "Congratulations, captain, you were just awarded England's highest civilian award, equivalent to the Victoria Cross," said Royce.

"I didn't do anything special."

"That's what they all say, son. What did the King say?"

"He invited me and Susan to tea and thanked me for saving his cousin, the King of Greece."

Royce noticed the Greek award and was impressed. "Captain, don't keep the King of England waiting. I will send a car to the Savoy to take you to Mildenhall at 0800hrs."

"Thank you, sir."

The King's major domo arrived. "Sir, His Majesty is requesting your presence. Please follow me."

Markos went over and grabbed Susan's arm. "Come with me. We are having tea with the King."

"She almost fell but he held on to her."

"What?"

"Just come along."

They followed the King's majordomo through several rooms and up a staircase to a nicely decorated sitting room where the King and his wife were having tea and cookies.

"Ah, nice of you and your lovely friend to join us," said the King.

Susan curtsied. "Thank you, Your Majesty. It's an honor."

"No, it is our honor to thank the captain for saving the lives of two of my subjects and thanking those that have sacrificed so much for this nation."

"Please have a seat," said the King's wife, Lady Elizabeth, the Duchess of York.

Both Markos and Susan sat down and were served their tea. "Well, young man, from all the decorations, I see that you have been around. Tell me of your experiences on Crete."

Markos related to the King his experiences during the battle for the island and of his latest unplanned visit to Crete. "This is why the Nazis must be defeated. They are murderers and the scourge of humanity," said the King after hearing of Markos' experiences.

After about another twenty minutes of conversation, the King got up from his seat. "Captain, let me return you to your party. They must be wondering what I am doing with you."

Markos thanked King George and his wife. They both followed the King's majordomo back to reception area, where they met Colonel Royce and were driven back to Susan's flat.

Savoy Hotel London
7 February 1942, 1930hrs

Markos and Susan took a taxi to the Savoy hotel. Susan was dressed in the same beautiful evening gown she wore to the palace and Markos was in his dress army uniform, wearing all his awards, the George Cross prominently displayed on his left jacket pocket. Tonight, they would eat and sleep in style. The hotel has two well-known restaurants, the Grill Room (usually known as the Savoy Grill), on the north side of the building, with its entrance off the Strand, and the Savoy Restaurant overlooking the river Thames, which is sometimes called the Grand River restaurant. The Grand River Restaurant has always been famous for its inventive chefs. Tonight, they would eat there.

Before having dinner, Markos and Susan stopped by the

famous American bar and had two White Lady cocktails made with Gin, Cointreau and fresh lemon juice. Many of the patrons in the bar recognized Markos from the newspapers and noticed the George Cross on his uniform. His popularity resulted in several rounds on the house. By the time they sat down for dinner both he and Susan were feeling a bit tipsy. Dinner consisted of roast saddle of lamb and steak and kidney pie. Dessert was *baisers de Vierge* (meringue with vanilla cream, and crystallized white rose and violet petals

After dinner, they retired to their room. Susan was amazed at the elegance and the décor. Even the bathroom had a telephone in it and ever room had 24 hour service. All the guest rooms were steam heated and there was hot water and a huge bathtub that she decided to use.

"I love this bathtub I'm going to use it," she said, as she quickly stripped off her evening dress and turned on the water to fill the tub.

After a few minutes, she stepped into the hot tub.

"Oh luv, this is marvelous, unlimited hot water."

Markos joined her in the tub several minutes later. "All we're missing is the rubber ducks," he said.

Thirty minutes later, they were both lying between freshly pressed cotton sheets in nice queen sized bed. "Thank you Markos, for all you did for me today. Never in my wildest fantasy, had I ever dreamed I would meet the King, much less have tea and crumpets with him. This has been one of the best days in my life."

"No, I thank you for taking me into your life and showing me around."

"I will miss you," she said teary eyed.

"I will keep in touch and visit you every time I come through London. I promise."

"I will be waiting. Now let's get some use out of this nice bed" she said, as she turned and kissed him passionately.

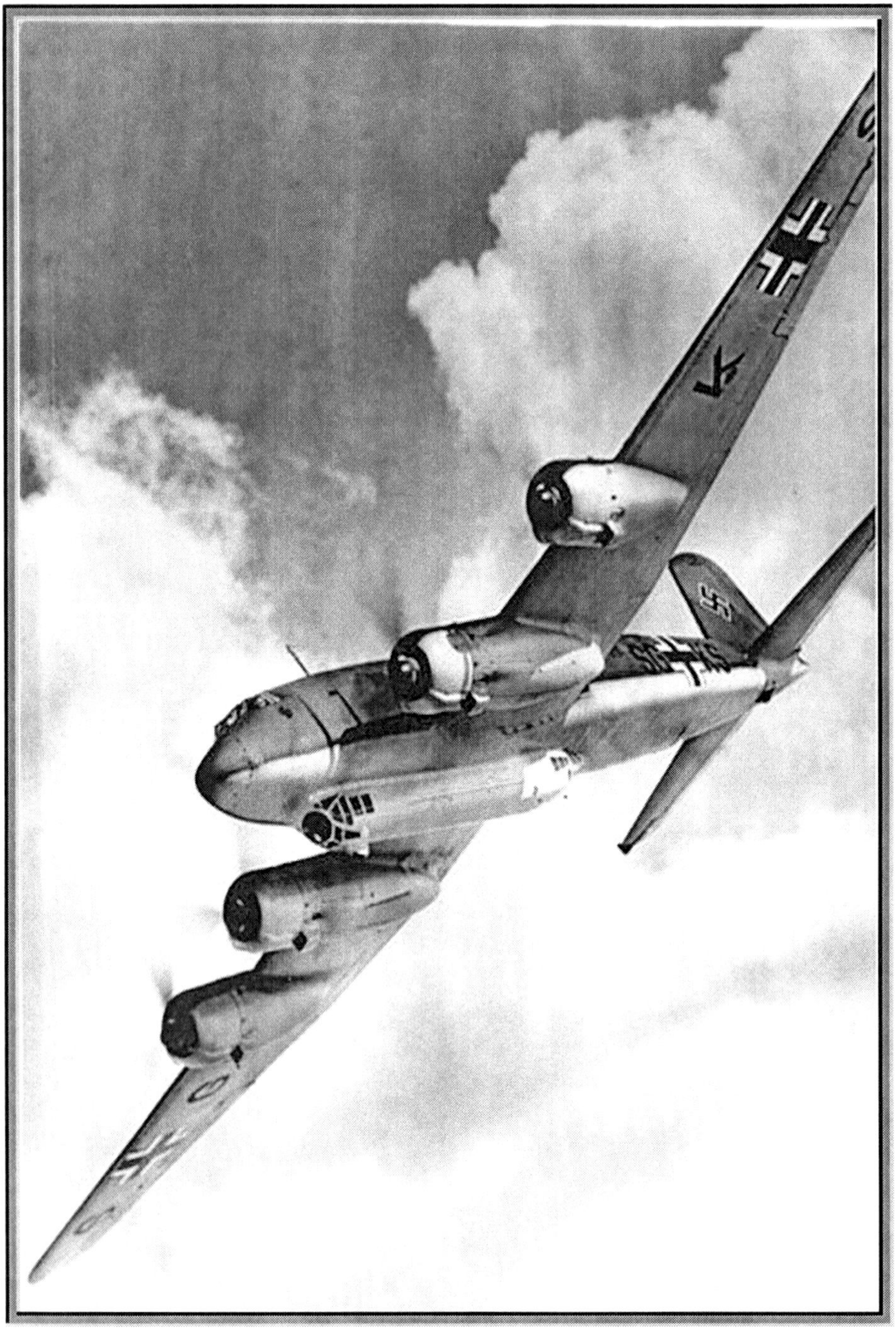

CHAPTER 14

500 Miles west of the British Isles
8 February 1942, 1530hrs

The four engine B-17E bomber known as "The Bitch is Back", was winging its way westward, at 210 miles per hour, at an altitude of 18,000 feet. Three and a half miles below them, were the frigid waters of the north Atlantic. The temperature in the unheated and unpressurized aircraft was five below zero and Markos was feeling the cold. He was dressed in a thick fleece lined fight suit and a thick leather bomber flight jacket. Once the plane had climbed above 12,000 feet, the air was too thin and the crew had to wear oxygen masks not to pass out. The mask, connected to a portable yellow oxygen tank, was uncomfortable but he soon got used to it. They had given him a jump seat, up in the cockpit, so he could sit up front with the flight crew.

Markos thought back to the events of the last couple of days. True to his word, Colonel Royce had arrived at the Savoy at 0800hrs with the embassy car and gave Susan a ride back to her flat and transported Markos to the air strip where he was introduced to the aircrew by the Colonel. The aircraft commander, Major Wilson, had quickly given Markos an aircraft safety briefing and turned him over to his copilot Captain Johnson, who issued him his flight suit and parachute prior to take off. The B-17 had departed Mildenhall a little past noon. The large bomber quickly climbed to cruising altitude and headed westward towards Gander Newfoundland, where it would be landing for fuel and crew rest late that evening.

Markos could not stop thinking of Susan as he observed the

flight crew going about their duties in the cockpit. His feelings towards her were still confusing. He liked her lot, that much he was sure of, and he had promised her that he would stay in touch and see her again. He would have to figure out just how he would do that. Hopefully, he could visit between trips to America and the Middle East. Only time would tell if their relationship went anywhere.

The B-17E had emerged out of a large cloudbank into a clear sky. Markos looked out the Plexiglas cockpit windows and could see the ocean white caps far below. "Hey major, take a look at that, at 3 o' clock, just below us. It's a large aircraft," said the bombardier who was sitting in the nose turret.

Major Wilson peered out the cockpit window. Several thousand feet below them was another four engine aircraft. "I think it's a FW 200 Condor reconnaissance and anti-shipping patrol plane," said the pilot.

"What's he doing way out here?" asked the copilot.

"He is looking for convoys to route his U boat buddies to and lone ships to attack. He carries sea mines and up to a ton of bombs."

"Why don't we take him out? We're armed with nine machine guns; eight of them are 50 calibers. That is a lot of fire power, sir,'" said the bombardier.

"We are also faster than him," said the copilot.

The pilot got on the intercom, "Attention everybody, there is a German FW 2000 reconnaissance plane right below us. We are going to try and shoot him down. We are heavier armed and faster than he is. I want all he gunners at their stations. The target will be on our starboard side."

Markos was glued to his seat. The last time he was in an aerial battle, he ended up having to swim for his life in the Mediterranean.

"Let's do it, sir," said the bombardier who also served as the nose gunner.

"I want all gunners to open fire as soon as we are in range," said the pilot.

The B-17E bomber went into a shallow dive, the pilot aiming for the lumbering FW 200. The large plane quickly came into view. The German tail gunner had seen the big four engine American bomber bearing down on them with fire spitting out of its nose gun. He quickly advised the pilot who immediately began evasive action. But it was too late. The B-17 had the speed advantage and passed the enemy plane on it port side, guns blazing, raking the Condor with bullets. The German gunners had attempted to fire back and the B-17 was hit by several 13mm rounds fired by the dorsal machine gunner as it flew by. The American pilot slowly pulled the plane out of its dive and began a 180 degree turn searching for the German plane. The German pilot had given his plane full throttle and headed for the deck. His dorsal gunner had been killed and his copilot wounded.

"There he is, headed for the deck," shouted the copilot.

Wilson pushed his throttles to full power and his four 1200hp Wright R-1820-65 Cyclone engines quickly responded and the American bomber began to gain on the German aircraft. "Sir, we can't keep this up for long. We are burning up too much fuel," said the copilot.

"Just one more pass."

As they got closer, the 30 caliber machine gun in the nose turret roared to life. They could see the German tail gunner responding in kind. Markos felt several bullets strike the B-17. Soon the waste gunners opened up as the B-17 flew by. Markos heard a yell come from one of the gunners. The B-17 went into a steep climbing turn as the Condor zoomed by, less than 200 yards distant.

"Got the bastard!"

"You sure did, Thorsten! He's smoking and got a long way to make it back to France," said the tail gunner, as he watched the FW 2000 disappear from view, trailing smoke.

The pilot put the plane back on course towards Newfoundland and turned to Markos. "So captain, what do you think about joining the air corps?" he said jokingly.

"I think I have had just about enough of flying. I'll take the infantry any day!" That brought a laugh from the cockpit flight crew.

"Okay, guys, I need a damage report," said the pilot.

"Just a few bullet holes in the fuselage," replied the waste gunner.

"Thanks, guys, good job back there. I think we just made military history turning a heavy bomber into a fighter. If those krauts make it back to the mainland they'll have a story to tell."

"So do we, sir. It should be worth a few drinks at the club," replied the copilot.

"I am sure it will, Johnson."

The rest of the fight was uneventful. The large bomber landed in Gander Newfoundland at 2100hrs that evening. Markos and the crew departed the aircraft to get something to eat and rest. They would continue their trip to the US in the morning. The news of their tangle with the German FW 200 had quickly gotten around the base. Captain Johnson's prediction had in fact come true, their story was worth numerous rounds of drinks as they told and retold the story of their air battle with the Condor. By midnight, most of the Crew of the "Bitch IS Back," was passed out and had to be helped or carried to their rooms. Markos was lucky enough to make it back to his room under his own power where he passed out on his bed, still wearing his clothes.

COI Headquarters, Washington D.C
10 February 1942, 1012hrs

It had been several weeks since Markos had last sat behind his desk at the Greek section of COI headquarters. Many changes had taken place during his absence. The agency was growing by leaps and bounds and several other national offices had been added to the Asia and Europe departments. Markos was enjoying his morning cup of coffee when Bill Donovan walked in. Markos stood up out of respect for his Boss, but Donovan gave him a bear hug and motioned for him to sit. "Glad to have you back and in one piece, Markos."

"Glad to be back, sir. Thanks for your assistance in getting me off the island."

"Had to call in some favors with the Brits, but you are a valuable asset."

"I really appreciate that or I would still be a guest of Standartenführer Mueller, or on my way to a German prison camp."

"I heard that from Bill Eddy. You and that SS man seem to be linked by fate."

"He is a ruthless, murderous bastard."

"As most of his kind are. They rule by fear and violence. They are only creating more enemies."

"Yes, but they are murdering hundreds of innocent civilians and caused the death of thousands by starvation on the mainland."

"That is why I want us to be ready to carry out missions in Greece by this summer and take the war to those bastards."

"We will be ready, at least on Crete. It will take a lot more work before we can operate on the mainland," said Markos.

"That is why I want you working closely with Eddy to develop Greek assets. Eddy told me about one of your former men that you brought out of Crete and of your conversation with the Greek King. It seems that he is willing to work with us."

"You must be speaking of Pavlos. I think he will be a big plus for us. As for the King, he wants his country liberated, but he is thinking of post war politics. Seems the communists are planning a guerrilla army on the mainland. He is worried about what happens after the German withdrawal."

"That's a long time from now. We'll even work with the devil, if he is fighting the Nazis."

"That's what I told him, sir. He is only asking that we give every resistance group equal treatment."

"I can agree to that as long as they are fighting the Germans."

"That's all he wanted, sir. He agreed to have Pavlos as a liaison with Colonel Eddy."

"I also heard of your adventures in London."

"Sir, I did not do anything special."

"Yes, you did Markos. You displayed what our alliance stands for. Respect for human life and freedom. You ran into that burning building, saving two British nationals, and was almost killed by a delayed action bomb. That showed the British public that their American allies are willing to risks their lives for them. You gave them a well needed morale boost."

"Anyone would have done the same, sir."

"Maybe, but you were the one that did it. Congratulations on receiving the George Cross, England's highest civilian award."

"Thanks, sir."

"We're expected at the White House at 1000hrs tomorrow

morning. The President will award you the Purple Heart for your wounds in combat and the Distinguished Service Cross for your actions on the island."

"Not another medal. I don't want or deserve another medal."

"Captain, the Pacific fleet is at the bottom of Pearl Harbor, the Japanese are advancing on all fronts and we will probably lose the Philippines too. The nation needs heroes at this moment, so there will be a lot of photographers there. So you are it. Are we clear?"

"Yes, sir,"

"Starting tomorrow, you will be on leave for a week. Go visit your family. Oh, I almost forgot Lieutenant Antonis Mavroyiannis graduates Friday at Fort Monmouth. See if you can be there."

"I'll be there, sir. I won't miss it for the world."

"Great, see you in dress uniform at 0900hrs, the car will be waiting."

White House Washington DC
11 February 1942, 1000hrs

Markos was standing at attention in the east room of the White House, waiting for his award. The room was filled with reporters and other dignitaries. He glimpsed at the President who was sitting in his wheel chair waiting for the ceremony to begin. He had woken up early that morning, showered, shaved and prepared his dress uniform for his visit with the commander in chief. He met Donovan downstairs in the driveway and they were transported to the White House.

Markos, stood at attention as the Army Chief of Staff, General George Marshall, walked up to the podium and read the Citation:

> **Attention to Orders to accompany the Citation of the Distinguished Service Cross and the Purple Heart**
>
> On 25 January 1942, Captain Markos Androlakis while being held prisoner and under armed guard by the German occupation forces, in the village of Loutro on the island of Crete, Greece, was able during a partisan attack against the enemy, to grab a weapon and escape custody. Even though he had been wounded by an enemy grenade from personnel attempting to recapture him, he was able to fight his way to friendly forces causing casualties to the enemy. As a result of his actions, he has brought credit to himself and to the United States Army."

General Marshal, with the accompaniment of a dozen light bulb flashes from reporters' cameras, pinned both the Distinguished Service Cross and the Purple Heart on Markos' right uniform breast pocket.

"Congratulations, captain," said the Army Chief of Staff, as he shook Markos' hand.

"Thank you, sir," replied Markos, as he saluted the general.

"Now please step over to the President."

Markos walked over to the President. Roosevelt grabbed his crutches, got up and shook Markos's hand as the press took dozens of pictures. Even though the nation knew he was stricken with polio, he never wanted to be seen as an invalid, confined to a wheelchair.

"Congratulations, son, on your actions in Greece and London. I did receive a phone call from Prime Minister Churchill. The British are ever grateful for your actions and so am I. This nation needs its heroes right now. We will talk more in a bit."

"Thank you, Mr. President." Roosevelt sat back down in his wheelchair. The strain of standing was evident in his face.

General Marshall turned to the reporters, "Gentlemen, you have been given the report from the Department of the Army. Captain Androlakis, for national security reasons, will not be taking or answering any of your questions concerning his actions on Crete. He can answer your questions on his actions in London, England, where he received the George Cross, England's highest civilian award, for which we are all very proud of him. Thank you very much."

Within seconds Markos was mobbed by the reporters with questions concerning his heroic actions during the London bombing raid. He answered most of their questions and was finally rescued by General Marshall who called an end to the conference. Donovan, Marshall and Markos were escorted by the secret service to the Oval Office where President Roosevelt was waiting for them. Several chairs had been brought in as well as a small table with a tray of coffee, sandwiches and beverages.

"Welcome gentlemen, have a seat and grab a snack," he said, as he motioned for them so sit down from behind his desk.

Markos grabbed a ham and cheese sandwich and sat down as did Donovan and Marshall. General Marshall spoke first. "So captain, you are probably the first person in the US army to have fought the Germans. Tell me how they as are soldiers. I remember them in the first war. By the time we got involved their morale was crumbling and they were in retreat."

"They are very good soldiers, sir. They are professional, well led, highly motivated and ruthless. Especially their Nazi indoctrinated special troops, such as the SS. They would shoot 50 civilians for every German soldier killed by the resistance."

"Yes, we have reports of their atrocities in Poland and now

the Soviet Union," said the President.

"I saw them, personally in action Mr. President," said Markos, as he related his run in with Mueller and the execution of the mayor of Loutro, to the president and General Marshall.

"My God," those bastards will pay once this war is over," said the President.

"Don't blame yourself, son. This is war and we are fighting an evil enemy that does not abide by the rules of war. The Greeks knew the risks when they helped you," said General Marshall.

"This is why you need to get your organization up and running, Bill. I want us to go after those Nazi bastards and harass them at every opportunity. They can be beaten. The Russians stopped them at the gates of Moscow and pushed them back 200 miles."

"Yes, Mr. President. Our recruiting is picking up, but we still need at least six months to train these people and organize our assets in Western Europe. Thanks to Markos and the great job he is doing things are moving a lot faster. I am hoping, by this summer, to begin operations on Crete, and by the fall on the mainland. Word has it that various resistance movements are forming in Greece and we will work with them against the Nazis. Captain Androlakis spoke to the Hellenic King while in Cairo. King George has agreed to cooperate with us and help us in any way he can."

"That's exactly what I want to hear, Bill. It seems the King has taken a liking to you, young man."

"Well, Mr. President, I did save his life twice and helped evacuate him from Crete."

"I dare say that is a pretty compelling reason," replied the President.

"Tell us about the Greek resistance," said Marshall."

"Well general, there are organized groups already on Crete being aided by British SOE agents. They formed on the first day of the German invasion. That is the nature of the Cretans. They do not take to invaders kindly. Now the mainland is a different story. They are taking longer to organize. The best organized at the moment are the communists or EAM (the National Liberation Front). This is due to their being persecuted by General Metaxas' secret police in the late 30s. They were forced to go underground so when the Germans arrived, their cadre was already in place. I heard that they will field a guerrilla army by this summer. The Nationalists are the EDES (The National Greek Republican League), they're former republicans and monarchists, but they are taking their time in forming a resistance force. The King has asked the British to try and help them organize faster. He wants a counter force to the communists. He does not trust them."

"I can also see why the communists won't trust him either after what Metaxas did to them," said the President.

"The King asked me to relay his request that all resistance groups be treated equal and receive equal amounts of aid."

"I think that is a fair request. What do you think, Bill?" asked Roosevelt.

"Mr. President as I said before, I will work with the devil if he is fighting the Nazis. I don't want us to get involved in the internal affairs of an allied nation unless they are totally against our war interests."

"I agree with Bill," said General Marshall.

"Well, that's the first time you said anything positive about the COI, George."

"Mr. President, I respect Bill but you know my opinion that the army should control all intelligence operations."

"Yes, I do, George." The president turned to Markos.

"Well son, when you are back in Cairo tell the King that we agree to his request. As long as the resistance groups are fighting the Germans and are not against allied interest, we will assist them equally. We will not favor anyone at this time."

"Yes, Mr. President."

"Now before I go take my thirty minute nap, I want to congratulate you again on your actions in London. You really helped the Anglo-American alliance and gave a boost to British morale."

The phone buzzed on the president's desk. Roosevelt picked it up and said a few words and hung it up.

"George, Bill does he know?

"Donovan shook his head. "No, Mr. President," replied Marshall.

"Captain, the next time you go to Cairo, you will be a major. You earned the rank and we want you to be at least a field grade officer when dealing with the Greeks and British there."

"Your promotion is effective today."

Markos was shocked. "Thank you, sir."

General Marshall took out a box from his pocket containing two gold Major leaves. The President nodded and Donovan opened the door and to Markos' total surprise both his parents and his sister and an army photographer were escorted in by the secret service. The President stood up and shook all their hands and sat down.

"I apologize I could not have them here sooner, but there was a short flight delay. George, let his parents do the honors of pinning on his major leafs."

General Marshall showed his parents where to put the insignia on. Markos stood at attention as the gold leafs were pinned on his epaulets and the photographer took pictures.

"Mr. and Mrs. Androlakis, you have a fine boy there, I am

sure you are very proud of him."

"Yes, Mr. President, we are very proud of our son. And thank you for bringing us here," replied Markos' father.

"America honors its heroes. Your son acted very bravely on Crete."

"Crete?"

"Yes, Crete. He can fill you in on the details," replied the president.

"I hope you can help our former country."

"We will do whatever we can, Mrs. Androlakis. The Greeks are a brave people and are making life difficult for the Nazis but they are paying a heavy price."

"Thank you, Mr. President."

"Now, Bill, please put them up in the Hay-Adams, the US government will pick up the tab. Now I need to take a 30 minute nap before I meet with the British Ambassador."

Roosevelt pressed a button under his desk and several seconds later, a black man, the President's butler arrived and wheeled him out of the office while Markos, his family, Donovan and Marshall were escorted to their Limos. Markos and his family were driven to their hotel, the Hay-Adams on 16th and H St. where they would spend the night and in the morning tour the city. In the evening, they would board a C-47 and be flown back to New York along with Markos who had two weeks of leave.

Fort Monmouth, NJ
13 Feb 1942, 1300hrs

Markos watched with pride as his friend, Antonis Mavroyiannis and the rest of the graduating class took their oath as 2nd lieutenants in the United States army. Markos wondered how many of those young men would still be alive when the war finally ended. He was glad Antonis had graduated, he really needed his services. There were several other Greek American agents going through various military training schools, but Antonis would be his right hand and his communications officer. When the ceremony had finally ended, Markos waited for Antonis to come to the guest reception area where many other VIPS waited along with family members of the graduating class. Markos finally spotted his friend who was saying his goodbyes to several of the recently minted 2nd lieutenants and former classmates. As he approached the group, someone noticed him and called the group to attention and they all saluted him.

"Markos! What are you doing here? And a major at that." H said Antonis, as he embraced his friend.

"I could not miss my best friend's graduation and commissioning. I had offered your parents a ride, but they said they were busy."

"My father is still pissed off that I joined the army."

"You would have been probably drafted anyway. This way you got to choose, you became an officer and you will be helping Greece."

"You know what a thick headed, stubborn old Greek he is. He knows that, but he does not want to admit it."

"He will get over it once he sees you in your uniform."

"So I see you made major. Read about your award at the White House in the papers. Congratulations, buddy."

"Thanks. Let's get out of here, I will tell you more on the way home."

Both of them took a cab into nearby Red Bank, New Jersey and caught the Pennsylvania-Reading Seashore Lines train to Penn Station. During the hour ride, both men went into the dining car and ordered a couple of beers.

"Antonis, you did it! Congratulations again and "Stin Igia sou" (to your health)," said Markos, in Greek, as he raised his beer in a toast.

"Thanks, Markos. It was a bit rough at first but then it became a breeze. The radio course was excellent, lots of new stuff coming out. Much smaller in size and more powerful."

"That's good news. Radio equipment that is easy to use and carry will aid greatly in our future missions. I have been assigned to be Colonel Eddy's operation officer for Greece. That is one of the reasons I was promoted to major. You are going to be my communications officer and executive officer. We will be working out of the Cairo office."

"I met a couple of Greek Americans going through the radio course, they will be graduating in the next few weeks."

"That's good news. I want to start building a network of agents all throughout Greece and start kicking some Nazi ass."

"So how was it back on Crete?"

"Well, the Germans rule with an iron fist. Any acts committed against them get paid back, tenfold, in blood. But the people want to fight. The Cretans have fought every invader that ever occupied the island. There is plenty food available, not like the mainland and Athens."

"We all heard about the mass starvation in Athens. Rumor has it that tens of thousands have died of starvation."

"It's not rumor, Antonis. It's even worse. Intelligence thinks that well over 100,000 Greeks may have starved to death or died by disease so far."

"My God! Let's hope the Greeks on the mainland decide to fight soon, Markos."

"There are movements both on the left and right. We should see partisans taking the field at least by the EAM communist movement by this summer. It's possible even the Republicans

/Monarchists may field men by this summer."

"We should be there on the ground equipping them and assisting them to get organized."

"That's the plan, Antonis. We should have several agents finishing their training by this summer. We will get them into the field quickly to help train and equip the partisan groups. The Brits have men already on Crete and plan to send agents to the mainland once there is organized resistance groups formed." Markos continued, "I just hope that these groups work together, but I have a bad feeling as did the King, that there are other agendas at work. Time will tell. For now, we need to fight and beat the Nazis."

"That is just so typical of the Greeks. They have not changed much since the old days, though they did manage to unite for once and beat the Italians."

"I just hope that holds, Antonis. The President said US policy will be to provide aid to any and all groups fighting the Nazis and furthering the allied cause. We will be treating everyone equal for now."

"So when are we going to Egypt?"

"Probably sometime in April, after we finish jump school at Fort Benning, Georgia. We report there on the 23rd."

"Jump school?"

"Yes, jump school. There will be times that we may have to jump in, so all agents will be jump qualified."

"Never flown before, much less jumped out of a plane, but whatever it takes."

"Now enjoy your leave, Antonis. I know I will," said Markos, as he thought of Anna Theofanis.

Broadway, New York
20 February 1942, 2130hrs

Markos and Anna had stopped to grab a hot dog off one of the many Greek pushcart food stands that dotted every corner in downtown New York. He and Anna had gone and seen the new Humphrey Bogart movie, Casablanca. Both of them had enjoyed it, but Markos had to laugh at the Hollywood stereotype Nazis that were depicted in the movie. He knew from personal experience that Hollywood was not even close to depicting the brutality they were capable of. It was pretty cold and he could see that Anna was shivering as she munched on her hotdog.

"Anna, let's go to Hector's to warm up and get a cup of coffee."

"Sure, I'm freezing."

They both quickly walked to Hector's cafeteria in Times Square. Markos got them a couple of Crème Puffs and coffee.

"Got us some dessert."

"Thanks, I like cream puffs," she replied.

"Ja, my dear, ve vill have cream puffs," he said jokingly."

"Ja, eat them quick before the Gestapo catches us," she said.

"I wish the Germans were like Hollywood. We would win the war tomorrow. They are very good soldiers but ruthless. I have seen them in action and witnessed them murder innocent people."

She looked at him with her beautiful, large green eyes and took his hand. "Was it bad this time?"

"I was captured by the Germans on Crete, and escaped during a partisan attack to free me. They killed the man that helped me right in front of me. Had the partisans not intervened, they would have also murdered his two sons. I feel responsible for his death."

"War is terrible. Men do horrible things to one another."

"I know, Anna, but the Germans disregard any rules that were written to protect civilians. Tens of thousands have starved to death in Athens and hundreds have been executed on Crete alone. The faster they are defeated, the better for all."

"When are you going back?"

"Probably sometime in March. I will be in Cairo. Antonis Mavroyiannis is coming along."

"His father is still mad at him?"

"As soon as he saw him in uniform, he got over it."

Markos looked at his watch. "Let's get going. I promised your father I would have you back home by midnight."

They both got up and walked to the corner subway entrance. Markos dropped two subway tokens into the turn style and they walked down to the platform and caught the IRT line to Brooklyn. Markos walked Anna to her tenement. "Goodnight Anna. I enjoyed the last few days with you. I am leaving for Georgia on Sunday."

"Wait,", she turned hugged him and gave him a long kiss.

"Please be careful and come back safe. I will write you." She turned around and went inside.

CHAPTER 15

Berlin, Germany
28 February 1942, 1100hrs

It was a beautiful sunny Saturday morning on the Kurfurststendamm as Sophia and George Mueller sat in a café and had breakfast. Mueller had been summoned to Berlin for a meeting with his superiors. He and Sophia had taken a Ju 52 transport from Elefsis to Rome, Italy. They both spent the day touring the eternal City and then caught an express train to Berlin. Mueller glanced at his watch.

"Sophia, I must leave for my meeting."

"I will walk around and visit some of the stores then meet you back at the hotel."

Mueller hailed a cab and was dropped off at the Reich

Chancellery. The SS guard at the gate snapped to attention and rendered a smart Nazi salute. Mueller walked up the lavishly decorated marble staircase to Himmler's office and noticed two SS guards at the entrance. They both rendered the Nazi salute and let him in office. Once inside, Mueller noticed several men sitting around a table, drinking coffee and eating pastries. He recognized three of them Himmler, Heydrich and SS-Gruppenführer Muller (Major General), the dreaded head of the Gestapo. The other man he did not recognize.

"Glad you could make it, Herr Standartenführer," said the Reichsfuhrer.

Not that anyone in the SS would commit career suicide and not come when asked by Himmler.

"Thank you, sir. It is always a pleasure to see you."

"The pleasure is mine, Mueller. I think you know everyone here except for Obersturmbanfuhrer Adolf Eichmann. He is the Chief Reichssicherheitshauptamt of Jewish affairs."

Eichmann came to attention clicking his heels. Mueller held out his hand and the tall thin man took it with a strong grip "I have heard of your exploits in Poland and Paris, Herr Standartenführer."

"Just dealing with enemies of the Reich, Herr Obersturmbanfuhrer."

"You are being too modest, Mueller. My subordinates reported that you did an excellent job in Paris for the Gestapo," said Muller.

"That is our Standartenführer, never taking credit for his work. Never the less we value him," said Himmler.

"Thank you, Herr Reichsfuhrer."

"This is the reason you are here, Mueller. Now take a seat have some coffee and Kuchen. (Cake)."

Even though he had breakfast earlier, he thought it rude to

refuse. He poured some coffee into a cup and had a sip. His taste buds were suddenly shocked, It was real coffee which he had not tasted had since 1940. Well if the second most powerful man in the Reich did not have real coffee, then who would. Himmler, ever observant, noticed Mueller's reaction.

"Hope you like the coffee, it's Brazilian, comes in via diplomatic pouch from Switzerland."

"It is excellent, sir."

"I will give you some for you and your lady friend, what's her name? I am so bad with names."

"Sophia, sir."

"Yes, yes, Sophia. Tell me how are things in Greece?"

"It's been a rough winter, Herr Reichsfuhrer. Tens of thousands of Greeks have starved to death in the capital and they and the world are blaming us."

"The world can go to hell. The British blockade is to blame. No food ships are allowed in."

"Yes, Herr Reichsfuhrer."

Mueller would point out but didn't for obvious reasons that the Wehrmacht had seized all the food in warehouses and means of transportation. Not to add that Germany had forced the Greek government to pay for the occupation, thus causing rampant inflation, making the Greek currency worthless.

"What about armed resistance? I have read your report, but give us an honest opinion."

All three pairs of eyes were on Mueller. He thought for a second of what to say as to not ruin his career.

"Crete has been a hotbed of resistance, but they have always been this way. It is in their blood. Of course, they are helped by the British with arms and training. Every act of terrorism is dealt with accordingly."

"As it should be, I would……," said Muller.

Himmler held up his hand and motioned Muller to stop talking. "Continue, Standartenführer."

"It has been a fairly quiet winter on the mainland and in the capital, but I do fear though that due to the mass starvation and British instigation, things may change."

"The filthy British Jew lovers with their naval blockade which caused the death of so many Greeks are turning the population against us," said Himmler.

"As are the communists, Herr Reichsfuhrer," added Mueller.

"We must root them out and destroy them before they organize," said Himmler.

"You have the use of my entire organization, Mueller."

"Thank you, Herr Gruppenführer."

"Thank you for your frank report, Mueller. Now the reason I called you here. You are to be entrusted with a "Special" mission. You will be doing a great service both to the Reich and to the human race. What you hear in this room can't be repeated to the general public or the regular military."

"What is that, sir?"

"Last week there was a conference at Wannsee, attended by very senior party officials and officers of the SS. The subject was the final solution of the Jewish question. The Fuhrer has finally decided to cleanse the human race of this subhuman vermin. He has given the Jews many warnings and promised that they would pay a steep price if they plunged the world into a war again. Well, the Jewish warmongers have gotten us into another world war. You, Mueller, will play a historical role in this great undertaking."

"I will be honored, Herr Reichsfuhrer," he replied, knowing very well that he could not reply otherwise. Not that he had any sympathy for Jews, but he had enough on his plate with the growing resistance movements.

"You will be in charge of the final solution in Greece. You will be the one known in history as the man that made Greece Juden Frei." (Jewish Free)

"There are over 70,000 Jews in Greece. How will I accomplish this?"

"This is where Obersturmbanfuhrer Eichmann comes into play. He is charged with managing the trains that will transport the Jews to camps and work centers in the east. The healthy will perform hard labor for the German war effort. The weak and sick will be liquidated by using Zyklon B gas. You two will be working closely together."

"How many Jews are we talking about, Herr Reichsfuhrer?"

"Several million."

Mueller was shocked at the audacity of what Himmler had just proposed. Yes, he had shot a few Jews and rounded up several hundred while in Warsaw as enemies of the Reich, but this? The systematic and organized extermination of an entire race of people, genocide! He would go down in history alright, with the likes of Genghis khan and Stalin. If Germany lost the war, he would be a hunted war criminal. But as a soldier and senior officer of the SS he had no choice but to obey and carry out his order to the best of his ability.

"Jawol, Herr Reichsfuhrer." He was now committed.

Fort Benning, Georgia
17 March 1942, 1030hrs

The noise in the open C47 was deafening as the plane cruised at 2000 feet above the plains of Georgia. The doors were open and the 20 students were preparing to do their first jump. Markos and Antonis were part of the group. They were waiting for the order to hook their static lines to the plane's interior wire.

"Markos, are you sure you want to do this?"

"Not really, but we are here and we graduate in a week."

"Okay, everybody, hook up," yelled the jump master.

Everyone attached their static lines and glued their eyes to the red jump light, waiting for it to turn green. Suddenly, the light turned green.

"Go! Go! Go!" yelled the jump master.

The first man was quickly out the door, followed by the rest of the group. Markos reached the door, hesitated for a second, and jumped. He looked up and saw his parachute canopy blossom. Hopefully Antonis' chute opened without incident. The view was spectacular as he floated down. If and when he would make a combat jump into enemy territory, it would be during the black of night.

The ground quickly was coming up; the impact was jarring as his feet hit the ground. He fell to the ground and was dragged by his parachute for several feet until he was able to remove the harness. He quickly got up to his feet and ran and recovered his chute.

"Hey, Markos you made it in one piece I see."

Markos turned and saw Antonis walking his way with a slight limp.

"You okay?"

"Just a light sprain, landed pretty hard. I will be okay for next week's night jump. It was fun. The view was spectacular."

"Yes, I must admit it was. Unfortunately, most of our insertion jumps will be at night and you don't know who or what is waiting for you upon landing."

They saw an army duce and a half coming their way.

"Guess that's our ride," said Antonis.

The duce and a half pulled up and a private jumped out and grabbed their chutes and helped them up into the truck. The truck went around and picked up several more jump students, one of them being another Greek American, Sergeant George Papadakis, a short stocky young man who had recently been recruited by Markos. He had just finished explosives demolition school and was now finishing jump school.

"Yiassou, (Greetings) George. How's everything going?" asked Markos.

"Pretty good, sir, just want to graduate and get out of here. I hope you both had a good jump."

"Seems we made all made it down in one piece," replied Antonis.

"One more week and we're done then we can get back to the business of fighting the Nazis," said Markos.

"Yes sir, I'm looking forward to it."

"I will keep you in mind, George. I heard that you are pretty good in your trade. We will definitely use your skills.

"Thanks, sir."

The duce and a half finally arrived on base and took everyone back to the jump school center where they reported in and returned their equipment. Because their day had started at 0500hrs, everyone was let go for the rest of the afternoon to relax and take care of any personal matters.

Officers Club, Fort Benning Georgia
17 March 1942, 1307hrs,

After turning in their gear, both Markos and Antonis walked over to get some lunch at the base's officers club. They were seated by a waitress at their table where they both ordered the daily special, cheese steak sandwiches, which they washed down with a cold beer. Antonis gestured to the waitress.

"Two more beers, please." She acknowledged him with a smile.

"She is cute."

"That she is," replied Markos.

She quickly brought them the two beers and Antonis noticed her name tag, it said Kathy.

"Thanks, Kathy."

"You're welcome. Are you here at the jump school?" she asked with a sexy southern drawl.

"Yes we will be here another week," replied Antonis.

She smiled at Antonis as she picked up the empty olive drab Budweiser cans.

"So, Markos, are we still headed to Egypt next month?"

"I want us to get there soon and set up our operations and build our network. I want all our operatives to come over and train with the Brits and gain some in theater, experience. We are also taking Sergeant Papadakis with us. He doesn't know it yet. We need a good explosive expert."

"Sounds like a winner. We need to start kicking some Kraut ass!"

"It won't be easy, my friend. The Germans are excellent soldiers and don't play by the rules. Many of us will die before Greece is liberated and Germany defeated."

"You know best about that Markos, you have firsthand experience. Well at least I will get to see the pyramids first."

"You will like it there. Lots of Greek girls from rich families. Especially in Alexandria."

"Can't wait to get there."

Markos gestured to the waitress to bring the check. A couple of minutes later, she brought the check and handed it to Antonis.

"I got this one, Markos."

Antonis looked at the check. "Oh, nice of her to leave me a note that she gets off at 1800hrs and she also left me her phone number too. Now that's what I call great service. This warrants a good tip," he said with a smile.

Thessaloniki, Greece
29 March 1942, 1410hrs

Standartenführer Mueller had just finished his meeting with General von Krenzski, the Wehrmacht commander of northern Greece, who briefed him on the local military and security situation. The facts that von Krenzski had presented to him revealed that anti occupation activities were beginning to pick up in this area of the country. That was not very good news for Mueller which meant that sooner or later activities would spread to other areas of the country. Athens was already a hot bed of communist subversive activities. There had been several strikes and demonstrations that had to be broken up by gunfire which had resulted in civilian casualties. He had put in a request to Berlin for more SS personnel to help with the security situation in the capital.

Mueller had arrived in the city by plane from Athens the night before in company with Sophia, Hauptscharführer Bruner and Hauptsturmführer Lantz. They had all taken a room at the Ritz hotel. Special orders had been sent by Heydrich, which had been signed by Himmler to begin the planning for the extermination of the Jewish population of Thessaloniki that had lived there since 1492 and numbered over 40,000.

Earlier in the morning, Mueller had met with Max Merten, the city's civil administrator, and senior SS commander, Obersturmbanfuhrer Schmitz, who briefed him on the latest measures taken against Thessaloniki's Jews and the work of the Rosenberg Sonder Kommandos (Special details), named after Hitler's chief ideologue, Alfred Rosenberg. This unit had scoured the countryside and the city and looted Jewish manuscripts, synagogues and Jewish homes, appropriating some of them for occupation authorities.

Mueller had also asked for a meeting with Thessaloniki's Jewish elders to be held at the city's central synagogue which Schmitz had arranged. They were driven there by a heavily armed SS escort, more as an intimidation factor than for security. Mueller stepped out of the vehicle in front of the synagogue and helped Sophia out. They were met outside the temple by several prominent Jews including The Grand Rabbi of Thessaloniki, Zvi Koretz.

"I am Standartenführer Georg Mueller," he said in accented Greek. The rabbi held out his hand but Mueller refused to take it.

"I am Rabbi Zvi Koretz, leader of the Jewish community. Please let us go inside and talk," he replied in fluent German.

Mueller had taken Sophia along as his interpreter, but she would not be needed since this Jew spoke fluent German. No matter, this only made it easier for him.

They passed through the main entrance, the rabbi leading the way inside to his office. Mueller and his entourage followed him inside into a very ornate room with a beautiful and probably very expensive crystal chandelier hanging from the ceiling. On the walls were portraits of past rabbis of the city. Mueller felt unclean surrounded by all this Jewry.

"Please have a seat; we will bring some baklava and coffee."

"No we don't want anything, Jew. We are here to discuss the future of the Jewish community of this city. I need your immediate cooperation."

"Ja, of course, of course, we will cooperate with the German authorities, Herr Mueller." He really disliked this sniveling Jew, but he figured the rabbi would prove very useful.

"As long as you Jews obey all the orders of the German

occupation authority and pay any fines and taxes imposed by the German Reich, you have nothing to fear. Now you will translate this to the rest of the Jews in here."

The rabbi quickly translated Mueller's words and there was an audible sigh. This was just what Mueller wanted.

"So, rabbi, we will need a detailed list of every Jew and their address in this city by next week."

"But, Herr Mueller, that is impossible. There are over 50,000 Jews in Thessaloniki alone."

"What did you say, you filthy Jew?" Mueller was almost screaming.

The rabbi began to tremble. He had spent several months in a Vienna prison as a guest of the SS and he knew their cruelty knew no bounds.

"You will do as I say. Now tell the others."

The rabbi told the other elders and they began to argue. One of the younger men shook his head and turned to Mueller.

"Sir, It's impossible, we can't..." before he could finish his sentence, he was backhanded hard in the face by Mueller and knocked to the ground. He nodded to Bruner who in turn kicked the man in the face and beat him to unconsciousness. The quick turn of events had shocked Sophia; she had not seen the business side of Mueller to this extent.

"Anyone else have anything to say or add? We will have the list by next Friday! I was kind enough to give you an extra day," said Mueller, who now appeared totally normal.

The rabbi was trembling from fear as were some of the other elders. The man that Bruner had beaten senseless was beginning to moan.

"Will someone get that piece of Jew shit out of here before I shoot him."

The rabbi said something to one of the elders and two of

them quickly picked up the bleeding man and dragged him outside. "So we will be waiting for you to come through rabbi. I am appointing you as the Jewish liaison to the SS special detachment on Jewish affairs. Do not be late with the list. You will deliver it to Sturmbanfuhrer Schmitz."

"Yes, Herr Mueller."

"Oh, before I forget, you will clean and pack this chandelier in a wooden crate and deliver it to Wehrmacht headquarters within the next 48 hours. I intend to send this as a gift to Reichsfuhrer Himmler. Understood Jew?"

"Yes, Herr Standartenführer."

"Have a good day," he said sarcastically and departed the synagogue.

Thessaloniki, Greece, Ritz Hotel
29 March 1942, 1744hrs

Both Mueller and Sophia returned to their hotel room which was located on Liberty square in the downtown section of the city. Two guards were posted at the entrance for security since this was a favorite hotel for visiting Germans. Sophia was still visibly agitated from what she had seen transpire at the synagogue and it had not gone unnoticed by Mueller. "What's wrong, Sophia?"

"Nothing, Georg."

"I know there is something wrong, I can see it in your face. What is it?"

"Just the way you dealt with the Jews. You had Bruner almost beat that other man to death."

He was about to say, "it probably would have been more merciful in the long run," but he did not want to tell her about the meeting he had with Himmler concerning the "Final Solution."

"My dear, the Jews are enemies of the greater German Reich. Their greed and intransience is what got us into this terrible war. They are a parasite. Our Fuehrer has plans for the Jews."

"What plans?"

"The forcible resettlement of the Jews to our eastern territories. There, the Jews will build new communities and work for the betterment of the Reich and the rest of humanity."

"So all the Jews of Thessaloniki will be resettled? What's your role in this?"

"To carry out the orders given to me."

"And what are those orders, Georg?"

"To prepare for the forcible removal of all the Greek Jews to the east."

Sophia was stunned. "This may result in the death of hundreds of women, children and invalids. You are a soldier; this should not be your job."

"I am an officer and I obey my orders."

"And what if Germany loses this war? America is now on the side of the British. You may be declared a war criminal, a murderer, Georg. I love you too much to see that happen to you."

"Germany will not lose the war, Sophia! We are winning on every front. Yes, we had a minor setback in front of Moscow, but we will finish the Slav untermensch (sub humans) off this summer. Then we will deal with the British before America can intervene."

"I hope so, Georg, for all our sakes."

"I am a soldier, Sophia, and I must obey the orders given to me by my superiors," he replied, knowing good and well that she was right. If Germany lost the war, he would be a hunted war criminal.

She hugged him and looked at him with tears in her eyes.

She could tell that he was putting up a front. "Oh, my Georg, I just fear for you." she said, as she pulled him towards the bed.

"Don't worry, Sophia, everything will be fine," he said, as he went to her.

COI Headquarters, Washington DC
8 April 1942, 1100hrs

Markos had just exited Donovan's staff meeting. He had received the okay to leave for Egypt and begin planning operations against the German occupation forces in Greece. He walked into his small office and found both Antonis and George Papadakis, his demolition expert, waiting for him.

"How did it go, Markos?"

"We leave this weekend, for Egypt and George, you are coming along."

"Thanks, sir. I am honored."

"Don't worry, you will earn your keep, Georgos," said Markos calling him by his Greek name.

"That is not a problem, sir. I am looking forward to it."

"I am appointing you, our demolitions expert. Your instructors said you were the best in your class."

"I do like playing with things that go bang."

"I am promoting you to staff sergeant, effective one April."

"Thanks, sir."

"How we getting there, sir?" asked Antonis.

"We will be flying out at 1200hrs this Sunday from Fort Dix army airfield to England, then from there to Egypt. You guys can take the rest of the week as leave and say goodbye to your families. Your orders have already been cut. Pick them up before you leave along with your transportation chit for the train to New York."

London, England
14 April 1942, 1700hrs

The long flight to England had been uneventful. Markos, Antonis and George had boarded a C 47 which flew from Fort Dix army airfield to Gander Newfoundland and then on to England where they would rest and catch a flight to Egypt on Thursday afternoon, the 16th. During the long flight, Markos reflected on the last few days he had spent in New York. He had seen Anna only once and she had told him that she could not commit to anything serious since he was going off to war. He was disappointed, but could not fault her for that because in his line of work, getting killed was a good possibility.

After the plane had landed in England, both Antonis and George had gotten a room for the night in billeting. They would meet Markos at Kings Cross Station, London the next morning and spend the day there. Markos noticed that more Americans were arriving daily and that a Military Air Transport office had been opened at RAF Mildenhall. Markos got a ride to the nearby train station and caught the Express train to London. There, he caught a cab to Knightsbridge where Susan's flat was located. He was dropped off in front of the flat, climbed the two flights of stairs and knocked on her door.

"Just a minute."

She opened the door and Markos saw her pretty face. Susan was totally caught by surprise, seeing Markos there in front of her.

"Markos!"

She pulled him inside, closed the door, wrapped her arms around him and planted a kiss on his lips.

"What a great surprise. How long are you staying?"

"I am leaving for Egypt Thursday, on an afternoon flight."

"Then we don't have much time, so let's make the most of it.

Are you hungry? I can make some sausage and potatoes if you like?

"Sure I would like that."

"Let me take your coat."

Markos pulled out a small package from his pocket and handed to her.

"I got this for you." She quickly tore it open.

"Oh my, nylons and perfume. Chanel#5! You shouldn't have, this must have cost you a small fortune."

"Used my pay raise after being promoted to Major," he said with a smile.

"You would not believe how hard it was to find nylon stockings now that the government has classified nylon as a strategic resource, critical for the war effort."

"My, my, a major at that. Congratulations, my sweet."

"Thanks, my parents pinned the rank on me at a White House ceremony in the company of President Roosevelt. He showed her the picture and article he had clipped from the NY Times."

"You are a hero."

"I don't know about that? I was just doing my duty and had lots of good luck, which I hope does not run out on me."

"You will always be my hero. Now let me make you dinner."

Forty five minutes later, having eaten and drunk several beers, Markos felt lightheaded and tired. The last 48 hours were beginning to catch up with him.

"Let's go to bed. I am exhausted."

"Mmmm, with pleasure," she said.

"I need to get up early and meet my two friends that came over with me at Kings Cross station. They are catching the 8 am train from Cambridge. I want to show them some of the sights of London."

"I've got an idea. I'll take tomorrow off, call two of my girlfriends and introduce them to your friends. What do you think?"

"I think that's a great idea."

"Are they good looking, Markos? Both my girlfriends are attractive."

"I am a guy and I don't have a taste toward other men, but they seem okay to me."

"Okay, I'll go call them and be right back."

"Sure, I'll be waiting for you."

By the time she had returned twenty minutes later, Markos was fast asleep and snoring loudly. Even though she wanted him badly, she did not have the heart to wake him. In the morning she would collect on what was owed to her.

London, England
15 April 1942, 1039hrs

Markos had met up with both Antonis and George at the Kings Cross train station and took a taxi back to Susan's flat where they hooked up with the other two girls. Markos introduced his friends to Susan who in turn introduced them to her friends, a pretty brunette named Shelly who immediately was attracted to George and a stunning well-proportioned blond named Jane.

"Susan, you did say your friends were attractive, but that was an understatement," said Markos.

"Yes," replied both George and Antonis.

"Thank you, Markos, you are such a gentlemen," replied Jane.

"Just as Susan described you," added Shelly.

"Thank you, ladies. Flattery will get you everywhere," he added, bringing a laugh to all there.

"Oh come on; let's get moving if you want to show London to your friends." said Susan.

For the rest of the day, they all visited some of London's famous sites, Buckingham palace being the best. Being a winner of England's highest civilian award, Antonis was able to get them a special tour. Afterwards, they all went to lunch and both Antonis and George were introduced to fish and chips which they liked immensely. Then they all visited the tower of London, but did not see the crown Jewels. They were stored in a secret location for safekeeping in case the building was hit in a bombing raid.

After dinner, they all went to a dance hall where Susan had reserved a table for them. The orchestra there was playing many of Glen Miller's latest tunes. It seemed that the two girls had taken a liking to both Antonis and George. Markos had noticed several kisses exchanged during some of the slower dances. The orchestra started playing Sun Valley Serenade.

"Markos, let's dance," said Susan.

"Sure." He grabbed her hand and pulled her to the dance floor and they both started dancing and swaying to the music.

"You are leaving tomorrow and going into harms' way. I can't bear to have anything happen to you too Markos."

"Don't worry Susan, I will be much safer than the guys on the front lines who are getting shot at."

"What you do is just as dangerous if not more so. You have no one watching your back, no one you can trust."

"I do have people watching my back. There is Antonis and George I am bringing them with me."

"At least they are trusted friends. You will need them where you are going."

Markos glanced at his two friends; they were having a good time. He was happy for them for he knew, sooner or later, they would all be in harm's way. "I'll write you from Cairo."

"I will be waiting for your letters, Markos."

"The music stopped and Markos and his two friends all sat down around the table with their dates.

"It's getting late, let's call it a night. We need to catch the last train back to Cambridge."

"Sir, we will meet you at the plane tomorrow. We decided to spend the night with the girls," said George, as Antonis nodded his head in consent.

"Well, guess I'll stay too," he said squeezing Susan's hand.

Cairo, Egypt
19 April 1942, 2000hrs

After they all spent the night in the great fortress base of Gibraltar, the RAF Dakota (C 47) took off at 0700hrs for the long flight to Egypt. The plane landed at 1900hrs, without incident, at the Almaza RAF field, in Cairo. Markos and his men were met at the tarmac by a marine driver in a duce and a half who drove them the short distance to the embassy.

When they reached the embassy, the marine guards waved them through the gates and at the same time called Colonel Eddy letting him know that Markos had arrived. The car pulled into the drive way and stopped at the back entrance just as Colonel Eddy was stepping out with Gunny Parker, the senior marine NCO in charge of the embassy marine guards. Markos got out of the vehicle, followed by Antonis and George. Markos saluted his boss. "Hello, sir. It's great to be back. Let me introduce you to Lieutenant Antonis Mavroyiannis, our new communications officer and radio expert, and this is Staff Sergeant Papadakis, our explosive and demolitions expert."

"Welcome to Egypt, men." The colonel shook everyone's hand. "Congratulations on your promotion to major and recent commendations, Markos."

"Thank you, sir."

"Nice to see you again, sir and congratulations on your promotion to major," said Parker.

"Thanks, gunny."

The colonel sized up both George and Antonis. I am really glad to meet you men and very happy you are all finally here so we can start getting to business and fighting this war."

"We're ready for action, sir. We brought along some of the latest radio gear for the field and spare parts to upgrade the equipment here," said Markos.

"I'll have the communications NCO come down to fetch the gear and lock it up in the armory."

"I'll get Sparks, sir."

"Thanks, gunny. Are you men hungry? I am sure the cook can make you some sandwiches?"

"Yes, sir, that will be good," replied Markos.

"Sergeant, please arrange for everyone's bags to be taken to their assigned rooms. Gunny Parker will tell you where their bunks are."

"Yes, sir."

"Let's go grab some roast beef sandwiches, I am getting hungry too."

"Lead the way sir," replied Markos.

Prefecture of Evritania, Greece
21 April 1942, 1210hrs

Thanasis Klaras, a heavy set, middle aged dark haired man, was sitting in a coffee shop in the town of Karpenisi, high in the mountains of Evritania, Greece. He was sipping on a glass of retsina wine and eating a slice of bread and cheese as he contemplated his next move. He was thankful that the party had sent him to central Greece. Food here, if though not very plentiful, was still available. Not like Athens where tens of thousands had been starved to death by the fascists.

A senior member of the Communist party (KKE), he had been sent to Central Greece (Roumeli) in order to assess the capacity for the development of a guerrilla movement against the Nazis. Thanasis had been a member of leftist movements since his early university days. He had been estranged from his wealthy middle class family for many years. His father a prominent lawyer, disowned him for his leftist beliefs and for disgracing the family by joining the KKE.

During the Metaxas dictatorship, he had been arrested and jailed in the Aegina prison. During his trial he escaped and joined the then illegal communist party of Greece. Thanasis was arrested again in 1939 and was sent to the Corfu prison and he stayed there until he signed a "statement of renouncement" of the Communist Party which had been a very humiliating act for him. When the war broke out against the Italians, he had fought the fascists in Albania as a corporal in an artillery unit. Now he was ready to fight them again.

Fortunately, Thanasis' proposals had been approved by the party's central committee. He had been dispatched in late January by the party, back into the region to begin building a people's resistance force. Thanasis spent much of his days traveling throughout the countryside and with the help of local communist cells, began setting up guerrilla groups. Soon the Greek people's liberation army would sally forth and begin the long hard struggle against the Greek collaborationist, and the fascist occupation forces. Once the fascist invaders were ousted from Greece, he would ensure the people's liberation forces would continue the fight for full national liberation, for the consolidation of the independence and integrity of Greece and for the annihilation of domestic fascism and armed traitor formations, no matter what the cost. Thanasis had even come up with a Nom de guerre he would use to spread terror amongst the occupation forces and Greek collaborationists. He would take the name of Aris Velouchiotis, Aris, in honor of the ancient Greek god of war and Velouchi, a local mountain.

CHAPTER 16

RAF Station Kibrit, 70 Miles East of Cairo
22 April 1942, 1350hrs

Sergeant George Papadakis set the fuse for 60 seconds on the Lewes bomb that he had attached to the wing of the aircraft and ran for cover. Sixty seconds later the Lewes bomb, a blast-incendiary field expedient explosive device, manufactured by mixing diesel oil and Nobel 808 (plastic explosive) detonated, ripping a hole in the wing of the old Bristol Blenheim bomber. The bomber had been grounded due to sever combat damage and parked in a remote area of the RAF airfield used by the SOE for training.

Markos and Captain Lewes of the Special Air Services (SAS), who was the inventor of the Lewes bomb, and who had been observing the exercise, got out of the half ton Ford truck and walked up to George.

"Good job, Sergeant. So what do you think of my little invention?"

George got up, dusted himself off and looked back at the burning plane. "It's a nice bomb, Captain Lewes. It's light, simple to use and very effective."

"It only weighs one pound, thus several can be carried by one man."

"So one person can hit several targets and cause lots of mischief."

"That was the original idea, sergeant. A team is operationally limited, when on a special mission, to what they can carry in their packs. Conventional bombs can weigh several pounds, each limiting the amount that can be carried. With these new bombs, one man can do the job of three or four men."

"I am looking forward to using them, sir."

"That may be sooner than you think, George," Markos added.

"I am ready, sir. It's time to start hitting back at the Nazis."

"Yes it is. I'm hoping that a joint operation with our British allies in the SOE may be in the making. In the meantime I want you to learn how to make and use these."

"How about you leave the sergeant, here major, and I will show him how to make them in the morning. It's not very difficult, only takes a few hours of instruction and some practice. I will deliver him back to you tomorrow afternoon."

"Sounds like a winner. That's why we came here. George, you mind staying the night?"

"Not at all, sir, I have taken a liking to British beer and intend to indulge in a few pints."

"We do appreciate all assistance, captain. Sergeant Papadakis is all yours."

"Thank you, major. I'll take good care of him. Would you

like a beer before you take off on your long drive back to Cairo?"

"Sure, why not. I've also developed a fondness for British beer."

"Let's go then. I think we all could use a cold one," said Lewes, as they all jumped into the truck and drove to the base RAF pub.

Cairo, COI Headquarters
29 April 1942, 1108hrs

The meeting of the combined American COI and British SOE leadership in Egypt had been in session for most of the morning. Colonel Eddy and Colonel Meyers had decided that the time had come for a joint operation against the Nazis. The target they selected was Crete. The island's airfields of Heraklion, Kastelli, Pediados, Tympaki and Maleme were being used by the Germans to provide logistic support to Rommel's Afrika Korps advance towards the Nile delta. Furthermore, Luftwaffe aircraft based on Crete operated photo-reconnaissance, bombing and convoy attack missions covering the south-east Mediterranean.

The British general staff were pressing that something had to be done soon to damage the Germans' ability to reinforce and resupply Rommel. The SOE already had agents in place and there was somewhat of an organized resistance movement which would make any action against the Germans a bit easier.

Mediterranean Sea

> The Mediterranean Sea is a sea connected to the Atlantic Ocean surrounded by the Mediterranean region and almost completely enclosed by land: on the north by Anatolia and Europe, on the south by North Africa, and on the east by the Levant...

Markos and Antonis were also in the meeting as were other members from Colonel Meyer's staff. Also attending was Lieutenant Pavlos Mitsakis, the Hellenic army's Special Forces representative. A large map of Crete hung on the wall with all the island's major Luftwaffe airfields circled in red.

"Colonel Eddy, Major Androlakis, Major Woodhouse and Lieutenant Mitsakis are our resident experts on the island," Let's ask their opinions, said Colonel Meyers.

"Major Androlakis, do you think we can pull these raids off with limited casualties?"

"I know we can pull them off, sir. The Cretans will help us."

"What do you think, Woody?"

"The Cretan people will pay dearly afterwards, but I do agree with the Major Androlakis."

"Dozens will be shot in retribution by the Nazis."

"It's a cost that unfortunately, we will have to bear, Markos."

Lieutenant Mitsakis, what do you think?"

"The Cretan resistance will do whatever is needed, it can be done."

"Then Operation Albumen is a go for the first week in June."

"I also concur with Colonel Myers. Anything we can do to disrupt the supplies and aid to Rommel will set back his time table. It will help buy time for the British 8th Army to prepare their defenses and increase their strength," added Colonel Eddy.

"There will be five teams, one for each target. They will be made up of SBS and SAS British and allied personnel. Each team will be delivered near their targets by boat or submarine," said Myers.

"Markos, we are assigning your team to hit the airfield at Iraklion. If there are any unforeseen complications, your knowledge of the area and fluency in Greek will prove vital in helping your team find shelter and assistance in the nearby city."

"Yes, sir, I do know Heraklion very well. I spent a couple of weeks there during the summer of 1940. I was working at a dig in Knossos, which is only a couple of miles from the city."

"Colonel Myers stood up and looked at everyone gathered around the table. "Gentlemen, right now the war is not going very well for us. Singapore is in trouble and may fall; Corregidor in the Philippines may surrender at any moment. Our position in North Africa is very tenuous. We need a morale lifter. This is going to be our first act of sabotage of many more to come against the Nazis in occupied Europe. Let's show the world that the Germans are not supermen and are vulnerable. Let's hurt them where they will feel it the most and help cut off the supplies to Rommel. We will begin training for the mission in two weeks at Kibrit air station."

RAF Station Kibrit, 70 Miles East of Cairo
17 May 1942, 0350hrs

Markos and the rest of the team waited in one of the numerous gullies that surrounded the base perimeter for the guard patrol to drive by. Once the RAF security patrol had departed the area, he sent two of his team members to cut the wire. After breaching the fence, the commando team entered the guarded area and crawled toward the parked aircraft to place their Lewis bombs. Antonis remained outside and covered their escape route. Besides Antonis and George, the team also consisted of four Free French forces personnel from the 1st Marine Parachute Regiment, Captain Georges Bergé, Corporal Pierre Mouhot, Sergeant Jack Sibard and 17 year old Private Pierre Léostic. The French men, whose nation was also under the Nazi boot, had volunteered to go on the mission and strike a blow against the Nazis.

This would be the second time in a week that the team was attempting to penetrate the base and RAF security. The first time, they had been detected and captured while attempting to exit the base after planting the explosives. As a result Markos and the team monitored the Security patrol cycles for 24 hours and estimated that they had 20 minutes to enter the base, set the explosives and get out.

Markos and Jack Sibard had taken up position and provided cover for George and the rest of the team. They were armed with blank ammunition, as was the RAF security force, to prevent any accidents. Pierre quietly snuck up on the guard and quickly silenced him. According to the training rules, once a person was officially taken out, they had to "play dead" and could no longer participate in the exercise. Once the guard was neutralized, George and the rest of the sappers quickly ran to the parked training aircraft and began planting the demolition charges.

"Sir, the charges have been set for five minutes," said George.

"Okay, let's get the hell out of here. We may just pull this off."

They all quickly headed for the hole they had cut into the

wire fence and upon reaching it, crawled out of the base, Markos being the last to exit. The sound of an approaching vehicle made the team scurry across the perimeter road and hide in the gully where Antonis was hiding.

"Welcome back, sir. You did it!"

"Yes, we did, Antonis. Here comes the RAF security patrol. They are three minutes early too. Let them have it! Wait for my shot."

As the RAF Ford truck approached, Markos pulled back on the charging handle of his Thompson submachine gun and yelled, "Fire."

Everybody stood up and fired at the approaching vehicle. Caught by surprise, the vehicle veered to the left and its passengers jumped out.

"You are all dead," shouted Markos, as he and the team began laughing. A few seconds later, the training charges exploded in a cloud of smoke. Within thirty seconds, alarms and sirens began sounding throughout the airfield.

"You got us, sir. Congratulations," said the RAF Sergeant.

"Thank you, sergeant. Now, will you give us a ride back to the barracks?"

Before the RAF flight sergeant could answer they all spotted a man in the trucks headlights. He was dressed in camouflage and was walking towards the vehicle. Markos recognized him immediately. It was their SAS instructor Captain George Jellicoe, 2nd Earl Jellicoe and the son of Admiral Jellicoe who commanded the British grand fleet to victory at the battle of Jutland. Markos had developed a liking for the man. He was very knowledgeable, not arrogant like many Brits of the nobility class and he had actually seen combat.

"Good job, major! You and your blokes were splendid. It was a flawless textbook operation. I have been observing you since you left the barracks."

Markos was flabbergasted that they had not noticed they were being followed. In a real mission such carelessness could cost them all their lives. But Jellicoe was SAS, they had perfected the art of sabotage and special operations.

"Thank you, captain. We could not have done it without your guidance."

"You're being too modest, major. I can only teach you the theory and show you the "tricks of the trade," but ultimately, you have to use what you learn and survive."

"George, you are a good teacher. Anyway, I think we could all use a beer and some sleep."

"I will second that, sir," replied Jellicoe.

"Sergeant, how about that ride back to the barracks?"

"Sure, sir, jump in." Markos got in the truck and the rest of the team hopped in the back of the bed.

"Oh, by the way, sergeant, we left your guard tied up and gagged back there."

"Serves the bloody bastard right for making us lose to you guys tonight, major. Let him sweat a little. The responding patrols will eventually untie him."

Athens, Greece
22 May, 1942, 1300hrs

Napoleon Zervas, the appointed leader of the resistance group EDES, was basking in his glory. A staunch republican and anti-communist, he had been recognized as a major political and military leader by the British high command in the Middle East. The British, earlier that spring had delivered the princely sum of 24,000 gold sovereigns to EDES to finance the forming of a guerilla resistance army.

Enjoying a Carafe of Ouzo with some bread and cheese, with

his second in command and political advisor, Komninos Pyromaglou, he contemplated the future of the movement. Zervas raised his glass in a toast. "To the glory of EDES and the future liberation of our nation from the Fascists."

His political advisor also raised his glass. "To the success of our future army, Napoleon!"

"Come on Komninos, we will soon leave for Epirus to raise our guerilla army to fight our enemies. I still need to tie up lots of loose ends here in the capital. The movement here in Athens needs capable leaders to manage its affairs once we leave for the countryside."

"My friend, the British are getting restless. They have given us a large amount of money. They are waiting for us to begin raising a force to fight the Germans. They are starting to get nasty and are threatening to expose us to the Germans."

"They are bluffing, Komninos. There is no one else to challenge the communists except EDES and they know that."

"I hope you are right, Napoleon."

"Don't worry, we will soon sally forth to the mountains of Epirus to begin the great struggle to free Greece from the fascist invader. It is my destiny to lead this struggle."

"Well, we better start soon, Napoleon. Rumor has it that the communists have already begun recruiting a guerilla force in Evritania. We must act quickly before they overwhelm us both in the field and on the political stage. Look at their power base here in the capital. They were able to bring down the collaborationist government with their general strike last April. Who would have ever imagined that EAM would control the government civil service?"

"A lot of good that did! The prime minister was replaced by the traitorous pro-Nazi, Rallis. But you are right, the communists have infiltrated everywhere. They plan to seize control of this nation once the Germans are thrown out. The British know this that is why they are aiding EDES. We can't allow that to happen."

"This is why we must build a nationalist force to counter them, Napoleon."

"You are right, my friend. We will leave for Epirus in a month. We will call our army the EOEA (*Ethnikes Omades Ellinon Antarton*, National Groups of Greek Guerrillas."

"A wise choice, my friend. It should resonate well with the British and the King. I will let the British know of your decision."

Domnista, Evritania, Greece
7 June, 1942, 1200hrs

Andreas Kanelopolos was tending to his olive orchard on the outskirts of the village of Domnista, when he spotted a group of a dozen armed men approaching. The men were dressed in a mixture of Greek army uniforms and civilian clothes and armed with old Gras and Mannlicher rifles. The group halted about 20 meters from Yiannis and a large stocky man with a long black beard approached him.

"Greetings, comrade. I'm Major of artillery Aris Velouchiotis. We are part of the ELAS, The Greek Peoples Liberation Army."

Andreas was shocked the armed man had spoken in Greek. He had never heard of ELAS. He was afraid for his life. He had heard that there were armed bandits roaming the mountains, making their living by stealing and murdering the local villagers.

"Please sir, don't hurt me. I have a family. I am only a simple farmer. Take everything I own."

Aris smiled to calm the man down. "Comrade, we are here

to liberate you and all the Greek people from the fascist occupiers. Please run ahead and tell everyone in the village to meet us in the square."

Andreas did not need to be told a second time. He took off running toward the village. Ten minutes later, he was telling everyone in the coffee shop that armed (Kleftes) bandits were coming to the village. Several minutes later the ELAS partisans entered the village and walked toward the coffee shop where a dozen men had gathered.

"Greetings, comrades, I am major of artillery Aris Velouchiotis, commander of the Greek Peoples Liberation Army (ELAS). We are here to begin the liberation of the Greek nation from the German and Italian fascists and their collaborators. Thousands of ELAS fighters will soon follow in our tracks. Once we throw the invaders out, we will build a new democratic Greece where everyone is equal and Greeks rule their own fate, not foreigners dictating it," said Aris. "We only ask you to help feed and clothe the people's army. ELAS is also looking for men to fight the occupiers."

"We never heard of you before," said the village mayor.

"Comrade, have you heard of EAM, The National Liberation Front?"

"Yes, I have," said the man. Several others also nodded in agreement indicating that they had also heard of EAM.

"Comrades, we are EAMs' army. An army of the proletariat that will fight the nation's enemies tooth and nail and show them no mercy."

That got everyone's attention. "Does anyone want to join ELAS and the fight against the fascists?"

Aris stared at the men. One of the younger men raised his hand; soon he was joined by another. Aris smiled, he knew that the struggle against the fascists had finally begun.

Kastelli, Crete
9 June 1942, 1405hrs

Standartenführer Mueller, was sitting in the airfield's commandant's office and was beside himself. He and Hauptsturmführer Lantz, had earlier that morning, viewed the destroyed and damaged aircraft from the sabotage raid that had taken place on the night of 7th by persons unknown. Five Luftwaffe aircraft had been destroyed and 29 damaged to various degrees with no losses to the attackers. Worst of all was the loss of 200 tons of precious aviation fuel, several refueling tanker vehicles and a considerable number of military supplies destined for North Africa. The losses came at a critical time. Rommel and his Afrika Korps were preparing to advance on Egypt and every bit of supplies and air support were needed to defeat the allies. Heads would role for this, starting with the island's Wehrmacht commander.

He had been dispatched to the island by Berlin, to help tighten security at this critical juncture in the North African campaign. Crete had become a major hub for running supplies to Rommel. Mueller was almost positive that several of the locals had given shelter and assisted the saboteurs with detailed knowledge of the base. Somehow he would get to the bottom of who was responsible. A knock on the door made him look up from the incident report he had been reading.

"Come in."

Hauptscharführer Bruner entered the office. His uniform was spotted with blood.

"Yes, Willi?"

"Sir, the prisoner does not have any knowledge of who conducted the raid. All he knows is the rumors they had heard in the local coffee house that the saboteurs were British and had possibly been helped by local bandits. He is not lying, Herr

Standartenführer. I had his family also arrested and threatened to have them executed."

"Good work, Willi. I also suspected the British had local assistance. We will spend the week here on the island inspecting the security of all the airfields. The Luftwaffe is too lax. I am having the commandant of this base replaced immediately and having him sent to the Russian front as an example to the rest of them."

"Great idea, sir."

"I think I will try the carrot and stick approach," said Mueller. Willi, have the mayor hanged as punishment for his town's people giving assistance to the British. Also have all the Wehrmacht security detachments on the island put out a proclamation that any information leading to the arrest of saboteurs and bandits will be handsomely rewarded, but any further act of sabotage will lead to the execution of 50 locals."

"Jawol, Her Standartenführer!"

Gulf of Malia, Crete
10 June 1942, 0300hrs

The Hellenic navy submarine Triton rose to periscope depth while the ASDIC operator listened for any enemy activity. "Sir the area is clear of any enemy patrols."

Lt. Commander Kontoyiannis raised the periscope and scanned the horizon. There was no moon out and the Germans had forced all coastal villages to observe a blackout. "Thank you, George," said the sub's captain. "Looks clear up above, Mr. Vassiliou. Our position should be a couple of kilometers east of Karteros beach. Can't see too much out there though, with no moon and the coast blacked out."

"That's exactly what the Germans want, sir, to make navigation difficult for potential saboteurs wanting to land on shore."

"You are right Yiannis, it sure does not help not being able to see any landmarks," said the boats' captain. "Helmsman, set our speed to dead slow."

"Aye, Aye, sir, dead slow it is."

"We will surface in about 20 minutes. Notify our passengers, Mr. Vassiliou."

"Yes, sir, I'll tell them."

The Triton had departed Alexandria on the morning of the 8th of June bound for Crete with a team of allied saboteurs. Word had come in while the sub was enroute to the island that the attack on Kastelli airfield had been a success. Several aircraft had been destroyed along with a large number of supplies and fuel stores. The mission had been so successful that the commando team had suffered no casualties. Everyone hoped the same could be repeated at Iraklion.

Yiannis walked down toward the torpedo storage section where the commando team was preparing their gear. All the men were wearing black outfits and their skin was covered in dark camouflage paint. Their gear was tightly secured so it would not make any noise that could give them away.

"Gentlemen, we will be surfacing in about 15 minutes," Yiannis said in accented English.

"Thank you, Yiannis," replied Captain George Jellicoe the SAS commander of the mission. "I think we're all ready to hit the beach."

Captain Jellicoe had been appointed mission commander at the last minute due to the insistence of the Free French command. Since most of the team consisted of French personnel, the French wanted an experienced commander leading the mission. For the good of inter-allied cooperation, Colonel Eddy had finally agreed to a compromise and Captain Jellicoe had been appointed to command the mission. Markos was disappointed, but he was happy that George Jellicoe, their former instructor, had been selected to lead them. Also prior to their departure from Egypt, a message from William Donavan had arrived notifying everyone that as of 13 June, the COI would be renamed the Office of Strategic Services (OSS) and that he, Donovan, was being reinstated in the US army to the rank of Colonel. Markos and Staff Sergeant George Papadakis would be the first American OSS agents participating on a mission against the Nazis in occupied Europe.

"Well, Markos, you will soon be back on Crete."

"Yeah, Yiannis, but this time I hope to cause the Germans some pain."

"I wish I was coming along."

"You can volunteer for the special forces, Yiannis. You can see some real action," said Jellicoe.

"Captain, I will take the commandoes and fighting Germans nonstop any day over being a submariner," said Markos. "You have never been under a depth charge attack. I got the pleasure of experiencing one the last time I left Crete. It's hell. You don't know if the next depth bomb will make the sub your steel coffin. I don't know how these guys do it," added Markos.

"I guess you have a point, major. I don't think I ever want to experience that pleasure. I am semi claustrophobic as it is," said Jellicoe

"You never know, guys, I may take you up on the offer one of these days and try land warfare, but for now I'll stay here," said Yiannis.

A few seconds later, they all felt the boat's angle change toward the surface, soon followed by the hiss of escaping stale air as the submarine's hatch was opened. The boat's diesel engines soon came to life and the Triton began slowly inching closer to shore.

"Prepare to launch the boats," blared over the Tannoy.

"Sorry we can't take you any closer, but we can't take the risk of grounding," said Lieutenant Vassiliou.

"Gentlemen, till we meet again for a drink in Cairo. Give the Germans hell! I wish you all luck and may God look after all of you," Yiannis said, as he shook everyone's hand not knowing if he'd ever see them again. The men jumped into two rubber rafts, and with another one in tow, began their long row to shore.

Malia Beach, Crete
10 June 1942, 0530hrs

After a grueling three hour row, the team reached the shore just as day was beginning to break over the gulf of Malia. The daylight quickly brought the realization that they had been dropped off over 20 kilometers east of their intended landing zone of Karteros beach. Not only were they over 30 kilometers from their intended target, they were now also behind schedule. They would have to travel at night and hide during the day to avoid enemy patrols and being spotted by the locals and possibly turned in to the Germans for a bounty.

After slashing open and sinking the rubber inflatable rafts in deeper water, they headed inland, away from the coast. The terrain was rocky and covered with thick shrubs which made travel very difficult. After a couple of hours, they found a small empty cave on the side of a hill which was used by the local sheep herders during the winter. During the summer, herders moved their animals to higher elevation where there was ample grazing. Captain Jellicoe decided they would all rest there and wait until nightfall.

"Major, we'll stay here for the day, to rest and avoid enemy patrols," said Jellicoe. "I am pretty beat. Get a guard rotation going, then get some sleep too."

"Sure, I do need some rest too. It's been a very long 24 hours. Sergeant Papadakis, you can take the first shift. Rotate every two hours."

"Will do, sir."

George turned and looked at the young Frenchman who was pulling out a sleeping bag from his pack. "Pierre, you will take the second watch two hours from now. I will take the first one."

"Yes, sergeant."

"If I see anyone coming, I'll wake you guys."

"Okay, sergeant, just try to lay low we don't want anyone to know we are here," said Captain Jellicoe.

"I will, sir. See you guys in a couple of hours," said Sergeant Papadakis as he grabbed his Thompson and walked out of the cave and walked about 100 meters from the entrance until he spotted a tree that provided some cover and had a clear field of view of anyone approaching their hideout. It would be a long haul till they reached Iraklion.

Maleme Airfield, Crete
11 June 1942, 1507hrs

The Luftwaffe sentry snapped to attention and saluted as Standartenführer Georg Mueller left the base headquarters building and walked towards the Kubel Wagen that was waiting to take him to Iraklion. The meeting with the Luftwaffe airfield commander and his staff had taken a little less than an hour. Mueller was satisfied at the increased security measures the Luftwaffe had taken to secure the airfield. Extra sentries had been posted along with additional machine gun emplacements that guarded the approaches to the base. Best of all, was the new electrified fence that surrounded the entire airfield which would make it very difficult for saboteurs to penetrate the base perimeter.

At the meeting, Mueller had stressed that the battle for North Africa was at a critical juncture and that Crete was the main focal point for much of the supplies transiting to Rommel's Afrika Korps. Those supplies were vital if the Africa Korps was going to defeat the British 8th army and capture Egypt and the important Suez Canal. He had made it perfectly clear to the Luftwaffe officer commanding the airfield, a Lt. Colonel, that Berlin would not tolerate any more security lapses. Mueller though, did commend the man for the extra measures he had taken to increase security on the airfield which resulted in an audible sigh of relief from the Luftwaffe officer. A senior Sicherdienst (SD) officer showing up on your doorstep in his black SS uniform did have a way of intimidating people.

As Mueller approached the parked vehicle, both Lantz and Bruner got out and saluted. Mueller returned their salute and got into the Kubel Wagen. Bruner closed the door behind his commander, got in, started the engine and put the vehicle in gear. "Everything went well sir? asked Lantz."

"Yes, it did. The base is locked down and with the addition of the electrified fence it would make it pretty difficult for saboteurs to enter the perimeter."

"That's good news for once, sir."

"Yes, Lantz, for once it is," Mueller said.

"Willi where are we going first?"

"I think we should spend the night in Chania, Herr Standartenführer and head for Iraklion in the morning," said Bruner. "I don't want to risk driving at night, sir, the roads are bad and we could meet bandits on the way. Besides, I got the scoop on a great seafood taverna on the Chania waterfront that serves delicious grilled Porgies and shrimp."

"Good idea, Willi. We'll go to Iraklion in the morning. Let's go get some good seafood."

"Jawol, Herr Standartenführer!" replied Bruner. In his mind, he could already taste the charcoal grilled Porgies and shrimp.

Amnisos, Crete
12 June 1942, 0430hrs

The commando team had been trudging westward toward Iraklion for the last two nights. Markos, familiar with the area had been steering them clear of the main roads to avoid German patrols and roadblocks. The team was near the small fishing village of Amnisos, less than seven kilometers from their target. Daylight would soon be upon them so they needed a place to rest and hide out. They were behind schedule, the attack should have occurred last night, but they had been more than 20 kilometers from the airfield. Hopefully, they would hit the airfield tonight.

The team had been resting for several minutes inside a small orange grove when they heard approaching footsteps. Everyone held their breath hoping it was not a German patrol.

"Don't shoot, it's us." Markos recognized the voice of Sergeant Papadakis.

"Easy lads, it's our guys," Captain Jellicoe said. Both Captain Georges Berge and Sergeant Papadakis who had been scouting several hundred meters ahead of the rest of the team entered the grove.

"There is a small empty hut up ahead. It's in an olive grove about 300 meters from here. It can't be seen from the road," said Sergeant Papadakis.

"It should offer us some security, Mon Capitan," said Georges Berge with a heavy French accent.

"Thank you, gentlemen," said Jellicoe. "Let's check it out, we do need a place to stay and get some rest for tonight. What do you think major? asked Jellicoe out of respect since Markos was the senior officer.

"It's almost day break and we do need to get off the trail. Let's take a look."

Ten minutes later, they had all entered the small one story structure. The hut was built out of stone and mud and smelled of manure. A small table and several chairs were set up in the middle of the room. The hut also contained two cots and several farm implements and a fireplace.

"Looks like no one has been in for a while," said Markos. I guess it must be used in the spring by the farmer that owns these fields.

"That's perfect for us. We don't want anyone suddenly dropping in on us," Jellicoe added.

"We will soon be running out of food and we will have to make contact with the locals if we want to eat, but only after we hit the Krauts."

"Hopefully, major, we'll hit them tonight," said Jellicoe. " Oh, Captain Berge, please let Cairo know our status."

"Oui, Captain I will string the antenna to send a quick status report and let them know we will hit the airfield tonight."

"Thank you, Georges."

Chapter 17

Iraklion airfield, Crete
13 June 1942, 0215hrs

    The allied commando team had been hiding in a grove of olive trees 500 meters east of the airfield. They had been monitoring the Luftwaffe airfield for the last few hours. However, they had been unable to mount an assault due to the increased traffic caused by a succession of night sorties that was in progress. The attack would have to be called off and they would have to return and try again the following night. The only problem was that the team was running out of food and would have to seek help from the local population. Markos would have to go into the city of Iraklion and try to make contact with the resistance forces and get their assistance.

"I'll meet you all back at the hut after I make contact with my friend and get us some food," said Markos." I do know Iraklion fairly well and should be able to avoid any German patrols."

"We do need food and water, sir, "said Jellicoe. We don't have much of a choice at this point. We were dealt a bad hand to begin with," he added. "I hope you know and can trust your friend. Our lives depend on it."

"He was my archeology professor and a true patriot. He had been an officer during the Balkan wars. When the Italians invaded, he tried to volunteer to go to the front but was turned down because of his age."

"Let me go with you, sir," Sergeant Papadakis said.

"No, George. I will be less conspicuous traveling alone.

"Then good luck, sir. We'll see you back at the hut."

One hour later, Markos was knocking on the door of Professor Stellios Pertrolakis' home which was located on the outskirts of Iraklion. He had not seen a soul on the way into the city. For a Friday night in June, the roads had been empty. Prewar it would have been full of merry makers leaving the tavernas. After several minutes, Markos saw a light come on in the modest two story house. The door opened and he was greeted by his friend and former mentor.

"Markos, what in god's name are you doing here?" Professor Pertrolakis noticed the uniform Markos was wearing. "You are an American officer? Come in quickly before someone notices you."

"Thank you, for letting me in, professor. Yes, I am an American officer on a mission here against the Nazis. I do apologize for coming to you at this late hour and putting you at risk, but I need your help."

"Nonsense, Markos it's my duty to assist in fighting the

occupier," he said with emotion. "What can I do to help?"

"I need food and water for six men and also need to get in contact with the local resistance."

"I can help you with some food, but as for contacting the resistance, I will have to ask around. People here are very frightened. Word has it that there is a new high ranking Nazi SS security officer in town. He showed up after the sabotage at Kastelli airfield. The Germans have been putting up posters offering large rewards for information and threatening reprisals if the locals aid the resistance."

Markos thought for a moment and he hoped he was wrong. "Did you catch the German's name by any chance, professor?"

"No I don't remember it, but I can find out. He is here with two of his henchmen. They spoke to the mayor of Iraklion and threatened to shoot hostages if the Germans are attacked again."

Markos hoped it was not that bastard Mueller again. He would find out soon enough. He explained to the professor where they were holed up. He gave Markos what food he could spare and promised to contact the local resistance and bring some more supplies to their location around noon. Markos thanked the man and took off into the night.

Wehrmacht Headquarters, Iraklion Crete
13 June 1942, 1131hrs

Mueller and his team had finished the security review of German forces on the island and hoped to spend the rest of the weekend relaxing. They had planned to catch a Monday morning flight back to the mainland. He really missed Sophia and was ready to return to the capital. His report to Berlin would recommend that occupation forces take strict action against the local population when there were acts of sabotage and attacks against German military targets. Force had to be met with force. The Cretans had to be made to understand that attacks against the occupation forces and giving assistance to allied agents would cost them dearly. There was no real way that attacks could totally be stopped due to allied involvement, but they could be blunted with the additional security measures he had recommended to the local commanders.

There was a knock on the door of the temporary office he had been given. "Come in!" It was his executive officer and aid Hauptsturmführer Lantz.

"Her Standartenführer, we were wondering if you would like to go for lunch and then go sightseeing to see the ancient ruins of Knossos, it's about 20 kilometers from here. Bruner has the Kubel Wagen (VW jeep) all gassed up and ready."

"Sure, why not. I always wanted to see Knossos from my days at the gymnasium when we were learning about ancient Greece."

"You know sir, that an Englishman, Sir Arthur Evans, excavated most of the ruins and rebuilt portions of the ancient palace as to what he thought they looked like back in antiquity."

"Typical corrupt and arrogant British aristocracy. He should have never damaged such a historical monument. What gave him the right to experiment on such a great treasure?"

"The British ruled the world at the time, sir. They could do whatever they liked. Plundering their colonies to make Jewish bankers in England richer and richer at the expense of the indigenous populations they ruled."

"Times are changing, Lantz. The corrupt Jew run British Empire is full of rot. Look at the humiliation they just suffered at the hands of the Japanese at Singapore. Not only did they lose their so called impregnable Asian fortress, they also lost two of their best warships to the inferior Japs. Soon we will take Egypt and the Suez and chase them out of the Middle East.

After that, they will be finished. The British people will throw out that pompous drunken Jew lover Churchill and England will beg the fuehrer for peace terms," said Mueller. "Anyway, I am getting hungry. Let's go get something to eat and then go see the sights."

"Yes, sir. The vehicle is right outside."

Amnisos, Crete
13 June 1942, 1300hrs

Markos stood guard a couple of hundred meters from where the team was resting and was observing the road that bordered the field the farm hut was situated on. The road, which ran east to west, had very little vehicle traffic since gasoline was almost nonexistent for civilians. The only traffic that Markos had observed in the last hour was a few farm carts pulled by donkeys or horses and a German military vehicle.

The sound of an approaching vehicle coming from the direction of Iraklion made Markos crouch behind a tree. It was a Wehrmacht Kubel Wagen. As the vehicle drove by with its top down, Markos noticed that there were three occupants inside. Markos could not believe his eyes; one of them looked like Standartenführer Georg Mueller. His hunch back at the professors' house had proven to be correct. Mueller was a formidable and ruthless foe that would pursue them with a vengeance once they attacked the airfield. They would now have to be more careful and take fewer chances, but the attack would still go on.

Markos heard the sound of voices and spotted a cart pulled by an old worn out farm horse approaching from the west. He recognized professor Petrolakis as one of the men; the other, he did not know, but suspected that he was probably with the local resistance. Markos stepped out of his hiding spot holding his

Thompson ready but pointed towards the ground.

"Yiassas, (Hello) gentlemen, I hope your trip out here was pleasant?"

"Markos, I am glad to see you again. Yes, the ride was enjoyable," said professor Petrolakis. "Let me introduce you to Sotiris Vangelakis. He is one of the local resistance leaders."

The man jumped off the cart and took Markos' hand in greeting. Sotiris was tall and muscular and probably in his early forties. He had the natural air of a leader about him.

"Markos Androlakis! I am so glad to finally meet you. Your name has become something of a legend on the island."

"I did not know I was so famous?"

"Your exploits in saving the King from the hands of the Nazis is known by everyone on the island. You are a true Cretan warrior!" he added. "Though I do suggest we get off the road to avoid any German patrols."

"Suggestion well taken, let's go to the farm hut," said Markos, as he climbed aboard the cart and guided them through the fields to the hut.

When they reached the hut, Markos had Sergeant Papadakis, who was posted as a sentry outside the hut, go take the position by the roadside he had just left. He went inside and woke everyone up to come outside and unload the food and water that had been brought to them. He introduced both professor Petrolakis and Sotiris to Jellicoe.

"Captain Jellicoe, any relation to the famous Admiral Jellicoe who led the Grand fleet to victory at Jutland? asked professor Petrolakis.

"Jellico smiled, "Yes, he is my father."

"It is an honor to meet his son."

"I am flattered, I hope I live up to his name, professor," said Jellico. "So, will the resistance be able to assist us? We will need your help to leave the area and get back to Egypt."

Professor Petrolakis translated Jellicoe's question to Sotiris. Without any hesitation, the resistance leader replied that he would help them in any way possible. Jellicoe was satisfied with the answer. He even offered assistance for any operation against the Germans. Unfortunately, Jellicoe could not tell them of the pending attack on the airfield for security reasons.

"Tell Sotiris that we will really appreciate that and we would like to meet him back here early tomorrow at 0500hrs. We will need their assistance to reach the south coast," said Jellicoe.

Sotiris agreed and shook Jellicoe's hand. "We'd better get back," said professor Petrolakis.

"Thanks for all the food supplies. We will see you in the morning," Markos said.

Iraklion airfield
13 June 1942, 2342hours

Jellicoe and Markos scanned the base perimeter for German patrols from their hiding place. The team had been observing the base for more than an hour. They saw that it would be very risky to attempt the penetration. The Germans had instituted walking and numerous vehicle patrols that scoured the base perimeter looking for holes in the fence and saboteurs.

"Major, this does not look good. It's too risky. The Jerries have really increased their security. Guess the attack on Kastelli must have caused a major shakeup"

Markos knew that Jellicoe was right. He wondered if Mueller had anything to do with it. He had not told anyone that he had spotted Mueller. What good would it do anyway? "It sure does look that way, captain. They are being very vigilant."

"What's that rumbling?" Jellicoe asked.

Markos listened for a while as the rumbling got closer. "It's aircraft. Here is our chance. The RAF is paying the Germans a visit tonight," Markos answered. As if on cue, the lights went out on the base and an air raid siren came to life.

"We may get killed by our own side, but now is the opportunity. Let's do it, men," Jellicoe said.

The Germans had gone to ground. They would only have a small window of opportunity to enter the base and plant the explosives. Jellico, followed by three Free French soldiers and Sergeant Papadakis, ran towards the perimeter wire which was a hundred meters distant. Markos and one of the French men stayed behind to guard their escape route.

After Jellicoe cut the wire, the men entered the base and headed toward the aircraft parking area. The night sky was suddenly lit up with the search lights and the relative quiet night, was ripped asunder by the sound of antiaircraft guns, exploding bombs. The group ran up to one of the tanker trucks used for refueling. They were approximately 100 meters from the parked aircraft.

"Sergeant Papadakis, take Pierre and Jack with you, I will take care of the sentries."

"On our way, sir."

Jellicoe and Georges Bergé quickly and silently eliminated the three German sentries that were guarding the aircraft and neutralized a machine gun nest that was watching the area paving the way for the rest of the team to set the explosives. The RAF air raid was still in progress so they would have to work quickly. Sergeant Papadakis and his French counterparts quickly began planting the assembled Lewis bombs on the wings of the parked aircraft, setting the pencil detonators for 30 minutes. They found two Luftwaffe mechanics that were working on the planes, they too were quickly dispatched.

Fifteen minutes later, Sergeant Papadakis and the two Frenchmen had completed their task and joined Jellico and Captain Bergé. They had successfully planted their charges on 20 Luftwaffe bombers and on several refueling tankers.

"Sir, we're done. Those charges will blow in less than fifteen minutes" said George.

"Let's get the hell out of here then," Jellicoe said.

Iraklion airfield, Crete
14 June 1942, 0040hrs

Standartenführer Mueller and his team had just settled down for the night when the air raid sirens sounded. They were spending the night at the airfield so they could catch a Sunday evening transport back to the mainland. Mueller quickly got dressed, grabbed his pistol and ran toward the nearest air raid shelter, about 100 meters from billeting where he was staying. He was immediately joined by both Lantz and Bruner and a couple of other Luftwaffe personnel. Soon they heard the sound of falling bombs and explosions. The explosions kept coming closer and closer.

"Never been on the receiving end before, sir. I hope their aim is bad," said Bruner.

"I hope so too, Willi, I don't relish being taken out by a British bomb while sitting in an air raid shelter." Finally the explosions ended. "The raid must be over. Let's see if we can offer any assistance," said Mueller.

They exited the air raid shelter just as the all clear sounded. In the distance, they could see others coming out of their shelters and a couple of hangers on fire that had been hit by bombs. One of the nearby antiaircraft guns had been up-ended by a near hit. The crew had been killed and body parts littered the area.

"Seems they really plastered the place," said Lance.

Before Mueller could comment, a series of explosions rippled across the airfield and lit up the sky even more. More explosions soon followed "Must be delayed action bombs, sir," said Lantz.

"I don't think so, Lantz, they are all coming from the aircraft parking area. Let's go see what's going on," said Mueller. Before they could go more than 50 meters, another siren sounded across the base.

"That's not an air raid siren, that's an alarm siren. We are being attacked. Follow me!"

They headed towards the command section which was a couple of hundred meters from their position. When they reached the headquarters building, they spotted the base commander. He immediately came to attention and saluted Mueller. Both Bruner and Lantz could see that he was terrified at seeing Mueller.

"What is going on, major?"

"Herr Standartenführer, we were attacked during the RAF bombing raid. Saboteurs have destroyed several aircraft and killed five of my men that were guarding the planes. I am sending response forces to hunt the saboteurs down."

"You idiot, it's too late now," yelled Mueller. "I will be taking charge of your response force. Have your men sweep the perimeter inside and out immediately. I will deal with you later!"

"The Luftwaffe major was trying to keep his composure and mumbled his reply. "Ja ja, Jawohl, Herr Standartenführer."

Mueller gave orders to several Luftwaffe junior officers to take their men and scour the base perimeter.

"Lantz, Bruner, let's go see what is going on." Mueller jumped into the major's Kubel Wagen and drove towards the flight line. Three minutes later, they reached the aircraft parking area which was now swarming with Luftwaffe fire fighters and security forces. They were greeted by the sight of almost two dozen JU-88 fighter bombers burning as well as several refueling vehicles.

"My God! They really did a job on us, Herr Standartenführer," Lantz said.

"Yes they did, Lantz, and they will pay dearly for it!"

Iraklion airfield, Base Perimeter
14 June 1942, 0100hrs

The RAF bombing raid on the airfield had ended. The Germans would soon start coming out of their shelters to check on the bomb damage. The commandos had almost made it to the wire when the charges blew one after the other. Almost immediately, a klaxon sounded initiating a base-wide alarm. The Germans would now be on full alert.

"We're almost to the exit," said Jellicoe. The Jerries will be looking for us." As if on cue, a German patrol was driving down the perimeter road.

"Everybody down!" Jellicoe said.

"We're fucked," said Sergeant Papadakis. "They can't miss the hole in the fence, captain."

The German patrol came to a sudden stop right next to the hole that had been cut in the perimeter fence. The three man security team exited the Kubel Wagen and checked the hole. One of the soldiers could be seen talking in a radio. "We can't stay here Mon Capitan. They called for reinforcements, we'll be trapped here if we don't do something," said Captain Bergé.

"You are right, Georges," Jellicoe replied.. "We need to take them out now." Before Jellicoe could give the order, a hail of gunfire ripped into the Germans.

"Open fire!" Jellicoe stood up and also poured fired on the German patrol. Hit by two sides the Germans had no chance and were quickly dispatched.

"Quickly, out the wire," yelled Jellicoe. Markos and Corporal Jacques Mouhot were waiting for them as they all exited through the perimeter fence. "Glad to see you major, for a while I thought we were screwed."

"Let's use their vehicle and put some distance from here before more Germans show up. We'll ditch the vehicle and double back to the farm house and wait for the resistance."

"Good idea, major, said Jellicoe. "Okay everybody in the vehicle.

Iraklion airfield, Base Perimeter
14 June 1942, 0115hrs

Mueller had heard the shots and ordered Bruner to drive toward the location they had come from. Within a few minutes they had reached the area of the shooting.

"Herr Standartenführer, look over there," said Bruner. "There is the cut in the fence."

"Stop the vehicle everyone out and take cover," ordered Mueller. "They could still be around."

Bruner slammed on the brakes and everyone exited and quickly went to ground. "Bruner, we have you covered. Crawl up to the cut in the fence and check it out," said Mueller.

"Jawohl, Herr Standartenführer." Bruner, an experienced soldier, quickly crawled up to the cut in the wire and shined his Daimon Wehrmacht issue flashlight outside. "Sir, I can see three bodies outside. It looks like they are wearing Luftwaffe uniforms. I am going outside."

"Just a minute, Willi, wait for us," Mueller said. Both Mueller and Lantz crawled to Bruner's position and shined their flashlights outside.

"Willi is correct, sir. They are Luftwaffe," Lantz said.

"We will all go through the wire. Willi, you first, we will cover you."

Bruner went through the wire, dashed forward a few steps and hit the dirt. Mueller and Lantz quickly followed. "Check the bodies, Willi."

Bruner crawled over and checked each body. "They are all dead Herr Standartenführer. Bruner shined his flashlight into the tree line." I believe they are gone, sir. They must have taken the security detail's vehicle."

Both Mueller and Lantz stood up and were joined by Bruner. "The bastards are gone, but we will find them and make them and the locals that helped them pay dearly," Mueller said.

They heard the sound of a vehicle approaching from the north and soon viewed its headlights. It was a Luftwaffe Opel Blitz truck. The truck stopped by the three SS men and a Luftwaffe lieutenant got out, snapped to attention and saluted Mueller.

"Lieutenant Stoffer and my men at your service, sir."

Mueller eyed the younger man; he looked like a capable officer. "Lieutenant, the bodies of your three comrades are over there. The saboteurs are long gone; you will not find them now. We will, though, hunt them down," said Mueller. "I will need you and your men's assistance. You will meet me in front of the command center at 0630hrs."

"Jawohl, Herr Standartenführer!"

Amnisos Farm House, Crete
14 June, 0835hrs

After their successful attack and escape from Iraklion airfield, the joint SAS-OSS team had abandoned the Kubel

Wagen a few kilometers from the airfield and trudged back to their farm hut at Amnisos to await the arrival of the resistance. They had taken turns trying to get some rest for the long journey that awaited them. In the interval, Jellicoe had sent a message to Egypt notifying them of the successful attack and destruction of over 20 enemy aircraft. Cairo had advised them to head for the south coast to await transportation back to Egypt.

The team had been having breakfast with the last of their food supplies when the door burst open.

"Sir, there are several armed men approaching," said Pierre Léostic, one of the sentries posted outside. Everyone grabbed their weapons and ran outside and quickly took cover. Less than a minute later, Jack Sibard and two other men, dressed in traditional Cretan garb, were approaching the hut. Jack was drinking out of a bottle.

"Capitan Jellicoe, our help is here," Jack said.

Markos and Jellicoe stood up and walked towards the two men. Markos recognized one of them as Sotiris Vangelakis, the leader of the resistance in Iraklion. "Yiassou Sotiris," said Markos.

"Markos, my friend, I told you I would be here to help you get to the south coast and safely," said Sotiris. "We need to leave here quickly, the Germans are all over the place. They entered Iraklion and are searching houses and rounding up hostages. I brought you all some civilian clothes."

Markos translated what Sotiris had just told him to Jellicoe. He thought back of his seeing Mueller the other day as he drove by him. Markos would bet his life that Mueller and his henchmen were behind the German's actions. This would make their escape from the island more difficult. The Nazis would be ruthless in their crackdown towards the local inhabitants and leave no stone unturned in their search for the saboteurs, he was certain of that.

"We need to move right away. Captain Bergé, get the men ready we leave in 10 minutes," Jellicoe said. "Everyone can wear the civilian clothes over their uniforms. I personally don't want to be caught without a uniform and get shot as a spy."

"I don't think it will make much of a difference at this point. If I am right, a certain Standartenführer Georg Mueller and his boys are running the German security efforts to capture us. He is one sadistic bastard. Mueller and I have a long history," Markos said, as he quickly related his past run-ins with Mueller.

"My God! It seems, major, that you and this Mueller fellow seem to share the same twisted fate or rotten luck, especially in your part," Jellicoe remarked.

"How do you know this Mueller is running the show now, Major?" Captain Bergé asked.

"I saw him with two of his protégés driving down the road towards the east yesterday, while I was taking a guard shift."

"And you did not think about mentioning it to anyone?"

"No, Captain Bergé. Everyone was under enough stress before the mission and in the grand scheme of things what difference would it make? The Germans would be looking for us anyway. Only now, they will be looking a little harder."

"That is true sir, you do have a point. But if this SS bastard somehow finds out you are here, he will take it personally and hunt us down like dogs."

"So let's get the hell out of here. Everyone is packed and ready," Jellicoe said.

Markos looked at the resistance leader. "Lead the way Sotiris, our fate is in your hands."

Iraklion, Crete, Central Square
14 June 1942, 1244hrs

After the successful night sabotage attack on the airfield, all hell had broken loose the next morning in Iraklion. Mueller, with the assistance of both Luftwaffe and Wehrmacht units, had his forces fan out throughout the city and began searching homes and rounding up suspects and hostages. He was insistent that the Greeks pay a heavy price for the destruction and loss of German lives at the airfield. Fifty male hostages had been selected to be shot at noon. Mueller had selected an area in the outskirts of Iraklion for the place of execution and had the hostages transported there. Two Opel Blitz trucks, one carrying an MG 42 with an SS crew manning the gun and the other carrying the hostages, pulled up in a dried riverbed known as Xeropotamos (dried river) where Mueller and many of the relatives and mayor of Iraklion were waiting.

"Sir, the hostages are here," Bruner said. "So is the gun crew."

"Let's get this over with quickly. Line them up."

"Jawohl, Herr Standartenführer."

Bruner and several Wehrmacht Feld Polizei (Military Police) armed with MP38 machine pistols dragged the people from the truck and lined them up along the dried river bed. Included in the hostages were several Jews, an old priest and a former governor general of the island. "Sir, here comes the town mayor with Basil V, Archbishop of Crete along with several relatives of the hostages," said Lantz.

"I'll take care of this, Lantz."

"Please, Herr Mueller, these are innocent people, they have not done anything," The mayor said.

"Herr Mayor, you were warned that any further actions of sabotage against German forces would result in the execution of

50 hostages. Not only were several aircraft destroyed, twelve German soldiers lost their lives," Mueller said.

"Please, in the name of God do not execute these people. They were not responsible for the sabotage. Show mercy," pleaded the archbishop.

"Sorry, your eminence. This is war and you were forewarned of the consequences. Your people are helping the enemy kill German soldiers and destroy military property. I am also showing mercy and not executing any women or ten Greeks for every German soldier that was killed."

"All ready, sir," Lantz said.

The hostages, which had been lined up in the dried riverbed, began singing the Greek national anthem. The remaining Opel Blitz drove up, dropped its tailgate and revealed a MG 42 machine gun with its SS crew and awaited Mueller's order to open fire.

"Fire!"

The buzz saw sound of the MG 42, spitting out 1500 rounds a minute, quickly silenced the singing. When the gun ceased fire the only thing that could still be heard was moaning from some of the machine gunned hostages, but was quickly stopped by a bullet in the head from Bruner.

The mayor of Iraklion and the archbishop stood silent in utter shock at what had just taken place before their eyes. "I hope this serves as a warning to all," said Mueller. "Any more sabotage or bandit activities against German forces will be dealt with more severely. Good day, gentlemen."

Both Lantz and Bruner had pulled up in the Kubel Wagen and Mueller jumped inside the back seat. Bruner gunned the vehicle and drove off from the place of slaughter along with the rest of the German military forces that had taken part in the reprisal execution of the Greek civilians.

Chapter 18

Allied Headquarters Cairo Egypt
15 June 1942, 1310hrs

Colonel Eddy glanced over the latest photos that Colonel Meyers had handed him. They were taken by a Mosquito reconnaissance bird of Iraklion airfield earlier that morning. "Well, Myers, these photos prove that our boys did a great job over there. They took out over 20 fighter bombers and support equipment. The mission was a great success and hurt the Germans."

"Unfortunately, it cost the lives of 50 Greeks," said Myers. "The Germans rounded up and executed the hostages yesterday."

"Oh Jesus! How did you hear about this, Meyers?"

"From our agents on this island."

"Well that certainly will make the Cretans hate the Germans

even more."

"Yes, but it certainly doesn't endear them to us either."

"There is more," said Meyers. "Standartenführer George Mueller was in charge of executing the hostages."

"If that ruthless bastard finds out Major Androlakis was part of the mission, he will scour the island and leave a trail of bodies until he captures or kills the entire team."

"I heard they have a history," Meyers said.

"He humiliated Mueller when he rescued the King of Greece twice from under his clutches," Colonel Eddy said. "We have to get the team off the island as soon as possible before he turns the locals against us with his barbarity."

"That will never happen, you don't know the Cretans," said Meyers. "They will never cooperate with the Germans. They will fight them at every opportunity, as they have fought invaders for centuries."

"I hope you're right, Meyers. We still need to get our people out."

"I'll get my assets on it," Meyers replied.

25 kilometers south of Iraklion, Crete
16 June 1942, 2100hrs

The SAS and OSS commando group traveled deeper into the island's heartland and continued to be handed off to various resistance groups as it headed towards the south coast and eventual transport back to Egypt. They had stopped for the night at the small agricultural village of Karkadioutisa which was situated in the central Cretan highlands. When the village's occupants saw the commandos and heard of their exploits, they broke out the alcohol and even slaughtered a sheep to celebrate the successful attack against the Germans. So far, everything had gone according to plan for Jellico's team, but the euphoria was about to come to a sudden end.

Markos had been sitting at one of the several tables that had been set up in the square. He looked up from his plate of roast lamb and salad and noticed Sergeant George Papadakis approaching with another man. "Major, we found this guy on the trail, he is armed and says he is part of Sotiris' resistance group," said Sergeant Papadakis, who had not been taking part in the festivities and had been watching the approaches to the village with Pierre instead.

"Who are you?" Markos asked the middle aged, well-built man.

"I'm Andreas Minakis from Iraklion," answered the man.

"Ask Sotiris. I am one of his lieutenants."

"Sergeant, go find Sotiris, he is at the town Mayor's home."

A few minutes later, both Sotiris and Jellicoe arrived. "Yiassou, Andrea. What are you doing here," asked the guerrilla leader.

"I have bad news from Iraklion, Sotiris. The Germans have executed 50 hostages in reprisal for the raid."

The jovial mood quickly went downhill as the realization that their successful raid against the Germans cost the lives of 50 Greek civilians. "Oh, my God, the bastards!" Markos said in anguish. "This had to be Mueller's handy work."

"The Germans are searching everywhere and will be here in a day or two. They have a huge reward on your heads," Andreas said.

"We need to move first thing in the morning," Captain Bergé said.

"You are right, Georges; we will head deeper into the mountains to avoid the German patrols that are searching for us. We can't risk anymore innocent people's lives," said Jellicoe.

"I know this Nazi SS bastard. Mueller is ruthless and he will not stop looking for us until he has hunted us down or we escape from the island."

"Well, we will make it as difficult as possible for the Germans to find us,"Captain Bergé added..

"We will double the sentries to the village approaches for tonight with the help of your men Sotiris and leave first thing at daybreak."

"You will have our help, Captain Jellicoe,"the partisan leader replied.

Iraklion, Crete
17 June 1942, 1315hrs

Standartenführer Mueller looked at the bleeding prisoner who was tied to a chair in the Iraklion Wehrmacht headquarters interrogation room. The man, who was in his middle thirties. had been caught with a pistol and two grenades at a security check point. He was beginning to lose his patience. Bruner had been working him over for the last hour, but the man still refused to talk. Mueller was almost certain that their prisoner was a member of the local resistance and probably had knowledge of the raid.

"I will ask you one more time. Where are the allied agents?"

"I don't know. I am just a farmer, I found the weapons hidden in my barn."

Mueller struck the man a sharp blow to the face. "You are a liar. If you tell us, we will spare you and your family and even reward you."

"I told you, I don't know anything about saboteurs," the man screamed.

The door opened and Lantz walked in with a pretty woman in her late twenties, holding a young child. She saw her bloodied husband in the chair and began to cry. "Finally, we may now get some cooperation," Mueller said.

The prisoner suddenly began to fight with his bonds and yell. "Why is my family here?"

"To get your cooperation, my friend," Mueller answered.

"But I told you, I don't know anything."

Mueller nodded to Lantz and took the child by the hand and led him out of the room while Lantz dragged the helpless woman to another part of the building. He returned twenty minutes later with two other SS troopers. "Where are my wife and child?" The prisoner asked Mueller.

"Your child is enjoying some sweets with one of our female administrative specialists," Mueller answered.

A look of relief came upon the man's face. "Where is my wife? I want to see her."

Mueller motioned to the two SS Sergeants who untied the prisoner and dragged him to a nearby room. The man screamed in rage when he saw his wife hanging naked from the ceiling. Her mouth had been gagged shut and she had been beaten all over her body with rubber hoses and burned with cigarettes, blood was oozing from several cuts on her body. "Are you ready to talk now?"

"Go fuck yourself, you German pig."

"Lantz, bring the boy."

"Jawohl, Her Standartenführer."

A minute later Lantz returned with the young child. Mueller took the child, pulled out his Walter P1, 9mm pistol and put it to the child's head. "My patience has run out. If you don't tell me what I want, I will shoot the boy."

"I told you I don't know anything."

"I will count till three," said Mueller. "One."

"Please don't hurt my son."

"Two," Muller pulled back on the hammer.

"Okay, I will tell you, if you let my wife and son go."

"I will let them go once you tell me what I want to know.
"You have my word," Mueller said.

"They left Iraklion and are heading towards the south coast to be evacuated to Egypt. They are being assisted by the local resistance. That is all I know I swear."

"How many saboteurs were there? asked Mueller.

"I am not sure six or seven."

"Were any of them Greek."

"Two of them spoke Greek but they wore American uniforms. One of them was an officer."

"What was the officer's name?"

"I don't remember. I am not sure."

Mueller slapped the man across the face. "You better remember! Mueller was now visibly agitated. "Or I will shoot the boy!"

"I think his name was Markos."

"Markos Androlakis?"

"Yes, yes that was it."

Mueller glanced at Lantz. "Now he is a major! I can never rid myself of that man. It seems that our fates are intertwined."

"He is proving to be very resourceful, sir."

"Let's put an end to his career. Notify the garrison commander that I want a platoon of men to go after these saboteurs," said Mueller. "Oh, and you can let this man and his family go. The locals will take care of him once they find out he talked."

"Jawohl, Herr Standartenführer!"

Vassilika, Central Crete
19 June 1942, 1321hrs

After leaving the village of Karkadioutisa, the commando team was whisked south to the village of Vassilika by the local resistance. It was known from resistance sources that the group had a price on its head by the Germans. Reports from locals said a large force of Germans was scouring the island's interior to catch them. Jellicoe decided that they would camp on some high ground, a couple of kilometers from the village, not to be caught by surprise by any German troops. The Cretan resistance was going to escort them to the beach the following morning, but until then, they had to stay tight.

Jellicoe, Markos and Sergeant Papadakis had left the Frenchmen at the camp to try and forage some food supplies, which they were running low on. As the three men walked down the steep rocky trail and neared the village of Vassilika, they spotted a large group of Germans moving through the village.

"Jellicoe, run over there," said Markos pointing to a grove of olive trees, less than a hundred feet from the path.

"Did they see us?" asked Jellicoe, as they hid in the trees.

"We'll know in a minute," replied Markos.

A couple of minutes passed and the Germans did not seem to be taking any aggressive moves toward their location. "I don't think they've seen us," said Sergeant Papadakis. "I think I may have spoken too soon. There is a group heading this way. Shit, we're screwed."

A squad of heavily armed Gebirgsjagers walked past where the three commandoes were taking cover. "They have not seen us, probably advanced scouts securing the approaches to the village. We will have to wait them out here," said Jellicoe.

Back down in the Vassilika, Mueller and his men had finished securing the village and were beginning a systematic house to house search. Along with the platoon of mountain troops, Muller brought a squad of SS Einsatz commandos (Special Detail Troop) under the command of an SS-Untersturmführer (2nd Lieutenant). They were doing the house to house search and any dirty work that needed to be done. Mueller had rounded up the town mayor and priest and had rather forcefully asked them if they had any knowledge of the allied band of saboteurs. He knew they were close; a couple of captured partisan, had talked and had told him the general direction the commandoes were travelling. The men had sworn they had no knowledge of the allied agent.

"Sir, there is a Greek man being held by Bruner that says he wants to speak to the commanding officer," said one of the SS NCOS that Mueller had brought along.

"Bring him here."

"Yes, sir."

A couple of minutes later, he returned with a younger man who appeared to be a farmer. The man was carrying a hoe and had been apparently tilling his field when Mueller's troops arrived in the area.

Mueller, who for the last year had been studying Greek with Sophia's tutoring, was now almost semi fluent in the language. Mueller studied the man for a moment. He showed no fear of him. "I am the commanding officer here. Who do I have the privilege of speaking to," Mueller said in accented Greek.

"I am Kostas Milonakis. I live in this village and I am a farmer. Is it true that there is a reward for information about the allied soldiers in the area?"

Mueller was almost speechless. His first big break without even trying. "Yes, there is 100 gold Sovereigns reward for friends of the German Reich."

"I have information. Too many Cretans have died for these men. We don't need more death here."

"You are correct, my friend. The English don't care if Greeks die for them,"

"I will show you. Their camp is at a hill, a couple of kilometers from the village."

"Lantz, I am taking half the men and going after them. Block all escape routes and see to it that any escaping saboteurs towards the village are killed or captured."

"Jawohl, Herr Standartenführer."

One kilometer North of Vassilika Crete
19 June 42, 1400hrs

The three allied agents watched in horror from their hiding place as the strong German force with Mueller and the Greek informant headed toward the direction of the their encampment. There was nothing they could do against such a strong enemy contingent. Neither could they go towards the direction of the village because the Germans had set up blocking positions to capture or kill any that would be fleeing toward that direction.

"Georges Bergé and his men are fucked," whispered Markos. "The worst of it is we can't do anything to help them."

"They're on their own," replied Jellicoe. "We can't move from here until the Jerries leave, so it may be a long wait."

"I'm glad I took my canteen, at least we will have something to drink in this sweltering heat," said Sergeant Papadakis.

Captain Bergé and his men had just finished having their lunch and sending a SITREP report to Cairo when they heard commotion coming from below their position. Sergeant Jack Sibard came running.

"Sir, there is a large German force approaching."

"Grab your weapons, some water and destroy the radio. We are leaving."

"Yes, Sir."

Bergé quickly ripped up the code book pages and threw them into the camp fire and watched them burn as Sergeant Sibard smashed the radio. "Let's move now!" Bergé said.

The Frenchmen grabbed their weapons and what meager water supplies they could and took off running. They took one of the escape routes they had selected with Private Pierre Léostic leading the way. They had not gone more than a couple of hundred meters when a gun shot rang out.

"Halt!" The well trained commandoes quickly reacted and opened fired at the direction of the ambush.

"Pull back, up the hill," Captain Bergé yelled.

The four Frenchman started to pull back when a German machine gun opened fire. Bergé heard a scream and looked back and saw that Pierre Léostic had fallen. Corporal Jacques Mouhot quickly crawled to where Léostic was lying and under cover fire from the three other Frenchmen dragged their seriously wounded comrade to safety. The four commandoes carried the wounded young soldier to a rock outcrop that offered cover.

"Sir, he is wounded very badly," Sibard said, shaking his head.

"Merde! He is only seventeen," Bergé said as he went over to the young soldier. Sibard had given him a shot of morphine from the first aid kit. The young man had taken a machine gun round through the stomach and was bleeding out. "Hold on, Pierre, we will get you help."

"No, sir. Don't surrender for me. I know I'm a not going to make it. Just take out some Bosch (French derogatory name for

Germans) for me."

"We will do our best and fight for the glory of France, son. Our country will be free one day again."

"Tell my mother I….I fell for France. Hold my hand, sir."

"I am here, Pierre. Pierre?"

"He is gone, Mon Capitan," Sibard said.

"If we have to fall for the glory of France, let's take some of the Bosch bastards with us." Both Sibard and Mouhot tacitly acknowledged their Captain with a nod and began returning fire.

Jellicoe, Markos and Sergeant Papadakis heard the gunfire coming from the direction of their camp. For the moment, they were secure in their hiding place.

"Sounds like the Frenchmen are giving the Krauts a run for their money," said Sergeant Papadakis.

"I expected no less from Captain Bergé and his men, sergeant. They are professional soldiers. They escaped occupied France to fight the Nazis," Jellicoe replied. "I wish we could assist them, but it would be sheer suicide. Before we could go a couple of hundred meters, they would cut us to pieces."

"You're right, captain. We will have to stay here till dark and hope the Germans leave," Markos said. "Pass me that water, sergeant, we may be here for a good while."

Two Kilometers North of Vassilika, Crete
19 June 1942, 1520hrs

It had been more than an hour since the firefight had started. Mueller was starting to get impatient and wanted to get this over with. He had dispatched Bruner to find the young SS Lieutenant that was leading the attack. They had set up a small command post in a clearing, 200 meters from where the fighting was taking place. Several men had been wounded and were receiving first aid from a Wehrmacht Corpsmen. This was starting to get costly.

"Sir, here is the untersturmführer," Bruner said.

"The man snapped to attention and saluted. "Untersturmführer Schultz reporting as ordered, Herr Standartenführer.

"Relax, Schultz,' you are on the battlefield, not the SS academy."

"Yes, sir."

"I want those enemy saboteurs eradicated. This has gone on for too long."

"They're held up in those rocks 150 meters up the path, sir, four of my men have been wounded."

"They will eventually run out of ammo, but we don't have all night. They may try to escape when it gets dark," said Mueller. "Where is the small mortar we brought with us?"

"The 5 CM mortar is with Hauptsturmführer Lantz, sir. I will send some men to retrieve it.

"Yes, we will blow them out of their hiding place," replied Mueller,

Ten minutes later, three men arrived with the mortar and two tubes of ammo, each tube carrying ten two pound high explosive shells. The mortar crew quickly began assembling the weapon for use.

Even though they were outnumbered ten to one, Captain George Bergé and his men had accounted for themselves with great valor. They had, thus far, held off the Germans for more than an hour against all odds. Luckily, Sergeant Sibard had grabbed the pack with the spare ammo or the Germans would have already overrun them.

"Sir, there is something going on. The Germans rights below

us are pulling back. I wonder what they're doing?" said Corporal Mouhot.

He soon got his answer. They heard a bang and a loud whistle coming their way. "Incoming," screamed Bergé. They all dived for cover as the mortar round exploded, 15 meters to their left. A few seconds later the second round impacted less than ten meters to their left.

"Sir, they are bracketing us," Sibard said.

"Further resistance is useless. We will die for nothing," replied Bergé. "I will surrender us, so we may live and possibly fight again."

"We are with you, sir," replied both men, as a mortar round landed several meters away and showered them with dirt and hot metal.

Bergé tied a white handkerchief to the end of his gun barrel and raised it over his head. A few seconds later, the firing died down and someone shouted to them. "This is Standartenführer Mueller. Come out with your hands raised or we will open fire. You have one minute to comply."

"Well, gentlemen, this is it. Let's go."

The three men stood up, saluted the body of their fallen comrade and walked out into the open with their hands raised. They were immediately surrounded by Germans soldiers and frisked for weapons and had their hands secured behind their backs. Mueller walked up to Bergé.

"Who are you?" He asked.

"I am Captain Georges Bergé. Free French Forces and these are my men."

"You are saboteurs and nothing more," Mueller said.

"Where is the rest of your group?"

"There are no more, just us and the dead soldier back there."

Mueller slapped the Frenchman hard. "You are a liar. I

know there are more of you, including an American officer!"

"I don't know any Americans. It is just us."

"Lying French pig," Muller punched Bergé hard, knocking him down. I will have you all shot as saboteurs!"

"Lieutenant, take the prisoners to Hauptsturmführer Lantz."

"Jawol, Herr Standartenführer,"

Mueller took several men and trudged up to where the commando's base camp was. When he reached the summit, he found the busted radio and burned documents. After searching for a few minutes, one of the soldiers found three more packs which proved to Mueller that there were others with Bergé. In a fashion, he could sympathize with the Frenchman. As an officer, he too, would be honor bound if taken prisoner not to say anything. But that was him. His job was to catch the enemies of the Reich. He would deal with these Frenchmen once he got them back to Iraklion.

One kilometer North of Vassilika Crete
19 June 1942, 1700hrs

They had heard the mortar rounds go off from their hiding place followed by total silence several minutes later. The three men had initially thought that their friends had all been killed in the firefight, but their grief turned to joy when Bergé, Sibard and Mouhot walked by under heavy enemy escort. Their joy quickly turned to sorrow when they saw the Germans carrying the body of young Pierre Léostic. A minute later, Markos noticed Mueller walking in the company of several soldiers. He was tempted to shoot him then and there for the good of humanity, but most likely that would end up costing him his life and the lives of his two friends.

After the Germans had all gone by the three men waited for another hour and left their hiding place. They were all hot and thirsty, having drunk the little water they had with them while hiding from the enemy.

"Major, here is where your knowledge of the area and language skills, come to play, Jellicoe said. "As you can see we are screwed. We have no food or water, no radio, no means of getting off the island and the Jerries are hell bent for our hide."

"That's putting it rather bluntly, but I see your point," Markos said. Mueller will take Bergé back to Iraklion, but they won't talk. Not that they know much anyway. We were going to receive extraction instructions once we reached the coast."

"I'm sure the Germans will figure that out too and start looking for us. We need to start moving towards the south coast and get there before them."

"You're right, captain. We'll bypass Vassilika, just in case Mueller left some of his men behind."

"I'll scout ahead, sir, said Sergeant Papadakis. I think I know where there is a well and we may be able to get some drinking water."

"Great idea, lead the way, sergeant," said Jellicoe.

CHAPTER 19

Wehrmacht Headquarters Iraklion Crete
21 June 1942, 1500hrs

After almost 48 hours of continuous interrogation of the prisoners, Mueller was exhausted. He was getting nothing out of them. Either they were very highly trained in resisting interrogation or they really did not know much. He was beginning to suspect the latter. He had lost his temper several times with the Frenchman Bergé who had a broken nose and several broken teeth to show for it. Bergé was tied to a chair in one of the interrogation rooms and blood was seeping from several cuts on his face.

"Captain Bergé, I will ask you one more time before I have you and your men shot as saboteurs and terrorists", said Mueller. "Now tell me, how were you going to escape the island? Who was helping you?"

"We were going to swim," answered Bergé who, despite the pain and bruises, began laughing at Mueller. But he was answered by a slap across the face from Bruner.

"I have had just about enough of them," said Mueller. "Bruner, take them out and shoot them immediately as spies and saboteurs."

"Jawohl, Herr Standartenführer!"

"No you won't," said Bergé in flawless German. "We will shoot German officers held as POWs in Egypt in reprisal if you execute allied prisoners. It is against the Geneva Convention which Germany is a signatory to. You know this very well, Colonel."

Mueller thought about what Bergé had just said. He did not want to be responsible for the execution of German prisoners and have to answer to Berlin. It was bad enough that he would have to give a full report on the entire operation on the island; he did not need any other blemishes on his stellar record.

"Bruner disregard that last order. Ensure the prisoners are transported to the mainland and shipped to a POW camp in Germany."

"I will, sir."

After Bruner had left with the prisoner, Mueller looked back on the last couple of days. The American and the other two men had managed to escape, but they were still on Crete, he was almost certain of it. He wondered how and where they were going to get off the island. Suddenly it hit him, the smashed radio. They would have received their instructions via radio on where their pick up would be. The American and his friends were trapped on the island. They would have to try and make for the south coast either to find a boat or make contact with the resistance. He would rest tonight and head for the south coast in the morning.

Lentas, South coast of Crete
22 June 1942, 1720hrs

After leaving Vassilika Crete, the three remaining allied agents carefully made their way south toward the coast and camped near the tiny fishing village of Lentas. Markos and George, the two Greek speakers, had been able to find food and water supplies along the way and make contact with the resistance. The resistance had informed them that the SOE team that had struck Kastelli airfield was also hiding in the general vicinity. Arrangements had been made for them to be extracted by a Cacique sometime after midnight the following morning from Tripiti beach, five kilometers east of where they were hiding.

Markos was hastily making his way back to the encampment from a foray into Lentas with some food and water for Jellicoe and Sergeant Papadakis. In Lentas, he had been warned by the local resistance members that a large German force was bearing down on the area. When he reached their encampment, which was a kilometer west of the village, in an orange grove, a hundred meters from the water's edge, he found both Jellicoe and Sergeant Papadakis enjoying a meal of fish and bread.

"Hey major, I netted some fish in the surf," said Sergeant Papadakis.

"No time, I'll eat on the go. The Germans will be here soon. We got to get the hell out of here and head for Tripiti beach. Our ride will be there just after midnight."

Within minutes, the three men grabbed their gear and headed out. They circumvented the village of Lentas and took the small path east which began just west of the small harbor and headed toward Tripiti beach. An hour later, they were stopped by a band of armed Greeks who were part of a resistance group in the Vassilika area. The Greeks had traveled the road leading down from the village of Vassilika ten kilometers to the north of Tripiti. Once the Greeks realized that they were allied agents, they warned Markos that the Vassilika area was swarming with Germans and offered to safely escort them to where the Kastelli raiding force was camped.

Five Kilometers North of Lentas, Crete
22 June 1942, 2200hrs

With a large raiding force of Wehrmacht and SS troops under his command, Mueller departed Iraklion at daybreak and made towards the island's south coast searching every village along the way. Mueller had taken the carrot and stick approach, offering a large reward for information leading to the capture of the allied saboteurs and execution to anyone caught harboring or assisting them.

After coming up empty handed for most of the day, his luck finally changed. One of the local resistance members turned the allied commandoes in after Mueller had taken hostages which included his wife and son and threatened to shoot them. The man told him of their impending evacuation from Tripiti beach and the time it was going to happen. Unfortunately for the man, Mueller put him in front of the German column as their guide which branded him as a collaborator and traitor to the locals. He would not have long to live if he stayed in the area or left German protection.

Mueller glanced at his watch; the luminous dial showed that it was 2210hrs. They had all been on forced march for the last hour trudging toward the coast. The raiding force had reached the gorge of Agios Savvas. The dim light of the quarter moon showed the outline of spectacular rock walls that lined the narrow gorge. "The scenery is very beautiful, sir, " Lantz said, who was walking beside him.

"Yes it is and it would be a great spot to stage an ambush. They could have us pinned down in here till daybreak."

"That is why I have taken precautions, sir. I have sent scouts up ahead to check out the road and look for any potential ambushes."

"Good job, Lantz."

"Thank you, sir."

Twenty minutes later they were through the gorge and entered a forest of olive and carob trees. They were now within a few kilometers from the beach and their quarry.

Tripiti Beach, Crete
23 June 1942, 2245hrs,

Markos, Jellicoe and Sergeant Papadakis had been safely delivered to Tripiti beach by the Greek resistance where they met up with the Kastelli raiding group, commanded by an Irishman, Captain G.I A Duncan. Duncan's team consisted of three British NCOs and Vassilis Dramoundanis, a Greek Gendarmes whom Markos and Sergeant Papadakis knew from Egypt. Their raid on Kastelli airfield had also been successful and had cost them no casualties, unlike Jellicoe's team. Each of the groups that participated in the raids on the German airfield had trained together in Egypt and knew each other very well. They were all finishing the bread and cheese that had been provided by the Greeks and drinking the wine that had also been brought to them.

"Well, gents, in the next hour we should all be on our way back to Egypt, with two successful operations against the Germans," Jellicoe said, raising his wine bottle "To our fallen comrade in arms, Pierre Léostic, and to his comrades who may at this moment either be dead or on their way to a POW camp." They all raised their bottles in salute.

Before they could finish their drink, one of the resistance fighters came running down the path. "We have spotted a strong German force headed this way and they're less than 30 minutes away. We have to delay them until the Cacique arrives."

"We are with you," Markos replied. Before Jellicoe could say anything Markos and Sergeant Papadakis grabbed their weapon and took off running up the trail to assist the resistance fighters to help buy them time.

Gorge of Tripiti, Crete
23 June 1942, 2320hrs

The Germans had entered the narrow confines of Tripiti gorge. They were now only a couple of kilometers from the beach. Mueller sensed that victory was close. If he managed to capture the entire raiding force and kill or capture the bandits helping them, it would be a major propaganda coup for the Reich. The entire area inside the gorge was suddenly lit up by a parachute flare. The landscape took on an eerie look as the German force looked around them and saw that they were surrounded by high cliffs.

"Get down," Mueller screamed, as a fusillade of gunfire erupted around them. Several men were hit before they could even react. He heard a grunt from Lantz.

"Are you okay, Lantz?"

"I have been hit in the leg, sir. The bullet went clean through the fleshy part. It did not hit a bone."

Mueller reached into Lantz's first aid pack and got out the bandages and placed them on the wound." Put pressure on the bandages to stop the bleeding. And stay under cover until a medic arrives."

"Sorry, Herr Standartenführer, bad time to get wounded," said Lantz. "The scouts should have spotted them."

"You did nothing wrong Lantz, they let the scouts pass. I would have done the same thing. The Greeks know the terrain better than us. Just be thankful it's only a flesh wound. You will be back in service in no time. Stay put. I need to get us out of this ambush."

With bullets landing all around him, Mueller crawled to where Bruner was taking cover behind a bolder. "Where is our Greek guide?"

"He is lying over there, sir. He won't have to worry about being recognized as an informer. The first shots took him out."

"Damn it! We are pinned down here and time is running out. I don't want them escaping. Reminds me of the last time we were pinned down in Samaria gorge when we first arrived on this accursed island," Muller said.

"I remember it well, sir. The Greek King managed to escape us."

"Well they're not getting away this time if I can help it," said Mueller. "Where is the mortar, Willie? We need it."

"It's coming, sir. The mortar crew was about 5-10 minutes behind us. They are lugging it and lots of ammo for it."

"As soon as it gets here, I want it deployed and firing star shells and HE."

"Jawohl, Herr Standartenführer."

Gorge of Tripiti, Crete

A hundred meters to the south, Markos and the Greeks were taking cover behind the numerous rock formations that littered the bottom of the canyon and firing towards the German positions. So far, they had been keeping them at bay, buying them time until the boat arrived to take them back to the Middle

East. They were soon joined by Jellicoe and two of Duncan's men.

"Major, it's your buddy Mueller out there. The Greeks captured two of his scouts and they confirmed it's him," said Jellicoe.

"Why does that not surprise me. So we have two of his men as prisoners?"

"Yes, they're being held on the beach. We will take them as POWs to Egypt. We don't want them identifying any of the local resistance members. The Greeks were going to shoot them.

"Sergeant Papadakis, I want you to go back to the beach."

"But, sir."

"That's an order, sergeant."

"Yes, sir. Sergeant Papadakis turned and departed.

"Okay everybody, cease fire, cease fire," yelled Markos and repeated the command in Greek. Once the shooting stopped on the Greek side, the Germans also followed.

"Hey, Mueller! Markos yelled toward the German positions. "I know you are out there, Mueller. This is your old acquaintance, Major Markos Androlakis, US army."

"My, my, you are now a major. The US army must be desperate for officers," Mueller hollered back. "What can I do for you, major?"

"We have two of your men as prisoners. They will not be harmed. What of Captain Bergé and his men? We know you took them and you have a bad reputation when dealing with prisoners."

"Major, you don't have to insult me. They are unharmed and on their way to a POW camp in Germany. You have my word as a German officer."

"Thank you, colonel."

"Now major, why don't you and your men surrender. You will be treated honorably and join your French friends as POWs. You are not going to escape. We know about the boat."

"Sir, the mortar is here and will be set up in another minute," whispered Bruner." Mueller nodded in acknowledgement.

"Prepare to fire on my command."

"Sorry, but we must refuse your hospitality. I believe you are pinned down and we seem to be controlling the only way forward," answered Markos.

"Major, the Cacique has been spotted a few miles out, it has signaled us," said one of the Greeks that had come running from the beach."

"Okay everybody, let's fall back. The Greeks will hold here for about five minutes before they fall back. Let's move." Markos and the rest of the commandoes quickly started to fall back.

A minute later, everyone on the Greek side heard the distinct sound of a mortar firing and hugged the ground for cover. A star shell lit up the Greek positions and was immediately followed by a withering hail of machine gunfire from the Germans. Soon 50mm mortar bombs were dropping amongst the resistance fighters spreading death and destruction everywhere. Even professional soldiers could not have withstood that intense fire for long. Soon the resistance fighters began falling back, leaving two of their men dead and another seriously wounded behind. Mueller's well trained and disciplined troops began a slow but methodical advance toward the gorge's exit which led to the beach. The mortar kept up a steady rate of fire as the gunners shifted their aim to keep the shells dropping in front of the advancing infantry.

"Cease fire before you start dropping them on our men,"

yelled Bruner to the mortar crew. "This thing only has about a 500 meter range. Pack up that tube and let's move forward quickly and meet up with the Standartenführer. I'm sure he will need our support." The mortar was dismantled and Bruner and the crew headed towards the beach.

Tripiti Beach Crete
23 June 1942, 2355hrs

Markos and the rest of the team had heard the mortar fire. They knew it would only be a matter a time before Mueller and his men pushed through to the beach. They headed toward the shore as quickly as possible. A few minutes later the mortar had stopped firing. Except for a few random rifle shots and an occasional bout of automatic weapons fire there was silence. They all knew what that meant, the Germans had broken through.

"Someone's coming," yelled one of the British NCOs from Duncan's command. They all quickly hit the dirt. It was several of the resistance fighters and they were helping a wounded man. They spotted Markos and stopped..

"The Germans broke through, we could not hold them once they started dropping mortar shells on us. They are about five minutes behind us," said the man that was helping his wounded comrade along. Markos recognized him as "Stellios," the district leader of the resistance in this part of the island.

"It's not your fault," Markos said. "They have superior fire power."

"I lost three good men back there. They all had families. We will set up another perimeter on the beach a couple of hundred meters from the water, now hurry."

"What about you and the Germans?"

"Don't worry about us, we will manage."

"Good luck and may God be with you," Markos said.

"What did he say?" Jellicoe asked.

"That the Germans broke through and they're only a few minutes behind us. Stellios' men will set up a blocking force a couple of hundred meters from the waterfront."

"Let's move it then," Jellicoe said.

Ten minutes later, they were less than 100 meters from the water's edge. They could hear heavy firing, punctuated by the occasional explosions of the mortar shells only a few hundred meters behind them. The Germans had moved quicker than they had anticipated. The boat was just arriving and had beached on the sandy shore. "We are not going to make it," said Markos.

"You men run along," said Jellicoe to the two NCOs that had accompanied them. "The major and I will try to buy you all a couple of minutes. Now go."

"Yes, sir."

Markos and Jellico ran toward the sound of firing. They did not have too far to go before they saw the Cretans. There were only about a dozen left fighting. The rest had been killed or had fled.

"Markos, to your right, screamed Jellicoe to be heard over the din of battle. Markos turned and let go a burst from his Thompson, taking down the German infantry man.

Soon mortar rounds began dropping all around them. Someone shouted to pull back in Greek and the resistance fighters began a fighting retreat. A mortar round landed by two of the fighters, shredding them with shrapnel. The rest of the survivors began to run towards the water and away from the Germans.

Markos grabbed Jellicoe, "Let's head for the boat, it's over, the German have broken through. There is nothing left to stop them"

The two men got up and started running toward the boat. Mortar rounds began to follow them. Rounds were starting to fall in the water. A mortar bomb exploded only a few meters away, showering them with rocks and shrapnel. Jellico looked back and saw that Markos had fallen. He turned around and tried to help him to his feet. "I am hit in the leg, leave me, save yourself," Markos said.

"Come on, mate. Get up, we are only a hundred meters away." Jellicoe helped Markos up and the two men headed for the shore.

Tripiti Beach, Crete
24 June 42, 0015hrs,

Mueller was elated. The firing that was coming from the Greeks and the commando teams had subsided. His men were telling him that the Greek bandits along with the British were fleeing the battle. He knew that in a real fight the Greek bandits could never stand up to well-trained German infantry.

"Bruner, I am pushing forward to the water. I want the mortar crew to drop a few more rounds on the shoreline to keep the enemy's heads down and then cease firing so you don't hit us," said Mueller. "I do though want you to fire illumination rounds so we can better see where we are going."

"I will relay the order, sir. Good luck."

Mueller motioned for the bulk of his force to advance. The skilled German soldiers moved forward cautiously in the darkness. Finding no opposition, they advanced quickly. Mueller was only a few meters behind his frontline. The mortar fire suddenly halted. A few seconds later, an illumination round lit up the darkness above the shoreline. He could see the boat, less than 300 meters away. "Advance, don't let them get away," he yelled to his men.

The German line began to surge forward, shooting their weapons at the Cacique that had just begun backing out. Mueller opened his mouth to yell an order to his advancing men when two large explosions ripped through the German line. Mueller was picked up by the force of the explosion and slammed back onto the ground. He thought he heard screaming, but it was coming out of his mouth. Soon everything went black.

The Cacique had a stinger of its own mounted on the bow, a 20MM Oerlikon cannon which opened fire on the remaining Germans quickly decimating many of them and forcing the survivors to retreat. The Cacique had started to pull away when Jellicoe, carrying Markos on his back, was spotted by Sergeant Papadakis who alerted the crew and made them return to the beach. A couple of men jumped in the water and helped Jellicoe carry their wounded comrade onto the boat. Once aboard, the captain put his engines in reverse and backed away from the beach. When it reached deeper water, the boat, which had its original engines replaced with a high speed diesels, went to full power and raced away at 25 knots leaving the coast of Crete rapidly behind.

After they were several miles out to sea, one of the boat's crewmen, a Royal Navy corpsman, went to the main cabin where Marko was.

"Ouch, what are you doing?"

"Trying to dig out all the shrapnel from your leg and thigh, sir," answered the corpsman. "Got one." He pulled out the bloody one and a half inch sliver of metal with large tweezers and showed it to Markos.

"How's the leg look? Is it bad?"

"I have seen a lot worse, nothing vital was hit, but you will be limping for a while. Another couple of inches to the left and you would be now singing Soprano, sir."

Jellicoe and Sergeant Papadakis, who were sitting on the deck next to Markos, began laughing. "I think you will be in for some R and R, (rest and relaxation) once you get out of the hospital, sir," said the corpsman.

Markos had a fleeting thought of Susan back in London. If he had enough R and R he just might be able to finagle a plane ride to England. But first, they would have to get back safely to Egypt.

"How's our Yank doing," asked Captain Duncan who had walked over to see how Markos was doing.

"I'll live Duncan. At least that's what the corpsman is telling me."

"We pulled it off," Jellicoe said.

"Yes, we did. I just hope it was worth it," said Markos as he thought of the dead young French soldier, all the executed civilians and the Cretan resistance fighters that gave their lives so they could escape.

"History will tell," Jellicoe said.

"We barely made it out of there. What were those large explosions that hit the Germans? I thought for a moment that we were goners."

"You owe that to your man Sergeant Papadakis," said Captain Duncan. "We had a bit of C4 left and the good Sergeant was able to leave a couple of surprises for the Jerries.

"I had rigged the bombs to explode simultaneously. I gave the detonator switch to one of the Greeks who hid in the shadows and set them off when the Germans reached the charges."

"Well, you saved all our asses," Jellicoe said.

"George, I believe you also earned some R and R. After I get out of the hospital, I think I can get us a couple of seats to

England," Markos said.

"That would be just swell, sir," said Sergeant Papadakis. "I wouldn't mind one bit seeing Shelly again."

"Ouch, what was that?"

"I administered a pain killer and a sedative, sir. You will be sleeping soundly very soon."

As Markos began to doze off, he thought of his run in with Mueller. Somehow their fates were intertwined and being manipulated by the ancient gods, he thought to himself and grinned. He was almost positive that he would be running into that man again, Somehow somewhere, their fate would be determined.

Tripiti Beach, Crete
24 June 1942, 0110hrs

Once the shooting had ended, Bruner took a detail of men to search for survivors. He had seen and heard the explosions and the firing of the Oerlikon cannon and had a feeling that there would not be many. Out of the 30 men that had accompanied Mueller on his wild charge to the beach, ten had made it back. He had the mortar team fire star shells to light up the beach to make the search for survivors easier. The ground looked like a charnel house. Bodies and body parts lay everywhere along the beach.

After a hectic ten minute search, he found Mueller. He was lying under another body which probably had shielded him from most of the effects of the blast. Bruner checked him for a pulse and heard a groan; he was still alive, but hurt pretty badly. Most likely, he had a concussion and some broken bones. Thankfully, he would recover. He called for a stretcher bearer and helped gently to lift his friend and commander on to it. The American had managed to escape once more. He was not a superstitious man but wondered how Mueller's and this American's fates were intertwined. He remembered reading Greek mythology as a young boy and how the Olympian gods fooled with and determined a man's fate. Somehow, he thought, Mueller's and this American's destiny was, in fact, in the hands of the gods.

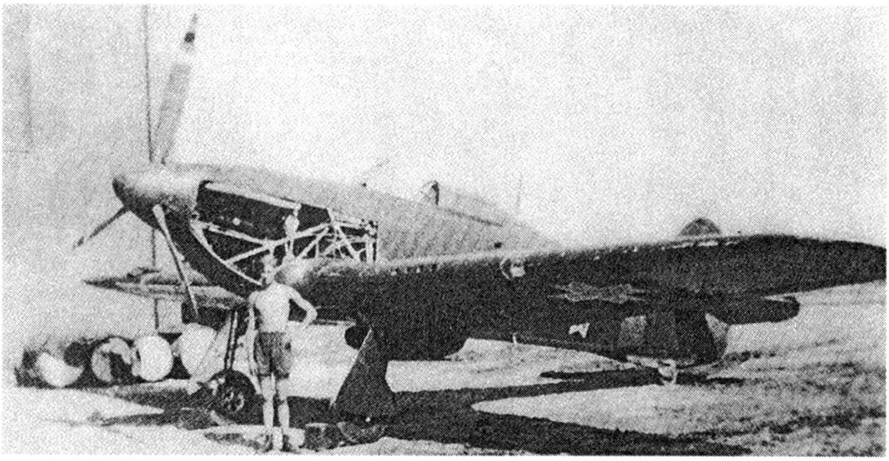

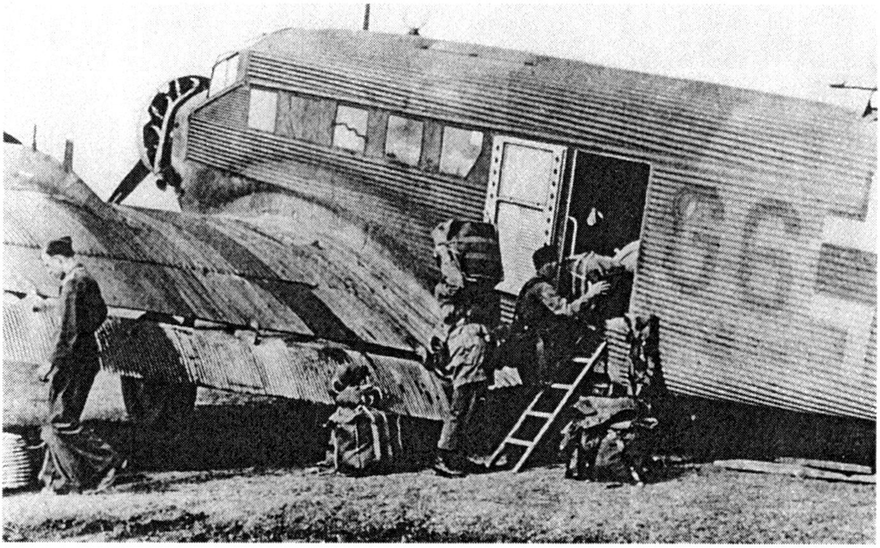

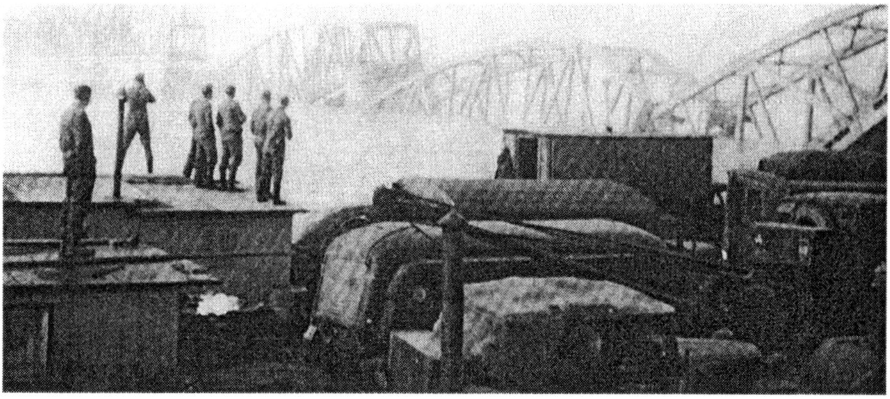

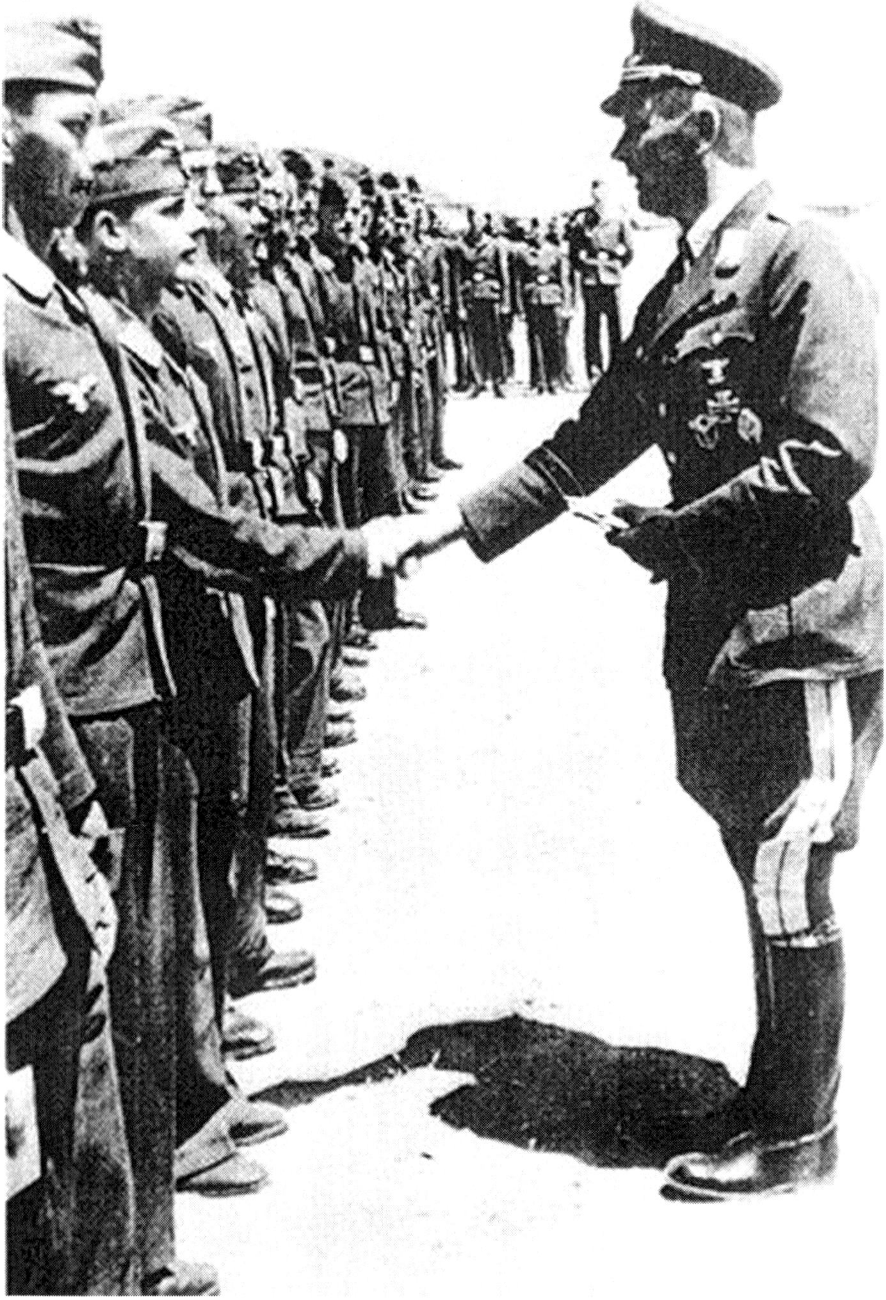

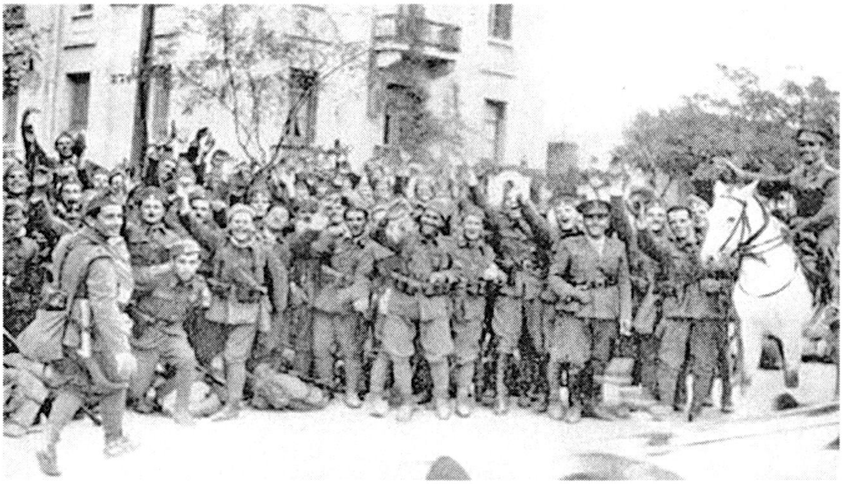

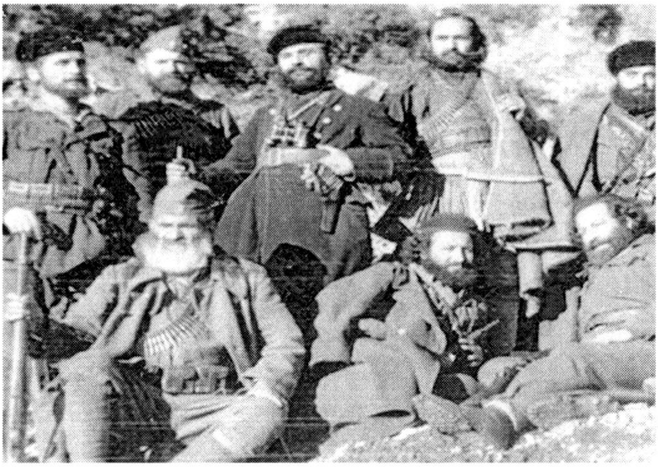

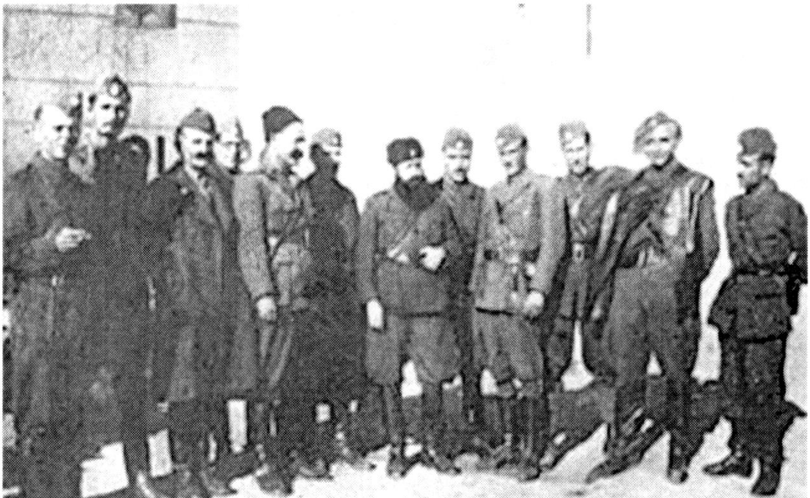

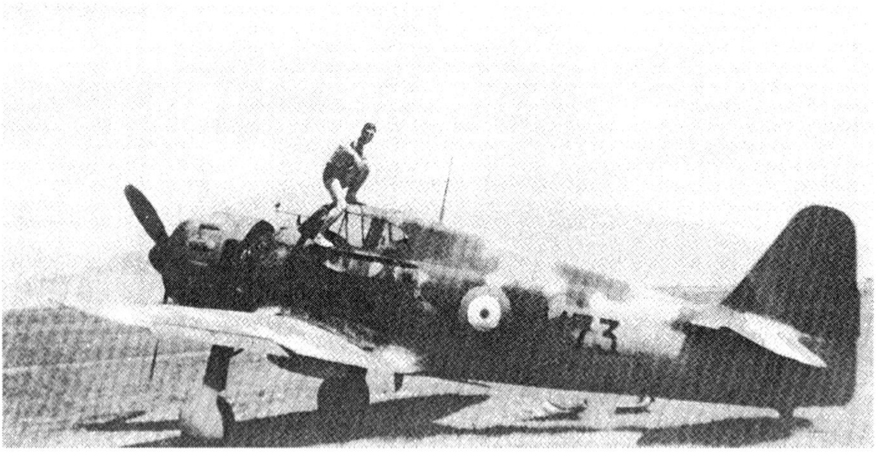
73

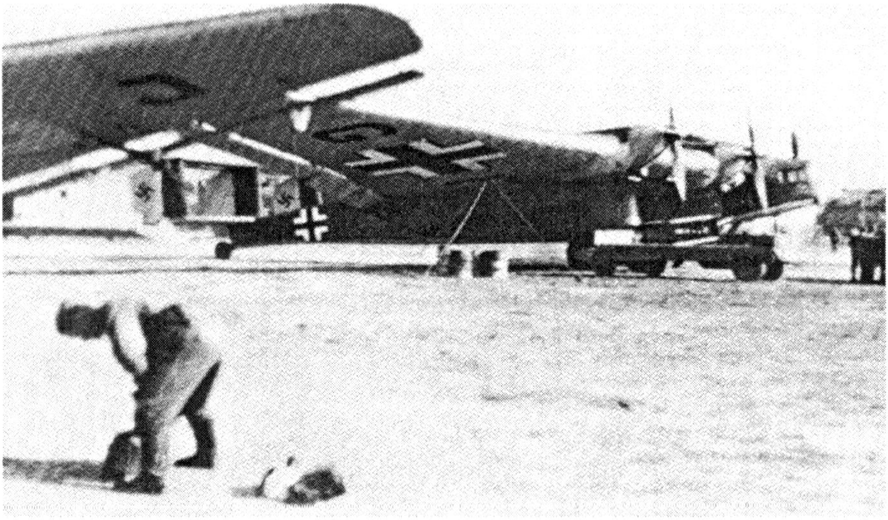

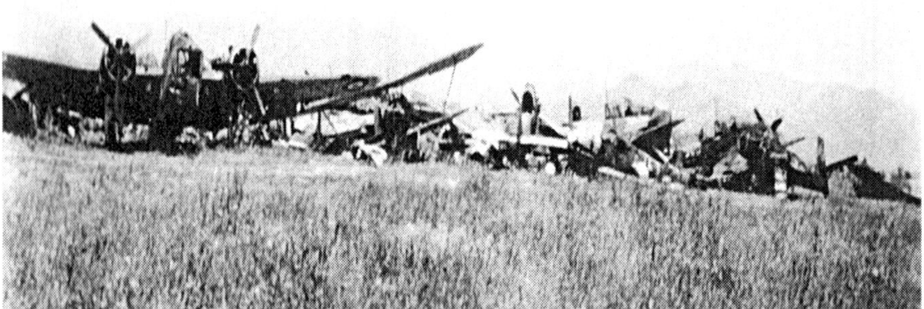

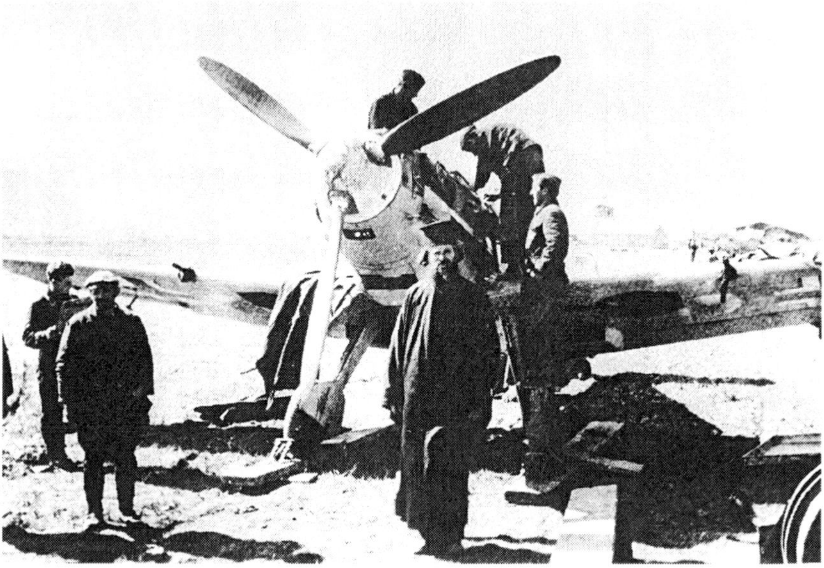

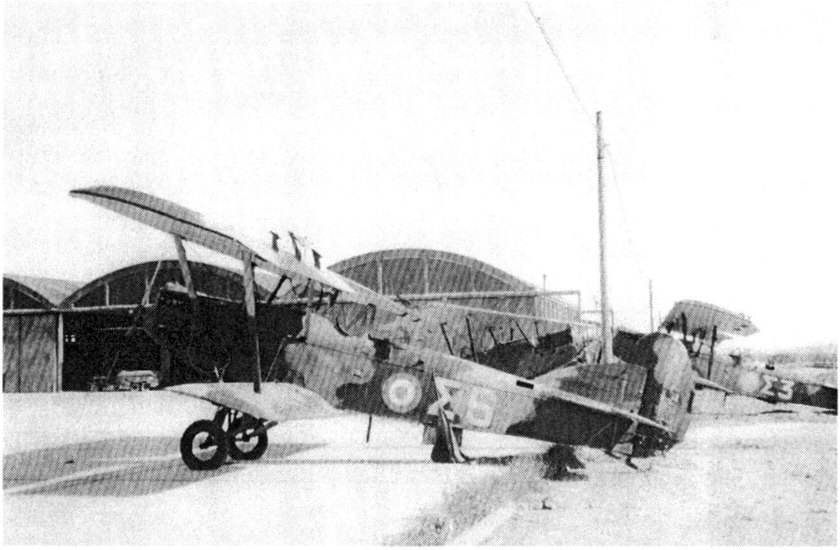

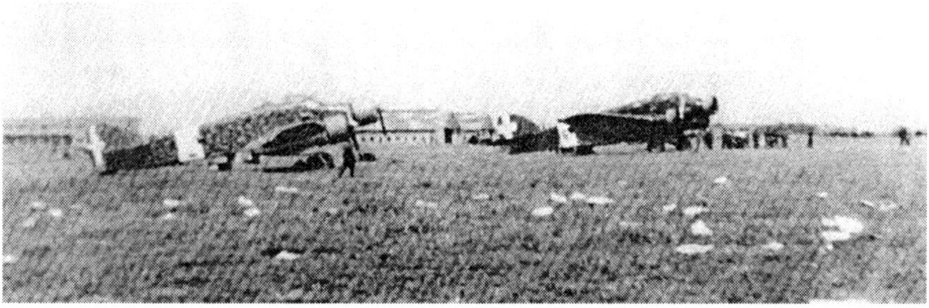

- Title: Operation Medina™: The Jihad
- Author: George Mavro
- Price: $27.95
- Publisher: TotalRecall Publications, Inc.
- Format: HARDCOVER, 6.14" x 9.21"
- Number of pages: 320
- 13-digit ISBN: 978-1-59095-747-9
- Publication: 2011

The Balkans and Mideast, a region very much in the news, is the setting for this action novel which takes place in the not too distant future. The secular pro-western government of Turkey has been overthrown in a violent revolution and replaced by an Islamic fundamentalist regime. Her fanatical leader, General Muhammad Kemal, has contrived a devious plan to restore the Ottoman Empire in the Balkans and unite the Islamic world under his evil rule. To accomplish this, Kemal will launch a devastating war with all the tools in his arsenal including Islamic Jihadist terrorists and WMDs. His first targets are US alley Greece and the few remaining American forces stationed in the region.

For his diabolic scheme to be successful, Kemal must eliminate any source of possible outside interference. To accomplish this, he sends a terrorist team to take out the USAF fighters.

A thousand miles to the south, a Palestinian terrorist sails a boat loaded with anti-ship missiles into Greek waters and delivers a devastating attack in the Mediterranean. The next morning, Turkey and her allies launch a devastating surprise attack against Greece.

With the Greeks facing certain defeat, the U.S. President quickly dispatches to Greece, a fighter squadron and a small USAF Security force contingent for airbase ground defense. The USAF expeditionary force is under the command Lieutenant Colonel Jack Logan a veteran fighter pilot. Logan will be faced with the greatest challenge of his career; he must use every bit of his skills to keep his outnumbered command from being annihilated and help stop the enemy onslaught.

- Title: Operation Medina™: The Crusade
- Author: George Mavro
- Price: $27.95
- Publisher: TotalRecall Publications, Inc.
- Format: HARDCOVER, 6.14" x 9.21"
- Number of pages: 352
- 13-digit ISBN: 978-1-59095-663-2
- Publication: 2012

The second book of the series Operation Medina, Crusade, opens up with the Greeks retreating on all fronts from the Turkish onslaught. The U.S. has dispatched an expeditionary force consisting of a fighter squadron and a small USAF Security Force to assist the Greeks.

As the Americans join the fight against the Turks, they begin to exact a heavy toll on the enemy. The Greeks manage to stabilize their Albanian and Macedonian fronts, yet are unable to halt the Turks, who continue to push them back. As the tide of battle begins to turn against General Kemal, he plans a final act of madness. A daring plan is formulated involving a simultaneous attack from both air and land to stop the madman from carrying out his deadly scheme. If the plan fails, the Americans will use the only other alternative left to stop him, a B-2 bomber with a nuclear payload which could lead to a nuclear showdown with other Islamic states. With the odds stacked highly against them, the allies must find a way to stop Kemal and avert a nuclear holocaust.

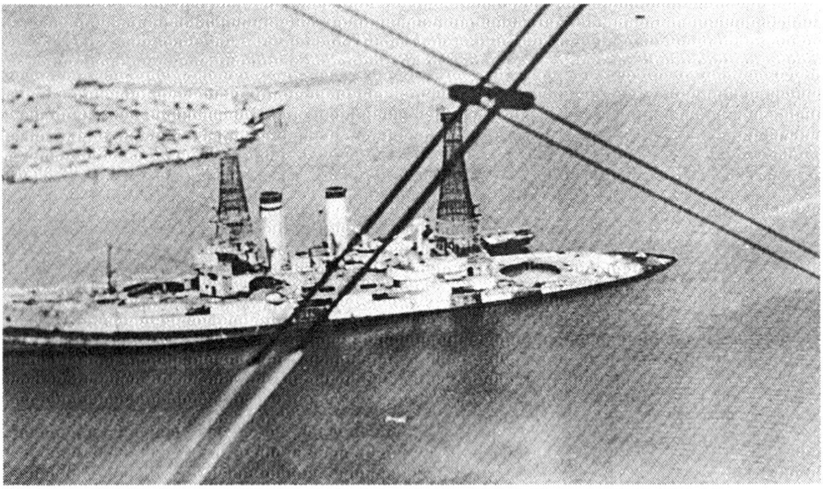

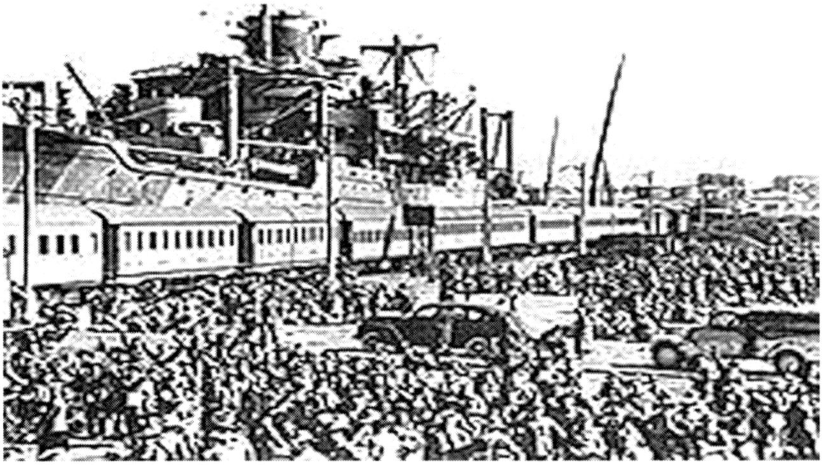

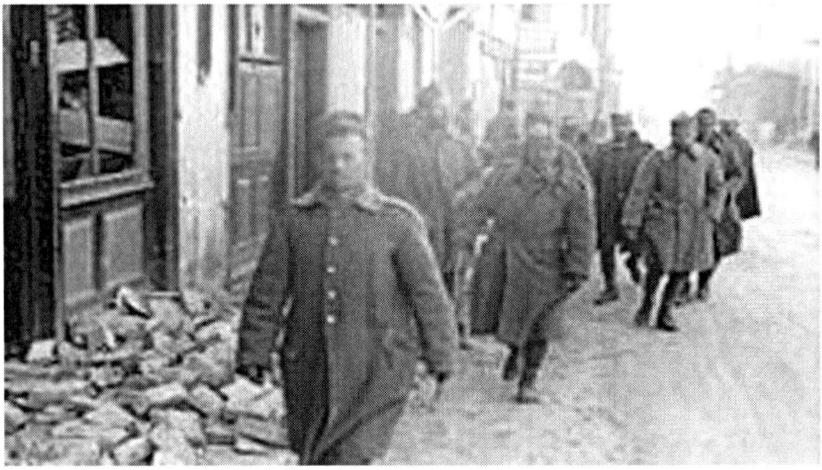

CPSIA information can be obtained at www.ICGtesting.com
Printed in the USA
BVOW04*0034260913

332151BV00003B/24/P